Away – A Romance

Sarah Pain

Published by Sarah Pain, 2022.

AWAY – A ROMANCE

First edition. May 22, 2022.

ISBN: 979-8201161828

Written by Sarah Pain.

AWAY

CHAPTER 1

I could barely contain my excitement when I saw the big metal cut out sign that said, "Howdy! From the Town of Hudson". Above the welcoming was a cut out silhouette of a cowboy tipping his hat. Under the great big sign was a wooden sign that was hand crafted and said, "Small, but mighty population of 2,208." Well at least it's grown in the last two years of my absence.

I was born and raised in the little town located in Montana, Hudson was all I knew. Well that, and the life of a cowgirl. I've been raising cattle, roping steers, pickin' eggs, going to church every Sunday, and riding horses since I came out of the womb. Seriously, before I could even walk, my parents had me riding horses.

My family owns the very famous CJ Ranch. It's one of the most successful and popular ranches between Montana and other states. Earning my family a lot of respect, and may I say, lots of money. Also, my family is evolved in one of my favorite sports, rodeo. My dad won the National Finals for team roping and steer wrestling. My beautiful mother was an amazing barrel racer and also won the National Finals. My crazy brother is one of the best saddle bronc riders in the world.

Horses and other animals are my passion. My dream job is to be a farm veterinarian, and I am real close, even though I'm 18. You're probably thinking, how could she be close to becoming a vet, she's so young? Well, I'm basically a hometown prodigy. I was advanced in everything.

I could talk, walk, and wipe my own ass before everyone else my age. I am super smart, like five grades above. Honestly, I wish I wasn't this smart. It's a waste, I wanna be a farm vet, not some scientist who someday creates a cure for cancer or something. I actually hate science.

Being so advanced for my age had many perks. By the age of three, I was starting the stage of creativity. So all the beads I had from my girly barbie packages, I used them for making my own jewelry. I obviously had no idea what I was doing, but my mom helped me out a lot. I was starting to help my family earn some extra cash on the side.

By the age of eight, I was already competing in rodeos. My specialty, barrel racing. I would have to have special saddles, to keep me from flying of my speedy horses. I was one of the few girls that actually competed in rodeo, besides my best friend Taylor, and a couple other girls. The rest of the girls either jumped horses, and didn't live on a farm, or the other girls hated the small town and left when they had the chance.

And by the age of 11, I was again earning my own money from skull decoration. I didn't rip people off, like the the big name brands do. I usually sold the skull for around $100. My creativity was well built over the eight years. We had a lot of skulls around the ranch, and the beading around here was cheap, so I earned a lot of money growing up. When I was 13, I worked for my dad at the Livestock Barn, earning me more cash.

Being in rodeo had me missing a lot of school, so I had to do some online classes. That made me even more advanced, because on the car rides I was bored, and chose to do more courses than I was suppose to. I actually like learning, just not science, that I hated doing. But the hatred I had, pushed me more to finish it.

But the thing I am most proud of is the diner. DaKota's Diner, to be exact. That's right, its my diner. I didn't do it by myself, my family obviously took care of the finical and other stuff, but I managed the menu, location, interior and exterior, and the staff.

The Diner turned out to be a major success! For the first year, it was almost full every night. I quit my job at the Livestock Barn and became a waitress at my Diner. The best thing about the diner, is the famous homemade ice cream. In reality, any one can make homemade ice cream, but this recipe was a family secret. It earned a lot of tourists and daily customers.

So ya, you could say I had a kick-ass childhood..

So why would I leave this heaven on earth? I didn't have a choice. It makes me sick thinking about it, and I can feel bile coming up my throat, but I stop it, because it's completely behind me. And I made sure of that back in Bismarck.

I was raped two years ago. I wasn't just raped, I was stalked. I wasn't just stalked, I was robbed of my innocence, my virginity to a stranger. It was only a matter of time before I knew someone was following me, then he kidnapped me and raped me on the same night. Wade was his name. It just sounds creepy. This guy was absolutely crazy, mentally ill. He went every where I went, he took pictures of me and kept a journal about me.

The pictures he took varied from me serving people, riding my horses on the ranch, even some pictures of me changing, following me to rodeos, and the ones that made me sick to my stomach were the ones of me sleeping. Wade completely changed my life.

After I was raped, the police tracked him and arrested him and he was quickly sentenced to life in prison. They dug into his personal life and told me what they had found. They showed me the horrid pictures, the worst part is there were thousands of pictures that covered his walls and hung over his bed. People like Wade made me question the world we live in, and why God created people like this.

It is only the police and my family who know about it, it is a miracle we manage to keep it a secret. Word travels fast small towns. I didn't even tell Taylor, my best friend, but she knew something was up with me. I was always on edge, and constantly looking around, because I felt like someone was always watching me. It was absolutely horrible, I loathed the feeling of being invaded.

It was about two months after Wade was put into jail, when he escaped. The police automatically informed my parents about his escape, and I will always remember that feeling of being scared, and telling myself I'd rather die than be his little toy.

They knew he was coming for me again because in his journal they let him have he wrote, "My beautiful DaKota will feel me again.. I'll feel her long soft hair, touch her angelic facial structures, and worship her body.. I'll continue taking her pictures because her face is too sexy to be forgotten. I'll see my flower soon.." He wrote that and other stuff, everyday.

That's when my family and I sat down and discussed what I needed to do. Our plan was for me to live on my own, because we all knew I was capable to do so. I would go somewhere I'd never been to. Bismarck, North Dakota seemed like the place to go. I'd get a fake ID and keep it on the down low. Get a simple job, catch up on school, and only drive when I needed to. No social media. I had no contact with my parents, except when they helped me by putting money into my account. Only being 16 at the time, it strained my family's relationship.

I hated thinking about my past, I hated how weak it made me feel. It is behind me, and now I am finally home! I get to see my parents, my brother, my diner, my friends, my horses, and my pets! Well I got to take my Bernese Mountain Dog, Micah, and my yellow lab, Gauge, with me, but I had other pets too.

I was also excited to see my brother's girlfriend, Ashley. She was my other best friend. She really knew how to put Caleb in his place, and she wrapped him around her finger so fast, it was awesome. Ashley and I bonded all the time, she was a sister to me. I wonder if they have gotten more serious?

I DROVE UNDER OUR BIG ranch entrance sign, and a smile pulled on my face, because my dad left the Christmas lights on there, and it's the middle of May. The sign was made of dark oak logs, and a metal sign with, "CJ Ranch" and our brand designed into it.

I pressed down on the pedal more and watched the dirt fly behind me, I couldn't wait to see that house again. I finally saw our cute white house, and I saw my dad's, mom's and Caleb's pickups, and Ashley's SUV in the grass. With all of my money I had managed to buy a midnight black six inch lifted 2016 Chevy Silverado.

As I reached the grass, I saw a certain blonde haired cowboy on the porch and he looked at my pickup. He couldn't see through my windows because of my dark tint. So I parked quickly and turned my truck off and opened the door and hopped out. I watched the dogs get out too, they ran loose, they knew they were home.

As I stepped aside so he could see me, I swear he peed himself with excitement. I smile so cheekily I thought my cheeks were going to fall off. "She's home!!!" Caleb yelled very loud and charged down the porch steps and I ran towards him.

"Caleb!" I cheered as I ran into his arms and we both tightly wrapped our arms around each other. I hated to admit it, but tears started to come out. God, I missed him so much it hurts.

"God, I can't believe you're actually here right now." He laughed and began to spin me around. We finally let go of each other, and I looked him up and down and he did the same to me.

"Wow, you grew nicely into your body." I said, noticing his taller and more muscular body. He turned into a very handsome cowboy.

"I can't say the same.." He says and makes a face at me and I shove him. As I do this I notice a ring on his finger. No way!!!

I take his left hand and raise it, "Married?!!" I ask him and he shakes his head.

"En-" Caleb was cut off, by a feminine voice.

"We weren't going to get married without you silly!" A familiar voice said, and I turned toward the porch and there stood a very gorgeous Ashley.

"Ash!!" I yell and we both run to each other and hug each other tightly, just like Caleb and I had done so a moment ago.

"Dang, you're hot!!" Was the first thing she said to me. Even though it was Ash, I blushed at her comment. I got compliments all the time, but I always felt awkward about them.

"So are you!" I playfully shoved her and Caleb came behind her and wrapped his arms around her and kissed her cheek.

"Yes she is." Gosh, Caleb was so in love with her, it was a beautiful sight to see. As always, Ashley rolled her eyes at him.

"Where's mom and dad?" I ask Caleb and he returns his attention back to me and not his bride-to-be.

"They're riding right now." He informs me and I nod to him and look around the place. The barn had done some remodeling and touched up a bit on the outside. We had the big read cliche barn and almost 500 acres of land, we were blessed to have great land for ranching. I really missed this place.

"Caleb, go help your sister unload her stuff." Ashley commanded.

"She's been here two minuets and she's already the queen again." Caleb joked and I rolled my eyes at him and started walking back to the pickup again.

MY PARENTS WERE FINALLY back from their ride, and I couldn't wait to see them. I wonder what hair color my mom had. She always went from black, to brown, to brown with gold highlights, to a dark red, and back to a very dark brown. She was very beautiful, everyone says I look like her. I have dark green/ gray eyes, while my mom had blue eyes and my father has a dark green and brown. I have always been his little cowgirl, very much a daddy's girl.

I sat in an island chair in the kitchen as I waiting for my parents to walk in any second. Ash and Caleb were sitting at dining table, chatting about something. The door knob of the door turned and the screen door creaked and my father's voice filled the air, "Caleb who's pickup is that?" My father's head was turned towards the table, while the island was behind them. My mother was standing behind my father. She had midnight black hair, classic. Her motherly instincts must of kicked in, because she looked turned the other direction and locked eyes with me.

She gasped and covered her mouth with her hand, I could see the tears in her eyes, as well as mine. "What Shey?" My dad said and then turned his head too. He was shocked and was at a loss of words.

I stood up and rushed over to my parents to give them the biggest hug ever. My right arm was tucked around my mother, and the other with my father and they engulfed me in the hug. Me and mom were crying, "My little girl." My mom cried happily and I hugged them tighter.

"I missed you guys." I said as I stepped back and wiped my tears away. I looked at my dad and he even had tears in his eyes, that really meant something to me. My dad still seemed astonished to see me. "What, dad?" I chuckled at him.

"Low how beautiful my little girl is." He said and I smiled and hugged him again.

"I love you dad." I said to him and kissed him on the cheek.

"I love you too sweetie." He says back. My mom and I calm ourselves down and we all sat down at the dinning table together.

"Hows the diner?" I ask them and they laugh. They all know how much that diner means to me, it's like my baby.

"Not the same without you, but it's going well." My mom said while wiping her eyes with a tissue.

"Okay, I wasn't sure if I could leave her in your guys' hands." I joke with them and Caleb is the only one who takes offence to it.

"Hey! I'll let you know I had to serve to cover your butt." He says and Ash puts her hand around his arm.

"Honey, that was for an hour." I chuckled at them, but it's Caleb we're talking about. His life is rodeo, and nothing else. I couldn't even imagine him serving people their food. It just didn't suit him.

"I love that you are here right now, but are you sure?" The way he said it made all of us know what he was talking about. Everyone went silent for my answer, and I gulped and nodded.

"I am sure. Wade is gone, and won't be bothering us ever again." I say confidently.

"How do you know?" My mother asks me.

"He's in a much more bigger and secure jail this time. Now that he's back in jail, they have a better security and better technology. There's no way he's gettin' out." I inform them, trying to put my best poker face on.

"Well those bastards should of had a bigger eye on him before!" My dad says sternly, and we all know it's true, but choose not to say anything. "Well this causes for a celebration!" My dad brings the mood back to happy with these words.

"We don't need to-" I start to protest, because I hated attention being brought on me. It made me feel superior over others, and I didn't like being the center of attention.

"Nonsense! A cook out on Friday evening?" My dad says and looks at my mother and she nods in agreement. I wasn't going to protest, because you hardly changed my dad's mind. It wasn't worth the time.

"Well I think I'm gonna go start to unpack." I announced to my family and then I looked outside to the pasture. "Where's Pharaoh?" I ask my parents and every looks at everyone weirdly. Pharaoh was my horse that I broke when I was 13. He was a mustang, but I roped him one day in the pasture and brought him home, against my parent's rules.

Pharaoh and I have a very special bond, he only lets me ride him. He'll let people tack, feed, brush, and other stuff. But if he sees you put a foot in that left stirrup, he will make sure you don't do it again. He's overall a really good horse, I raced him, he was as fast as lightning. It was shocking to some, but it wasn't unusual for a mustang to be wicked fast and strong.

"He's probably down by the creek." My mom says and every one remains quite. What the hell is going on? I'm too tired to figure out right now, I'll leave it for tomorrow.

I walked upstairs to my room, down the hall. I took a deep breath before I opened the door, and it looked like everything was still in the same place. Except for all the boxes on the floor, but that will go away.

My bed was perfectly made, and my furniture was neat in it's place. I looked around my room and looked at all of my pictures. Pictures of me and family, horses, friends, and competitions. There was a couple of photos of the first opening day of the diner, it made me smile at how young I was. There was other photos of branding, fishing, and hunting.

Looking at my balcony door, I smiled and skipped over to the doors and pulled them open, letting the fresh mountain air into my room. I smiled as the cool wind came in contact with my skin, but my smiled dimmed when I realized I had to unpack. Eh, I'll do it tomorrow.

I looked at my bed and ran and jumped on the soft blue and gray Aztec printed comforter. The memory foam sunk to fit my body and I groaned at how good it felt. I rolled over so I was staring at the ceiling, with my limbs sprawled out over the bed. "It's good to be home."

I walked downstairs to the rich smell of farm-fresh eggs, bacon, and waffles. It made my stomach growl and made my nerves go all fuzzy inside. "Good morning." Every one said at the same time, I wasn't surprised Ash stayed over last night.

"Morning!" I said and took the plates from the cabinets and placed them on the table. I took my place at the table, next to Ashley. Ash was across from Caleb, and my parents were at the ends of the table.

Before we dug into our delicious breakfast we joined hands and bowed our heads. "Lord, thank you for blessing us with this nutritious meal, letting us live another day, and doing what we love. Thank you for letting us have our daughter and sister back and keeping her safe. Thank you for a great life. Amen." My father said and then we all finished the Amen, together.

Mom put the big spoon in the eggs and we passed the very hot dish around. I took two scoops of the eggs, three slices of bacon, and just one Belgium waffle. "Mom, this looks good." I said to her and she just smiled at me. "So Caleb, Ash, when's the wedding?" I ask them and they both smile, probably at the thought of them being together forever.

"July 18." Ashley said and I smiled, holy that is just around the corner!!

"Oh my goodness, that's really soon!!" I gasped and they both nodded towards me, while Caleb was scarfing his food down his throat, he was always a messy eater. Best of luck to Ashley.

"Do you want to review some things with me later today?" Ash asks me and I turn towards her and nod with a sweet smile.

After breakfast the girls cleaned everything up and washed and dried the dishes, now it was time for chores. I pulled my very long hair into a high ponytail and pulled on my Ariat square toe boots and started walking to the barn.

It was a really nice morning, already about 60 degrees, it was perfect. I walked through the huge barn doors and went to the feed area, and decided to start with the pigs. I loved the pigs, even though they were loud, and kinda disgusting, they had a cute thing about them. I poured their feed into a bucket and walked out to their pen, where they were squealing when they saw me, or the bucket of food.

IT WAS ABOUT TEN O'CLOCK when I was done with my chores, and now it was time to take a warm and relaxing shower. Having to shovel poop and be around dirty animals didn't leave a good smell on you, plus the sweat I worked up didn't help.

I walked up to my room and took off my shirt, leaving me in a sports bra and jeans. I looked for box that was labeled, 'Bathroom', and I threw it on my bed and opened it. I unpacked the box and it all went into the bathroom in my room, and it was the only boxed unpacked..

I felt great when I was done with my shower, I felt energized and I was getting excited to go to the diner. I looked at myself in the mirror when I was moisturizing my face. I was one of the few girls who actually liked their natural look, not to be self centered though. I don't know how, but my natural face glowed and looked smooth and young. I already had long eyelashes, so that also gave me an edge, and my dark hair complemented my face and skin tone.

My makeup just consisted of foundation and mascara, but not a lot of foundation because I still wanted a natural look. It was a simple and easy process and only took about ten minuets. My hair was a different story. My natural hair is a very beach curl, not like the nice pictures you see on the internet, it is curlier and thicker. Sometimes it was nice to wear down, but other times I either straighten it or curl it.

I walked out of the bathroom and sat in my cushioned chair grabbed the journal from my nightstand. I know, how girly of me to keep a journal. But I just don't it for fun, I started doing it after I got raped. It help me let out my anger out, and everything I wanted to say out loud but I couldn't. Sometimes I did a paragraph, or as long as three pages.

I wrote everyday, except for last night, I was too tired to write about my day. So while my hair is drying, I might as well do it. I clicked the pen so the ink side was out, and I got comfortable and started writing.

My hand cramped from writing while I was on my second and final page. My hair was almost dry to the point it would only take a minuet to blow dry it. I added the last period and closed the book and clicked the pen so it closed.

I did not want anyone to read this, so I had to think of a clever way to hide the journal. The nightstand is way too obvious, under the pillow is too cliche, but under the cushion of the chair was good. I stuck it under there and sat on top to see if I could feel it, nope. Alright, it's staying there.

Being the lazy person I am, instead of unpacking the boxes, I just threw clothes around my room as I was looking for something to wear. I walked out to the balcony to see if I wanted to wear skinny jeans, boot cut jeans, or jean shorts.. I'm gonna go with jean shorts on this warm day.

I picked out a simple loose army green shirt and the jean shorts that had some loosely distressed strings around the pockets, and were the right length in the back. Now was time to do my hair, and I think I'm going to curl it.

I finally curled my hair and I flipped it up and down a couple of times, to give it a natural look. I looked one last time at the big 1.75 inch curls, that were very romantic and bouncy. Okay, now it was time to go to the diner!

DAKOTA'S DINER, IN big cursive letters was on display on top of the retro stainless steal building. It was your typical diner look, and the main colors were baby blue and a soft pink. Blue was my favorite and my family picked pink that went with that blue. The waitresses also had cute uniforms, it was just shirt they had to wear, and they could either where jeans, a skirt, or just simple black pants.

I pulled into a parking spot and noticed it wasn't packed, nor empty, just enough. Before I got out of my truck I checked my hair and makeup, all good. I noticed all the trucks parked in the front row, and they looked familiar to me.

As I pulled the door open, the bells dinged, signaling a customer and attention to yourself. A big smiled formed on my face as I looked around and then I heard, "DaKota?!" And by the voice I knew who it was, Maybell! Maybell and I were really close since she worked here, and she told me that I reminded her of herself when she was younger. Maybell was in her late 50's now, but she sure didn't act like it.

She came racing from the counter island and she engulfed me in a hug. "Hi Maybell." I hugged her back, she still uses that perfume older people use, it makes me laugh. We pulled back from each other and I looked at her more clearly. "You haven't aged a day!" I say and she rolls her eyes at me.

"Look at you! Such a beautiful young woman." She emphasizes young because she hates getting older. I always teased her about it, but she was gorgeous for her age. She had dark hazel eyes, a very good completion, and short curly blonde hair.

"Thank you," I blushed at her and tuck a piece of hair behind my hair, I always did that when I was embarrassed or tongue tied. "How's business?" I ask her as we walk over to the counter, to get more privacy in our conversation.

"Pretty good, but I bet it will be even more better once people know you're back. Definitely more boys." She winks at me and I shake my head at her. "So how was your cousins house?" She asks me, at first I'm confused, but I realize what my family told everyone for a cover story.

"Oh it was good, but I really missed this place, especially the diner." I say as she's doing something with the register.

"Well that's good to hear. Hudson wasn't the same without you." She says to me.

"Oh I don't that's true." I laugh awkwardly.

"Just trust me honey, now I have to get back to work. I'll talk to you later, yeah?" She says as she grabs her notepad and walks over to a table. I grab a menu from under the counter and begin to look through it until I hear, "Hey wolf girl!!" I haven't heard someone call me that in a very long time.

I smiled and turned around on the stool and looked around until I saw Rusty, Jake, and some other guy at the round booth. Jake and Rusty were some of my close friends before I left. They were very good friends with Caleb, which is how I met them. I pushed myself off the stool and walked over to their table. Rusty and Jake slid out of the booth and both hugged me in a tight embrace. "Hey guys!" I chuckle as they let me go and plop right back into their original spots.

My eyes go towards the stranger under a black cowboy hat, holy sweet virgin Mary. This stranger was the most beautiful cowboy I had ever laid eyes on. He had a perfectly structured face, an impressive jawline, and broad shoulders. When we made eye contact, I could just melt into his brown eyes. His lips pulled into a very cute crooked grin. "I don't ever think we've met, I'm sure I would remember such a pretty face." This is the very first thing he says to me, wow. My cheeks rush into a dark pink color, and I tuck a piece behind my ear, damn it! His voice was so attractive and he had a light accent from the south, when did he get here?

"I'm DaKota Jones." I say to him and he smiles.

"I'm Cooper Blackwood." He says, why does he have to have such a hot name to go with his face?! I had to stop looking at him, so I turn my attention to Rusty.

"Cooper moved here a few months after you left," Rusty informed me. "When did you get back?" Rusty asks me.

"Just last night." I say back to him.

"Where did you go again?" Jake scratches his head, trying to think.

"Uh, my cousins." I say and clasp my hands in front of me and look down.

"Why again?" Jake questions me more, and I think hard about the answer. I don't remember what my family told everyone. Hurry up Kota, think!

"Family business." I answer blankly to him and I think of something else to say. "I'd thought I'd come up and see how things were going today." I say looking around the diner.

"Well not to be rude, but when I was here last week, that really young waitress really fucked up my order," Jake said and I chuckled since he said that she was a new waitress.

"Well maybe I could talk to Maybell about the way she trains newbies." I am slightly joking, but serious at the same time.

"You think you can do that because you're Colby's daughter, huh?" Cooper says to me, and I was slightly taken back. Did he think just because I was my dad's daughter, that I got everything I wanted? I looked at Rusty and Jake and they looked sorry for him. Did he just forget my name, or was he dumb?

"Did you forget my name?" I ask him, placing a hand on my hip.

"No." He scoffs and he sounds like's confused and also offended.

" What's the diner called?" I ask him and he looks at the menu, and I can tell by his face, that he realized, but I wanted to clear it to him. "I own this place." I smirk at him and lean down put my hands on the table, leaning in a bit, and he just clenches his jaw, but looks sorry at the same time. I have no idea where this confidence came from.

"Well it's very good and I love it." He tries to make up for his false accusation, but I just shrug it off. I look at him one last time and put my eyes somewhere else.

"So my dad's throwing this cook out tomorrow evening, you guys interested?" I say to them and they look at each other and nod.

"If there's free food, I'm always there." Jake says making me laugh and I nodded because it was true.

"Okay, great. Well I'm gonna go say hi to some other people, it was really nice to see you guys and good to meet you Cooper." I say and Cooper sends me a golden boy smile, and I look a little bit too long for my liking, damn his good looks.

"See ya DaKota." Jake and Rusty say as I leave their booth, and I start to go talk to The Jefferson family.

COOPER

THE BOYS AND I WERE laughing about something stupid Jake had just said, and I stopped laughing heavily when I heard the bells ring, ans saw an angel walk through the door. Seriously, this girl was a jaw dropper. Her long tan legs caught my attention, toned and perfect.

Even with her hair curled, I could tell it reached her tailbone. But her face, she was the most beautiful girl I had ever seen, and I've been around. She looked innocent and very sweet. And when Maybell said what I'm guessing was her name, it made me smile softly. DaKota, such a unique and pretty name.

Her smile was the real show-stopper, she had straight and pearly-white teeth that could brighten anyone's day.

The weird thing was I felt something turning in my stomach. I'd never had this feeling in my life before, what could it be? Was I nervous? Why would I be, it was just a girl. I flirt with girls all the time, why would she be different?

I was looking at menu when I heard Rusty say, "No way, Jake look." He sounded astonished and taken back. Curious, I look up to where he was looking and it was the girl.

Jake turned back to us and smiled widely, "Holy shit!"

"Hey Wolf girl!" Wolf girl, what kind of name is that? "DaKota" looked back at Rusty and she smiled at them and walked over to the table. How would go about this? Go right to the flirting, play around, or just say hi?

Rusty and Jake go up to hug her, and that feeling is back into my stomach. What the hell is going on with my body? Her voice intrigues me when she says, "Hey guys!" I can't help but stare at her, she was so damn cute. Her eyes met mine. Jesus, what didn't this girl have? She had a perfect body, face, and now she has these eyes that I could look at all day.

"I don't ever think we've met, I'm sure I would remember such a pretty face." I say to her, using my charm I'm rumored to have. I see her cheeks turn into a pink shade and she tucks a piece of her hair behind her face. Hah, my charm strikes again!

"I'm DaKota Jones." She says to me, she made her name sound perfect.

"I'm Cooper Blackwood." I introduce myself to the pretty lady and she gives me a small grin.

"Cooper moved here a few months after you left," Rusty says and then adds, "When did you get back?"

"Just last night." She says, leaving my eye contact to his. Making me smirk, gosh I'm so full of myself.

"Where did you go again?" Jake scratches his head, trying to think.

"Uh, my cousins." She hesitated with her answer.

"Why again?" Jake questions.

16

"Family business." She says and then no one says anything. "I'd thought I'd come up and see how things were going today." She says and checks out the diner.

"Well not to be rude, but when I was here last week, that really young waitress really fucked up my order," Jake said and she laughs at him. That laugh...

"Well maybe I could talk to Maybell about the way she trains newbies." She said to him. She's kidding right? Just when I thought there would be a different kind of girl in this town, another stuck up one comes in.

"You think you can do that because you're Colby's daughter, huh?" I say to her and she looks taken back like no one has ever talked to her like that.

"Did you forget my name?" She says and puts her hand on her hip. Well I do know her name.

"No." I scoff, does she think I'm dumb?

"What's the diner called?" She sasses to me and I look down at the diner, even though I already knew the name. Oh God, I just set myself up for a burn. "I own this place." She evilly smirks at me, and puts her hands on the table and leans down more. I see she's got some fire to her, I like it.

"Well it's very good and I love it." I actually felt a little bad about accusing her of being a snob.

"So my dad's throwing this cook out tomorrow evening, you guys interested?" She changes the subject, which I am grateful for.

"If there's free food, I'm always there." Jake says making us laugh.

"Okay, great. Well I'm gonna go say hi to some other people, it was really nice to see you guys and good to meet you Cooper." She sweetly smiles at us, and I send her my best goodbye smile and she looks a little longer at me and then leaves.

"See ya DaKota." Jake and Rusty say, and I watch her walk away, paying more attention to her bake side. Oh good Lord.

Maybell passed me walking to the kitchen, "Table 5, dear." She said and I nodded and made my way over there, it was just a single person. As I got closer, I noticed the blonde hair. Could it be? As I got to the table, my insides busted with excitement! "Taylor!" I say and she looks to her left and her jaw drops.

"DaKota!" She beams and she stands up and we hug it out. I've missed her so much, she's my best friend. We've been friends since diapers, seriously, our moms are best friends, too.

Taylor was a gorgeous girl, inside and out. She had blue eyes that sparkled all the time, she had perfect blonde hair, a bubbly personality, and a great smile. We had everything in common. We're basically sisters.

"Here come to the counter so we can talk." I say and take her menu for her and place it on a spot with a stool under it.

"I just came here to see if the rumors were true." She smiled at me.

"So you're not going to order?" I joke with her and rolls her eyes at me.

"I'll have a water because I have a lot to tell you about." She gives me a devil's grin and I smirk too, gossip time.

"Okay, I'll just take my break now, since I wasn't really signed up to work." I said to her and walked away to go get her a glass of water.

When I came back she was looking at her phone and texting, but she was smiling like an idiot. Could it be a boyfriend? "Who ya texting?" I ask her as I go across the counter from her on the other side.

She looked up at me and blushed a little bit, "Beau." She sheepishly said and my jaw dropped.

"Are you guys dating?" I ask her, please say yes! Everyone knew Beau had a crush on Tay since we were in Elementary school. Tay just denied it because she thought it was crazy the most popular boy in school liked her. Beau is the star football and basketball player here, and he also does some rodeo. He also had a lot of good looks, and he was really nice. Overall, he was perfect for Taylor. I considered him more of my friend, because I knew of his crush with Tay.

"Yeah." Really, that's all she gives me? I raise my eyebrows at her and she giggles. "Since last August." The thought of them together warms my heart.

"I want details." I rest my elbows on the counter and place my head in my hands, and wait for her to begin what has happened these past two years.

TAY WAS FINALLY DONE spilling everything, man I missed a lot. A lot of party drama, rodeo drama, and relationship drama. I didn't like to be evolved in drama, but I sure did like hearing about it. Most of it was about Avery and her little group.

Avery Johnson and I have never gotten along, and I would like to keep it like that. Avery is a spoiled little girl who has never worked a day for anything she "owns", and she acts like she's the biggest deal around. Not saying that I am, but seriously.

Avery jumps horses, and she bashes anyone who owns or lives on a ranch. I always try to be nice to her, but once she starts something, I'll try to match her. I usually win an argument because I am way smarter than her, and more witty and sarcastic. At the end of an argument she crosses her arms and stomps her foot and walks away.

Two years ago she really hated my guts, because I was dating Mason Bishop. Mason wasn't a cowboy, but he tried to be one. That was only the really bad thing about Mason, he was sometimes fake around people. But when it was just us two, he was a really good guy.

My thoughts were interrupted by the bells on the doors. I looked up from Taylor talking, and saw that it was the boy I met yesterday, Cooper Blackwood. I looked away before he could see me staring at him. Today he was wearing light blue jeans and a fitted black tee. His arms were very toned and very tan, and the t-shirt wasn't the only thing that fitted him in the right places. He went over to a table and started talking to Mr. Daniels.

I grabbed a rag from under the counter and grabbed the disinfect spray and began to clean. Taylor had stopped talking, and I took a risk. "What do you know about Cooper Blackwood?" I asked Taylor and she slowly looked up at me and smirked, and she caught me looking at him. She turned around and looked at him, then back at me.

"I see you already met him." She said like it wasn't a shock to her. I raised my eyebrows at her, telling her to explain. "Every girl in this town is in love with him," She said. Well I don't blame them, look at him.. "He's very charming, and he's got a bad boy reputation to him." She said.

"What do you mean?" I ask her.

"He's gotten into a couple fights, he always comes out on top, and he's not afraid to speak his mind." She said.

"Well I don't think that's bad." I said and shrugged my shoulders.

"Fighting?" She questions me.

"No, the speaking his mind thing." I shake my head. "We need more people like that." I added.

"Did I tell you he's a bull rider?" She said and this really got my attention.

"Is he any good?" I ask her putting down the rag and looking at her.

"He's real good." She winked at me and I rolled my eyes. "Well I better be going, Beau and I got a date." She smiled, I was so happy for her.

"Okay, oh did you hear about the cookout tonight?" I ask and she nods to me. "Okay, I'll see you later. " I said and she hugged me over the counter and left the diner.

I bent down on my knees and I started to wipe the insides of the shelves on the other side of the counter, does no one care about this dust?

When I was almost done with the first one, I heard the call bell ding once. I looked up with just my eyes and I saw Cooper leaning over the counter and smiling at me. I blew the hair out of my face and I wiped off my hands and stood up. "Hi." I gave him a small shy smile and handed him a menu.

"Hey Kota, can I call you that?" He politely asked me, making me smile a bit.

"Sure. Can I get you something to drink?" I ask him.

"I'll take a short Coors Light." He says and I raise an eyebrow at him. He looked older than me, but not 21.

"I'm gonna need an ID." I say to him in an obvious tone and he reaches into his pocket and grabs his wallet. He opens it up and pulls the ID card out and hands it to me. I inspect it carefully, I know what to look for on a fake ID. The cops never noticed it though, or club bouncers. "Sorry, but I know this is fake." I smirk and hand it back over to him.

"I've gotten away with this bad boy so many times, how did you know it was fake?" He asks me and puts his wallet back into his pocket. He looked very intrigued and interested.

"What makes you think I don't have one?" I smirk at him and he looks a little shocked but he smirks and chuckles a bit. I leave as I go to the kitchen to get him a root beer. The root beer does come in a beer bottle shape.

"So you comin' tonight?" I ask him as I put the root beer in front of him. When he sees the bottle he laughs. His laugh was deep and attractive to me. The weird thing is that I actually feel comfortable talking to him.

"Plan on it, will there be beer there?" He asks me with a delighted grin on his face, he was too cute for his own good.

"Will you be 21?" I ask him and he drops his head and laughs with me. "They'll probably will be if my brother and his friends are there." I say and take my notepad out.

"I like your brother." He says to me and I look into his eyes.

"Do you guys hangout?" I ask him and he shrugs.

"Well we hangout with the same friends, but I don't think we would every hangout just us two." He says and I nod my head.

"Are you ready to order?" I ask him and he makes a sound like you would to call a horse. You know, the one where you pull one cheek back and it makes that sucking sound.

"Not quite yet." He says and I nod.

"Can I ask you a question?" I randomly say to him, shocking myself. He looks up from the menu and his eyes glimmer, man he had the most gorgeous eyes.

"You just did." He plays and with me and I roll my eyes at him. That just reminds me of when you would ask someone if you could go to the bathroom and they replied with, 'I don't know, can you?'. I thought it was weird. "But yeah, I'm an open book." Which is the total opposite of me.

"Do you have a problem with my father?" Cooper sighed at this question and shook his head. Taylor had told me that him and my father and had never seen being friendly towards each other.

"No, but I think he has a problem with me." He didn't seem to worked up about it so I decided to leave it. He was going to say something but that bell on the door stopped him. We both looked and it was Mason and his parents. Oh crap, I can't do this today.

Before he could see me, I ducked behind the counter. I could hear Cooper start laughing and I put my head against the wood and closed my eyes, because I probably looked stupid doing that.

What I wasn't expecting was Cooper to come around the counter and sit beside me. He was so close to me I could could smell him, which was not a bad thing, he smelt like the outdoors, and some kind of cologne. "What are we doing down here?" He whispers in my ear, I'm hoping he didn't see the goosebumps on my skin that he gave me.

"Ex-boyfriend." I whisper and he sucks in a breath, like he knew the awkward feeling.

"And how do you plan to get out, just sit down here for an hour?" He whispers to me, obviously knowing I had no exit plan.

"Well that's where you come in." I looked at him and he shook his head.

"Oh no." He continued to shake his head and I pouted my lip.

"Please Cooper!" I grabbed his arm, getting his full attention. I almost took my hand off his skin, because it felt like electricity running through my fingers and up my arm. We both looked at our skin-to-skin contact, and he looked at me in the yes. "Pretty please. I can't do it today, and his parents are here!" I said and he took a deep breath.

"What can I do." He sighed as he gave into me. I looked in front of me and tried to think of something.

"Can you look over the counter, and just see where he is?" I ask him and he gives me the are-you-serious- look and I nodded to encourage him. He pushes himself up by using his arms, which I watched his biceps flex as he did this motion.

He comes down and lets out a breath and looks at me like he did something wrong. "Uh we might have a problem.." He says and I widen my eyes at him..

"Well what is it?"I whisper yell at him.

"He kinda saw me, and I think he might be walking over here." He said and I slapped his arm and I looked at his cowboy hat on.

"Well I wonder how he saw you?" I sarcastically say to him and he begins to smirk.

"Taking of my hat wasn't part of the plan, sweetheart." I was suppose to be mad at him, but the way he called me sweetheart, made all of that go away.

"Well a little bit of common-" I whispered to him but was cut off from a deep voice above us.

"DaKota?" I slowly looked up and saw Mason leaning over the counter, just like Cooper had done earlier. I quickly put on a fake smile to get Mason to think I was excited to see him. "What are you doing down there?" He says and then frowns when he sees Cooper. I look at Cooper and he has an emotionless look on his face.

"I uh lost an earing and Cooper was helping me find it." I lied and then I stood up to met his eye level and Cooper did the same.

"Did you find it?" He asks and I nod to him, and then he looks at Cooper, and it wasn't a polite look. "Good."

Cooper then chuckles and uncrosses his arms, "Okay, I get it. I'll just be right here, Kota." Cooper says and walks around the counter and sits back in his spot.

"Can we go talk?" Mason asks me and I really do not want to deal with this right now. If I hadn't talked to Taylor earlier, I would of been fine with talking to him. But Taylor told me everything he's done since I've been gone. Hooked up with a lot of girls, and even bashed me and my family. I don't really care about the hooking up, since we broke up.

"Now's not a good time, I have to go wait and figure out some things with the diner." I try to lie my best to him, the look on his face told me he that he didn't believe me.

"I've seen a lot of waitresses around here, DaKota." He says and I didn't look at him.

"Mason, you know this is small town right? People always hear what you say." I finally say and he looks confused but then he realizes.

"So you've talked to Taylor I see," He says and puts his hands on his hips and clenches his jaw. "That girl."

23

"Hey, you are talking about my best friend." I warn him and he sighs and drops his head. "Look, Mason. Can we just do this another day?" I plead him, but he doesn't budge. He reaches down and takes my hands into his.

"C'mon DaKota, I miss you and I miss us.. Let's just go back to my place and we can talk." He softly says to me and I shake my head and pull my hands away.

"I-" I was just going to turn him down again, but the call bell rang three times. Mason and I both looked over to Cooper, who had a inpatient look on his face. Telling me, that he was ready to order. "I have to go Mason." I say and walk back behind the counter.

I return my position in front of Cooper and side-eyed Mason looking at us and then leaving out the door. I put my hands on the counter and drop my head in between my shoulders.

I JUST FINISHED UNPACKING my boxes and I was really glad I did it because it was drivin' me crazy. But now I was gonna have a little fun at the cook out, but first I had to get myself lookin' pretty.

I walk over to my newly packed closet and I go through all of my dresses. It was a beautiful warm summer night, and just a light breeze to cool you down. I decided to take a shower before, just cause I had some time to do so.

As I was letting the water get my hair wet and ready for shampooing, I started thinking about Cooper. I started working at the diner at 9 and I ended at 5, and 95% of that time, I was talking to Cooper. I found it easy to talk to Cooper and I really liked it. He knew how to keep a conversation and he sure knew how to make me laugh and smile.

Cooper and I mostly talked about me, I tried to get him to talk about his life, but he somehow avoided it. It was really fun talking to him. He even did some flirting, and I shocked myself because I even flirted back.

I shook my head because I doubted he was thinking about me like I was thinking about him. From what Taylor had told me, he was quite the flirt to every girl he could talk to.

I flipped my hair up and down a couple of time after my shower and then wrapped it in a towel. I tied my robe belt in a knot and walked out into my bedroom. I still hadn't picked out my outfit, and now was a good time to do so.

I hummed along to a Willie Nelson song as I searched my closet and I finally found it. It was a light blue, spaghetti strap dress, it was so perfect for tonight. But since it was spaghetti strap, I had to wear a cardigan over it. I had gotten a tattoo while in Bismarck, and my parents were not big fans of tattoos, but it's not their skin. The tattoo had a special place to my heart, and it was on my left shoulder blade. I picked out a cream flowing caridigan to match with the dress, and I laid the outfit on the bed.

I heard a truck coming down the rode and I walked out to my balcony that faced our huge front yard. My jaw dropped when I saw a whole lot of people already here and mingling. I automatically spun on my heel and ran into my room. My heart was pounding in my chest, what time was it?! I grabbed my phone and it was already 7:18, and the party started at 7! My mom is going to kill me!

I slipped on the dress and then added my wolf and moon necklace and then stood in front of the mirror. The dress made me look even more tan than I already was, and my dark hair complimented the dress. I fixed my makeup a bit and then divided my hair into three and started to braid my hair behind my head.

My hair was so long, even in a braid it went down all the wall down my back, just to my tailbone. I also had a black anklet on my right foot with little diamond horseshoes on it, it was adorable. "DaKota Annie Jones! Are you almost done?" My mother barged into my room and looked around until she saw me.

"Yes mom." I say back to her and she smiles at me. She comes over to me and wraps her arms around me and mine go up her back.

"You look stunning." She says in the the hug and we pull back and she wraps an arm around my shoulder and my left arm goes around her waist and we start to walk out of my room.

"Well I got it from my mama." I say and kiss her cheek. My mom was my biggest role model and my best friend.

As I walked on the porch I realized how many people were here, a lot more than I expected. I saw Caleb standing with some buddies, he was wearing a black cowboy hat, a red, blue, and black flannel hoodie, and was holding a beer. Classic Caleb.

"There she is!" My father's voice sticks out from the crowd and I see everyone's head turn towards me. My fingers find the hem of my dress and start playing with it. I looked up and gave everyone a smile and my eyes landed on Cooper's glance. He shows me his crooked smile and it made me a blush a little.

After a couple of moments, everyone went back to talking, letting me relax now. I walk down the steps and I'm automatically greeted by Miss Kale. Miss Kale was a local who owned the giftshop I used to go to all the time. "Oh dear, it's great to have you back!" Her elder voice made me smile, she was very cute.

"It's good to be back." I smile back at her.

"I missed you so much! I didn't have no one to talk to about my Shetlands!" Miss Kale had two very cute Shetland ponies, they were like her children, since she wasn't married. She was happy though and didn't mind being single. I really admired her for that, she was a very positive person.

"Aw, I missed ya too!" I said and touched her shoulder.

"Well I'll let ya be, I'm sure you have other people who miss you!" She said and turned away from me. I swung my arms and put my hands together and turned on my bare heal. I looked around and started looking around for Ashley.

"Burgers, brats, and hot dogs are ready!" My father's voice boomed over the hungry people's voices.

"Finally!" The group of boys say and they're the first ones at the grill, and food table. I stayed back to let the guests get their food first.

I WAS CURRENTLY LAUGHING at Ashley and Taylor on the porch swing as we were finishing our burgers, and watching people. I was laughing because Taylor and Ash were arguing about the show Orange is the New Black. I had no idea what they were talking about, but they really were getting into it.

"If you don't agree with me, you're uninvited to my wedding!" Ashley pointed her finger at Taylor, and she gasped at Ash. Taylor was going to say something but closed her mouth and crossed her arms and huffed. I chuckled at them, they were always fun together.

"Hey Kota," Taylor said and I looked at her to see her and Ash smirking. They looked like they had just secretly made up a plan, and they end result wasn't good for me. "Looks like you got an admirer." She finished and elbowed me in the side.

I looked up to where Ashley was looking and I saw Cooper talking to some other guys and then he looked at me, and he gave me a polite smile. I returned it, but I had a blush upon my cheeks. He looked good tonight, and he changed his clothes from earlier today. He was wearing dark blue jeans, and an dark green RVCA shirt. "Oooo, does someone have a little crush?" Ashley mocked me and I rolled my eyes and shook my head.

"I don't know." I quietly said, did I like him? It was kinda too soon to tell, but I always did get this feeling in my stomach when I saw him. I guess time would only tell. "Are you done with your plates?" I ask them, avoiding the subject.

"Yeah, but why don't Ash and I take them?" Taylor says in a very suspicious voice, but I shake it off.

"Are you sure, you guys are my guests." I tell them, it would be rude of me to have them take their plates back.

"Oh no!" Asheley says and takes my plate. She again looks at Taylor and they smile like little girls, "Consider it our little welcome back gift." After they had walked down the porch steps, they high-fived each other. They are so weird.

But once my eye averted to my left, I saw what they were doing. Cooper was now walking towards the porch and I looked back to were the girls were. They were "innocently" standing there and waving, those sneaky little bitches.

I looked up when I heard his boots on the wood of the porch. I met his eyes and they sparkled down at me, as he was walking to me. "What's the guest of honor doing all by herself?" He smoothly says as he leans against the railing.

"Well my friends kind of ditched me." I say and direct my hand in the direction of Ash and Tay. He turns to look at them, but they turn around before he can see them. They are unbelievable. "You can sit if you want." I say and gesture right beside me.

He takes me up on my offer and sits closer than I thought he would. Our legs were an inch apart, it started to make my hands sweat. "You don't like attention do you?" He asks me and I turn my head towards him. How could he know that?

"Am I that readable?" I chuckle and he shakes his head and looks at the guests.

"Nah, but when you came out and your dad announced you, your cheeks were as red as a sharpie." He says and what he said made me think, sharpie?

I raise my eyebrows at him, "A Sharpie?" I question his simile and he looks confused.

"Yeah, what about it?" He asks as he looks at me if I was crazy.

"Well usually people say like tomato, or firetruck. Not a sharpie." I giggle a bit and tuck a loose piece behind my ear and look at him again.

I was a little taken back when he leaned down and whispered, "I do what I want, sugar." Now I was furiously blushing, why did he have to do that to me?

THE PARTY WAS OVER but close friends were still inside the house, it was all the girls inside the house and the boys were still outside. Every woman here was my mother's friend, because Ash and Taylor had left a while ago.

I was laying on the couch, under a quilt, reading one of my favorite books, "White Fang." Ever since I was a little girl I was very interested in Native American culture, and wolves were my second favorite animals.

I was interrupted reading my book, by the sound of a horse whinnying. I sat up and pulled the covers off me and walked over to the window. The sun was still shining on the land, and it looked like it would go down in about an hour.

My jaw dropped at what I saw. At least 10 men standing in the pasture, and a white horse trailer being backed in. My heart broke at what I was seeing. They had my horse Pharaoh cooped up in a round pen. Pharaoh was running around in circles, occasionally stopping to rear. He was panicking. What the hell are they doing!

I started to run past the kitchen where the woman were at and my mother had stopped me, "Dakota, just stay inside.." She softly said and I was disgusted by her words. I scoffed at her and ran to the door and outside.

I climbed the fence to get into the pasture and ran towards the chaos. I noticed everyone had ropes in their hands, what are they doing to my horse? I was looking around for my father and brother. They came out from behind the horse trailer on their horses. "What the hell is going on?" I yell at them and every one turns to look at me.

"Go inside DaKota." Caleb says in a deep-over-protective-brotherly-tone. I look up and glare at him.

"Not until someone tells me what is going on!" I demand back, holding my own ground.

"That horse has got to go." My father shocks me. Why would they give up Pharaoh, he's one of the best horses we've ever had.

"What? I don't understand." I run a hand through my loosely braided hair.

"Look at it," My dad says and turns back and looks at the scared beast. "A couple months after you left that horse went back to it's ways. It was very short-tempered and was very dangerous! It even tried to attack other horses and damaged the barns, and kicked down a gate. We can't afford to keep-" My father said and it was breaking my heart. I could never imagine Pharaoh doing this, he was such a sweet horse.

"He's just scared right now, if I go in there and tr-" I was cut off by my older brother.

"No Dakota." Caleb had a very deep voice, but it didn't strike me. I was used to his protests, he didn't scare me. I started walking to the corral while every one watch.

"Young lady you come back here!" My father's voice yelled at me, but I continued walking. I knew he wasn't going to do anything, he always gave into me.

"Is she crazy?" I heard voices say, but I paid no attention. I couldn't give a damn about what they thought, this was my horse. I was the one who broke him, and the one he trusted. Horses are very intelligent, he would definitely recognize me.

CHAPTER 2

I was almost to the gate when someone's hand pulled me back causing me to stop. I looked at the hand on my left forearm, and my eyes traveled up the arm and to the face of Cooper. What was he doing here? "DaKota what are you doing? You'll get yourself killed if you go in there!" He pleaded me, didn't he know not to mess with a girl and her horse?

"Get your hands off me," I snapped at him and he looked shocked, "I know what I am doing, he'll listen to me." I said and my eyes glanced down and saw the halter he had in his hands. I quickly snatched the halter from his left hand and pulled my arm away from him, and I ran to the gate and climbed over the gate.

"DaKota!" Cooper yelled, but my brother did to.

I softly landed on the ground, and I gasped at Pharaoh. His mane and tail were tangled up, and he had a lot of muck on him, hiding his beautiful wild coloration. I slung the halter around my shoulder and walked into the middle of the corral.

Amazingly, Pharaoh had stopped running and now stood on the other side of the corral, across from me. I looked him in the eyes and spoke to him, "Hey boy, remember me?" And I actually smiled when I said it.

He just stomped his foot at me and thrashed his head. I walked a little more towards him, still having eye contact. I held out my hand in the middle of the corral, "C'mon Phar, it's me, DaKota." I softly spoke to him, and he came forward to me.

It made me smile widely, but once my fingertips brushed against his soft nose, he got scared. In a flash he bucked up and kicked his legs, barely missing me. But I didn't flinch. "That's it Dakota!" Caleb yelled behind me, climbing the gate.

"Caleb, go away.. You'll scare him." I said and he gave me the too-late look and continued. I ran over to him, "Please Caleb, just one more try.. I have to do this." I beg him, trying to use my best puppy eyes. I was his little sister, he could never say no to me.

"Fine." He growled at me and climbed back down. Even if this didn't work, I still wouldn't let anyone touch my horse.

I was honestly trying to come up with another way to get Pharaoh to recognize me.. I again stopped across from him and he did to. "C'mon Pharaoh, it's me.." I say with tears in my eyes, I couldn't loose this horse, he meant to much to me.

Pharaoh's eyes showed lots of fear and confusion. I again held my hand out and walked to the middle. Pharaoh took a couple of steps towards me, but then stopped. "Hey good boy. Right? You're my good handsome boy.." I say.

I drop the bridle off my shoulder and take off my flannel very slowly. My front side was in front of everyone, so no one would see my tattoo. Maybe I could use my flannel to get him to smell my scent, I know it's weird, but it's gotta work.

I cautiously throw my flannel in front of him, and then he lowers his neck to sniff it. He stomped on it a couple of times, and continued to sniff it. Then the next thing he did surprised me, he picked it up between his teeth and he walked over to me. A tear fell down my cheek as I grabbed the flannel from him. I put my hand on his face and put my forehead to his. "Good boy." I smiled.

I walked back a couple of steps and Pharaoh followed me, I bent down and grabbed the halter. I turned around and let Pharaoh smell it and then I slid it over his head. I kissed his forehead and went to the gate and opened it. As I did, I looked up and saw Cooper completely shocked to death with his jaw dropped.

I walked to Pharaoh's left side and I put the lead rope over his head. I grabbed onto his mane and pulled myself up. I grabbed the reins in my hands and got settled on him, I haven't done this in a long time. I took a deep breath and kicked his sides and he bolted off. Showing off to every guy there, that's my boy.

RIDING PHARAOH WAS my antidote. Everything just seemed to go away when it was just me and him, out in wide open spaces. Riding along the land that God had blessed us with, it was surreal. Pharaoh rid so smoothly, I barely used the rope.

It was getting pretty dark so I decided to head back to the main pasture. I knew I was in trouble when I got home because I disobeyed him and all that crap. I could care less because I got my horse back.

After I had put Pharaoh back into his stall, I had began walking to the house. I saw there were still lamps on, indicating they were waiting for me. I took a deep breath and jogged to the house because it was getting cold out here.

I opened the door and automatically looked at the dining table, yep, there they were. "I don't need a lecture." I told them and my dad stood up, he didn't look too happy with me, nor did my mom.

"That was reckless, did you even think what could of happened to you?" I really wanted to roll my eyes at him, but I knew I'd pay big time for doing so.

"Obviously I did.. What were you going to do with him?" I asked him, afraid of the answer.

"Sell him to Mr. Erickson." He said, and I gulped. Well it could be worse. Mr. Erickson raised the top bucking horses around, and had made quite the name for himself.

"You didn't even try did you?" I snapped at him. He never did like that horse because it was a mustang, he never supported me while I was breaking him.

"DaKota, you better watch it." My dad warns me, my dad hated being told off, especially of one of the opposite sex.

"Look, everything is okay now. So I don't see what's the big deal, it's over with." I reasoned with them, I hated getting into fights with my parents. "I just want to go to bed, it's been a long day." I say to them, really tired about talking about this.

"Goodnight." He surprisingly says.

"Night." I say back to him.

After I was done in the bathroom, I changed into a big t-shirt and some running shorts. I put my hair into a messy bun, and climbed into my bed. Before I laid down I reached down under my bed and reached into my boots and grabbed the container.

I dumped a pill into my hand and grabbed the glass of water on my nightstand, and I downed the pill. My parents didn't know about these pills and they won't. These pills helped me not get nightmares.

I got these pills back in Bismarck, because my nightmares were really bad after that night. I never had flashbacks during the day, it happened when I would close my eyes and be in the dark. Or when ever there was a storm.

During my nightmares, I wake up screaming or covering my mouth with my hand, trying to get me to stop screaming, causing me to almost suffocate. I would be dripping with sweat and I would have a hard time breathing. After a nightmare I wouldn't go back to sleep, even sometimes the pills wouldn't work. The only thing I had to hope for was my strength..

As I looked at myself in my long body mirror I straightened out my tank top. I was wearing boot cut jeans, and a loose light gray tee. I also had a golden square belt buckle on, it was my own barrel racing buckle. My hair was pulled back into a low bun, and I made it look a little messy.

Today is Sunday, so you know what that means, church! I loved going to church, and our church, St. Mary's. It wasn't small but not your average size of a church. Our priest was very kind and very wise, our family was close to him.

Sunday was also a very busy day at the diner, especially after church. Sundays were also by binge watching day, I only watched my TV shows and movies on Sunday.

We always traveled in one truck when we went to church. Even Ashley came with us, she already basically in the family. So it was Ashley in the middle, and Caleb and I beside her. "So who sings now?" I ask my parents as we pull up to the white church.

"Avery.." My mother says and my neck snaps towards her. Well, good for her.

We walked into the church together and we walked to our usual spot. It was in the fourth row in the front and we took up the whole pew, except for a couple of spaces, but no one sat there anyways. We said hi to a few people we knew as we walked to the pew. I was a little shocked when I saw Cooper on the other side in the third pew up.

He didn't see me, but he was facing forward. He was standing beside a woman with blonde hair and she stood at his biceps, must be his mom. But I was confused when I saw a smaller figure standing besides his mom. "Stop staring." Ashley smirks beside me and pokes me with her finger. I didn't say anything but just start to wait for mass to start.

WE WAITED OUR TURN to exit the pew, and when we did I genuflected, and then rose. I was in front of everyone as we walked through the door and greeted Father Robert. Like an cliche church, everyone was talking out front. "Oh Dakota! If I would of saw you earlier, I would of asked you!" Mrs. Ingleheart said to me.

"Asked me what?" I say, not picking up on what she was trying to say.

"To sing again! You and Avery would make a great pair!" She said and I put my best fake smile on, because the thought of us singing together made me puke inside.

"Oh, what a shame." I force out of my mouth, still having the fake smile on my face, trying to be polite.

"Next Sunday for sure!" She said and winked at me and walked away to go to her husband. My mother wrapped an arm my shoulder and side-hugged me. As we were walking down the steps my eyes landed on a certain pair of brown eyes. I sent him a polite smile and he returned it and then I looked away.

My dad pulled into a parking spot at the Diner, and we all piled out. I pulled the door open, it revealed every seat in the spot in the Diner full. I looked around and it was mostly people coming from church, I sighed and left my family to go help out.

I RANG THE KITCHEN bell and yelled, "Martin!" I yelled to the the head chef to let him know another ticket was on the spiny deal. I walked back out around to the dining area and walked to my tables to see how they were doing, I was a great waitress. "Thanks for coming today, y'all have a great day." I say to a family as I return their change and receipt.

"Thanks DaKota." The mother sweetly smiled and I smiled back and walked away. I noticed a new couple of customers at the counter, my area. I quickly walked to the other side of the counter and grabbed two menus and walked over to the customers. Most people would feel overwhelmed by the amount of customers, but it made me happy because I'm glad people chose to come here.

When I saw who my new customers I smiled to myself. It was Cooper and the small boy he was with in church earlier. "Hey Cooper, who ya got here?" I smiled brightly as I placed down there menus for them.

I stared at the little kid and I almost 'awed' at his big brown eyes, they reminded me of Cooper's. "This right here, is my little brother Reese." He smiled down to his little brother and wrapped an arm around him. I was shocked he had a little brother, he had never brought Reese up in one of conversations. Reese was on of the cutest kids I had seen.

"Hi, what's your name?" He had such a little voice, sweet and southern. He made me melt inside, he was going to be a heart breaker when he grows up. Just like his brother.

"I'm DaKota." I say to him and he giggles. I look at Cooper and he raises an eyebrow at his little brother.

"What?" Cooper asks while adding a light chuckle.

"Just like the states? That's funny." I don't take offense to it, I did have an unusual name, and he was just a kid. I even started laughing.

"Well I think it's a beautiful name." Cooper says and looks up at me, his eyes sparkle at me. How does he do that? When he said that I dropped my head and blushed, hard core. After I'm done blushing I get back to my job.

"So what can I get you to drink?" I ask Reese.

"Can I have a chocolate milk?" He asks, but he sounds a little shy for asking. It was so cute.

"Sure thing, and I suppose you want a raspberry iced tea, Cooper?" Cooper always ordered that when he's been here.

"Yes ma'am." He says and I nod and walk away from them. I grab two glasses from the shelf and go to the fridge and pour Reese's glass of chocolate milk and then Cooper's iced tea. I put one in each hand and returned, to just Cooper. I looked around and I saw Reese going to the bathroom on crutches, aw what happened to him?

As I sat the glasses down I looked at Cooper, "Why is he on crutches?" I ask Cooper and he sighs and turns his head around to look at Reese, then back at me.

"When he was about four, he got Osteosarcoma Cancer." That broke my heart, "A tumor started to grow in his tibia, and as it got bigger when he was six. So to stop the cancer from spreading, they amputated his leg until his femur." I could hear my heart break some more, no kid should have to go through that.

"I'm so sorry Coop, is he okay?" I ask him.

"Yeah, it's kind of funny, he thinks his leg is so cool. Although, he really didn't understand the cancer part of it.. He's a really good kid." He smiles at the end, which makes me smile.

"Why haven't you ever mentioned him before, you guys seem to have a good relationship." I say to him, even though I should be waiting other tables, but other waitresses are doing it, since I volunteered.

"I don't really like talking bout it." He says a little rough but I completely understand because I don't talk about me being raped. "Sorry, it's ju-"

"No, I understand what's it like." I say to him and then Reese comes back. I give Reese a toothless smile and then Cooper stands up and helps Reese up on the stool.

COOPER

I WATCHED HER COME out of the church and she was immediately was greeted by other people. People were always with her, unless we were at the diner. That was my time to talk to her, I really liked talking to DaKota. She was real sweet, understanding, funny, had a good spirit, and wasn't afraid to say what was on her mind. And I didn't mind looking at her face for awhile, too.

DaKota made me feel some type of way when we spoke, some way I had never felt before with any other girl. I was lucky, because in church I kept turning my head to look at her and she didn't catch me. But sometimes, Caleb did and that's when I would look away.

I liked Caleb, he was really fun to be around and he was laid back. But somehow, I don't think that would be the same with his sister.

Church was church, but I hated when they begun to sing. I sing along too, but I hated when Avery sang. Avery was my ex girlfriend, and worst mistake in awhile. She was really clingy and she always wanted to go party or go to one of the bigger cities to shop, or some shit like that.

She didn't even come watch me bull ride or sometimes bull dog. I even went to go watch show jump, which was absolute hell for me. I needed a real cowgirl, and that was DaKota.

I was going to go talk to her, but then her mother pulled her away. I let out a frustrated breath and returned to helping Reese.

I HELPED REESE ONTO the stool at DaKota's Diner, I would have got a booth, but the place was packed. "What are you hungry for buddy?" I turn towards Reese as he gets settled.

"Foooooooood!" He says making me laugh. Every time I look at Reese I think of my father, I hated that man for what he did to us.

I was hoping that DaKota would be serving us, because I really wanted to talk to her. My wish was on command when I saw her happily walking over to us. Maybe she was happy she was serving us. "Hey Cooper, who ya got here?" She smiled brightly at us, her smile was hypnotizing to me. She was still wearing her outfit from church, and her hair was done perfectly to me.

"This right here, is my little brother Reese." I said proudly to my little brother and wrapped my left arm around his shoulder and ruffed up his hair. He giggled slightly and then I let him go.

"Hi, what's your name?" Reese politely said to her and she looked impressed.

"I'm DaKota." When she says her name he starts to laugh, I was confused and so was she. I looked down at him and raised my eyebrow.

"What?" I ask him to see what's going on in his tiny mind.

"Just like the states? That's funny." He explained himself. I had just taught him the states, and he was talking about North and South Dakota.

"Well I think it's a beautiful name." I compliment her. She wasn't trying to smile, but it broke out and I saw her cheeks get red before she hid it. I liked when I did that to her, it gave me hope.

"So what can I get you to drink?" She side-steps me, and begins to be a waitress again.

"Can I have a chocolate milk?" He said, chocolate milk was his favorite.

"Sure thing, and I suppose you want a raspberry iced tea, Cooper?" I smiled when she remembered what I ordered, she continued to get me every time.

"Yes ma'am." I say with a nod and she smiles and walks away.

"Why are you watching her?" Reese's voice says beside me and I break my gaze from DaKota and look at him.

"One day you'll understand." I sigh as I say.

"Can I go to the bathroom?" He asks me and I nod.

"Do you need me to help you?" I ask him and he shakes head at me. I know he can go to the bathroom on his own, but I always asked just in case.

"No thank you." He says in a matter-of-fact tone, but I do help him down from the stool.

I watch him all the way to the bathroom, until I heard, "Why is he on crutches?" It was her sweet voice behind me.

"When he was about 4, he got Osteosarcoma Cancer." When I said it, her lips turned into a sad frown, "A tumor started to grow in his tibia, and as it got bigger when he was six. So to stop the cancer from spreading, they amputated his leg until his femur." I hated talking about his case, because I was always scared the cancer would come back.. Reese was so strong.

"I'm so sorry Coop, is he okay?" When she called me 'Coop' I almost exploded. My name sounded so good off her tongue.

"Yeah, it's kind of funny, he thinks his leg is so cool. Although, he really didn't understand the cancer part of it.. He's a really good kid." I smile, thinking about him playing the end of his amputated leg. My mom and I were hoping to get a prosthetic pretty soon for his birthday.

"Why haven't you ever mentioned him before, you guys seem to have a good relationship." She sounded a bit hurt that I didn't tell her, but I hated talking about my family.

"I don't really like talking bout it." I say a little too mean for my liking and I automatically felt bad. "Sorry, it's ju-" I was going to apologize but she stopped me.

"No, I understand what's it like." She says and I wanna know what she means by that.

I would ask her more about why she left Hudson, and she was always so cautious about what she said. I also asked her what she did in Bismarck, and she would stumble on her words. Almost if she couldn't remember. But I doubt she would have a reason to lie to me.

I was hoping to talk to her more today because the rest of my week is busy. This last week I had a week off of work, but now I had to work from 9-7, and also do chores at my house. There was no time I would be able to come to the diner, well maybe on Wednesday, those are my off days.

Maybe I could get her to hangout with me, or even a date. I would have to ask her dad first, because I like to be a gentleman and make a good impression.

"Cooper?" Her voice wakes me up from my thoughts and I look at her and she has a pad in her hands, she must be taking our orders.

"Oh," I smirk a bit, "I'll have a bacon cheeseburger, cheddar, and sweet potato fries." I tell her and hand her my menu. When I do my fingertips touch hers and I literally felt a spark, and I could tell she did to by the way she looked at me. That has never happened before.. What do I do? She's driving me crazy, a good crazy of course.

"Ever since that night I always had trouble talking to guys, or being comfortable, or not trying to think of those nights. If a boy would ever get too close to me, I would flinch or even close my eyes. In Bismarck, I tried to go out with a lot of guys to see if I could handle it better. Some went well and others went bad. With the some that went well, I would get them to make out with me. Everything would go okay, until they would slip their hand under my shirt, and then I would have a flashback.. Sometimes even bare skin contact sent me back to that night.. But lately there has been a few times I wouldn't think, I would feel something different. Those times have been with Cooper. His fingers have brushed against mine, he has grabbed my arm once, and one time he accidentally put his hand on my thigh. Cooper always gave me these huge butterflies in my stomach when I was talking to him, or even if I just saw him. I never had these feelings before and they were hella confusing to me. I haven't seen Cooper in about four days, and the weird thing is that I think I actually miss him walking into the diner. I guess he didn't feel the same as I did for him, figures.." I wrote in my diary and then closed the book and shoved it back under the cushion of my chair.

It's been a normal week for me: work at diner, online school, chores, and try to busy myself. On Tuesday I started working with my mom again at the Vet Clinic again. My mom owned the Vet Clinic and I used to go on calls with her all the time. I was a very quick learner and I would keep notes in my notebook I would bring with.

Seeing how my mom would treat and care for the animals inspired me to be just like my mom, a veterinarian. I loved working with animals and treating the unusual animals, like llamas.

Today and tomorrow were going to awesome! It was the first day of the Hudson Rodeo! My dad had managed to get me entered for barrels and team roping. I would be teaming roping with Taylor, who was the header and I was the heeler. Taylor also did barrels, she had a great quarter horse. Caleb would be bare backing, and Ashley would be worrying from the stands. Broncs weren't near as nerve wrecking as bulls. I didn't know if my dad would be competing today or tomorrow.

When my dad was younger he did every event, except bulls and barrels. His best event was broncs and then it was bull dogging. My dad was one of the best.

AS I GOT OUT OF MY truck I looked at myself in my extension mirror of the Dodge 3500 dually. I straightened out my black felt cowboy hat and looked at my big curls, I was satisfied. I had some dark blue jeans on and a white barrel racing shirt on, I had one of my gold belt buckles on, and some buckskin Ariat square-toed boots on.

I went back to our trailer and opened it and there stood my beautiful Pharaoh, "Hey boy." I smiled at him and scratched his head. I walked over to the other side and grabbed his saddle blanket and his saddle.

I looked at Pharaoh's customized breast collar and ran my fingers over it. It was hand carved leather with turquoise and white and gold studded diamonds. I was only getting ready now because I had to sing the national anthem.

I was extremely nervous to sing, even though I had done it a number of times. I loved doing it though because I loved holding the Flag and then having Pharaoh ride along the gates of the arena was the best feeling in the world. Along with the crowd's cheers and yells.

I had Pharaoh's reins in my right hand and started walking him to the back gates of the arena. I watched the bleachers start to fill up and my heart started racing a bit, but I had done this plenty of times, why was I so nervous today? "Hey DaKota!" I heard a voice from behind me, I turned my head and saw Mason jogging towards me.

"Oh boy." I mumbled to myself and waited for him to get to my side. "Hey Mason, what are you doing here?" I say to him, and he lets out a breath from just jogging.

"Well I thought I'd make an appearance, but then I heard you were competing again, so I decided to come early so I could hear you sing." He says, trying to be cute, but I didn't by into it.

"Well thanks." I chuckle, not really knowing what to say to him.

"Yeah Avery was pissed when she heard you were singing and competing." He says and then I finally look at him. "She took your spot when you were gone." He informed me and I just nodded. Avery never barrel raced, she must of started when I was gone.

"Well I'm back so.." I say in kind of of bitchy voice but I didn't care, Avery always tried to compete with me. I hated it!

"When she found out, she almost screamed.. But I think she's jealous and knows that your better than her. I think she's threatened that your back, and that you will steal all of the attention from her." He rambles on and I really didn't care about her anymore.

"She can have the attention, I don't want it." I directly say and he smiles a bit and nods. "Well I should be going, see you later." I say to him and give him my best polite smile and pull Pharaoh away from him.

I looked up and saw Taylor and a few other girls already mounted and ready to go. The other girls were Jessica, Molly, and Reyna. They were very sweet and nice girls, all of us grew up together. I pulled Pharaoh over to them and then mounted myself. "Hey DaKota." They sweetly smiled to me and a slight wave.

"Hey girls." I say as I grab the reins and stop Pharaoh. We all place our horses beside each other in a neat straight line.

"Wasn't Avery suppose to come?" Jessica says as she leans back in her saddle.

"She was and then she found out big-mean-ol'-DaKota was coming." Taylor says and we all laugh together. I lean up up on my saddle and rest my arms on the horn of the saddle.

"Ow ow! Look who's coming over here girls!" Molly says in a loud but quiet voice, just for us to hear. Then she adds a quick cat whistle, I laugh at her. She had lots of fire inside her, and she was a crazy cowgirl.

"He fits in those jeans so well, if he bent over I'd fall off my horse." Jessica sweet talks, they are so crazy. I finally turn my head to the left where they were looking, and I saw they were talking about the one and only, Cooper Blackwood. It was weird, I started blushing.

He looked up and smiled at me, and then he walked over to my horse. "Hey DaKota, girls." His charming voice says and looks at me and tips his hat at the other girls. I side look the girls and I could tell they were trying not to giggle like little school girls.

"Hey Coop, what's up?" I speak clearly to him, kinda happy I finally get to see him after a while. He then walked over to my left side and placed his left hand on Pharaoh's mane and he looked up at me.

"Well I was just gonna ask if you were gonna watch bull riding and wrestlin'." His charming southern voice says and it makes me a grin a bit.

"I might, depends what I got going on." I say and he frowns a bit, but then smirks.

"Well you should, I could use a good luck charm." He smoothly says and slightly cocks his head to the side, revealing a crooked grin to me. I felt my cheeks heat up and I smiled down at him.

"Okay I'll come." I sheepishly said to him and couldn't stop smiling at him.

"C'mon girls!!" A voice yelled from behind us, and we all turned and Mrs. Ellington was waving at us.

"Well we gotta go, good luck later!" I say and return in my posture and grab the reins.

"Thanks you too, see ya girls." Cooper says and we all pull our reins and walk away.

"Bye!" The girls say and when we started to walk our horses, it started, "Oh my gosh DaKota! You are sooo lucky!" Reyna, Jess, and Molly gasp at me. I shake my head at them and laugh, I didn't know what to say! Because I didn't know where him and I stood, ugh.

"Well girls, looks like he'll be bent over for DaKota." Taylor says and I gasp at her, but we all laugh. Taylor was always like that, I loved her for it.

THE GIRLS AND I JUST finished riding the sponsors flag around the arena, and now it was time for the National Anthem. One of the judges handed me the American Flag and I took it in my right hand, and the microphone. "Cowgirls and Cowboys, please rise and remove your hats." The announcers deep southern voice says and then I ride out into the middle.

I hold the flag in my left hand and drop the reins and hold the mic with my left. I took a big gulp and cleared my throat, and waited for the music to start. "Oh, say can you see, By the dawn's early light, What so proudly we hailed, At the twilight's last gleaming? Whose broad stripes and bright stars, Through the perilous fight, O'er the ramparts we watched, Were so gallantly streaming. And the rocket's red glare, The bombs bursting in air, Gave proof through the night, That our flag was still there. Oh say does that star spangled banner yet wave, For the land of the free, and the home of the brave!" I sung into the micro phone and then picked up the reins with my fingers and rode to the gate and threw the mic to the judge and then kicked Pharaoh in the sides and he exploded around the arena.

Everyone was clapping and yelling, as the Flag waved in the air from Pharaoh and I. I held it proudly and smiled wide for the crowd. Even with all the noise, I could hear Phar breathing hard and his shoes pounding into the soft dirt. I loved riding him, and loved the way the air from his speed felt in my face. As I passed the bucking chutes I heard, "That's my little sister!!" Obviously it was Caleb and it made me smile even bigger.

I rode around one more time and then stopped my horse at the entrance gate and then walked Pharaoh out. "Oh sweetie, you sang so good!!" My mother says to me as I slid down my horse and she gives me a light hug.

"Thanks mama." I say and she lets go of me. I give the flag back to the judge, "Great job." He says and I give him a smile and thank him.

TAYLOR AND I WERE WAITING our turn for team roping, we were up next. The top time already was 4.9 seconds, that was going to be tricky. Taylor and I were the third to last, so we had to beat it to make top three. Taylor was the header and I was the heeler. "C'mon girls." The judge said and we entered onto the dirt.

I took my place in the right box and backed Pharaoh into the padded corner. I raised my throwing arm up above my head and looked at Taylor and gave her a nod. She got situated and then she nodded her head.

The steer broke out and then we were hot on it's trail. We were real close to breaking the barrier but we didn't. Taylor made a sweet throw over the horns and then she turned her horse and the rope got tight and ripped the steer to turn and then I swung a couple of times and released the rope out of my fingers and it went right around the two hind legs! Yes! When the legs were pulled, I looked at the clock, 5 on the dot! Sweet!

Taylor and I high-fived and exited the arena, and stood by the gates. I straightened out my hat and put my rope loops over my saddle horn. "That was a great throw." I told Taylor and she shrugged cockily, but I knew she was joking.

"Well you looked like Jade Corkill!" She said, comparing me to the best heeler in the world. I was no way near as good as him, but I'll take the compliment.

The other two teams, their times were 5.1 and 8.4, so Taylor and I were in second! The next event was steer wrestling, so that meant I had to go watch Cooper.

Molly, Reyna, Jess, Tay, and I were all sitting in the front bleacher watching the steer wrestling, and there was some pretty impressive times. Cooper still hasn't gone yet, and I was really interested to see if he was good enough. There was no doubt that he had the strength to bring the steer down fast.

I couldn't help but stare at Avery and her groupies standing near the gates, they were so annoying. I almost rolled my eyes every time they laughed. After this event was barrels, then tie down, then broncs, and the last event was bulls. "Our next bull dogger is the young and furious

46

Cooper Blackwood!" The announcer boomed and we all cheered. Avery cheered a little more than others, whore.

I didn't know who was his 'hazer', but I hope he did his job well. Cooper had a beautiful buckskin quarter horse, and it had a really unique hair color, kinda like a graphite color. The horse went in a couple of circles and then Cooper smoothly backed the horse into the box.

When Cooper nodded, the steer bolted out of the chute. It was just like lightning! I thought the steer was fast, but damn, Cooper's horse was faster. Also the hazer's horse also had amazing speed, making them a great pair. It felt like Cooper was on the steer in a blink of an eye.

Cooper wrapped his arm behind the horns and planted his feet and got a hold of the steer. With one quick movement of his muscular body, the steer fell into the dirt, and the crowd roared with life. "Wooooo-hooooo!" All of us girls yelled and threw up our hands, and we all laughed after it.

Cooper stood up and watched the steer run away and then he walked over to get his hat and gave the crowd a small thank you wave. Before he got mounted on his horse, he found my gaze and gave me a quick wink and I winked back, but I was the only one who blushed. Obviously Avery must of saw because she turned to look at me and she gave me a death glare. I couldn't help but laugh and stick my tongue at her.

IT'S NOW MY TURN FOR barrels and I took a long deep breath. I can do this, just like old times. I've been practicing for a couple days and it looked promising, I just hoped Pharaoh was thinking the same. "And now, our last barrel racer of the night, DaKota Joooonnnnessss!" The announcer yelled into the mic, but before he even announced me being the last rider, I had already took off. "She's so fast I didn't even finish!" He laughed into the mic.

Pharaoh quickly and tightly turn the first barrel, letting me relax some. I kicked him more and lead him to the next barrel, it was a little sloppy, but we didn't tip the barrel. Making up for the sloppiness, I pushed him harder to the last barrel.

She turned the barrel perfectly, and very quickly. I gave him butt a quick slap before we headed for the home stretch. "C'mon babe!" I said to him, I was flying in the saddle. I could hear his hard breathing and I watched his muscles contract and push with all his might.

Once we reached the line I sat up on the saddle and pulled the reins up. I knew it was a good run because the crowd was going nuts, "DaKota and her horse Pharaoh with a time of 13.6, earning her the top spot. Way to end the night, DaKota!" He said, and it made me smile ear-to-ear.

I was still mounted on my house, walking Pharaoh back to my trailer. On my way the girls caught up to me, all with their horses. "Good job Kota!" Molly said to me and I gave her a kind smile.

"Thanks, Molls, you did great too." I said back to her and she rolled her eyes at me.

"Always have to beat me, don't you?" Taylor pipped in and I shook my head at her.

"Someone's gotta keep you in line." I said and she rolled her eyes at me.

"Did anyone hear what Avery got?" Jessica says and no one says anything, I don't really think I even heard her name being called. Or maybe I trained my brain to block out her name.

"She hit two barrels, I think she got like 30 seconds." Reyna said, making me snicker a bit. I knew it was mean, but it's Avery we're talking about.

"Speak of the she-devil." Taylor says making us all confused, until we look to our right and Avery is walking over towards us. Surprisingly she doesn't have her little 'city posse' with her.

"Lord help us." Molly mumbles, making me smirk to myself.

"Well isn't this a classic DaKota move? Comes back and steals all of the attention, doing whatever she can to beat me." Avery says and crosses her arms and cocks her head to the side.

"Let's be real Avery." I say with a stern look, and then I break out into a smirk, "I wasn't the only one who beat you tonight, about every other girl was in front of your time." I say and Taylor and the other girls snicker.

"You've been gone for two years, and you're trying to steal singing the National Anthem, my popularity, and my Cooper." My Cooper? She had a bitch tone going on, and I really wanted her to shut up. What was she even talking about, my Cooper? Psht, they couldn't be dating.. What if they were?

"You're overreacting." I said to Avery, she was pushing it too far and she needed to stop.

"Cooper obviously likes her more," Jessica says and I just look at the ground, because I couldn't get the image of Cooper flirting with Avery. "She's his good luck charm." Jess says in a mater-of-fact-tone.

"Oh really?" Avery laughs, causing me to scrunch my eyebrows. "He's told me that at least a thousand times." She says like I should of expected it. I wasn't going to lie, I was hurt. But how could I know if she was telling the truth. "Don't believe me?" She raises her eyebrow at me. "Did he ask you if you were staying for the events? Then he probably made you feel like you were the only girl in the world. And if you said no, did he use that cute crooked-smile on you? Or if y-" She walked closer to me, giving me a your-so-dumb look.

I had to cut her off, "Okay Avery, that's enough." I raised my voice lightly, because I knew she was right. I couldn't what I was saying, I actually believed Avery Johnson. "Let's go." I said to the girls and I pulled Pharaoh's reins and started walking to my trailer.

Why was I so butt-hurt about this? Cooper and I weren't anything. I didn't even know if I liked her. But I think it was the part where I fell for his ways. What Avery described to me was exactly how it happened. Cooper used his charm on me, like he had practiced it a million of times. "You don't actually believe her do you?" Taylor says to me while we dismount.

"I don't want to, but it's what happened." I say in a dull tone and start to untack Pharaoh.

"C'mon Kota, it's Avery!" Taylor says and sits down on the edge of the trailer floor.

"I know Tay," I say and turn to look at her with my saddle in my hands. "Do you remember when you talked about what happened when I was away? I asked you about Cooper and you said all he did was flirt? Why should I be shocked then, it's Cooper Blackwood, we're talking about." But even I didn't believe myself.

It was almost Cooper's time to ride, and I don't really know what I was feeling. Mostly betrayed because I actually thought what he said was real, and he was trying to impress me. Taylor and I looked at each other, "Am I stupid?" I ask her and she frowns and shakes her head at me.

"DaKota, you are like the most smart person I know." She said to me, and then I looked at the ground.

"Smartest." I corrected her, and she rolled her eyes at me.

"Exactly! But honey, no girl is smart or stupid when it comes to guys. Trust me." She says and I sigh and nod. "How bout we go to the parking lot and go find some dogs." She said and I smiled. Taylor and I used to go into the parking lot and go pet some random people's dogs that were tied to a tree or trailer, it was actually fun.

"Let's go, I hope we see some Blue Heelers!" I smile at her as we stand up. Ironically as we start to walk down on the bleachers the announcer says, "The young and furious Cooper Blackwood, riding the lovely Texas Sweetheart!" I looked at Cooper in the chutes, and kind of felt bad I wasn't staying to watch him, but sucks to suck.

"HEY DAKOTA!" I HEARD a familiar voice call from behind me. I turned around and saw a jogging Cooper coming towards me. Oh jeez. It was only five minuets ago since Taylor left me to go home, and I was now walking around by myself.

"Oh hey Cooper." I say quietly as he comes to my left shoulder. I wrap my arms around myself, because the wind turned into a crisp-cool wind.

"How come I saw you leave before my ride?" He asks me, his voice is soft and very confused. Okay, maybe I could just play this out. Yeah, that's what I will do.

"Well I'm sure your other good luck charms where there to help you." I snapped at him.. I wanted to face palm myself, nicely played DaKota... "Sorry, I didn't mean it like that." I said and then I shivered.

"Are you cold? Here." He said and took off his jacket and tried to hand it to me.

"No, keep it." I said and pushed his hand back towards him.

"No, it's cold out here.. Seriously, take it." He says and I again shake my head at him. Then he sighs and keeps his jacket. "And what did you mean, 'other good luck charms'?" He asked me.

"I know I wasn't your only good luck charm tonight." I say looking forward and clenching my jaw.

"DaKota what are you talking about?" He says and grabs my arm, stopping me from walking.

"Avery told me that you said that to her and other girls tonight." I almost growled at him.

"You can't honestly believe her. Does she think we're still dating?" Cooper says and puts both his hands on his hips.

"She said that you were hers, and you guys dated?" I was genuinely shocked about this. I honestly couldn't think of them like together. Doing all the cute romance stuff, nope, can't see it.

"For like a month, and I broke it off like four months ago.. I swear DaKota, I didn't tell any other girl that she was my good luck charm.. Just you, I swear DaKota.. I'm not that kind of guy.." He said, and I knew he was telling the truth. I could hear it in his voice.

"Okay, I believe you and I'm sorry." I say and I feel so insecure about myself right now. Cooper and I didn't have a thing going on, so why was I being like this?

"It's okay, but why were you so mad about it?" Cooper said with too big of a smirk on his face. Like he was onto something. He was thinking about what I was thinking, did I like him?

"I don't know," I said a little too quickly, "I don't like being lied to.." I say and he nods, but still has the smirk on his face, like he didn't believe me.

"Oh really, or was someone a little jealous?" Cooper says with a cocky smirk on his face. I opened my mouth to speak, but nothing came out. Instead a little dry laugh came out, and I felt like there was no moisture in my mouth to speak.

Cooper walked towards me and I started walking backwards. After two steps my back hit a horse trailer and I was stuck with a dangerous-looking Cooper. I felt my heart pace to quicken, and my hands began to sweat. Cooper's body was inches from mine, and his 6'2" height made me look up to him. His left forearm went above my head and he looked down at me. "W-what are y-you doing?" I ask him, but it came out as a whisper. Damn his good looks.

"Making you nervous." He confidently says, getting a little closer to me. "Is it working, lovely?" He whispered, he did not just call me lovely.. My hands began shaking, I couldn't get that word out of my head. In my head it wasn't Cooper saying it, it was Wade. That was Wade's pet-name for me, it was horrible.

FLASHBACK

I WAS SHAKING IN FEAR because Wade just stood above me, looking down at me, or should I say my body. My hands were chained, and his feet were pinning my legs down. My eyes started watering, "Please, don't do this.." I whimpered to him.

He came down and straddled my lap, making me flinch and almost throwing up in my mouth. He brought his hand up to my cheek and began caressing it, "Shhhh.. It's okay, lovely.. I'm gonna be gentle, unless you start crying.. Then I'm going to have to be rough, I know you like it that why, my lovely.." And then he took both his hands and removed my bra.

"Please, stop!" I say louder and then he covered my mouth and began to touch me.

PRESENT

"DAKOTA?" COOPER'S VOICE says and I feel something drip on my lip. I taste the salt and realize I had a couple tears on my cheeks. I looked up at him and he looked concerned. "Are you okay, what's wrong?"

"I'm sorry, I have to go." I slip under him and then run to the direction of my trailer. I couldn't believe that just happened in front of Cooper. I was still shaking and I could barely catch my breath, I had to go home and take my pills and write in my journal.. I just hoped that Cooper wouldn't bring this up again, I don't think I could face him again.

It was a pretty quite breakfast, but I didn't mind. I didn't feel like talking. I was tired from my sleepless night last night. It was one of those nights last night.. I had a nightmare, and I couldn't go back to sleep, so I spent last night reading the last chapters of my book. I didn't have anything special planned for today, just serving a couple of hours at the diner.

It's Tuesday, so it's been a couple of days since the rodeo, and I haven't talked to Cooper at all. He's tried texting me, but I've left him on read. I really don't want to have to try to explain to him what was with me, it would end up in a lie. Maybe I should tell him that I was on my period and it was symptoms, and I was acting up all day. Yeah, maybe that would work. Guys hate talking about periods. I know Ashley uses it on Caleb all the time. "Are you available Dakota?" My father's voice awoke me.

"I'm sorry what?" I say while putting my fork down and looking at everyone. Then everyone looked at each other suspiciously.

"We're branding tomorrow, are you able to help?" My dad asks me, but slowly, like I wouldn't understand.

"Yeah, I'd love to." I smile and then stand up with my plate. "Excuse me, I have to go to the diner."

I looked at myself in the mirror, only having my shirt and underwear on. I turned to my left side and looked at the scar running from the top of my underwear to about four inches down. I ran my finger down it, making my leg shiver. That night was the worst night of my life, and I will never talk about it again. I pealed off the bandage and threw it in the garbage, I didn't need it if I was wearing jeans.

There was a knock on my door, I finished buttoning my jeans, "Come in." I say and grab my belt off my bed. The door came open and in came my mom. "Hey mom, what's up?" I ask and slip the leather in the belt loops.

"You were a little quiet at breakfast this morning, everything okay?" She asks me, and I nod almost right away.. I was horrible at lying, when I didn't have a good cause.

"Yeah, just a little tired." I say to her and look her into eyes. She looked at me like she didn't totally believe me, but in the end she let it go.

"Okay, don't be too long at the diner, I have stuff for you to do when you get back." She says as she walks out of my room and into the hallway. I wonder what we are going to do after I get back. I looked at the clock and it was already 9:30, well I plan to be back here at 3.

IT WAS A RELAXED AFTERNOON at the diner, kinda busy at sometimes, sometimes it was chill. But later I think it will get more busy because it's suppose to rain later. Usually people stop in to have a coffee and read, or just to relax.

I grabbed a bus tray and started to clean off the table. Holy, this family left a mess, but a good tip, so I didn't care. I knelled on the booth seat and started wiping down the table. I also began humming, 'Fancy' by Reba. I looked up and out of the window when I heard a truck door close, I frowned at what I saw.

Cooper was walking away from his black 2013 Ford Powerstroke, oh boy, he looked damn good. But when didn't he? He was wearing a gray sweatshirt and some loose fitting jeans, very casual. His hair was getting a little longer than a short cut, but I'm sure he would look good with the long hair.

I slid out of the booth and took the bus tray to the kitchen for the other guys to mess with. When I came out from the kitchen, I noticed Cooper sitting in a booth, in my section. I really didn't want to talk to him right now, I don't think I could do it. "Hey May, can you cover for me?" I turn to her and throw my head back to motion towards Cooper. Maybell raised her eyebrows at me and laughed.

"Why would I do that? You always serve him, you guys seem to like each other." She then wiggles her eyebrows at me and I roll my eyes.

"Yeah I know, but today I don't want to. Please?" I say and put my hands together in front of me, begging her.

"DaKota, go buck up and figure out what's happening between you two." She smirks at me and I'm taken back, and my jaw drops a bit. She hands me my ordering pad and pen, with a fake smile.

I take my time walking to Cooper's booth, and he notices me, but I don't look at him. "Welcome to DaKota's Diner, I'm DaKota and I'll be serving you." I say in a monotone voice, trying to send him a message. Cooper snickers, making me finally look at him.

"Oh I see, still giving me the silent treatment, even though I don't know what I did wrong." Cooper says and I automatically feel bad, he was right. I was making up an excuse to cover my lies to him.

"I'm sorry Cooper," I sigh, admitting to my faults, "You really didn't do anything wrong, it's just complicated." I say and look at my pad.

"I just don't understand what happened-"

"Please don't ask," I cut him off, "You're my last customer before I get to go home." I say, trying to send him another message that he should just order.

"Okay, I only came here to try to get you to talk to me. I didn't like getting ignored by DaKota Jones." Cooper says with a gentle smile.

"I didn't like it either." I say with a small smirk, just to let him know I felt bad for ignoring him. He gave me a small gentle smile that said he was glad too. I turned on my heal and started walking away from him.

"Hey DaKota?" Cooper calls out from behind me, and I stopped walking and turned around, he looked a little unsure but then he disguised that with a smile, "Can I call you tomorrow?" Him asking that was the most heart warming thing. It was so gentleman like it made me melt inside.

I felt my cheeks heat up and I looked down quickly and looked back up at him, "I'd like that." I flash him an inviting smile, and turn back around and walked away.

COOPER

I WALKED OUT OF DAKOTA'S Diner feeling like a damn fool. Why didn't I just ask her? I opened the door into my baby(my pickup) and jumped into the seat. I turned the key into the ignition and then I just sat there. I thought I had balls, but when it came to her, I guess I had none.

I leaned up and rested my head on my steering wheel and groaned. Why did I just chicken out like that? Why couldn't I just ask her out on a date like everyone else? Because you don't know if she likes you, idiot. True, I had no idea if she was into me.

I flirt with her a lot, sometimes she even does it back. But there's something she's not saying, but I know she wants to. I really liked DaKota, she's perfect for me.

I liked the way she defended herself and the things she loved, it was attractive to me. Like the other night when I went to go help them round up that horse, that was amazing. I felt like I had seen the real DaKota, strong and stubborn. She also had a lot of confidence in herself, and she knew how to handle a horse. I don't know if she felt it to, but when I grabbed her, something shot throughout my body, it was a strange, but good feeling.

She looked so good that night, it was aw-strucking. The color of her dress made her goddess skin look more dark than it already was. I wonder if her skin was as soft as it looked. Every guy's eyes were on her that night, she looked so hot, but an elegant hot. Some loose strands fell out of place from her braided hair, and the braid went all the way down her back.

But my favorite part of the night is when I saw her on the balcony. She was in a robe and her head was wrapped in a towel. When she looked at my truck, her jaw dropped and she seemed shocked and worried. She spun so quickly around, it was just like a flash. She must of lost track of time in the shower. Hmm, DaKota in the shower. Okay, stop Cooper..

Maybe if DaKota and I hung out a little more, just us two, I could ask her on a date. I didn't want to eat everyday at the Diner just so I could talk to her.

I HATED MUCKING OUT the horse stalls, it was my least favorite chore. I'd rather be doing something more important and something that made me sweat and feel good. But at least I got to listen to some original country and sing along. My favorite singer was Charlie Daniels, he had real country songs. I've been listening to him since I was a kid, I'm starting to get Reese to listen to him. I know, I'm a great brother.

"Cooper!!!!" I heard my mother's voice yell from the barn and then I heard a cow. Is this what I think it is?! I dropped the rake and ran to the barn. I stopped myself from running by placing both my arms across the door frame and my jaw dropped at what I saw. Our cow, Bell, was in labor! I hope this goes well, she needs it.

My mom was sitting with her and my mom looked a little worried. My mom was trying to sooth her by running her hand across her pregnant stomach and making calm noises. I slowly walked to Bell and the water sac was already out. She's almost ready to start pushing! "Mom, I hope this goes well." I say to my mother and she sighs.

"I hope so, I don't think she could handle another miscarriage." My mom's soft voice speaks and then she stands up and goes to the sink. As my mom is washing her hands, Belle tries to get up, and I rush over to her.

"Oh no you don't." I say and gently push her back down. "We gotta hurry up." I say to my mom as she's putting on the arm gloves.

"Let's do this." She confidently says and smiles at me. I go in front of Bell and sooth her and my mother sticks her hand up the cow's ass, and Bell let's out a cry. My mother feels around and her face goes into a frown, this can't be good.

"Mom, what's wrong?" I quickly ask and then she slowly pulls her hands out.

"Call a vet, the calf is backwards." Oh Jesus, that's not good. I swear Bell has the worst luck calving. I didn't have the vet's number, but I did have DaKota's. I stood up quickly and pulled my phone out of my pocket and dialed her number.

Ring.. Ring... Ring... Oh c'mon DaKota, pick the damn phone up.. Ring.. Ring. "I thought you said you'd call tomorrow." Her sweet voice answers, making me relieved.

"DaKota is your mom available?" I quickly ask her, we desperately needed this.

"Um no, she's in Rowan helping a client. Is something wrong?" She asks me, she seems more worried than I am.

"DaKota, have you ever delivered a calf?" I ask her running my hands through my hair, and pacing around. Please say yes, please.

"Yes! Tons of times!"

"Great, I-uh- I mean we need you now!!" I say with a great amount of relief and thank the Lord above.

"Where do you live?" She asks me, and I'm kinda shocked she doesn't know where I live. Since I'm just down and around the corner from her.

"South of your house, Crazy Man Hill." I say to her.

"Oh wow, well I'm on my way!" She says and then I hang up the phone and go back into the barn.

I heard DaKota's truck make a quick stop on our gravel and then I heard a door slam. I stood up and walked to the door, "In here!" I say and look at her grabbing her vet gear and walking towards the barn.

She walks into the barn and her jaw drops, "What?" I ask her with worry in my voice.

"She's huge," She says and puts her box down and starts putting her hair into a high ponytail. "Okay, what's wrong?" She asks and picks up her gear and goes to Bell's rear, where my mom is.

"The calf's back hooves are in the front." My mom says and Kota nods to her.

"Okay, I've done this tons of times. I'll take good care of her." DaKota reassures my mom and goes to the sink and washes her hands. I notice DaKota's wearing a over sized tee shirt, that seems to be an old paint shirt, and some holy jeans. "What?" She says, catching my staring at her.

"Nothing." I smirk and she shakes her head and then dries her hands and pulls out her own gloves. Of course she would have turquoise gloves, her favorite color.

She kneels down behind Bell and sticks her hands in her, she made no facial expressions saying she was grossed out, God she's one of a kind. "Well she's definitely backwards, but in a good position for pulling." DaKota informs us.

Bell moos loudly and starts breathing heavy, "What's wrong?" Mom asks immediately.

"Don't worry, just mean's she's ready to help me." DaKota smiles, she seems so excited to do this. "Okay, I'm going to pull now." She says and goes deeper in Bell. Wow, what a woman.

DaKota seems to struggle a bit, biting her lip, and then I see the hooves of the calf in DaKota's hands. "Cooper, can you go get a cup of water for me?" She asks me and I nod and I go fetch her one.

When I come back, she already has almost the whole calf out, just needs the head. I place the water beside her as she continues to pull, and then she stops. "I'm going to let her to the rest." She says with a heavy breath. Bell knows what do and her stomach contracts and releases, moving the calf a bit, and then with one more, the calf is all the way out!

We all let out a breath of relief and all have smiles on our faces. You can see the steam coming off the calf, and it starts moving around and shakes his head continuously, allowing himself to breath. I look at Kota and she looks confused. "What's the matter?" I ask her.

"Well I'm just confused because she should of gotten up and came over to check out her calf, give me a sec." She says and gently picks up the calf and moves it to the side.

I look at my mother and we both look at each other confused what was happening. Kota already has her hands deep in Bell, and then she looks at us questionable eyes. "Did you know she's having twins?" Holy cow, how did we not know she was having twins?

"Twins?" My mother gasps and covers her mouth, "How is that possible?" She asks DaKota.

"Well sometimes during the ultrasounds, the other one can hide behind the other. Kinda like human fetus's do sometimes. But this one is in a critical position. It's head is under it's stomach, and it's rear is up, so I have to carefully turn it. I might need some help." She says looking up at us.

My mom looked at me with raised eyebrows, is she kidding?! I've never calved before! "Oh no." I drag out and my mother shoves me towards Kota. "I've never done this before." I nervously say and look at Kota's hands in Bell's ass.

"It's okay I'll help you." She says in a positive tone and then turns her attention to the sink, and I sigh. Maybe this could be the start to our bonding.

I took a deep breath before I kneeled down beside DaKota. "Come closer to me." She instructs me and I do until our legs are touching, making me looking down at our touching, and I look at her and give her a wink and she blushes, but shakes it off. "Okay, you have longer arms than me so you're going to move the body and I'm going under you to move the feet.. If you have any questions let me know." She says and I keep telling myself I can do it.

I move into position and place my hands in the cow, oh my gosh, how does she enjoy this?! It was warm, mushy, and just weird. Cowboy up, Cooper. I grow more confident and went deeper, "Do you feel the spine?" She asks me as she slides under my arms, spreading her legs out, so she fits. I finally feel the spine and I smile, this is actually kinda cool.

"Yeah, now what?" I ask her and she gives me a slight smile.

"Just gently push the calf towards the the back, and I'm gonna reach for the feet." She says. In order to reach deeper I scoot closer to her and my head is right next to hers and her back is touching my chest. Control yourself, Cooper.

I gently use my fingers to push him or her back towards. From my peripheral vision I see Kota looking at me with her eyes. "Got it?" I ask her and she looks caught off guard, and returns her vision to the anus.

She reaches a bit more, and returns to bit her lip. "Yes!" She says and I noticed her move her arms around, and then she leans back, making me lean back. She's now in between my legs, my lord we should always have pregnant cows.

"Is everything alright?" My mom says looking at our position.

"Very!" I say in a charming tone, looking down at her. Her cheeks light up in a rosy tone, success.

"Yeah, it's just putting up a fight, but I'll get it." She says and I look at her arms and she's flexing, telling me she's really pulling. She has impressive biceps, did she have any flaws? I notice a couple of beads on her forehead.

"Do you want help?" I ask her and she shakes her head.

"I'm almost there." She breaths and pulls a little harder and the feet pop out. I smile and she does to, then everything else is smoother. Next is the head, and there's the lovely smell and the steam.

And then everything falls out with the calf. The calf lays between her legs and we both wait for it to start shaking its head. "Give me the water." She says and I reach the left and grab the glass and hand it to her.

She takes the glass, our fingers brushing while doing so, and then she pours a little bit of water in the calf's ears. "The water will help it shake it's head, so it can get all of the stuff out of it's nose to breath." She explains to us and as she says, the calf thrashes its head.

DaKota sighs in relief and then she leans back into me, resting her head on my shoulder. "That was awesome." She says and then sits back up again, making me a little sad. I look up at my mother and she has tears in her eyes.

"Mom are you okay?" I ask her and DaKota looks from me to my mom.

"I'm sorry, I'm just so happy.. Twins!!" She exclaims.

"Bell's already had two miscarriages, she hasn't been acting the same, so this was really important to us and her." I inform Kota and she frowns. "But thanks to you, she now has two healthy babies." I say and we all look at Bell who is cleaning her calves.

"It was nothing." She says and stands up and shrugs it off.

"Oh honey, it wasn't nothing! I've heard of calves in that position and they've suffocated after an amount of time." My mom says and DaKota looks like she already knew that.

"Well I did have some help." Kota looks at me and I smile proudly.

"Oh and by the way I'm Desiree Blackwood." She says and holds her hand out for DaKota. DaKota reaches for her hand but then drops her hand.

"Um." Kota laughs and takes off the gloves, and then shakes my mom's hand. "DaKota Jones." She flashes her beautiful smile.

"Where did you learn to do that?" My mom asks in shock and wonder.

"Well I've been watching and learning from my mom since I was 10. I love working with animals." She says.

"Well in honor of helping today, would you like to name them?" Mom says, making me smile because Kota blushes in fluster.

"Oh no, I coul-"

"Oh don't be so bashful! I insist!" Mom says and Kota looks at me for permission and I nod towards the calves.

"How about that one is Otis," She says and points at the first born calf. "And how about Cupid for that one?" She says and we both nod in agreement.

"Great, well I have some cooking to do so I'll leave you two.. It was nice to finally meet you DaKota." Mom said to us.

"You too." DaKota smiles back and then she turns to me "Do I need to stay or can you handle it?" She asks me as she cleans up a bit.

"Um, I can do it." I say and then she turns around to wash her gloves. I'm such an idiot. I put my hands on top of my head and spin around. Ask her you idiot! "Um, DaKota do you wanna stay and hangout for a bit?" I say and she turns around slowly and bits down on her lip.

"Sounds like fun." She finally says and I act cool on the outside, but in the inside I was bouncing around.

"Do you wanna go ride?" I ask her and she smiles at me. Does she do that on purpose, you know drive my crazy with that smile?

"Do you even have to ask?" She says and I chuckle and rub the back of my neck, I guess she's right.

DAKOTA

COOPER'S HORSE CUT mine off, but I think it was more of Cooper cutting me off. Cooper turned around and gave me a cocky smile and I scoffed. I pulled the reins and gave Butterscotch a kick in the side and she turned and passed Cooper's horse. "Hey!" Cooper laughed as I was leaving him in our dust.

I now had Butterscotch in a canter and I looked back and Cooper had his horse coming after us. I saw the creek in front of us and decided that would be the finish line. I pulled the reins and she quickly stopped for me, and I gave her a pat on the back.

Cooper finally caught up with us, and was shaking his head at me. "That was unfair and you know it." He says as his horse stands beside mine.

"You cut me off! Totally fair!" I laugh at him, "You're just mad because you got beat by a girl." I say and he looks at me.

"I don't mind being beat by you." Why does he always do that! Does he want to make me blush and embarrass myself?

"So why'd you guys move here?" I ask him, changing the subject. Noticing my actions he laughs and gives me a pointed look.

"Complicated reasons." He says and looks the side. His voice sounded disappointed and hurt, making me very curious.

"Good or bad?" I ask him.

"Both, I guess." He blankly says, and I decide to leave it alone.

"What's little Reese doing?" I ask him, trying to get him back to his happy self. Since I feel like moving here is a sensitive subject.

"I wouldn't be surprised if he's playing with the calves now." He says and looks back the barn, way behind us.

"Oh my gosh! What if he wanted to name them! I feel so bad, it's okay if you want to change the names. I mean he's apart of the family, so that means he should have priority over me-"

"DaKota!" Cooper stops me from my freaking out. I was freaking out because I felt so bad. If I was a kid I would want to name the calves, and Reese was so cute. "He'll be fine, his middle name is actually Otis." Cooper says, but I still feel bad.

"I still feel bad!" I whine and Cooper laughs at me.

"He won't even notice!" Cooper says and I roll my eyes.

"But-"

"No, we're keeping the names!" Cooper says and I groan, because I didn't get my way.

We're back at the barn, brushing the horses and almost done. Hanging out with Cooper was really fun and I'm glad he asked me to stay. I hope we can do this a lot more often, and not just talk at the diner. "Are you ready to talk about what happened the other night?" Cooper's voice comes over the radio. Is he serious? I literally told him I didn't want to talk about it.

"Are you ready to tell me why you moved here?" I come back at him and he gives me the fair-enough-nod.

"I think I deserve to know why, you're just curious." Cooper points, he did have a point, but there was no way I was telling him.

"I think I should get home." I say and drop the brush in the bucket and start to walk away.

"DaKota!" Cooper catches up to me and pulls my arm, yanking me to a stop. "I'm sorry, but why won't you tell me? You seemed pretty shaken up, and I'm just worried about you. You seem so distant when I bring up why you moved.." He says and I sigh. I didn't like lying, but I had to!

"I get muscle spasms, okay?!" I blurt out, are you serious DaKota? Muscles spasms? Like he'll totally believe me... "It's embarrassing and painful." I hesitantly looked up at him and he had an unreadable look on his face.

"How come I've only seen it once? And you seem to have steady hands." Cooper eyed me and I looked away again.

"Well I take medication for it." I say, which is a partial lie. I don't have medication for muscle spasms, but I do have medication for the other thing.

"Oh." Oh, Is all he says? This boy is about to get slapped. Then he speaks again, "I'll find out the real reason." My phone buzzes in my back pocket and I reach for it and I see it's my dad calling me. "Hello?" I say.

"Where are you?" He asks me in a fatherly tone.

"The Blackwood's place." I reply in a confused voice because I don't know why he sounded so worked up. "Why?" I ask looking at Cooper.

"Did you ask to go over there?" He says, okay, who pissed in his coffee this morning?

"Cooper called me to ask if I could help deliver their calves, and I did. And now I'm just hanging with Cooper." I say like it's no big deal, because it isn't.

"Well you need to come home." He says and then hangs up, okay, now I'm worried.

"I guess I need to go home.." I'm so confused why I need to go home? We had nothing planned for tonight and it's not even supper time. Is my dad mad at me for hanging out with Cooper? I sure hope not, because I plan on doing this a lot more. But did Cooper really mean what he said? How hard was he going to try to figure out the truth?

I grabbed my cattlemen cowboy hat of the rack and placed it on top of my head, ready for a good day of branding. I opened the porch screen door and was welcomed to a warm breeze and the very bright sun. I was shocked when I already saw them bringing in the calves! They started without me!

I ran into the barn stalls and I grabbed Pharaoh's bridle and then his saddle, and tacked him up. I couldn't believe they were starting without me! On the way out of the barn, I grabbed my rope off the wall rack and I rid out of the barn and towards the arena.

There were a ton of guys here because we had a lot of cattle, and it takes a lot of work and lots of time. I rode up behind my dad and he turned around and scrunched his eyebrows at me. "Honey what are you doing here?" He says and I'm the one to scrunch my eyebrows at him. Didn't he ask me to help yesterday? I'm so confused right now. I feel everyone's attention turn towards me and not the cattle.

"I'm helping dad." I say in an obvious tone, "Didn't you ask me to help yesterday at breakfast?" I say and meet everyone's wondering looks, and they all look the same, is she okay?

"Oh sweetie, I meant helping your mom make lunch and food for the guys." He says like I should of already known it, and I am out of my mind. I always help brand, and I am offended I would be replaced by some guys I don't even know!! What the hell is this?

"Dad, why can't I help?" I ask him in a hurt tone.

"We already have enough guys, and you haven't done it in a while, so I thought this would just be quicker." He says, he is such an asshole lately! He's being one of those guys that thinks all women do is clean and make food! What changed with him? I used to do all kinds of things with him around the ranch with him, but now, something has changed. What did he think I forgot how to rope and take charge?

"Dad! I didn't forget how to brand! I-"

"Enough DaKota!" My dad orders and I have to stand down, or else it will only get worse. "If your not going to help your mother, you just stay out of the way and watch." He says and then walks away from me.

Did he get kicked in the head earlier today and forget who his daughter was?

Like little minions, the other guys followed my dad and got to work. Every one was scared of my dad, and nobody dared to question my dad's action. My dad was Satan when he was mad and the only person I had seen stand up to my dad was my brother and it was not pretty.

Caleb had wanted to go on a trip with some friends to Cancun for spring break, but my dad needed him on the ranch. Caleb had only go to a two-year college, but it was close to home so he could still work on the ranch. Anyways, Caleb really wanted to go because he was single and wanted to party like a regular college boy. Caleb just wanted two weeks of vacation and my dad wouldn't have it, so they started screaming at each other. No joke, the whole house was shaking and my mom and I were laying in my bed together and my mom was crying because she hated it. In the end, Caleb snuck out in the middle of the night and left for Cancun, with my help of course.

After that night, no one had ever stood up to my dad, because even Caleb was scared to. Trust me, there has been many times were I had wanted to, but I always think of that feeling I had that night, and I automatically shut my mouth.

Speaking of my brother, where is he? I pull Pharaoh's reins back and back him far enough to "stay out of the way", and then I look around for Caleb. Then I see him throwing a calf to the ground, with his buddies surrounding him. I was shocked to see Cooper here, I was surprised because of last night when I came home from his house.

Apparently, my dad did not trust "the Blackwood kid". He really didn't explain why, but I had an idea why. Maybe my dad had heard of Cooper being the 'player' type, that Taylor had explained to me. But Cooper wasn't like that with me, sometimes he actually got a little shy, it was really cute. My father said I wasn't allowed over at Cooper's without his permission, ever again. Yeah, not gonna happen. I'm 18, I'm able to make my own choices, and I have since the past two years.

THE BOYS WERE ALMOST done branding, and I was bored out of my mind, but I wasn't gonna leave that would just prove my dad right. During my boredom I had braided Pharaoh's hair, mane and tail. Also during my boredom, I paid lots of attention on how well Cooper was doing his job. His main job was to keep the cow's ass on the ground and still.

All of a sudden there was a loud noise of the arena gates shaking, and then I heard, "Two calves got loose!" I looked up and looked around for the steers and located it. I was the only one mounted on a horse and rope in my hands, this is my time to show my dad.

I grabbed the reins and kicked Pharaoh in the sides and we took off. We bolted through all of the cowboys, trying to get mounted, silly boys. I was swinging my right arm with my rope, getting closer and closer to the slowest calf. I finally release the rope and it goes perfectly over the neck and I pull the slack, tightening the loop. I mentally did a fist bump in my head, but then I tied the rest of the rope around the saddle horn.

Keeping Pharaoh running, I start to get closer to the other calf. Since I didn't have another rope, I would have to wrestle this calf and it would be tough. I kicked Phar harder and he got right next to the steer and I smoothly slid off the saddle and grabbed the ears of the run-away-calf.

I dug my heels into the hard dirt, trying to slow myself down and get control of the calf. Once I did I stood up a bit, and then put my butt into the calf and then wrapped my arm around the calf and then turned it's head and brought it down to the ground with me. I was out of breath and I looked up and saw Cooper, Caleb, Dad, Ryan, and Rusty coming over to me.

Rusty grabbed the other calf from my horse, and then I let the calf get up and Ryan successfully roped it. And now all I could see was three horse heads and chests, and then I saw a pair of boots come down from the stirrups. It was Cooper, he reached down and grabbed my arm and helped me up. "DaKota Annie Jones! What the hell was that!" My dad barks at me and I roll my eyes.

"Dad, she's just being herself. Look at my badass little sister." Caleb sighs and then proudly smirks at me.

"I don't care, I told her not to and she does it anyways! After your done here, go put your horse away and go into the house and help your mother." He orders again and I roll my eyes again. He turns his horse away and rides back to the arena. But what catches me, is when he said, 'when your done here'. Then I realize Cooper is still holding onto me, and my body is pressed against his.

I look at his hand and then up at him and he smirks down at me, and begins to open his mouth, but Caleb interrupts, "Cooper, I think she's standing okay now." Caleb says and then Cooper releases, and then Caleb leaves to.

I turn to stand in front of Cooper, and I see he has my hat in his dirty hands. "Here you are." He says and then puts it on for me.

"Thanks." I awkwardly chuckle with no smile, and then sigh.

"That was impressive and kind of hot." Coopers says to me with his really, really hot smirk.

"I guess not to my dad." I kick at the dirt and cross my arms.

"Well I hope your dad doesn't think that's hot!" Cooper jokes and I push his shoulder a bit, and smile a bit. "There's that smile." He says and then I frown again, being the stubborn girl I am.

"Ugh! I don't know what his deal is!" I groan and throw my arms in the air frustrated. "It's like he doesn't even remember who I am, and what I can handle." I complain to Cooper, who probably doesn't even care right now.

"Well you showed him, and knowing you you're gonna keep doing it, so might as well piss 'em off." Cooper says and I don't say anything back. "Just relax, I'm sure he's just being a good, protective father." Cooper says and touches my shoulder and squeezing a bit.

I WAS CURRENTLY ALONE on the porch swing, while everyone was eating inside. I would die in there, it's so loud and the guys spill all over the place. The main reason I am out here is because I tried sitting by Cooper, but my dad announced clearly I was not allowed to sit by him. God, it was embarrassing.

I heard the door open, but I didn't look, but I had an idea who it was. "Pretty girls should never be alone." Cooper's deep voice says as he sits down on the swing, and then slides right next to me.

"Well now I'm not thanks to you." I sigh and look at Cooper, he's already looking at me. He looks at me like he already knows why I'm out here.

"Can I ask why your dad doesn't like you around me." He says and I decide to go the safe route and not be rude, because I didn't want Cooper to go away.

"Like you said earlier, he's just being a protective dad." I sigh and again look at Cooper. His expression changed. He looked a little serious, determined, a little mysterious, and a little nervous.

"Are you still trying to pissing him off?" Cooper asks, as if he's confirming something to me. I don't say anything, but nod to him. "Well we could start with this." Cooper says quietly and then he starts to lean in!!!

His lips almost touch mine, but then the porch door swings open and crashes against the house, making us both jump and Cooper to sit upright. Oh my gosh, did he just try to kiss me?!! Was I going to let him kiss me? Talk about intense.

We both look to our right and here comes Ryan and Rusty, the dynamic duo. "DaKoootttttaaaa!" They boom and walk over to the swing. "Dude, scoot over!" Rusty says, and the two squeezes in between Cooper and I.

"What's up guys?" I ask hanging onto the metal chains of the swing.

"You were so rank earlier!" Rusty says, his voice like a sufer dude.

"Better than ol' Cooper over here." Ryan says and shoves Cooper, making the swing move along with the shove.

"I don't think so." I shyly say and tuck a piece of hair behind my ear.

"I bet she's a better bull rider too." Rusty challenges Cooper and I smirk to myself.

"Well now, I do think I am better than Cooper." I play along with them and lean forward to look at Cooper.

Playing along with me, he leans forward and smirks, "Oh really? Wanna find out?" He raises an eyebrow, challenging me.

"Only if you can handle it." I snark back at him and Ryan and Rusty cheer in joy.

"Okay it's settled," Rusty said and stood up. "We'll go down to the practice chutes and see who the real badass is!" He clapped his hands and I stood up along with Cooper and Ryan. I looked up at Cooper and gave him my best seductive smirk I could.

What the hell was I getting myself into?

COOPER

I REALLY HATE RUSTY and Ryan right now. Those two numb-nuts ruined my chance to kiss DaKota, and she looked like she wanted to kiss me too! And now Kota and I are going to see who's the best at bull riding. I don't know why the guys even set up the challenge, because I obviously have more experience.

I obviously wasn't going to let her do it because she could get seriously hurt, and her dad would hate me even more. But I think Caleb would kill me with one hand, and me begging for mercy. I had driven my own truck down here because I didn't want to face the possible wrath of the Jones men if something happened.

Ryan had already got a young bull into the chute and they tested the bull out to see if it would do the job, and it seemed okay. "Okay ladies first, get on up there Cooper!" Rusty jokes and everyone else laughs and I shake my head and flip him the bird and then climb up on the chute and get onto the bull.

I nodded my head and Ryan pulled the gate open and the bull slowly busted to the right, and I started to work my magic. I heard Ryan's lame ass buzzer and the boys cheered and I jumped off the bull. I landed on my feet and tipped my hat to DaKota, "Beat that." Then I winked at her.

When I helped DaKota onto the bull, I let her sit for a second and then I started to pull her up again, "What are you doing?" She asked confused.

"You're not serious are you?" I ask and she gives me the I'm-not-backing-down-look and I shake my head. "You could get seriously hurt, Kota!" I snap at her and she shakes her head at me.

"Not if I make the eight seconds." She says and then sits back down on the bull. Knowing she wasn't going to back off, I let it go.

I had to help DaKota with all the ropes and all the stuff she needed not to embarrass herself. As doing so we both looked as we saw trucks pull up and we all stopped when we saw her father. "You get off that bull right now!!" He yells over the fence and looks seriously pissed off.

DaKota didn't say anything but just concentrated on getting the rausen to stick to the rope. Her dad had enough and I guess he couldn't watch, so he got back into his truck and drove off. "Okay DaKota he's gone, you can get off now." I say to her, convincing her now she's only doing this to piss her dad off.

"I'm doing it Cooper." She says through her gritted teeth, telling me to back off. I mentally start to kick myself for letting her do this. She takes a deep breath and then nods her head and the gate comes open.

I immediately jump of the gate and wait for what is about to happen. The bull barely gets three inches off the ground, but it does spin a lot. Wow, she's doing really great. We start to cheer for her as she's almost done. And then the buzzer goes off, she actually made it! As she's trying to release the rope, the bull gets crazier, making me worried.

Right as she lets go, the bull jumps like hell and she comes flying off the bull and hits really hard into the dirt. I can tell she landed awkwardly, but then the bull starts to go towards her, but Rusty throws his hands, but I don't know if in time.

I run over to a definitely hurting DaKota and I kneel down beside her. "Oh my gosh, are you okay Kota?!!" I freak out, looking all over her body as she grabs her shoulder and rolls in place and seethes and groans.

"Not really, but I think I did better than you." She says in deep pain and I have to get her home.

"Can I pick you up?" I ask and she nods her head. I carefully pick up her light body and carry her like a groom does to his bride.

"That was awesome DaKota!!" Rusty cheers and I glare at him.

"No, that was stupid Rusty." I snap at him and he looks taken back. It was stupid of me to say, because I could of easily stopped her from doing it.

I looked down at DaKota who was trying to hold her pain in, but she squeezed her eyes together and began taking deep breaths. I hold her higher and tighter to let her know I was there for her. "I'm so sorry DaKota." I apologize, Lord I am such a douche bag. She'll never like me after this.

"I'm fine Cooper, and it was my fault. It was just a rough landing." She says, but I shake her off.

"Well I think your dad is going to be pissed at me more than he is you." I say and she smiles a bit up at me and finally opens her eyes.

"He won't be home, he has some type of meeting. So I'd be worried about Caleb." She chuckles and I gulp down, thinking about how Caleb would react.

"I can handle him." I scoff a bit and she chuckles.

"You know, I'm okay I can walk." She says and tries to get out of my arms.

"Let me just carry you to the truck, I feel bad." I offer her and then walk over to the truck and gently let her down. As doing so she glides her hands down my chest, making me shiver under her touch. I make sure she's standing okay, before I go to my side of the truck.

We don't say much as I start driving back to her house, but I side-eye her to make sure she's okay. Why did I let her do it? She could of got seriously hurt and I would of killed myself if that happened. But it did give me a good excuse to hold her, but a stupid reason it was. "You know there's other ways you could apologize." She speaks with a little cute smirk on her face, and I don't say anything back to her because I'm deciding if she's being flirty or snarky...

We walk into Kota's home and automatically Caleb comes up to his sister. Oh boy, here it comes. The over-protective brother speech and death threats from him. "My sister is a badass!!" He proudly smiles and laughs and smiles down at his sister, not acknowledging me. "I heard you kicked the bull's ass!" He said nodding with approval.

"I don't know about that, but I kicked his." DaKota says and nudges me a bit in the side, making me smile down at her. "Well I'm gonna take a shower, thanks for the ride Cooper." She says and I give her a nod of the head, she looks at me once and then slowly walks up the stairs.

"She took a really hard landing, I'm sorry Caleb I shouldn't of had her go down to the chutes and-" I start my apology before I get a lesson coming for me.

"Look I know my sister, she knows the difference between right and wrong. So I know if she didn't want to do something, she wouldn't of. So I know you didn't make her, and I can tell you care about her." He shocks me by this, and I start to worry.

"How di-"

"You're like the only guy who would bring a girl home and brave the wrath of a possible father and brother ass beating, after taking their daughter slash sister on a death machine. And you look at her like I look at Ashley. Don't worry, I won't tell her." He says and touches my shoulder and turns and leaves. Wow, that didn't go as I thought it would.

As Caleb leaves, his mother walks in and doesn't notice me at first. She seems to be reading something and then goes into their pantry.. Okay, awkward. I clear my throat, and then she turns around and smiles politely at me. "Hi ma'am, I'm Cooper Blackwood, one of DaKota's friends." I introduce myself and she puts her hands on her hips and smiles.

"I know who you are," She smirks at me, making me wonder what she meant. "I heard you just took my daughter to ride a bull." She says again.

"Yes ma'am, I am real sorry about that. I was just a joke and I didn't thi-"

"No need to explain, my girl is a cowgirl." She says and then she begins putting pots and pans out. "So why are you still here?" She asks.

"Well she took a rough landing, so I wanted to ask if it was okay to stay and see if she's okay." I say and stick my hands in my pockets and wait for her answer.

"Of course sweetie, her room is up the stairs and the last door of the hall on the left side." She says and I'm shocked she's letting me go into her room.

"Thanks ma'am." I say and give her a polite nod and head up the stairs to her room.

I can't help but look around DaKota's room and enjoy all the pictures she has. Most of them of her and her horses, some with friends, and some with family. Hopefully in the future I could make it up on the wall. Then I turned to the next wall and was amazed at what I saw, real photography. She took amazing pictures of nature, rodeo, farm pictures, and even made the inside of the diner look professional. These were really special and I wondered if she thought of doing it for a living.

Kota was in her bathroom, that happened to be in her room too. She was taking a shower, and I could faintly hear her singing, making me smile. I could totally see her going full-out in the shower, holding her conditioner bottle as a pretend microphone.

I think about sitting on her bed and waiting for her, but then I decide to play it safe and sit on her chair. As I sit down I feel something out of place and reach under between the cushion and then my fingers automatically hit something hard.

I pull the object up and it's a small little book. But then I realize it's a journal, no way. She kept a journal?! As I opened open the journal, I heard the shower water stop and then I slammed the book closed and shoved it back under the cushion. Soon after DaKota walks out, in just a towel and her hair was down and dripping water. I was in star-struck on how naturally beautiful she was.. But then I saw a huge blue, black, and purple bruise on her shoulder, did the ride do that?

DAKOTA

AFTER WRAPPING THE towel around myself, I looked in the mirror and gasped at what I saw. I had an ugly bruise on my right shoulder from the bull stepping on it. I was just lucky I didn't dislocate my shoulder. It sure did hurt like a bitch though. I didn't tell Cooper because I know he would freak out more than he already did.

It really warmed my heart on how Cooper cared about me after I landed. I think I should ride a bull everyday if it gets me in Cooper's arms, man that was great. Cooper was built and I felt safe and comfortable in his arms.

I forgot my clothes in my room and then I secured the towel with a knot by my left shoulder. I opened the bathroom door and turned to go towards my closet, but stopped abruptly when I saw him on my chair.

My heart began racing in my chest, and he looked just as shocked too. "Cooper, what are you doing here?" I ask and then I awkwardly move my hair over my right shoulder, hoping he didn't notice.

"I wanted to stay and see if you were okay." He said and pushed himself off the couch and walked over to me. I wanted to move but it was like my feet were cemented into the ground. Cooper's chest seemed overwhelming to me as his height overcame mine. I stared at his chest and noticed his left arm coming up and then moved my hair back away off my shoulder, revealing my bruise. "And I see you're not." He sighs and then I step back away from him.

"Cooper, it's nothing." I plead and look at Cooper who seems to be kicking himself over it.

"No it's not DaKota! This is my fault and-" I'm so sick of him apologizing, so I grab his hand and put it on the bruise.

"See it doesn't even hurt!" I say and his eyes turn a shade darker, but then he looks me in the eyes and sighs. "I'm okay Cooper, but I really appreciate you checking up on me. It's sweet." I offer him a smile and let his hand drop back beside him.

"Well you're welcome, well I should get going." He says and I turn to the side, to let him get to the door.

"Have a good night Coop." I say as I lean against the edge of the door as he walks out.

"Oh I will." He smirks at me, looking me up and down. I gasp and then shut the door quickly and then I hear his laughter behind the door. "Good night Kota." He says and then I hear his footsteps walk away from me.

Currently Ashley, Taylor, and I are in the pool, soaking up the sun on this very, very warm Friday afternoon. Ashley and I were on floaties and Taylor was just tanning on a pool chair, taking notes. Taking notes on what? Ashley's wedding, of course. Taylor was also one of bridesmaids, and she was very organized and liked to do this kind of stuff.

"I want those classic Christmas light bulbs and the tiny little round ones, the bigger ones have the cream light and the smaller ones have the blue." Ashley says and I nod in agreement.

"Okay, and what kinds of flowers again?" Taylor asks and then I hear Ashley giggle for a moment.

"Sunflowers and daisies, my mother hates those." She says in an evil tone, making me sit up and look at her and raise an eyebrow, questioning her. "Well you know how my mother hates Caleb?" She says and Taylor laughs after.

"No way, really? How is she letting you get married to him?" Taylor says in shock, while letting out a few chuckles.

"Not her choice is it? Anyways, Caleb got me those flowers on our first date. My mother thought they were too 'bumpkin', but I thought they were romantic for him." Ashley says like she's in a happy daze, as if remembering it was only yesterday it happened. "My mother hates the thought of my spending the rest of my life with some 'cowboy who rides ponies for a living', but what can she do, I love 'em." She swoons, making my heart melt and smile.

"I love you two." I say as I lay back down.

"I know, we're perfect."

WRITING IN MY JOURNAL today was mostly was about Ashley and Caleb, and my thoughts and wishing about what love is. I wrote down my ideal man and what I looked for in a guy, but with my case I would never allow myself to find it.

Keeping what happened in Bismarck is killing me inside. I feel like it's building up inside me like lava does in a volcano. But I can't let it out, it would make everything worse. I know my family would keep constant tabs on me, and it would put a major down fall on the family. I couldn't do that to them, after everything they have done for me. This is for me to deal with on my own.

Feeling the vibration under my leg, I flip over my phone and look at the screen and see that Cooper is calling me. "Hello?"

"Hey it's me, I was just wondering if you could come over and help me with a couple of horses." Cooper's voice says through the phone.

"Yeah sure, be right over." I say and close my journal and slide off my bed, my feet hitting the cold wooden floor of my bedroom.

I'm almost to my truck, when I see my dad and decide to tell him where I'm going. Dad's currently cutting some old wood, and then loading them in the truck bed. My dad had put a lot of time and effort into this ranch, and it made me really proud to be apart of it. "Hey dad I'm going to Cooper's to help him with his horses." I say and then he stops and puts down the chainsaw and looks at me with a confused look.

"Is this you asking me?" He says as he wipes his forehead with his handkerchief.

"Um, well I just though-"

"I told you that you have to ask before going to his house, so no, you can't go." He says very sternly, taking me way back because of his actions.

"What? Dad I'm just going over there to help him." I say back to him.

"Do you know what he did to me?" My dad says, as if he's had enough of me trying to defend Cooper. I cross my arms, waiting for him to inform me. "He stole money from the livestock barn!" He barks at me and I am shocked. Cooper wouldn't steal money, I know he has plenty enough for himself and his family.

"No he didn't." I scoff and roll my eyes at my dad.

"Are you going to believe your family, or some wild kid who likes to get into fights and doesn't care about anyone but himself?" My father throws at me. When I wasn't with Cooper, I did hear about his temper getting in the way, or he was very rude to people.

I've seen it before once.. It was at the diner, he didn't know I was there, but I picked up a late shift for Maybell that night. From behind the kitchen counter, I watched him confront someone and it was not pretty. I didn't see the man who he was talking to, but I couldn't make out what Cooper was saying. They were in the back corner, so no one else saw them. But I did see Cooper shove the man, making it seem like Cooper was giving him a warning.

I don't know why I hadn't thought more of it. Maybe I had believed Cooper had a rough day and was just letting off steam, but now that I think of it, that's still not a good reason to rough someone up like that. "Are you sure he did it?" I ask my dad.

"It was his jacket, I know it was. I want you to be careful around him." My dad says softly, making me realize he was telling the truth. I didn't say anything, I just turned around and walked into the house.

What would I tell Cooper? Tell him that my daddy said no, so I couldn't? Or after every conversation we've had, I just didn't want to anymore? I grabbed my phone from my back pocket, and hesitated before I called Cooper, but I just couldn't bring myself to call Cooper. How could he steal from my family? And I'm sure it wouldn't be a big deal if it was $100, I'm sure it had to be a lot more than that. Was Cooper, who I really thought he was? Or was he just trying to get on my good side so he could do other bad dead?

TONIGHT AT THE DINER was, "Friday Fun." Friday fun was just a night at the diner for kids still in high school. There was sometimes live music and the ice cream was buy one get one free, so lots of people of came. When I was in school everyone looked forward to it, I wonder if people still like to go.

I looked at my outfit before I headed out. My hair was curled, but I braided the front pieces of my hair and pinned them on the back of my head. I was wearing a white long sleeve shirt with the criss cross lase up strings, and some black ripped skinny jeans. I wore some flip flops and a Boot Barn belt.

Holy cow, there is a lot of people here tonight. I had to park on the street, it was so packed! I tucked my phone in my back pocket as I walked up to the entrance door. As I opened the door the noise overwhelmed my senses and I looked around at all the teens around me. When I was looking around my eyes landed on Cooper, who I didn't think who was going to be here.

He wasn't looking at me, and I was thankful. I really didn't want to explain myself to him for skipping on him, because quite frankly, I didn't have an answer for myself. I went behind the counter, to go talk to Maybell who was cashing into the cash register. "I didn't think it would be this busy." I say to May as I lean against the counter.

"Every Friday night, just like this. But most of them just kind of hang around, barely get anything." She shrugs and I nod to her.

"Hey May, can I ask you something?" I ask her as I return my eyes to her after looking at Cooper.

"Anything sugar." She sweetly says and stands in front of me, with a hand on her hip.

"What do you think about Cooper Blackwood?" I ask with a force sigh during the words.

"Honestly?" She asks and I nod, "From the amount of girls I've seen him here with, I'd assume he can't be in a committed relationship or it's for something else. And what he did to your daddy, makes me weary about him. He's also got a fighting side to him.. I'd be careful, D." She says and I just nod to her, not knowing what to think. Hearing Maybell say it made things a little bit easier, because now I know my dad isn't lying to me.

Looking at Cooper I remembered the text he sent me earlier, 'Hey what happened to ya?' and then another one, 'You okay?' Both I didn't reply to because I didn't have an answer for him. I didn't know what happened, and I didn't know if I was okay.

Caught in my thought, I had realized Cooper was looking at me to. His stare was mostly confused, but I saw a little bit of anger? Why would he be angry at me? After a second of staring I quickly looked down and began to think of something to occupy myself for an excuse.

I begin wiping the counter and from the top of my vision I see a figure sit in front of me, and I really hope it's not the person I am thinking of. I take a quick deep breath, set the old rag down, and then slowly look up. Well I didn't know what to think about this, it wasn't Cooper, but it was still someone I didn't want to talk to, Mason.

Although I can't help but feel relived when I see it's Mason, because I'm actually ready to talk to Mason, even though I don't want to. "What do you want Mason?" I ask as politely as I can to him.

"Hi to you to, sweetheart." He sarcastically says and I mentally kick myself for being rude to him.

"Sorry, I've had a weird day." I say to him and he nods if he understands.

"Well it wouldn't have to do with him, would it?" He says and turns his back to look at Cooper, and I follow him and look. Cooper turned his position, and now I see everyone he's sitting with and of course, Avery's there. Avery's sitting right next to him, twirling her finger through her fake hair and obnoxiously chewing her gum.

"How would you know?" I ask him turning my attention back to Mason.

"Please, I saw you guys exchanging weird looks ever since you walked in. What happened?" He asks me and I look at him and begin to laugh at him. He gives me a confused look and I stop laughing as I realize he's serious.

"Why do you care, Mason?" I ask him, placing both my hands on the counter.

"Because I care about you DaKota." He says seriously as he puts his right hand on my left hand. There it is, classic Mason. "I'm serious. Just listen to me. What ever happened between you two, has he tried to fix it?" He points out to me.

"Well no, but it's my fa-" I try to protest to him but he cuts me off.

"Who's ever fault it is, he should be over here talking to you, not talking to Avery right now." He says and then I peak around Mason and see Avery laughing at Cooper, ugh what a- be nice DaKota. "If he really wanted to make it right, he wouldn't be paying attention to her right now.. Remember how I would try to fix things?" He says and I give him a warning glare, for bringing up our old relationship.

Mason would always try to immediate fix things between us, but sometimes it got tiring because sometimes you just need space. But these wasn't one of those times. For once, Mason actually had a point. "Thanks Mason, but this really isn't your problem." I say in a nice tone because I wasn't trying to be mean to him.

"When you make up your mind, I'll be over there." He says with a small smirk and gentle smirk, and then he brings my hand to his lips and kisses it. Once again I shoot him a glare and he drops my hand and leaves the chair.

I decide I want a bowl of our famous ice cream, I could really use it right now. I go over to our ice cream station and whip it up in a quick motion because I've done it so many times. Once it's done, I stick my finger in there and stick in my mouth, tasting if it's right, sure is.

"DaKota." A deep serious voice says behind me and I internally groan to myself as I know who it is. I turn around to see Cooper right there, he has a very serious look on his face making me very confused. "Can we talk outside?" He says.

"Well I have to wait a c-"

"No you don't, you've haven't been working at all tonight." He catches me in my lie and I sigh and nod to him. When he turns to leave, I shove a big spoonful of ice cream in my mouth and then leave the bowl on the counter.

Cooper and I made it outside, off the side walk by the cars. Walking past him, I could faintly smell women's perfume and I knew it was Avery's. "Why have you been avoiding me?" He asks me while crossing his arms over his chest.

"I've just been really busy today, I'm sorry." I say without looking him straight in the eyes.

"Too busy to reply to a simple text?" He asks and I bit my lip, trying to think. "And what's going on with Mason and you?" He asks out of the blue.

"What does that have to do with this?" I turn back to him, actually looking at him.

"What are you avoiding that topic too?" He snaps at me and I start to question him in my mind.

"No I am not, there's nothing going on with him and that's it." I snap back at him and I see his jaw clench. "You and Avery seem to be enjoying yourselves." I return it to him and he looks offended. What he's the only one to ask questions?

"That has nothing to do with this." He blankly says and his voice is getting louder. What is his deal! He's acting like this is all my fault and he's all innocent.

"Just like Mason and I." I come back at him and he puts his hand on his hip.

"So there is something between you-"

"No, there isn't!" I yelled frustrated. "I am sorry that I told you I would come over but then I didn't." I say in a more calm voice, hoping he would figure out I was sincere.

"But why?" He asked in a pained voice. My mind was racing with lies I could tell him, but I didn't want to lie to Cooper.

"What's going on here?" I rolled my eyes when I heard Mason's voice. I was irritated that he came out here, can anyone just get some alone time in this town?!

"Go back inside Mason." I turn to him, and almost grit through my teeth at him.

"Why are you yelling at her, Blackwood?" He says and takes a step towards Cooper. Cooper squares his shoulders to Mason and glares at him. His expression was annoyed and tired of Mason.

"She told you to go inside, Bishop." Cooper warns and then mocks him at the end. I swear to the Lord if they start arguing, I'm going to loose my freaking mind.

"Well what are you saying?" Mason dangerously says to Cooper, and takes another threatening step towards Cooper, who clenches his jaw.

"I'm saying if you don't leave in the next 15 seconds, you'll be screaming for yer daddy to come help you." Cooper warns Mason, but Mason just smirks like he doesn't think Cooper will hit him, or he has something smart to say.

"Well at east my father is actually here." Mason says, and I look at Cooper and he looks like a whole new level of pissed off. I can tell Cooper is trying not to say something because his jaw is clenched so hard I think it might fall off. "That's right Blackwood, are you remembering the day your dad lef-"

Before Mason could say anymore, Cooper loaded his arm back and hit Mason so hard you could hear it. I was surprised when Mason got right back up and cocked his jaw at Cooper. "You don't know anything." Cooper spat at him and he took a step back from Mason, giving him room.

But then Mason did a stupid thing, he charged towards Cooper and tackled Cooper, bringing them to the ground. "Mason, stop!" I say as they both start fighting to get on top of each other.

Cooper got out of Mason's hold and stood back up and so did Mason. "Stop it you guys!!" I tried to yell at them, but then Cooper sent another blow to Mason's jaw. Mason had to take a few steps back after the impact and he shook his head, as if trying to set his jaw back in place.

"That's all you got, Blackwood?" Mason challenged Cooper and Cooper just smirked and grabbed Mason's shirt and pulled him closer and punched him square in the nose. There was definitely a crack after the punch, and Mason was on the ground rolling in pain holding his nose. "Cooper, stop it!" I yelled at Cooper and tried to pull his arm back, and then he looked at me square in the eyes. His eyes were dark, it made me feel scared and cowardly. This Cooper wasn't the one I knew, I was afraid of this Cooper.. I automatically dropped my hand from his arm and looked down at the ground.

Cooper hovered over the hurting Mason and he looked disgusted at Mason, "You call that a fight? You city boys make me laugh." Cooper evilly humored, and then his serious look came again. "If you ever talk about my family again, I'll be talking to you in your hospital bed." Cooper warned and it made me freeze in my spot.

But then I saw Mason open his mouth, "Shut up Mason!" I tried to warn him from saying something stupid that could get him seriously hurt.

"Let him say it." Cooper growled at me, but didn't look at me.

Mason smirked up at Cooper, "You're just like your father." Mason added a chuckle. As Cooper raised his fist behind his ear, I launched myself between Mason and Cooper. I was thankful Cooper had the strength to stop his firing fist, because if he didn't, I would be dead.

"What the hell DaKota!!" Cooper yelled at me.

"You need to leave." I try to say in the most stable voice I can right now, although in the inside I am shaking with fear.

"He needs a lesson on how to shut his mouth." Cooper tries to defend himself, and he can't take his eyes off Mason.

"And you need a lesson on how to know when to stop." I say back to him, and he clenches his jaw at me.

"Trust me I know how to stop, I just think he needed a little extra-" Before he can finish his lame ass reason to be tough, I cut him off.

"Really Cooper? Kicking someone when they're already down?" I glare at him and shake my head at him, telling him I had enough and this is not who I thought it was. This is the last thing I say to him before I grab Mason's hand and walk him over to my truck, he needs to go to the hospital and check out his nose. Even though you can clearly tell it is broken, from it's unusual positioning on his face.

I DECIDED TO WAIT FOR Mason to come out of the emergency room, mostly because I was his ride, but I wanted to see if he was okay. I really wanted to see if Cooper was okay too, even though he only got punched once, but I couldn't do it. After that, all I can see is Cooper's eyes. They were terrifying to me and they reminded me of Wade's eyes.. When I would constantly say no to Wade, he would have the same look in his eyes as Cooper just did, and that's why I am so freaked out.

I missed Cooper's crooked smirk, with his charming-bad-boy smile he would give me. I missed the glimmer in his eyes when he was talking about his passions. I felt like the Cooper I knew had just vanished, and this Cooper had crawled up from hell and took over his body.

When I saw the door open from examining room I looked up and there was Mason. His nose was wrapped up and he looked like shit. His hair was tousled, face stained with his own blood, and his shirt and shorts had blood on them, too. "It's broken, they said it should heal in about two-three weeks." Mason says as we begin to walk to the parking lot.

"I'm sorry Mason." I say and put a hand on his shoulder for a sec.

"It's alright I guess," He shrugs and I furrow my eyebrows, "You always said I had a big nose." He says making me have a big smile on my face. When I told him he had a big nose, I didn't mean it physically. I just meant he really liked to know everything, and be in everyone's business.

I'm taking Mason back to the diner, just because his Toyota is there. It was a really awkward ride, but at least there was music to help. I pulled up right beside his truck and we both looked at each other. "Well here ya are!" I fake smile at him, but he has a serious look on his face.

"Did you finally see who he really is?" Mason says and my jaw drops a little bit. What is he talking about? Obviously it's about Cooper, but why?

"What the hell does that mean?" I scoff at him.

"Back there, that was the real Cooper. He's nothing but bad, DaKota." He says to me and I am so fired up right now.

"Did you plan this just so I could watch him beat the shit out of you?!" By the look on his face, I can tell the answer is yes. "Get the hell out." I say and unlock the door and he opens the door and slides out.

"But just so you know, I wasn't predicting you would defend me and not him. Maybe you are realizing what kind of guy he is." And then he shut the door and I put my truck in reverse and got the hell out of there.

I WALKED INTO MY KITCHEN to see my dad doing some kind of paperwork, maybe bills of some kind. He had his reading glasses down on the tip of his nose, and then looked up at me. "Where have you been? I thought that thing went until 11." He says to me and I groan out loud.

"Don't worry, I was just helping Mason with something." I say as I grab the orange juice out of the fridge and pour it into a small glass.

"Mason," He raises hie eyebrow at me, "Like your ex-boyfriend Mason?" He confirms his question.

"Yeah." I say with a weird expression on my face. "What's the problem?" He asks.

"Well I'm just shocked is all." He says and then looks back down at the papers he's holding.

"Why are you shocked?" I say and then take a sip of my drink. Orange juice is my all time favorite drink, it's just so refreshing!

"I like him, he's not like us." And by the he means, he isn't a cowboy. "Or a bullrider." He mumbles under his breath, but I heard it..

"Okay," I say frustrated and my dad looks up at me shocked, "What is so wrong with Cooper that everyone seems to hate him!"

"Not now DaKota." Is all he says and I shake my head and stomp all the way up to my room. I need to write in my journal to let out my steam and anger I shouldn't take out on anyone. I am going to get to the bottom of this..

The lady behind me pull the dress strings and it sucked in all of my stomach. I almost gasped at the sudden movement and I looked at myself in the almost 360 degree mirror in the room. It was a blue bridesmaid dress with an open shoulder, but then on the biceps were big and poofy. The dress was also a skin tight mermaid style, with a mess of fabric at the bottom. What the hell is Ashley thinking? I thought to myself as I studied the dress.

The manager took me into the showing area where Ashley and Taylor were waiting for me. Taylor had already fitted her dress, and this was my appointment. This can't be the dress Ash picked for her wedding. I basically came out stomping, but it was hard to tell because the dress was so tight.

However, I knew it was a joke because right when they saw me coming out they started to burst with laughter. They smacked each other and held their chests, soaking in the humiliation. Everyone was staring at them, but their vision was too blurred by their tears.

"Okay, that's enough." I say standing in front of them and try to kick them, but the dress restricts me, making me look even more ridiculous.

"Just wait!" Ashley laughs and pulls out her phone and snaps a picture of me.

"You look so stupid!!" Taylor points and looks me up and down.

"Oh! You didn't look any better!" Ashley laughs and then I see her swipe through her phone and then she holds her phone out to me to look. I look at the picture and sure enough it's Tay in the same dress, and with my same expression.

"I still think she looks worse." Taylor crosses her arms with a chuckle at the end.

"Yeah she does." Ashley bursts again and I shake my head. "Hey 1970 called and wants her dress back!" She says in a cheesy voice and I glare at her.

"I fucking hate you." I whisper/yell at them, and turn around and walk away.

The manager zipped me up and I was completely shocked at this dress. It was a stunning rustic-pink dress with a halter top covering the chest, and it was knee length. The waistline was a natural fit and between the legs was a slight a slit, making it beautiful. It fit me really nice and I was getting more and more excited for the wedding. "I don't know, I think I like thee other one the best." The manager says in her Russian accent and adds a smile, making me realize she's joking with me.

I walked out into the showing area and Ashley and Taylor's reactions were completely different this time. They looked aw-struck and happy at the same time. "Ashley, this dress is amazing!" I say as I stand in front of the mirror and admire it more.

I see her have her clever smirk on and she shrugs, "I know, I have great taste." She says and elbows Taylor in the side.

"I can't wait for Cooper to see you in that." Taylor snickers and I glare at her.

"Taylor you know there's nothing between Cooper and I." I continue to glare at through the mirror and she looks at me like you-know-I-know-it.

"Wait, you like Cooper?" Ashley says, but something in her voice doesn't convince me that she just now thought it.

"No."

"Yes." Taylor and I interrupt each other with different statements.

"Can we just drop it? And plus I'm going to the bonfire with Mason tonight." I make my case and both their jaw drops.

"Mason Bishop?" Taylor says loudly and very announced, as if she didn't hear it right.

It was true, I was going to hangout with Mason tonight. He asked me yesterday at the Diner, it was a very tough spot to be in. If he would of asked me over text, I would of turned him down. It was hard to say no to Mason because of those big eyes he gives you, and it made me remember the fun times we used to have. I thought it would be a good excuse to go out and let loose a little, since I haven't done any of that since I've been here.

THE WIND AND WEATHER was absolutely perfect, scratch that it was magical. I re positioned myself on one of our Buckskin horses, Rango as I continued riding up to the ridge. With this great weather, I thought it would be nice to get away from soon-to-be-bridezilla Ashley. I needed to get away from them because now Caleb was evolved, and that will take hours to get Caleb to agree, and lots of yelling.

I had about four hours until Mason was going to pick me up for the bonfire. I was excited for the party, but I was just a little worried about how Mason and I would be around each other for that period of time. I wonder if I would loosen up and try to have some fun, or it would just be plain awkward for us. And I really wanted to hang out with Taylor, but if Mason is the same, he'll stay by my side the whole time.

Rango and I finally made it on top of the ridge and it was just simply breath taking.. Our ranch was surrounded by distant mountains, lots of forested areas, and lots of hills and plains. The trees were full and a luscious, vibrant green, and everything looked healthy and gorgeous.

I can't even describe the natural smell, it's so earthy and mountainous, if that makes sense. In Montana in general, and if I could, I would stay here everyday. I slid off Rango and dropped the split reins and tied them over a broken tree branch and then I walked over to the edge of the hill and looked down.

I looked down at the steepness of the cut off, and I looked to my left to the unforgettable hole. That hole lead me to what I say changed my life. That hole lead me to my nickname, "Wolf girl." I was only 9 when it happened, everyone says it was a miracle and very strange, but to me it meant so much more.

FLASHBACK

I HAD WANTED TO WATCH the sun set on the ridge, and I begged my parents to let me go alone. It took a lot of convincing, but they finally agreed, but I had to come right back. I was so excited to go, I ran to my horse and tacked him up and immediately took off for the ridge.

But the thing is, I wasn't at the main ridge. I had managed to find a secluded area, where I had never been, or anyone else. I only saw it because the wind was just right and I saw an opening through the trees, and decided to be adventurous.

Then I was amazed at what the new view was. "Wow." I gasped as I walked my horse around to inspect and I was in the happiest mood of all. To look more closer, I decided to tie Jasper to a branch. I walked to the edge of ridge and looked around. Being at a young age, I had never seen anything as breathtaking as this. It was a whole new world to me.

But then, I felt the earth beneath me break and the next thing I knew I was tumbling down a steep slope of dirt. I must have gotten to close to the weak edge, and broke the surface. It was a long way down, but I finally rolled to the bottom.

I was hurt and torn up. I was really dizzy from all the tumbling, I had scrap marks all over me, and I could barely move my right arm. I was at the bottom of a huge opening to be surrounded by a forest. I looked up at the ridge I had just fallen from, there was no way I could climb up, or another way to get around and climb. Good thing I knew my directions..

It was now cold and beginning to get very dark and spooky, but the full moon was on my side tonight and made the darkness brighter. I was starting to get scared, but I was worried about my parents. They must be out of their minds right now.

Then it started to rain, just great. I had to look for some kid of shelter, it would not be okay if I was soaked. From the moonlight, I saw an opening through the dirt and decided to check it out. I climbed into the hole, but only to drop down a foot down. I held my arm in pain, and smelled the earth around me. It wasn't a pleasant smell, it smelt like wild animals and some other scent.

Then I heard it.

I heard cries of something.

A little moonlight shined in the hole and I saw them, wolf pups. I gasped and was absolutely amazed at the little creatures. They had to be a month old or so, not old enough to care for themselves.

Their cries were small, and they seemed to be wondering what I was and if I was safe. One courageous slowly and carefully walked over to me, I stood still and just was prepared for anything to happen.

After the little pup sniffed me, and gave me a couple of ticklish licks, he seemed to communicate with the others and they walked over to me. There was seven of them, all about the same size, but the first one was the biggest and the only one who had 100% black fur. The others had some black, some gray, a brown, and even a reddish/orange fur. They all had blue eyes, but when they were mature they would turn into yellow.

"Hey little guys." I said and I started to pet them and they seemed to like it because they all laid on their backs and wagged their tails. They were so soft and very playful with me, it made me forget I was lost in a forest.

It all ended when I heard a loud growl, and I don't think it was the pups. I slowly looked up and saw a gray-black wolf standing at the entrance of the den. I gulped and started to crawl back. The pups ran to what I assume was their mother. They yipped and yelped at their guardian, and I couldn't take my eyes off the wolf's piercing yellow eyes.

She looked down at her pups and scrunched her eyes at the pups, and they were making all kinds of noises, I wish I understood. It was a miracle, the wolf came in and laid right beside me. I was just completely astonished by their actions. It was like the pups told their mother I was safe and she could trust me.

But then it got weird, mama wolf regurgitated some type of meat and the pups went crazy over it. As the pups were eating, the mother kept a very close eye on me the whole entire time.

I am proud to say, that entire night I slept in a wolf den with wolves.. No one would believe me.

PRESENT

I REMEMBER NO ONE BELIEVING me the next day, and my parents were super mad at me. But I wanted them to know I wasn't joking, so I took them back to the den. Then they believed me, oh, they sure did.

CURRENTLY SITTING ON a tailgate with the great Mason by my side. We've been here for an hour or so, and there's been little excitement. The only exciting thing was seeing Big John chugging a half gallon of beer and then tipping over. But other than that, I've watching the huge flames of the fire and rolling my eyes at Mason.

The whole time he's been trying to show off to me, and trying to be "cool" to his friends. Taylor wasn't here yet, but I guess a lot more "fun" people were coming soon. "Wanna drink DaKota?" As he's holding up a red solo cup to me.

"No thanks, again." I say because this is his sixth time asking me if I wanted a drink.

"Wanna to dance?" He asks me and I look over to where everyone was dancing, and it just looked so sweaty and really crowded.

"Maybe some other time." I say politely to him and he nods and looks a bit irritated.

"Well I'll be back then." Yup, definitely mad at me. Does it bother me? Nope.

And there I sat, all alone. All alone with a bunch drunk rednecks and some slutty girls. I was really glad I wasn't one of those girls, because I only pray that they don't get some kind of STD in their lifetime.

I checked my phone, it was already 11:50. If Taylor doesn't show up in the next couple of minuets, I'm walking home. I checked my messages to see if I missed anything from her, nothing. From the corner of my eye I saw something move beside me, and then I felt the tailgate lower from a new weight being added.

I looked to my right and it was good ol' Cooper. An overwhelming of feelings came over me at this moment. I was relieved and happy that someone was here, but I was still a little mad at him because of the fight. "You looked a little lonely, and I brought a blanket." He says a little quiet, like he didn't know if I was mad or not.

I didn't say anything, I just watched him grab the ends of the blanket and throw it out in the air and it slowly lands on our legs. The blanket was soft and rough at the same time, telling me he uses this a lot. It was a red, blue, and black Aztec pattern. "So where's Taylor?" He asks me.

"I was wondering the same thing." I say and finally look at him. He's wearing a hooded light blue and black flannel, with some dark jeans and some Twisted X mocs. To say the least, he looks good.

"What do you mean? You didn't come with Taylor?" He says really shocked and starts to look around. After I didn't say anything he asks again, "Then who did you come with?" He says in a voice that tells me he has a slight idea who it is.

"Who's truck is this.." I say and he looks around to inspect. I can tell when he figured it out, he stopped looking and he sat up straighter and slowly turned to me again.

"You did not come with him. " He says very slowly, as if he's trying to process it himself.

"Yeah I did, I did come with Mason." I say back to him, clenching my jaw. I watched his eyes go somewhere else, but then they lit up with something.. Humor?

"And where is he now?" His voice was filled with a sick humor and I watched his eyes again to where they were looking, and I looked. Of course, Mason was dancing with girls surrounding him. "C'mon I'll take you home." He says and takes the blanket off me.

"Thanks," I say and slid off the tailgate and stand in front of him. "But I'm capable of taking care of myself."

"DaKota, can you stop being mad at me?" He stubbornly says at me and I cross my arms. "Look, I apologized to you and him."

What did he just say? Did he actually apologize to Mason? Mason never mentioned anything about it, would Cooper do it? "You did?" I ask him, slowly looking up at him.

"Why do you sound so shocked?" He sounded surprised and really offended.

I didn't answer him right away, I turned my head and looked back at the intoxicated Mason. "He just-it's nothing." I blow off.

TAYLOR WAS FINALLY here and we're just chilling by the fire, almost ready to go home. The party got some what better since her and Beau got here, because they actually made me smile. And Mason, well he just Mason. I really don't know what I was thinking when I said yes to him.

"Are you ready to go home?" Taylor asks me.

"Yeah, I'll go get the truck started." I say and grab her keys since she and Beau had a beer tonight.

I wrapped my arms around myself because of the weather changing into a cool, chilly night. "DaKooootaaa!" Someone slurred behind me and I stopped and turned around. A almost stumbling Mason, holding a beer in his hand, trying to walk over to me. "Where ya going? I don't wanna leave yet!!" He says, throwing his hand behind him towards the party.

"Well I'm leaving without you, I'm going with Taylor." I explain to him as he stands right in front of me. I can smell the stench of alcohol all over Mason.

"I don't want you to leave.." He slurs all sadly. "You already left me once, please don't do it again.." He says as he wraps an arm around me.

"Mason.." I say but he sush's me.

"You're so lovely, let me kiss you." He says and pushes me up against the truck.

"Mason, stop!" I cry out and he's breathing heavy, and I can feel the anxiety coming. I can feel myself shaking and the tears are going to start. "Please.. Mas, stop." I said as he ran his hand up my thigh, and I felt his disgusting breath against my neck.

He started to kiss me now, I didn't even move my lips, it was all him. He was so drunk, he didn't know what he was doing. "Mason, no!" I tried shoving him away, but he just pinned me harder.

All I could see was Wade's face and what he would do to me.. His voice was all over my head and I couldn't get him out, and I remembered every detail about his disgusting self.

Now, the shaking had started and the tears were rolling. Right now I couldn't move a muscle I was shaking and panicking so bad. "P-ple-eas-ee s-top-p." I stutter.

"Get the hell off her!!" My hero's deep voice boomed as Mason was pushed off me. Once Mason was off me, I automatically fell to the ground and started shivering. "DaKota!" I was suddenly woke out of my haze and I slowly looked above me to Cooper hovering me.

He lifted my head onto his knee, he looked so scared, which made me even more scared. "Please talk to me, say something.." He said down to me.

"I'm okay, just help me up." I say and he looks at me like he had just seen me do something completely crazy.

He picked me up under my armpits and made sure I was stable, he let me go. I slowly turned to him. "Um, can you take me home?" I ask, just like nothing happened.

"Yes." He says and then wraps a blanket around my shoulder. We start walking the other direction of Taylor's truck, I grab the ends of the blanket in my hands and look over my shoulder. I see Mason laying on the ground, passed out with a bloody nose. He deserved it.

It was a short walk to Cooper's truck, and I was very thankful for it. Cooper comes to my side of the truck and he opens the door for me and I give him a small smile and get in. I unwrap the blanket and put on my seat belt as Cooper gets into his seat. He put the key into the ignition and the diesel starts and the lights flash on.

I heard him sigh and from the corner of my eye I see him look at me. I see his mouth open, but then it shuts. I just stare into the windshield and try to forget about what just happened.

It seemed like it took forever to get to my house, but Cooper finally pulled into my drive. I really needed to go into my room and let my thoughts go into words in my journal. Cooper parked his truck in the grass and we finally looked at each other. "Do you wanna talk about it?" Cooper says and I slowly shake my head.

"Thanks for the ride, Cooper." I say as I grab the door handle and open it up.

"Let me walk you in." I heard him say as he opens his door. Next thing, he's right beside me, walking to the porch steps.

We're at the door and stand in front of each other. "Goodnight." I say to him and look into his eyes. His eyes are full of concern and really curious.

"Goodnight, Kota.." He said and dug his hands into his pockets and walked off the steps.

As I thought about it, no one was home. My dad was off in another town, and Mom and Caleb were with Ashley visiting her parents. I really didn't want to be alone tonight. "Hey Cooper?" I say in a loud voice as he's almost to his truck. He turns around to look at me, "No one's home, can you stay with me?" I offer and he almost smiles and he starts walking to me, or the house I mean.

AS SOON AS I GOT INTO my room, I felt it in my stomach. I felt really sick, violated, and I had that feeling I had two years ago. And then the tears started to pour. "DaKota." He says with worry and I slowly turn around, sniffling and letting the tears slowly drop. "Hey come here." He says in a very calming voice and he steps towards me and wraps me in a hug.

It was weird, I felt actually good. Not just good, but like I fit in his arms so well I didn't want to leave. He smelt like a bonfire and the woods. We just stood there, I'm sure he didn't know what to say and I didn't blame him. What would you say to a girl in this situation, personally I'm glad he didn't say anything.

After I felt like I had cried enough, I gave Cooper a little squeeze and then stepped back. "I've just never seen that side of him." I said as I sat on my bed and started to rub my arms because I was cold.

"Drunk or pushy?" Cooper says as he sits beside me on the edge of the bed.

"Both, I guess." I shrugged. I suddenly looked up at him, "Cooper what would of happened if you weren't there?" I teared and he looked me in the eyes.

"DaKota, don't think like that.. Please don't say that, it makes me mad just thinking about it." He says and clenches his jaw, telling me he's really serious.

"Why would it make you mad?" I asked him out of curiosity.

"Because I care about you, Kota." He says and places his hand on my thigh, but only for a second because I moved my thigh. I didn't mean to, but it was a instinct for me.

"Sorry." We both at the same time.

"You should be getting to bed." Cooper says and looks over at my pillows.

"Yeah I should." I say and stand up and walk over to the other side and flip the sheets and slide under the covers.

Cooper comes over to me and pulls more covers for me and sits on the edge. "I'm sorry Kota, if you ever feel uncomfortable again, please call me. Call me for anything.. Goodnight." He says and I pause before I say anything.

"Thanks Coop." I say and grab his hand and I lean up and kiss his left cheek. "I really appreciate it." Then I lay back down and turn on my left side and mumble against the pillow, "Sweet dreams." I feel Cooper's weight leave the bed and then heard his footsteps leave my room. The last thing I remember is thinking about Cooper's brown eyes.

I woke up the next morning, smiling? I searched my brain as why I was smiling, and the only thing I could think of was Cooper. Cooper and his gorgeous eyes. Cooper with his charming smile. Cooper and his cheesy and funny jokes. Cooper and his punches... Cooper and his protective ways.. Cooper Blackwood..

I sat up in my bed and remembered last night. I only thought about the whole Mason situation for a second, because my mind was preoccupied with Cooper saving me. Honestly, I would never thought of Cooper handling it like he did.

I know he punched Mason, but I would of expected him to just pound on Mason. But no, just one shove and punch, sending him a message and he was done. He knew it was a delicate moment and he didn't try to get me to talk.

And that hug we had, oh that hug.. Least to say, it was perfect. I really wanted to do it again. But I couldn't, Cooper probably didn't want me to.

I know he said he cared, but so did Mason. Mason said he cared about me, but look at what happened. I think Cooper was just in the moment and it would only be last night...

I'M TAKING THE DOGS for a run, I'm planning to go to Crazy Man Hill. The dogs really enjoy going there and so do I. It was so open, the hills rolled and the mountains in the horizon seemed like they were glowing. Micah and Gauge were best buddies and they would run side by side with each other, stopping occasionally to have a quick fight.

It felt good to go on a run, it really got my steam out and my mind off things. I really need to do this often, I've ran two miles and I'm started to get pretty tired. I stopped on the top of hill to catch my breath.

Then it thundered, and I looked up at the sky and it was darkening by the second. Next thing I knew, it was pouring cats and dogs. I looked up, the rain droplets pounded my face. "Great." I mumbled. I looked around and dogs were sitting side by side looking at me basically saying, 'What are you gonna do?'

I looked around and saw a house, as I looked harder, it was Cooper's house. I turned around in the direction of my house, it would be too far to run in this rain and not get sick. I almost start to hit myself, because I wanted to go to his house, but at the same time I didn't. "Ugh, come on boys." I say and wipe the rain off my face and I start jogging. The dogs begin to bark as they run in the direction I am.

I reached Cooper's house in no time, because of the angle I was running down. By now, I was drenched and so were my dogs. I went onto their porch and rang the doorbell. The door opened and Cooper's mom answered it. She looked a little confused but then her lips turned into a smile. "Come in!" She waved her arm and opened the door.

"I am so sorry Desiree, I don't want to make your house a mess." I say and stay on the floor mat.

"Oh honey no worries! So what were you doing?" She yells as she walks into their bathroom.

"Well I was running with my dogs and it just started pouring!" I say louder so she can hear me.

"Well I'll go out there and take care of ya puppies! Here's a towel, you can go up stairs and use the shower."

"I hate to be a bother Desiree." I say taking the towel from her and start to dry myself.

"Oh it's not a bother! Oh and Cooper's in town right now, but he should be back any time." She says and she goes behind me and grabs an umbrella and puts her Muck boots on.

"Thanks Desiree." I say and she smiles and then goes outside.

I take off my shoes and look around Cooper's house. I like how rustic and charming it was. Little country decor was all over and pictures were neatly arranged on the walls. As I walked up the stairs I enjoyed the school pictures. Cooper was so cute as a little kid! Reese was equally as cute, and they looked very much alike.

I walked up stairs and opened every door to see which was the bathroom. I finally found it and honestly could not wait to get in.

AFTER MY SHOWER I REALIZED I have no clothes to wear. I looked in the drawers for a comb and I found one. After I combed my hair I re secured my towel around myself and then opened the door and stepped out. I walked down back the stairs, looking for Desiree. "Desiree?" I say and look around.

"In here sweetie!" She says and I follow her voice into another room. I enter and see that she's doing laundry.

"Um, I don't have any dry clothes." I say and she nods her head at me.

"Yeah, I hope you don't mind I picked 'em up and are washing them now. And I'm sure Cooper wouldn't mind you wearing his clothes." She shrugs and continues to do her laundry.

"Well do you think you have any clothes for me?" I ask shyly, it would be kind of awkward wearing something of Cooper's. I mean I wouldn't mind if he gave me a sweatshirt or something, I just don't want to take something.

"Come to think of it I do have a pair of PJ pants for you." She says and then stands up and walks away.

I enter their living room and I see someone sitting on the couch. It's Reese! "Hey Reese!" I smile and his head turns towards me. He looked a little confused.

"States?" He said which made me smile big.

"Yep, that's me." I laugh at him and go sit down next to him. I looked at the a the TV and he was watching Spongebob.

"Why are you in a towel?" He asks me and then I clutch the towel more.

"Um, your mom is getting me some clothes." I say to him and then look back at the TV.

"Here ya go." Desiree came in and holding a pile of clothes.

"Thank you so much!" I smile and stand up and take them from her.

I giggle at Reese as he plays with my hair. All he was really doing was flipping it up and down and putting in random ponytails. "Do you wanna go meet Gauge and Micah?" I ask him and I feel him stop playing with my hair.

"They're here?!" He excitedly says and then slides off the couch.

"Yeah, why don't you ask your mom if they can come in!" I say to him and stand up and grab his tiny hands and pull him up. He grabs his crutches off the side of the couch and goes into the other room.

Soon all I see is my dogs bursting into the living room and they playfully attack us. I'm not worried about them hurting Reese because dogs have this special sense about how old someone is, and they're actions change because of it.

Reese's giggle fills the room, making me smile and really appreciate how lucky Reese is. I'm sitting on the couch while Reese is on the floor, having the dogs lick all over his face. "Do you know what types of dogs these are?" I ask him.

"Gauge is a lab!! We used to have one, but dad took him." He says sadly as he scratches Gauge's stomach.

"And what was his name?" I ask him.

"Roofus." He smiles and starts to drum against his stomach.

"And where's your dad?" I ask him out of curiosity. Cooper has never mentioned his dad and if I do bring it up, he changes the subject. Reese seemed sad talking about his dog, which must of reminded him of his absent father.

Before Reese could answer, the screen door opened and in came in Cooper. He was wearing a long trench coat you see cowboys wear in the movies, and a straw hat on. "Cooper! Look!" Reese's little voice says and Cooper turns his attention to the living room.

His eyes lit up when he sees us, and he kicks off his boots and walks over to us. "What do we have here?" He says as he kneels down and starts to pet Micah.

"Well DaKota was running this morning it started raining, then she came here and then took a shower, and now is wearing mama's pants and your shirt." Reese rambles quickly and then I look at Cooper and he looks at his shirt.

It was an old baseball shirt, and Desiree didn't have a tee shirt for me. It was just a gray tee, but it was huge on me. Cooper smirks and says, "They say Farmers praise the rain." He looks me up and down and continues to pet the dogs. I blush at his flirty comment.

Cooper gets up and sits right next to me, so our legs are touching. "So what were you doing?" I ask him and nudge him a bit.

"Just doing some guy stuff." He said with a smirk and looked at me with his eyes.

"Guy stuff, huh?" I say and lean back on the couch and he copies me. "Like what?" I ask him.

"Cowboy shit." He whispers in my, making sure his voice sounds like a stereotypical cowboy. He makes me laugh and I elbow him in the side.

REESE WAS SLEEPING on the floor, cuddled up to the dogs and was sleeping like a baby, he was tired out by playing with the dogs. Cooper and I were just chilling on the couch, it was still raining outside. I was facing Cooper, laying at one end at the couch and he was facing me, laying on the other side. "Hey Cooper?" I ask him, while playing with the fringes of the couch pillow.

"Yes?" He says and opens his eyes to look at me.

"You didn't tell anyone about last night, did you?" I ask him, and he moves around uncomfortably.

"No." He said like he wouldn't even imagine of doing it, "Well, it wasn't just anyone.." He said softly and I immediately sat up and gaped at him.

"What does that mean!?" I asked through clenched teeth. Cooper's facial expression was sorry, but also not sorry.. "Who did you tell?"

"Caleb.." He says looking me in the eyes and I almost jump out of my skin! How could he tell my brother! That is worst person to tell about the situation! I'm going to kill Cooper!

"Cooper!!!! We have to go, now!!" I say and jump off the couch and stand in front of Cooper.

"Why?" He asks me, looking up.

"WE have to go see if Mason is still alive!" I say and crouch down and grab his hand and pull him up. "Come on dogs!" I hiss and they pop up and follow Cooper and I out the door.

Cooper and I pull into my drive and I'm happy to see Caleb's truck still here. My heart rate slows and I look at Cooper and he looks as relaxed as a bloodhound on a porch. "See wasn't that bad." Cooper says calmly.

"But you should of asked me first, what happened when you told him?" I ask him as I take off my seat belt.

"Well he just stood there, shook his head, and didn't really do anything. He wasn't calm but he didn't seem in a murderous mood." Cooper shrugs and I roll my eyes.

"Great, now Caleb won't let me out of the house again." I sigh, but I panic when I figure out what I just said.

"What was the first time he didn't let you out of his watch?" He asks, very amused. But he wouldn't be amused if he knew the real reason.

"Oh it was nothing." I awkwardly laugh. I hear the screen door shut and I see my father and brother coming out. Or should I say storming out.. They looked absolutely pissed and very determined. "Oh shit." I say and I open the door and jump out of Cooper's truck. "Where are you guys going?!" I yell at them.

"Settle some business.. You stay here! And we'll talk about that later!" My dad yells as he loads up into the truck, but I see him look at Cooper's truck.

"Yeah, right." I grumble and head back to Cooper's truck. I knew where they were off to and Cooper was going to take me there.

"Where we goin'?" Cooper asks as I climb into the truck and start to put on my seat belt.

"Just follow them!" I instruct and run my fingers through my hair. This is going to be very chaotic.

WE ARRIVED AT THE SCENE just as my dad and brother were jumping out of the truck. We were at Mason's house and he just so happened to be outside, I guess at the right time. I ripped off my seat belt and followed my dad. "You got some nerve kid!" My dad yelled and Mason looked scared shitless.

I started to run and I got in front of my raging dad and brother. "Please, stop.. He was drunk and didn't-"

"Shut up DaKota!" Caleb yells at me and I automatically feel stomped on by him.

"What's going on?" Mason says and starts walking backwards. If I was him, I would start running. My dad wouldn't catch him, and Caleb would try but I don't think he would catch him.

"You think it's okay to sexually harass girls?" My dad yells and then shoves Mason backwards. Mason looked very guilty, and very much ashamed of himself.

"Caleb, Dad!" I yell at them and then step in front of them. Both of them looked down at me, both steaming like a mad heifer. They don't say anything but my dad just shoves me out of the way, making me stumble a bit. Although, I was caught by Cooper.

"Cooper." Caleb says and then looks me up and down, motioning Cooper to keep me there. I try to get out of his grip, but Cooper just holds me tighter.

"Cooper, let me go!" I say, struggling more and more.

"You know he deserves this DaKota." Cooper says to me.. I know it wasn't right, but he didn't need to get punched until he pukes his guts out.

So there I stood, watching my dad and Caleb gain up on Mason. Mason just stood there, as if he was going to take it like a man.. This isn't right, I hate how they do this.

"Mason, run!-" I start to yell but then Coopers covers my mouth with his rough hand. I start to yell into his hand, but nothing is comprehensible because of my 'muzzle'.

Then the first punch is thrown by my father, and then Caleb jabs him one in the stomach. I couldn't watch them hurt Mason. "I can't watch." I say and then I turn into Mason's chest and clutch his shirt with my hands. I try to block out Mason's grunts and groans of pain, but they're just too loud to block out.

Cooper wraps his arms around me tighter, comforting me like he did last night. "Alright, he's had enough." Cooper speaks up and I pick my head up from Cooper's chest and look over at the boys.

I ripped out of Cooper's grasp and ran over to Mason. He had a bloody face, cuts and scraps on his eyebrows and a big ol' goose egg on his forehead. "Mason, oh my gosh.." I say as I kneel down next to him.

"I'm so sorry DaKota.." He cries out and painfully looks at me.

"No I'm sorr-"

"No what I did was stupid, I am so sorry! I'll be alright, please just go." Mason says and I nod and stand back up. I turn around and look at Caleb and my dad standing on guard, still with clenched fists at their sides. I was full of anger and sadness. Anger because of what they did to Mason, and sadness because of the reason they did it.

"You guys are so immature." I snarl at them as I walk past them. How could they just do something like this?!

THERE WE STOOD, ACROSS from each other, both with our arms crossed. We just stared at each other ready to blow off our steam. And in between us was mom, and ready for entertainment was Caleb. "How could you feel bad for him?!" My dad shouts at me and I roll my eyes and I see my mom sigh.

Her and I talked before my dad came here. She completely understood why I wasn't so mad at Mason, but no one could get through his thick head. See I knew Mason, I knew it wouldn't happen again. And after Caleb and dad kicked his ass, it definitely won't happen again.

"He was drunk and didn't know what he was doing! Mason isn't that type of guy and you know it!" I shout back at him.

"Yeah well it still happened! Have you not forgotten about the other time th-"

"Of course I haven't forgotten. How could you even say that?" I snap at him and he throws up his hands in frustration and looks at me, then away, then back at me.

"Because you're acting like it's not a big deal!" He says and then puts his hands on his hips.

"Dad it only happened for like 30 seconds!-"

"But if Cooper wasn't there it would of gotten worse.." Caleb's voice pops out of no where, cutting my voice off. Slowly my dad and I turn our heads to look at my idiotic brother. He just sits there looking like he did nothing wrong.

"Shut up, Caleb." We both say.

"It's over with now, you made him pay for it. Please don't hold it against him.." I say and I turn around and start towards the stairs to upstairs.

"You come back here young lady!!" My dad yelled as me as I was half way up the stairs. I internally groaned and rolled my eyes. What does he want now? I stomp back down the stairs and I lean against the wall, still on the bottom step. "We still need to talk about that Blackwood kid." Well I was not expecting this, I scrunched my eyebrows at him.

"What with Cooper?" I ask him.

"You didn't ask me to be hanging out with him." He says, using his big dad voice on me.

"Yes, I'm sorry dad. I should of asked you before. I am deeply sorry.." I say very sarcastically, but my dad is so egotistical he believed me. I knew how my dad worked, and I knew very well how to take advantage when I needed to.

"Okay, great." My dad nodded his head in approval and gave me an understanding small smile and slapped his hands together and turned on his heels away from me. I rolled my eyes and look at Caleb and he gave me a thumbs up.

When I got to my room I grabbed my phone and I texted Mason, "I'm really sorry what happened to you :(I know you weren't in the right state of mind, I hope you know I'm not mad at you."

I looked outside and it was getting dark, I grabbed my quilt and my headphones and I walked out to my balcony. I threw the quilt on my cushioned chair and then walked up to the balcony railing. I looked up at the rising half moon and admired it. It's the thing people dread when they see because it means the day is ending. But yet they admire it when it's at the highest point and they are laying under it's light.

I walked backwards and laid back on my chair and I pulled my quilt over my chest. This quilt I made with my grandma when I was 13, it had great memories with it. I missed her, she died in her sleep just before I left Hudson.

I plugged my headphones into my phone and went onto Pandora and clicked on Outlaw country radio. I could stay here all day if I could. It was so peaceful to look at the mountains and watch everything that passes by them. I turned my head and before I knew it my eyes began to close.

I blew the piece of hair out of my face as I was mucking out the stalls. I was sweating because of my hard work on this morning. I had already picked the garden, fed all the horses, fed the cows and chickens, and milked the cows. Why do these horses have to crap so much?

And to help it, Caleb wasn't even helping me. And I was working quickly because I had to go help organize the rodeo in the next town over, Smallsvielle. My dad was suppose to get everything organized for the rodeo but he "forgot" about it, so know I have to do it. I mean I shouldn't be complaining about it, he does this to me all the time.

Smallsvielle is only about twenty minuets away and it was bigger than Hudson by a couple thousand people. And it was a lot bigger rodeo than Hudson and others combined. I will be competing and so will Taylor and the girls, and unfortunately so would be Avery. I can't wait to beat her.

After I was done mucking the stalls I quickly put the fork away. When I was hustling I tripped over my boots and landed in a wheel barrel. Why is this wheel barrel here? Oh no, it's a wheel barrel full of cow shit. I'm going to kill Caleb!! He was suppose to get rid of this! Now I'm covered in sweat and poo. I pushed myself up and out and then I sprinted to the house. When I got in I kicked off my muck boots and I ran to the bathroom in my room but I couldn't get in because the door was locked. I pounded on the door, "Caleb!!!" I screamed, why the hell is he in my bathroom?

"What?" He yells back.

"Why are you in my shower?!" I yell at him, I'm so irritated at him right now.

"Rusty and Jake are in the down stairs shower!!" He yells back at me, what are they doing here? You know what, I probably don't even want to know..

"Ugh!"I screamed. "I'm covered in cow shit that you didn't take care of!!" I complained to him.

"Oh and DaKota?!" He says ignoring my complaint, "Can you make breakfast for us?" Is he joking? I praise Ashley for keeping up with him, and good luck to her when they live together.

"Are you serious, Caleb? Where's mom and dad?" I ask him as he is still showering.

"They went Jamestown for the company." He yells at me.

"Fine!" I roll my eyes and then I run back down stairs and start my slaving for the boys.

So far I have made omelets and french toast with Texas toast. I have also cut up some deer sausage and some fruit. I know what the boys

106

need to fuel up for the rodeo. I heard a door close and out came Rusty with wet hair, he looked up at me and stopped. "Hey DaKota..." He says looking me up and down. I can sense he's noticing my great appearance.

"Hi Rusty." I say as I bring over the big plate of french toast to the table and set it down in the center, "Come and eat." I smile the best I can right now. I can tell he can sense my stench but he doesn't say anything.

"Whoooo!! Something smells good!!" Jake screams in the house and uses his socks to slide against the wood floor. He's not wearing a shirt, shocker, and his jeans and belt buckle. "What's cookin' good lookin'?" He smoothly says as he pulls out the chair and sits down. Jake has always been the joking flirting type with me. It seriously means nothing, he just uses pick up lines all the time.

"French toast, your favorite." I say as I pat his shoulder.

"Your cooking is the best! Your smell.. Not so much.." He says as I begin to walk away but then I stand in my tracks and slowly turn around.

"Well if it wasn't for your ass, I wouldn't smell like this!!" I smacked the back side of his head and Rusty chuckled. "Just shut up and eat your breakfast." I say to both of them, hearing Caleb's footsteps coming down the stairs. Finally, I get to go take a shower.

AFTER MY SHOWER I LEFT on my towel and started to get my outfit on my bed. Hmm, what barrel racing shirt should I wear today? I think I'm gonna wear one of my Cinch shirts. I walked over to my closet and started to rummage my clothes. Ah-hah! I really like this one.

I pulled the burgundy shirt off the hanger and throw the shirt on the bed and then I go to my jean drawer and pull out a pair of my nicer Wrangler Jeans. I squat down beside my bed and pull out my glass case of my barrel racing belt buckles. I decide to wear the biggest one I have, oval shaped at least. After that I sit down at my makeup table and begin to do my mascara.

Before leaving my house for the rodeo, I made sure I had everything and I looked okay. I put the duffel bag strap and put it on my shoulder and then grabbed my steel colored Brim hat and opened the door and headed to my truck and trailer.

COOPER

WE ALL CHOKED WHEN we all breathed as one, and now we were rolling down the windows. Jake had just ripped a nasty one and Rusty and I were disgusted. Jake had the nastiest farts. "You're sick." I yelled at him in the back seat.

"Blame Wolf Girl, she gave me blackberries!!" He says while sitting forward and putting his head between Rusty and I. Wolf Girl? Oh ya, DaKota.

"Why were you with DaKota?" I ask him raising my eyebrow at him.

"Well Rusty and I were helping Caleb with some work and we got all dirty so-"

"Get to the point." I said to him as I turned onto the rodeo grounds.

"She made us breakfast, you should of seen her man.. She was covered in shit." He laughs sitting back into the seat again.

"In shit?" I clarify to them and they both nod. I could just see it. DaKota with dirt and shit hinted on her face, a little sweaty, her cute little muck boots, and her hair in a messy ponytail, what a cutie.

I turned my truck into the designated parking area for the competitors and I felt myself getting excited. I loved to compete, especially bulls. Bulls was definitely my favorite, but that doesn't mean I don't love bull-dogging, but I know I'll go far with bulls.

I was gaining more and more points and pretty soon I'll be competing in CBR, if I keep riding like I am. That means I'll be traveling more, going to bigger rodeos. That's my next step to my biggest goal, PBR.

"Here we go boys." Rusty said as we all opened our doors and stepped onto the dirt.

I HAD TOOK THE TOP time for bull dogging and earned a paycheck for $5,500. Bull ridin' is the the last event, right now it's team roping. I'm just walking around, trying to find familiar faces to talk with. It's a packed rodeo, I don't think there's one seat in the bleachers that isn't taken.

As people walked passed me, I gave some a small grin. I saw a lot of girls lookin at me when they pass by, some of them were cute, but I don't think they were named after a state. "Cooper!" I knew who said my name, but I kept walking. "Cooper! Cooper Blackwood!" I stopped walking and took in a deep breath.

I turned around and saw Avery walking towards me. She was wearing jeans tighter than tight and a shirt a little too shirt for her, making her stomach show. She did look pretty good I have to admit. "Hey Avery." I say to her and she sends me a smile.

"Whaddya doing by yaself?" She says and then sticks her hands in her back pockets and starts walking beside me.

"Look for a friendly face." I reply kindly to her and adjust my hat.

"Well now ya got one." She bashes her eyelashes, and while saying it she puts her hand on my arm for second, or maybe longer. I didn't say nothing back to her, I just kept walking. "Congrats on the win, Cooper." She says and then nudges me with her arm.

"Thanks Avery. Have you seen the Jones'?" I ask her, turning my head to look down at her. Her usual smirk turns into confused frown.

"I guess I saw them over by the kid's chutes." She said quietly and then I stopped and turned my head in that direction. I focused my eyes around the chutes and there they were, DaKota and her dad. DaKota had her arms crossed and talking about something to her dad, who looked like he wasn't even paying attention.

"Well I gotta go, see ya later Avery. Always a pleasure talking to you!" I turned towards Avery while walking backwards and tipped my hat at her.

I walked over to the chutes where DaKota once was, and I looked around for her. Then I saw her laying on the side hill by herself, what the hell is she doing? As I got closer to her I saw that she had her hat tipped over her face and her eyes closed. Just laying on the hill she still looked good. Now I'm right next to her, deciding to lay down next to her. "What are you doing?" I whispered in her ear and she shot up quicker than a bull out of the chutes.

She was holding her chest and had her head hung down. "God damn it Cooper." She chuckles and then puts her hat back on. I sit up along with her and use my arms to hold me up, my left arm is behind her back. "You scared the hell out of me." She said making eye contact with me, her eyes held something of sadness and amusement. Why could she be sad now? I'm here for Gods sake.

"I didn't think you were scared of anything." I say to her, but when I'm done saying it she breaks our eye contact and looks the other way. I notice what her hands are doing, her right hand is hovering over her right hip and looking at it weird.

"So what's up." She says in voice she usually doesn't use. But I remember her using it once when she avoided talking about her past.

"Just saw you over here and wanted to talk to you." I say to her and she nods and looks at me again.

"Oh my gosh! I just had a great idea!" Her green eyes lit up and turns her torso towards me. "Do you wanna do a favor with me?" She asks me with a begging smile on her face.

"Yeah sure, what is it?" I ask her and she squirms while sitting down.

"Yay!! Oh my gosh you're the best!" She says with a very bright smile that could of made the atmosphere lighter.

"DaKota what are we doing?" I chuckle at her excitement, but I'm curious on what the favor is. I noticed her smile fade a little, making me more curious. "Kota?"

"Helping me with the chicken chase.." When she said that I stood up and really started to rethink my answer to her.

"Woah now. The chicken chase?" I look down at her and she throws her head to the side and groans.

"C'mon Cooper! It won't be that bad." She begged while standing up in front of me.

"I don't know DaKota." I say and scratch the back of my neck..

"Oh pleeeeaaassseeee Cooper!" She says and puts both of her hands on my arms, now getting my attention. "I'll return the favor! C'mon for meeeee!" She pleads to me. God dammit, why does she have to be so adorable...

"Fine.. What do we have to do?" I give in to her and she jumped up a little.

"Okay! Come with me!" She grabbed my forearm, just above my wrist and she started to drag me with her. While we were walking I heard her spurs so I looked down, oh my I wish I didn't look down..

"FINAL CALL FOR THE chicken chase!!" DaKota's voice boomed from the microphone as she looked into the crowd. Her cheeks were getting red from all of the attention from the crowd, I thought it was cute. She handed over the microphone to the announcer and then started walking over to me.

I looked behind me, holy crap there are a lot of other kids here. It kind of made me sad because I started to think about Reese. If it wasn't for my little brother I would be a total mess, or worse be like my father. Reese has given me so much inspiration during his treatment for his cancer and how he still looks at life, overcoming every obstacle. "Ready Cooper?" DaKota's voice perks up from behind me.

I turn around and head over to the chicken cages, three cages, each have 5 chickens in it. They were stacked on top of each other and I bent over and picked them up and carried them over to the middle of the arena. I dropped the boxes carefully and they were still going bat-shit crazy, making me glad to drop them.

DaKota comes over to me and stands right next to me, our arms slightly touching. Why is she standing this close to me? We're the only two people around the arena. Believe me, I'm not complaining that she's standing so close, but makes me curious. I start to grin down at her as she was looking around at the kids. She looks up at me, but I don't stop smiling because her eyes were sparkling in the sun. "What?" She asks me while blushing a bit.

I bent down a little so my mouth was right next to her ear, "You look real beautiful today." I complimented her, I was so close her, I could hear her breath hitch. I regained my position and noticed her blushing a lot more now and she started to look at the dirt.

"Thanks Cooper." Shy shyly says making me smirk. Then she brought the microphone up to her dark pink lips and took a deep breath, "Hi everyone!! Y'all ready for the chicken chase?" She says and then turns on her heal to look at everyone in the stands.

The crowd cheered loudly at DaKota's question and she smiled brightly at them. "Alright!" She said and then turned towards the kids. "Okay, Cooper here is going to let the chickens loose when I count to three and say go. Also you guys will go also when I say go, okay?" She explains to them and some of them cheer. DaKota looked at me, and started to speak, "Okay Cooper.. 1..2...3..Goose!" She totally faked the kids out and everyone started to laugh.

She looked a little embarrassed from all the attention but then she looked a little more serious, "Okay, 1..2..3.. GO!" As soon as she said go I let the chickens loose and the kids went a flying. DaKota stood closer to me as kids were pushing and shoving each other in order to get a chicken. Even through the loudness of the crowd and the kids, I could still hear DaKota laugh and giggle at the kids. She had the prettiest laugh I had ever heard.

DAKOTA

IT WAS DARK OUT AND the rodeo was finished and I had taken first in the barrels, Pharaoh had a perfect run with a time of 14.54! Jessica and Molly took second and third, we all had close times. I was taking Pharaoh back to my trailer, I was actually hoping to see Cooper, I needed to thank him for earlier. Cooper was so nice with the kids and I actually think he had fun doing it.

I reached my trailer and I tied Phar's halter rope onto the loop of the trailer and I went to the back door and opened it. I walked back to Pharaoh and I saw a figure walking towards me, but I ignored it. I started to undo the cinch and then I heard, "Excuse me?" It was a masculine voice but I didn't know who they belonged to.

"Can I help you?" I ask the man who got closer to me so I could see his face, and I couldn't complain. He had a well structured face and looked very rugged, very attractive. I was still untacking my horse, while keeping eyes on the stranger.

"I don't mean to be a bother, but I was wondering if there was any restaurants around here? I'm new around here and I'm real hungry." He said to me as I slid down the saddle.

"Just one second." I say and then carry the saddle to the tack closet and put it correctly back. I quickly walk back to the cute stranger. "Well how hungry are you? I know a really good place about twenty minuets out." I say to him.

"Very." He chuckles.

"Well it's in Hudson and it's called DaKota's Diner. It's famous for it's homemade ice cream!" I smile at him, but slightly smirking.

"Sounds good! Excuse my manners, my name is River, River Haynes." He says and takes off his cowboy hat and sticks out his hand for me.

I hesitate but then stick out my hand, "DaKota Jones." I introduce myself with a smile. After I said my name he had a weird smile on his face, like he was trying to put the pieces together. "Wait, like the diner?" He smiles kindly.

"Yup, I own it." I say proudly while I scratch Pharaoh a bit.

"Well now I'm definitely going," He says and I automatically start to blush. "Can I tell you something?" He asks me.

"Sure, I guess." I tell him, slightly looking at him.

"You have a pretty rockin' smile." He compliments me again, making me blush more.

"Thank you!" I smile and then I stand in front of my horse, having Phar's head over my shoulder. "Well I hope you like the diner, I think you'll love it though.. Have a good night." I smile at him as I untie the halter.

"I can tell I already like it," He says and then looks me up and down and smirks, "Have a good night, DaKota." He says flirtatiously and then walks away. I bit my lip watching him walk away and then I pull Pharaoh to the back of the trailer and load him up.

The cliche saying of the rooster crowing in the morning is true, very true. But what it doesn't say is that the rooster won't shut up the hell up. I rolled over and grabbed the other pillow with my right hand it shoved the pillow over my face and groaned. I have a really busy day today for the diner, do I want to do it? Nope, but I have to.

I sat up in my very comfortable bed and threw my covers off my bare legs and slowly get my legs to stand on my cool wooden floor and I walk to my bathroom. I flipped on the switch and let my eyes adjust to the bathroom lights and then I started combing my bed head. I took off my PJ clothes and then opened the shower door and turned the shower handle to a medium heat and began my shower.

After my shower I put on a white tee shirt and some baby blue Nike running shorts. I ran my fingers through my wet hair and walked over to my chair and grabbed my journal and pen and walked over to my window seat and put a pillow against the wall for my back.

I looked out the window and smiled at the clear blue sky and the slight wind dancing through the sage grass. It looked like it was going to be a warm day, and I'll be inside all day doing paperwork!

"June 28, 2016

Dear Journal,

Last night was terrible, again. Although it was different from last time though. This time I actually had a shirt on, but I was handcuffed again. I was so scared, screaming for him to stop but his smile just got bigger. He took a fistful of my hair and smelt it and moaned, then he ran his finger over every inch of my body, humming as he did it. "My little flower, so lovely.. You're all mine.." He would whisper to my skin, making me cringe and shiver..

I woke up sweating and breathing heavily with my hair all over my face. I looked all around my room to see if he was any where close, I knew he couldn't be in my room, but I just thought. After I calmed down a bit, I reached under my bed for my pair of boots. I grabbed the left one and grabbed the pill container and counted my pills, forgot to take one last night. The pills don't always work, but they help and I'm thankful for that.

I'm feeling disgusting even though I just took a shower, lately I can't get Wade of my mind. I've picturing him taking pictures of me, him watching me, him being him.. But I have to cover it up, my parents can't know I'm still thinking about it. They would worry too much about me, and I can't have this small town suspecting anything."

I stopped writing because I heard a truck coming down our drive, a black Powerstroke, Cooper's black Powerstroke. What is he doing here so early? I saw him look up at my window, that small gesture made me blush. Why was I blushing about that? I looked back down at my journal and picked up the pen.

"Cooper, you know him.. Cowboy with good looks, soft but dark brown eyes, structured face, strong arms, funny, smart, and very charming.. We've grown close to each other and I consider him a close friend.. Yeah, I'll be honest, I've thought of him of more than just a friend. Especially when he tried to kiss me that night, man I wish he would of kissed me..

Dad doesn't like Cooper, or doesn't respect him. For what reason? I don't know. But I like him.. Cooper has been a lot more.. Flirty.. He's been giving me a lot of compliments, standing closer to me, and making romantic innuendos. It's making me feel different, a good different. He makes me forget about anything when we talk, he makes me feel good about myself again. But I can't like him is the thing.. I wish Cooper and I could ju-"

I stopped writing when my door came open. I was a deer in the headlights when I saw Cooper and my mom together in my doorway. "Hi sweetie," I slid the journal on the side of my thigh, keeping my cool. "Cooper's here." She said sweetly looking up at the much taller Cooper.

"I see that." I smile a bit and then finally make eye contact with him.

"I'll leave you two then.." My mother says as Cooper steps in my room and my mother swings the door close. I bring my legs off my window seat and sit upright and cross my ankles, putting my hands under my thighs.

"So what's up?" I ask him tilting my head a bit.

"Was that a journal I saw you writing in?" He says as he walks closer to me, with a smirk and humor and curiosity sparkling in his handsome eyes.

"No, why would I write in a journal?" I play off to him as I scoot back, pressing my back against my journal to the window.

"C'm DaKota, I've seen it before," He says and then looks over to my lounge chair, "I saw it when I felt it under that cushion."

My heart was started to race very rapidly, "You didn't read it did you?" I spit out very fast I wonder if he even understood me.

"If I did, what would I find in there?" He smirked, playing with me. I was relieved to find out Cooper hadn't read my journal full of my biggest secrets and thoughts. If would of read my journal, he would of talked to me before today, or did he even care?

"Just stupid stuff when I was like six years old." I chuckle and then he smiles at me.. Oh curses, his smile could just let me hand over the journal to him.

"I wanna hear about little DaKota!" His smile brightens as he says it. "C'mon let me see it!" He says and reaches around me for the book of secrets.

"Alright, I'll read one to you!" I fakely-playfully laugh at him as I slip the book to my other side and slide around Cooper. I back up away from Cooper, flipping through the pages, acting like I was searching for a certain story. "Oh! Here's a good one!" I fake a smile and then look up at Cooper and he's sitting on the left side of my bed, with his legs hanging off the end, making himself turn his torso to look at me..

"May 21, 2004.. I wish horses were like people. People suck, horses don't. Oh Lord forgive me I said suck, gosh I said it again! I'm sorry! Sometimes I wish people were raised like me, but I guess that is how the world works. Avery Johnson is a girl in my grade who is very mean and annoying. She is mean to me and other girls, and boys! She doesn't understand how my family works, and I really don't understand her family, but I don't make fun of her for it! Cuz my mamma taught me to bite my tongue, but I really want to bite Avery! But to calm down I grabbed my horse, Mushroom, and I rode her to the creek. Mushroom always rode so nice it made it a lot easier to control her with my small legs and arms. In the creek Mushroom and I would splash each other making me fall in love with the mare a lot more than I already am. Anyways I'm done for the day!

Love~ DaKota!"

I don't know how I made all that up in such small amount of time, but Cooper seemed to enjoy it. I closed the journal and looked at him and he was quietly laughing, looking down. "What's so funny?" I ask Cooper as I put the journal back in my desk.

He looked up at me and smiled again, making me blush a little bit. I go to sit on the other side of the bed, still waiting for him to answer. "That was cute." He slightly bit his lip, making me dream about his lips.

"What do you mean?" I ask him and then I pull my legs up and sit criss-cross to full look at the beautiful man in front of me.

"I really want to bite Avery!" He mocks me and I put my head down laughing with him. "And a horse named Mushroom? What's up with that darlin'?" I didn't mean to but my head shot up when he called me darlin', what the hell is he doing to me?

"W-well she was colored like a mushroom!" I laughed and he raised an eyebrow at me, "You know, she was white but had lighter brown spots, made her look like a mushroom!" Cooper was laughing, "Stop making fun of me! I was six!" I laugh and then I grabbed a pillow and threw it at him.

"Hey now!" He said and grabbed the pillow and threw it back at me, but I caught it.

"So what did you come here for anyways?" I ask him as I play with the corner of the pillow.

"Um well I was gonna ask if you uh-" He scratches the back of his neck and it seems if he's unsure of himself. "I just wanted to see how you are doing." He says a little weird, okay this is odd.

"Are you sure Cooper? Is everything okay?" I ask him and he nods.

"Yeah, so how are you DaKota? How's the diner?"

"I'm doing just fine, today I'm going to the diner to do some cleaning up and some paperwork and stuff like that. Also it's the 25 and under night tonight, so maybe that can take some stress off me." I say to him.

"Oh yeah I forgot about that, you'll be seeing me there." He smirks at me and I blush a little bit at him.

"Hey how's Reese doing?" I ask him, I'm smiling at him because of the thought of Reese, the cute little miniature of Cooper.

"He's okay, I think he needs a little play date with you again." Cooper says and it makes laugh. "He really likes you." Cooper adds.

"No, he likes my dogs." I chuckle while playing with my pillow again.

"I'm not kidding Kota, he talks about you a lot, and your dogs, and come to think about it, your ice-cream."

"I guess my ice cream is pretty mention able." I laugh looking into his eyes.

"Did you ever have braces?" He asked me.

"Yeah, why?" I ask him as I see him staring at my teeth.

"You have a great smile, DaKota." He shocks me with his openness, and I feel me cheeks heat up because of him.

"Thanks Coop.." I smile genuinely at him.

"Well I should get going, let you get your day going." He said and then got off my bed.

"I'll walk ya out." I say and hustle over to Cooper as he reaches for my door handle.

I walked in front of Cooper as we walked down the stairs to the kitchen, but I wasn't expecting my dad to be sitting at the table. My dad's eyes looked up at me and then behind me to Cooper. "Hi dad." I smile at him.

"Hi Mr. Jones." Cooper's deep voice says behind me.

"Hi sweetie, what's going on." He says and completely ignores Cooper, making stop in my tracks.

"Cooper and I were talking about the diner." I say to my dad, and I feel Cooper behind me, a little too close.

"Why couldn't you do it down here?" He asks setting down the newspaper and looking Cooper straight in the eyes.

"Because mom brought him up to my room and it's not a big deal, and don't be rude." I stand up to my dad because it was rude not to say hello.

My dad looks at me and gives me the you've-got-to-be-kidding-me look and I nod him on, "Hello Cooper."

"Hi, sir." Cooper said and I swear I heard him gulp.

"I'm walking him out." I say to my dad and raise an eyebrow to give my dad another hint of being hospitable.

"Bye Cooper." My dad grumbles and picks up the newspaper again.

"Bye Mr. Jones, sir." Cooper says and then he follows me to the door.

I'm standing right outside of Cooper's door, with my hands in my back pockets. Cooper's hand turn the key in the ignition and the diesel truck roared with life, I love that sound. Cooper reached onto the dash and put on his black felt hat and then looked down at me. "Well thanks for checking up on me." I smile at him.

Cooper pressed on the brake and shifted the gear into reverse, "Anytime darlin'." He winks as he drives away from me. Holy smoking pine cones I almost fell because of my weakening knees because of that handsome cowboy.

I STOOD BEHIND THE counter, looking at the almost full diner. Everyone seemed to be having a good time, laughing and smiling with each other. It looked good in here and I was satisfied that I could pull it out of me, but I also had some help from Taylor.

Ah, Taylor and Beau. Probably the cutest couple in the whole world. You should see the way Beau looks at Taylor when ever she talks or she laugh, you can't look away from the two. I'm glad Taylor is happy because she's always had trouble with relationships and trusting guys. Taylor really deserves Beau. They are so much a like that I wonder why they never got together before they did. "Hey DaKota! Can I have some chocolate ice cream?" Johnny's voice yelled out the loudness of the crowd.

I didn't bother to waist my voice, so I just nodded. I made my way over to our ice cream machine and pressed the chocolate button. I grabbed a bowl and swirled the deliciousness into the dish and when it was full enough I stopped it, and then I added a small piece of brownie on top.

I walked over to Johnny's table and smiled at everyone, Reed, Bonnie, Jared, Erica, and Jake. Johnny smiles excitedly at the bowl of ice cream as I set it down in front of him. "Thanks DaKota." He says and I smile and nod.

"How's everyone doing? I haven't talked to you guys in forever." I say to them, who I consider friends, good friends.

"Good." They all reply at the same time, "How about you Kota?" Bonnie says sweetly.

"I'm doing just fine, thanks."

"Hey, what's this I hear about you and-"

"Cooper! Hey!!" Jake cuts his girlfriend off and we all look at Cooper coming in the door, not just Cooper. Cooper and Avery.. Avery had a devilish smirk on her face as she had her hand wrapped around his arm, and Cooper had an emotionless face on, but he looked good. Avery had a low cut shirt on, with skin tight skinny jeans on, classic.

I decide to leave their table because Cooper and Avery were coming this way. I hope Cooper didn't see me, because I didn't want to talk to him right now. I went behind the counter again and started to wipe it down, glancing up at Cooper and Avery..

The way he let her hang onto him made me question Cooper, did he like her? I was stupid he would actually start to maybe like me, why would he like someone like me? Gosh, I could just slap Avery if I could. "DaKota, there's a man over there who asks for you." Maddie says to me as she walks past me and points to table 9.

I look and there's someone with their back to me, all I can see is a cowboy hat and a carhart sweatshirt. I threw the towel over my shoulder and started walking over to the stranger. I walked out of the island counter and looked at the guy waiting in the booth, it was the guy from the rodeo, River I think his is name. "Hey! You took my advice I see." I smiled at him and he smiles back.

"I did, and I decided I wanted to come back for some more." He says with a smirk, "Also I wanted to see you again." He adds, gaining my attention and making me blush. "You busy?" He asks, pointing to the open side of the booth. I look around and decide I can take a break for a while, so I sat down and River smiled.

120

HOLY, RIVER COULD MAKE me laugh! We've been talking non-stop with each other, just about different things. We talked about our families and what we do on our free time, and talked about farm problems. It took my mind off the diner, and I was thankful. Plus, he wasn't too bad to look at while talking this long.

"And don't you hate it when you have to fix a fence or post that you just fixed because that same damn cow did it again?!" River explains, throwing his head back and tossing his hands into the air, clearly frustrated just thinking about it again.

"Omg, yes!! We used to have a heifer do that all the time!!" I laugh with him.

"Used?" He asks me.

"We sold that bitch." I say serious, and then we both break out in laughter. Through the laughter, I see Cooper walking over here with a blank expression. My laughter stops and River looks at me weird, and I can only imagine what Cooper wants to talk about.

"What's up Cooper?" I ask him as he eyes River. Cooper stands on my side and I look up at him and see him glaring at River.

"Nice to see you, Cooper." River smiles weirdly at Cooper, but Cooper continues to glare.

"River." Cooper acknowledges him, I can literally feel the tension in the air.

"How do y'all know each other?" I ask them, looking between them. Cooper didn't look like he was going to answer, so River spoke.

"Oh me and ol' Coop go way back, we met in 4H." River says and slightly smirks.

"Cool, so-"

"How do you know River?" Cooper cuts me off with an aggressive question.

"Oh we met at the rodeo last week, and I told him about the diner." I said and he nodded.

"Well we need you over at our table." Cooper says and it sparks me with worry.

"What's wrong?" I ask him, sitting up straighter.

"Jake, Bonnie, and I want to talk to you." He says plainly, like I have nothing else to do.

"Huh-Cooper, I'm kinda busy right now." I say, making it obvious I'm talking to River.

"Okay, I see. Well bye." Cooper says quick and then leaves us and goes back to his table where Avery is glaring at me. Cooper sits right next to her and puts his arm around the back of her chair, making me mentally gag.

"I wonder what was up with him.." I mumble to myself.

"I don't think he likes me very much." River sighs and I crinkle my eyebrows.

"Why?" I ask.

"I'm not sure, he's always been like that towards me." River says and then it becomes silent.

"Want some ice cream? On the house." I winked at him and he smiled and smirked and nodded.

"Sounds great." He says and then I slide out of the booth and walk around to go behind the counter to the ice cream machine. I grab two bowls and begin to do vanilla and chocolate swirl in the bowls. I casually look over to my group of friends and Avery and they all seem to be enjoying themselves, until I saw Avery get out of her chair and walk over to me.

"Hi DaKota!" She fakely says to me with her devil smile.

"Hi Avery, what can I do for you?" I politely say, trying to get past her inner bitch.

"Well I just came over here to tell you that Cooper is mine." She says and I finally look her in her ice cold eyes.

"Well good for you Avery, you finally got a boy who can stand you." I gave her a fake smile and she gasped. "I'm sorry that was uncalled for." I quickly apologize to her, because I can't help but feel bad for what I said.

"At least I can get a man." She snares.

"What does that mean?" I ask her with shock.

"A man doesn't want a girl who does his work." She acts like she feels bad for me, I can not stand her. "He doesn't want a girl who makes him feel he's not good enough, or a girl who gets as dirty as him, or a girl who makes the same amount as him. A man wants someone like me." She flips her bleach blonde hair off her shoulder.

I am mad. Beyond mad. I am so mad that my fists are clenched at my sides and I am ready to pounce. She doesn't understand the way I was raised. She doesn't get who I am. She doesn't know how much I work and sweat my ass off. She hasn't worked a day in her life, she doesn't understand. She gets everything handed to her, and she's as dumb as a sack of rocks.

"You know what, Avery." I say very firmly and then I climb over the counter, making her back up a couple of steps as I stand right in front of her. I can feel everyone look at us, but anger is raging inside me. "I am so sick of you. You making fun of me. You making fun of my family. You wouldn't survive a day in my boots. So I ask you to stop staying those things, because you truly don't understand. I also don't understand because I never say those things to you." I manage to say in the nicest way I can, because everyone is watching.

Avery just smirked at me, "I wonder how your mother even married your father, or Ashley is agreeing to marry your dirty-cowboy-brother. What a waste of time.." She shakes her head and then she burned my last nerve. She doesn't know whats coming.

With out a second of hesitation I raised my fist and punched that girl right square in the nose. She fell hard on the ground and groaned with a lot of pain, but to my surprise she got up quicker than I thought. "You bitch!" She gasped, wiping the blood from her nose.

"Don't worry, daddy can probably fix that." I give her a bitch smirk and I hear other people start to talk and 'ooo'. Avery raises her hand to slap me, but I dodge and go behind her.

"Come here you ugly pig!" She screams at me turning around and charging.

I take this chance and I tackle her to the ground, clearly on top of her. I raise my arm to hit her again, but my hand is stopped by another's. I look up at the person and it's River, what the hell is he doing. Then he pulls me up and then I see Cooper pulling Avery up. Her nose looks pretty messed up, and I sickly smile. "At least my daddy doesn't have to work for his money!" Avery spat and I saw Cooper drop his head in abashment because of her stupid comment.

I gave her the are-you-kidding-me look and then I broke out of River's grasp and punched her right on the jaw, making me feel a lot better. "You whore!" She screamed again and came after me again but Cooper pulled her against him and she was still squirming, so I decided to go after her, until River pulled me into his arms.

His grip was solid on me, making me kick up my legs, "Let me have her!" I groaned.

"You slutty heifer!" She screamed and I rolled my eyes again at her..

"Let me go, I'm not gonna hit her." I say and I see River look at me and I nod for assurance and then he lets me go. I see Cooper slowly letting Avery go, and I can see a bruise forming on her face.

"I'm going to sue you and your nasty ranch for this!" She screamed at me.

I clenched my jaw and put my hands into fists and took a deep breath, "Get the hell out of my diner!!!" I almost screamed at her, but I kept my cool.

"I think everyone needs to leave." Cooper announces and then everyone gets up and walks past us.

As Jake walked past me he gave me a low high five, "Way to go wolf girl." He smirked, making me smirk.

THERE WE STOOD, COOPER, River and I. I was standing right across of Cooper, us staring right into each other's eyes. We didn't say anything to each other, I was still fuming. "DaKota, can I speak to you?" River says and my head snaps to him as he is backing away from Cooper and I's stare down.

I break our eye contact and walk with River. "I'm sorry for ruining our nice conversation." I apologize to him.

"Actually I wanted to talk about that. I wanted to ask you on a date." He shocks me, making me make eye contact with his dark blue eyes.

"Yeah, that would be great." I say with my best smile.

"Okay, how about tomorrow, at 6?" He asks and I nod, "I'll pick you up." He says and then bends down and plants a kiss on my cheek, leaving me dazed and my cheeks fiery. But my daze is over when my eyes meet Cooper's.

"What are you still doing here Cooper?" I ask him as I start cleaning up around the diner.

"Did he just ask you on a date?" Cooper asks me, why does he always do that?

"That's none of your business, but I see Avery is now, am I right?" I snap at him, looking at him for a second and then back to the dirty plates.

"Why do you care?" He asks, I can basically hear the smirk in his voice.

"Why do you care about River?" I return back to him.

"I don't, why do you care about Avery?"

"How can you stand her? You heard what she was saying!!! And you just stood there, watching her insult me and my family." I snapped at him and he looked guilty but I didn't care. "You know what, just go home Cooper." I said frustrated and then I accidentally pushed a glass off the counter and it broke in a million pieces, I wish Avery's nose would of done that.

"At least let me help you." Cooper says normally as we both bend down to the fallen glass.

"No Cooper! Go. Home." I growled at him and looked into his eyes, full of guilt and sadness.

"Okay, I'm sorry. I'll see you later, Kota." He says as he stands up and then he walks out the door. I throw down my rag and put my head into my hands. The only thing I can say about tonight is that I don't regret punching that bitch.

After I was done washing my face, I looked at myself in my full-length mirror. I looked at my long hair that probably needed a trim soon, I didn't mind it, it was my mother who hounded on me. The next thing that caught my attention made me shiver. It was the horrid scar on my upper leg that Wade gave me. The scar started from my hip and ran down 4 inches to my leg.

The scar originated in Bismarck and the story of the scar is staying in Bismarck. No one knows about it and I plan on keeping it that way. I did a good job hiding the scar, usually covered by shorts or my jeans, but when I went swimming with the girls, I just wore some jean shorts. I just told people I had a rash or something.

I pulled my shorts down and decided it would be best if I walked away from the mirror to stop reliving that night. Instead I went over to my closet an pulled out a pair of Cowgirl Tuff jeans and a black tank top and pulled my hair into a high ponytail. I was going to the diner to go meet River for breakfast and then we planned on riding later at home.

River and I have been going out for little under two weeks, and it's been going pretty well. Okay, I lied. I mean it's been going okay and all, but there's something in me that is tugging on something that is making me feel unsatisfied, but River is doing everything right. He's really nice and caring which is very important to me, but sometimes he acts strange. He hardly likes to talk to my family, and he barely likes to check cattle with me or even rope. He always makes up an excuse to get out of it, and my family has noticed. Everyone has actually.

CHAPTER 3

My dad and my brother always make fun of River because they think he is a sissy-boy because he doesn't do those things with me, but I think he has good reasons not to. Coming from me, I consider the real reasons behind an excuse. I don't know how many times Caleb has asked me why I am dating him, and I tell him every time, "He is a real nice guy and he likes me and I like him." I think that's a good enough answer.

BY MYSELF AT A BOOTH at the dinerI looked to see what time it was, 9:15. Great. River was suppose to meet me here 15 minuets ago. I dropped my head in my hands and sighed. I picked my head up and looked to my right, "Maybell." I said getting her attention and she gave me a sympathetic look and come around the island and to my table.

"Has he called you explaining himself?" She said as she placed her hand on her hip.

"No, but after I'm done ordering my food I'm going to call him." I say as I give her my menu and she raises her eyebrows, "I'll take french toast, with a side of two scrambled eggs. Orange juice please." I say and she nods and then goes to the kitchen.

I open my phone and go to call River.

Ring.

Ring.

Ring.

"Hello?" A very groggy-sounding River picks up the phone. That bugger is still sleeping!

"Hi, yes, this is your dense headed brain reminding you that you have a date with your girlfriend at her diner at 9:00 and it's 9:17." I fake being sweet and then he groans.

"Oh DaKota, I am so sorry! I am on my way!! I am so sorry again sweetie." He said and I could hear him getting out of bed.

"Okay, bye." I said and then I hung up the phone.

"Boyfriend troubles?" A voice comes from behind me and I look to my right and a body crossed my vision and then I heard the booth seat make a sound from a body sitting down.

I looked up and there was Mr. Cooper Blackwood with his devilish smirk. Just great, I did not need him getting involved right now. I haven't talked to him in a week, ever since the night he figured out I was dating River. "I guess you could call it that." I sigh and finally look him in his eyes.

"It? That's no way to talk about River." He says with humor in his eyes and I automatically roll my eyes at him when I lean back into the booth and close my eyes. "So what's wrong?" He asks and I pop one eye open.

"What are you? My therapist?" I say and he chuckles.

"Just trying to help a friend," He says and holds up his hands slightly. "Seriously though." He says and then I sigh.

"River was supposed to meet me here at 9:00 and instead he was sleeping in." After I said this Cooper breaks out in laughter. And I mean he is laughing, not playfully, he thinks it's actually funny! He clutches his stomach as I stare at him in confusion and then he finally settles down, but not without a smile, trying to keep it in. "Why is that funny?" I ask him and to my surprise a chuckle comes out of my mouth.

"Sleeping in?" He asks and then laughs again. I nod answering his question, "That kid has been sleeping in all his life!" Cooper blurts out with a slap-my-butt-and-call-me-sally smile on his face.

"What do you mean?" I ask him as Maybell brings out my food and I give her a grateful nod as she smirks and walks away.

"Okay," He says and straightens up and stops his laughter smiles. "What time do you usually get up every day?" He asks in an almost businessman type way.

"Around 6, depends on sunup." I shrug and then take a piece of my french toast and dip it in syrup and put it in my mouth.

"Yeah and I'm up around 5:45." He says and it makes me raise my eyebrows.

"Your point is?"

"River isn't like us. The only time that boy has woken up that early is because he wet the bed and scared himself half-to-death!" He says and then I let out a laugh but then cover it up because it was rude to laugh about River.

"That's not true, and how did you know that?" I ask him as I take a drink of my OJ.

"I have friends." He smugly smirks at me and then takes a piece of my french toast and puts in his mouth before I even have time to protest. "You do know that River thinks he's like us, cowboys?" Cooper says in a serious tone.

"He is." I defend.

"Name one thing he does at his daddy's ranch." Cooper says and then crosses his arms and then leans back on the booth.

"He rides the horses and...brushes the horses.. Oh! He uh-" I am at a loss of words because I can not think of another thing..

"Exactly. He goes to rodeos and dresses up and makes up an excuse that he's injured so he can't ride saddle bronc. How long does it take to recover from a sprained wrist! You know what I did when I broke my leg bull riding? I done gone on to the next one and cowboy'ed up!" Cooper says in a mater-of-fact tone, making me feel taken back. I couldn't help but realize that he was in-fact, right.

I was going to say something but then Cooper cut me off, "Well look who the cat dragged in! River over here bud!" Cooper said in a very inviting way, making me look wide-eyed at him. Cooper was acting very friendly to River, was he sick? Did he get mad cow disease?

I say this because this is not how Cooper usually reacted around River. When Cooper found out that I was dating River he went on a rampage, and I still don't know why he had a hissy about it, but he did. He asked me a shit load of questions and he looked like a very ticked off snake in the grass, let's just say he did not take it well. I haven't a clue why he acted the way he did, it shocked me, but it didn't seem to shock other people.

I scooted over to let River sit beside me and he plumped down right next to me and then planted a kiss on my cheek, making me flinch a bit. "Hey." Really?! Hey? Hey is all I get? I side glanced at Cooper and he looked confused at my flinch from River, if only he knew..

Remembering my grace, I held in my anger and just smiled at him. "Hey." And then I looked at Cooper who looked like he was having a hell of a time, almost like he enjoyed the obvious awkward tension in the air.

"River, good to see you. No hard feelings about last time?" He said and then offered a handshake.

I looked up at River and he looked just as confused as I am, "Yeah no problem." He says and then hesitantly shakes Cooper's hand. I say hesitantly because River told me that Cooper intimidates him. "Thanks for keeping DaKota company while I was busy with the horses."

The what? Oh man, River!

Cooper tries really hard to contain his laughter but his facial expression is about to come undone and River looks confused. I put my head in my hands and start praying for River. This boy just can't help himself. "What's so funny?" River asks with his best stay-cool face.

"She told me that you were- ow!" Cooper started to say but then I kicked him under the table.

"I told him that you were running late on your chores." I say with a fake smile while I side eye Cooper who rolls his eyes, but River doesn't see because he's looking at me.

"So what are y'all doing after this?" Cooper acts interested as River wraps an arm around me, and I again flinch. I couldn't help it, flinching to any male who made that kind of motion towards me.

"We were planning to go ride out at DaKota's place." River says and then I see Cooper's eyes light up with amusement.

"Really, so I am." Coop says and then I choke on my drink, but quickly regain myself. I raise an eyebrow at Cooper. "Your brother invited me and the boys to come over and get some practice in. Care to join River?" Cooper folds his hands, what a sneaky little bastard he is.

"Well we had already made plans, Cooper." I say and then wrap my arm around River's bicep to give a look to Cooper to knock it off. Cooper and I have an intense stare down, and I know River is noticing it because he scoots closer to me.

"It's only the start of the day! What do you say River?" Cooper says and then looks back at River.

"You don't have to do it if you don't want to Riv." I say to him and look up at him.

River looked both confident and nervous, and I expected an excuse but then he said, "Sure, why not!" I frowned but when he looked at me I smiled proudly and I looked at Cooper and gave him a mocking shrug. I'm sure if River agreed to practicing with them he knew how to rope and bulldog.

"Great! I'll see y'all in a half hour?" Cooper says as he slides out of the booth and smiles at us. River and I nodded in goodbye to Cooper and then he walked past us and I looked at River.

"What made you agree to practicing Riv?" I kindly say to him as I finish eating my breakfast.

"I think it's time for me to spend some time with your brother, and do some guy stuff and not just do the girly-riding-in-the-pasture stuff." He says, but I notice he deepens his voice and I wonder if he knows Cooper isn't here anymore. Why is he saying this? He hasn't seemed to mind riding in the field at all, what's got his britches in a twist.

"Oh well, that sounds like a good plan!" I smile at him and then he does to.

"I can't wait for you to watch me rope them steers." He says and then leans down and kisses me. I felt very uncomfortable kissing River, every damn time it gave me horrible images in my mind. But I had to keep the act up, or he would start acting questions, and I needed to avoid that.

I SAT ON THE GATE WATCHING Caleb, River, Cooper, Rusty, Ryan, and Jake rope the steer dummy. River was doing good, but missed more than the other guys. Cooper on the other hand, never missed one throw. I'd cheer River on, making my brother glare at me because he obviously doesn't like River and he thinks I'm annoying.

I couldn't hear what they were saying but they were laughing and River just looked lost in their conversation. The boys had devilish smiles on their faces as they talked to River, I bet they were secretly making fun of him! Those little dick heads! I was going to go over there and give them a piece of my mind but then River turns to me, "Hey Kota! Why don't you go inside and make us some grub? Oh and while you're in there put on some shorts!" He says in an macho tone, and my smile turns into a pissed off frown. My jaw literally drops, who did he think he was talking to? Especially coming from him, I could probably punch harder than him.

I was about to give him a lesson, but my brother recognizes my body language and then says, "He's just kidding!" But River looks like he was shocked my Caleb's words and then returns to talking with the boys.

Make us some grub my ass.

Now the boys are saddling up their horses, but River does not have a horse. But then I see Caleb come out with my buckskin American quarter horse mare, Scarlet, with her saddled and ready to go. Please River do not ruin my horse. Caleb hands River the reins and then River looks up at Caleb, "Can you give me a leg up?"

Shoot me, shoot me now..

I hang onto the bars of the gate and leaded back in embarrassment. "What's wrong DaK?" Ashley's voice comes from behind me and the comes and sits right beside me. Ash is wearing a cinch vest with a flannel underneath and some Silver jeans.

"Just look, I can't." I say and motion my hand to wear Caleb and River were.

"Oh no." Ashley snickers but then covers her mouth.

"What's happening?" I ask her, looking in the other direction.

"Okay well, River is struggling to get his boot into the stirrup." She informs me and I smack my forehead. I guess when River and I rode that I never paid attention how he mounted one of my horses.

I looked up and Caleb was looking at us and I gave him a sorrow look that said just please help the boy. Caleb looked flushed and stubbornly turned around and quickly helped River get on the saddle and then quickly left him. I felt Ashley pat my back and I sighed. It will get better, he knows how to ride a horse. "Did I just see your brother give your boyfriend a leg up?"

Kill me. Kill me now.

My dad's voice said behind us and I froze in my spot. Gee wiz, this is going to be ugly. I didn't even answer my dad as he climbed over the gate and stood against it beside me. The boys started to warm up the horses by trotting around the arena and warming up the arms, swinging the rope over their heads.

They started with bull dogging, they better not force River to do it because he could get hurt. Maybe River could be the hazer for one of the boys. Caleb was putting the steers into the chutes and pulling the gate when the boys nodded their heads. Jake was up first and Rusty was being the hazer. Jake gave the nod and Caleb let the steer loose, Rusty's horse was fast and did his job and then Jake slid down onto the steer, stuck his heels in the dirt, turned his head and brought him down to the ground. "4.6! Nice job Jake!" My dad says.

My dad loves watching the boys practice for rodeos. I can just tell he relives his days of practicing with his brother and father when he watches Caleb and me. Caleb was up next and he gave nod and I looked down at my dad's phone 5.8 seconds. "Excellent time Caleb!" My father cheers and Caleb nods in approval.

"Okay River, your turn." Cooper says mounted on his horse, leaning on his saddle horn.

"Oh okay." River says and then goes to the back of the box. He looked scared out of his mind and I looked at Cooper and he was smirking. He and I were going to have a talk after this. Cooper makes eye contact with me and we hold it, he better get my message. My attention adverts from his stare when the gate opens and the Scarlet with River take off.

River lets go of the reins and slides down the saddle, but completely misses the steer. So? He's never bulldogged before. He's not gonna get it right away. I jump down from the gate and jog to River laying in the dirt. "Riv, are you okay?" I say as I kneel down to him.

"Yeah, thanks babe." He groans as he stands himself up and then pulls me in for a kiss.

"Step away from my sister!" Caleb roared and I gladly pulled back from our very short kiss. I was not a fan of PDA, especially in front of my family. My eyes looked around and landed on Cooper, he had a straight face on and his jaw was tightly locked. "I'll show em how it's really done." Cooper drawls and then kicks his horse into the back of the box and quickly nods his head.

"3.6! Well done Blackwood!" My dad gives cudos to Cooper and Cooper flashes his lovely smile to every one. Stop DaKota! Remember River!

EVEN WORSE IDEA. PUTTING River on a horse and trying to get him team rope. The boys were tired of practicing so my dad took over. He got on Caleb's horse and wanted someone to head for him, and River blindly agreed. Caleb took over Rusty's gelding and I was sitting on the back of the horse, watching our father and my boyfriend.

Ryan let the steer out and then River jumped out of the box with Scarlet and threw the rope about ten feet over the steer and totally lost control of Scarlet. When River wasn't looking I covered my face with embarrassment, my lord. My dad looked at me and I gave him a begging look. "Come here." I say to River and he guides Scarlet over to me.

"What?" He asks and I grab his rope from him.

"Make your loop a little bigger like this," I say and then I grab the hondo and then slide the shank and make it bigger, "And keep your left hand in front of you, you gotta steer the horse." I say and give him a reassuring smile to let him know it was okay.

My advice did not help River at all. My dad gave him five more chances until he said, "DaKota, why don't you try?" My heart started to beat rapidly. I knew I could do it, I just didn't want to "show up" River.

"I think Caleb can do it." I say to my father and he shakes his head.

"Young lady I want you to do it, so get on that horse and rope that damn steer." My dad strictly says, making everyone's facial expression turn into a frown.

I have no choice but to obey my dad, so I slide off Rusty's horse and go over to my mare. "You did great, don't beat yourself up. And just remember I've been doing this a lot longer." I say and kiss River's cheek.

I mount onto my horse and River hands me the rope and I adjust it just how I like it. I grabbed the leather reins and backed my horse into the box and I raised my arm back behind my ear, and then I nodded my head. I had perfect timing with the steer and with two swings I was already pulling the slack and dallying the rope around the saddle horn and turning the steer for my dad, who easily catches the heels.

"Nice work honey!" My dad cheers and everyone whoops, while I quickly recoil the rope and go back to River. Gosh, I just feel so bad for him right now. He's such a nice guy, he doesn't deserve to be played like this.

I STABBED THE PIECE of stake with my fork and then took it off the fork with my teeth. I looked around the dinner table where every one was talking except for me. Ashley and Caleb were probably sweet talking each other and my parents were talking about the drama in the community.

I was thinking about River. After we had put away the horses, the boys had left, but not before I had gave a talk to Cooper. River was busy helping with the horses, so he couldn't hear our conversation. I had politely told Cooper to knock it off, trying to embarrass River. I had told him that it was perfectly normal not to know how to rope while riding, and not doing stuff that we do on normal basis. I told him that River did not deserve Cooper's rudeness and arrogance. Cooper didn't say much, but just look disappointed and angry at me. I don't know why he looked disappointed, but maybe he did feel sorry about doing that to River.

"I'm not too found of that kid, but Cooper was on fire today!" My dad's voice wakes me of my thoughts. Dad looked very impressed and

Caleb nodded his head to my dad. "I wonder why he doesn't do any timed events with roping. That kid has potential to be an All-Around Cowboy, like me." He adds at the end, making me roll my eyes without him seeing.

"Because he's an even better bull rider." I mumble under my breath and then I take a sip of my tea.

"I've never see him ride before," He says to me, "But I guess he thinks he would be a good riding teacher.." My dad raises his eyebrows and wipes his mouth with his napkin. Its clear what he is talking about, when Rusty and Ryan challenged me to ride a bull.

"It wasn't his idea!" I say for what seems the thousandth time.

"Don't raise your voice, DaKota." My dad says and then my lips turn into a frown.

"I'm sorry," I say, "But I just don't understand what you have against Cooper?" I say to him what I've been meaning to ask him for a while. I look at my mom who looks almost sad and is preparing herself for what is about to happen.

"That family is not to be trusted DaKota." My dad says and shakes his head slowly.

"Well we're going to our room, thanks for supper Mom." Caleb says like he's avoiding a fight coming on. I glare at him and Ashley gives me a sympathetic look and then she thanks my mom for dinner.

"What do you mean? Desiree and Cooper are one of the most respectful people in this town!"

"Honey, do you know who Bill Blackwood is?" My dad says very serious, making me wonder what makes him say it like that. I don't say anything but look at my mom who starts cleaning up. I would help her, but I wanna hear this. "In most basic terms, he's an outlaw..."

"An outlaw?" I laugh, "What is this? the 1800's?" I laugh more, but by the look on my dad's face is telling me this is no joke and that Bill Blackwood is truly an outlaw.

AS I LAID IN BED I couldn't stop thinking about what my dad told me about Cooper's dad. All those times I asked Cooper about his dad, he's always blew me off, and know I know why. I couldn't even imagine what it must be like to be Desiree, to be married to a guy like that. I wonder if Reese even knew about what his dad did.

Bill Blackwood was a true outlaw. No one knew how many laws he had broken, but people thought just about everyone of them. He robs banks, trains, and people. People even say that if it's bad enough he might even kill. Desiree took her kids away from her husband and now they live here.

But people round here even heard that Cooper was his dad's accomplice at some points. The weird thing is, I kind of believed it. It kind of makes sense. It's all about his temper and his bad boy ways. My dad did accuse Cooper of stealing money from the sale barn. But then there's the side of me that didn't because he wouldn't do it because of his mom. He would never admit it, but he loves his mom with everything he has.

Just when I was starting to figure things out..

I am going to kill my family. Instead of all of us going going to a rodeo in Esther, they ditched me so I could watch Nash. Who is Nash? Why, he is my 11 month old cousin who my aunt and uncle decided to drop on us because an opportunity came up from them to go on a cruise. Gotta love family. I really don't understand why I had to stay back and babysit Nash, I was entered to compete and my mother wasn't. My mom obviously has more experience than me, considering I only babysat once, and that was with 6 moth old and when I was 12!

They dropped him off around 6 last night, and right away he threw a temper tantrum because of separation anxiety, but he calmed down. He acted up in the middle of the night. I had to wake up 6 different times to feed him, burp him, and change him. To say the least, I'm exhausted. And now it's early in the morning, about 5:45 and time to feed Nash and do chores. It's one of those mornings that all I am wearing is a bra and tank-top and light blue flannel pj pants. I pulled my hair into a ponytail and walked into Nash's room. There the blue eyed boy stood in his crib, hugging his 'Bucky Bronc' stuffed animal. "Good morning my little Nashie boy." I say as I pick him up and bring him into my arms.

"Good morwing." He smiles back at me and then looks down at his stuffed animal.

"Do you want some yogurt for breakfast?" I ask him as we go down the stairs into the kitchen. I sit him down into his chair and turned the radio on, and the lovely sound of George Strait came on making me smile.

"Bwue Bewwy!" He exclaims and throws up his hands and I laugh and nod.

I reach into the fridge and pull out his blue berry yogurt and put it into a plastic bowl and grab a spoon for him. I sit down beside him encase he needs help eating, but Aunt Lisa said he could do it pretty well. So I checked all of my social media while Nash ate his nutritious yogurt.

I hear murming beside me and I looked over and Nash had eaten all of us yogurt. I did a gasp and widen my eyes, "You ate all of your food! Good job Nash!" I say and kissed his nose, while he laughed with delight. He was the cutest little boy ever! "Okay, do you wanna go say hi to the horses?" I ask him as I pick him up out of his chair and support him with one arm as I clean up the mess.

"Yes!" He throws his arms up in excitement making me laugh.

I had dressed Nash in his little Stetson hat and his adorable cowboy boots, this kid was going to be a heart breaker, he already is. I let Nash walk around the stall while I mucked it out and exchanged hay in the stall. All of the horses were out in the field after Nash helped me turn them out, a smile never left his lips. Seeing how happy it made Nash made me feel like the best baby sitter in the world.

I AM THE WORST BABYSITTER in the world.. Nash was taking his day time nap, until I had dropped a frying pan in the kitchen, waking him up. Ever since then he will not stop crying! My insides were freaking out, panicking to stop the crying child. I had tried everything. I tried rocking him, feeding him, reading to him, changing him, and even trying to put him back to sleep! I even called my mother and my grandmother, they both said that they couldn't do anything unless they were there.

One thing was for sure, I needed someone here with me because I was going to loose my shit pretty soon. I needed a mother. Actually, maybe River could help me. Still rocking Nash, I grabbed my phone and dialed River. "Hey DaKota." His voice comes through the other end of the line.

"Do you know anything about kids?" I quickly ask him, making him chuckle.

"How old?" He asks.

"11 months." I reply to him and then he sighs.

"Nope, never babysat in my life." He says making me groan.

"Wait, why did it matter how old-never mind. I'll talk to you later." I say and then I hang up on him.

Right then, Nash let's out another blood-curdling scream, making me flinch with anxiety. That's it, I needed a mom here right now. So I grabbed my mother's address book and called every mother I knew.

God must of woken up today and said, 'Let's not make it DaKota's day today.' because every one was either at a rodeo, or they were taking care of their child. Wait, there's a mother I am missing, Desiree Blackwood. Of course! She raised two children, boys especially.

I positioned Nash so his stomach was against my shoulder and I bounced on my legs and patted his back as he continued to cry. I went to my recent phone calls and looked at the date, Desiree had called me about two weeks ago to ask me a vet related question. I clicked on her number and hoped for the best.

Ring.

Ring.

Ring.

"Hello?" Her sweet southern voice answered the phone. Thank you Jesus!

I breathed with a sigh of relief, "Hi Desiree it's DaKota." I say into the phone.

"Oh my! Hello DaKota! What do I owe this call?" She says.

"Long story short, I am babysitting and I accidentally woke him from his nap, and ever since then he will not stop crying! I've tried everything!" I almost cry into the phone, "I really need a mother's help right now.." I beg her.

She chuckles into the phone, "Okay, I'll be over in about ten minuets." She answers my prayers and I almost do a fist pump, but I contain myself.

"Oh my gosh! You are the best! Thank you so much! See you soon!" I say and then I wait for her good bye and then I hang up the phone. I hold Nash in front of me and see his watery eyes and his continuous crying face and kiss his face.

"Don't worry big guy, mama Blackwood is coming!" I say with a bright smile because right now, she is my only hope.

NASH'S FACE JUST SIMPLY said 'don't-you-see-me-crying-fix-it!'. I felt so bad for him, there was nothing I could do! I looked at the oven clock and figured out he had been crying for about 35 minuets now, this was not good.

When I heard the knocking on the door I thought I heard the sound of angle wings. I picked up Nash and carried him with arm as I walked to door. I was glad it was only Desiree coming because I didn't doubt I looked like a slob at the moment. I kept my eyes on Nash as I opened the door because he seemed to cry louder as the door creaked. "Desiree I can not thank-" I cut myself off as I looked up at the person at the door, that was definitely not Desiree. Instead it was her cowboy of a son, Cooper.

Cooper looked at Nash, and then he slowly looked me up and down. Curious to what I looked like, I also looked down. My tank top was a little pulled up, showing some of my lower stomach, and to make it an even better day, the top of my Victoria Secret underwear was showing, not so secret anymore. Great. Immediately I pulled my pants up and scrunched my eyebrows. But he for one, looked good. Light blue jeans and a white tee that showed off his tanned and toned upper body. His hair was neatly done, he didn't need to do anything to it because of it's slight curl to it. "I am your reinforcement, my mom got called into the hospital." He says and then Nash cries more.

"Cooper, you can just go home if you want. I'm sure I can handle this." I sigh in disappointment and I look him in the eyes, but he just smirks at me.

"What, do you think I don't know anything about babies?" He asked me. I didn't answer him, just gave him a curious look, "Did you forget I have a little brother." He says and then steps into my home and takes Nash from my arms.

"Hey little guy." Cooper coos to Nash. "What's your name?" He asks Nash as he sits him down on the island counter.

For a split second Nash stops crying, "Nash Kacey Jones." He says and then I sigh in relief that he stopped crying, but my happiness is destroyed when I hear sobbing again.

Cooper looks at me with question, "I don't know. I've tried everything!" I say and collapsed into the island chair and throw my head back.

"How long as he been crying?" Cooper asks me and then I pop my head up and see he is inspecting Nash.

"About 40 minuets." I reply to him.

"He has an ear infection." Cooper says in the straightest tone of voice ever. I was in shock at Cooper's words.

"Wh-what? How do you know that?" I stumbled with my words.

"Come here." He says and I scoot the chair back and go where to Cooper was and looked at Nash. "Look at his ear. It's redder than this one, little swollen, and it's very sensitive, 100% classic ear infection.." Cooper says with a lot of confidence and I see what he is talking about.

"How did you know?" I ask him as I rub my hand up and down Nash's arm.

"My brother used to get them all of the time." He replies simply as he plays with Nash's feet.

"So I should take him to the pediatrician?" I say to Cooper, looking at his side profile. I couldn't help but think of what my father had told me the other night..

"Lucky for you this cowboy has his own home remedy that cures the infection." Cooper says and turns his head to look at me and winks. It was weird, right when I looked into Cooper's eyes I couldn't hear Nash's cries, so I stared into his eye's more..

I break my focus from his chocolate eyes, "Are you sure? Will it hurt him?"

"No, my brother actually liked the way it felt." Cooper says, "May I?" He says as he goes toward the pantry and fridge.

"Go ahead." I encourage him as I start to play with Nash's arms, trying to get him to smile. I watch as Cooper pulls out stuff he needs for his 'remedy', this better work.

COOPER

"DESIREE I CAN NOT THANK-" DaKota starts to ramble, not noticing it's me and not my mother. My mother was on her way to go to DaKota's house but then she got a call from the hospital saying someone overdosed and they needed her right away, so she told me to go, and I happily obliged.

I looked at the cute little dude she had in her arms, and then I noticed her. She was wearing a tight tank top that came up a little bit to show off her tanned flat stomach, and then I was surprised when I saw a gray fabric peaking under her pj's. She looked like she was tired and flustered. Her face didn't look tired at all, she still looked cute as always.

She notices me looking at her, so I cleared my throat, "I am your reinforcement, my mom got called into the hospital." As I said that, the little boy cries more and she closes her eyes in frustration.

"Cooper, you can just go home if you want. I'm sure I can handle this." She says to me in sadness, and it makes me a little sad hearing it.

"What, do you think I don't know anything about babies?" I question her, putting a little humor in my voice. "Did you forget I have a little brother." I say and then step inside her house and grab the child from her arms. I look into his bright blue eyes and smile at him.

"Hey little guy." I say lightly. "What's your name?"

He stops crying, "Nash Kacey Jones." He hiccups, but I understood him. After he said his name, he went right back to crying, weird. I look at DaKota for her to explain to me.

"I don't know. I've tried everything!" She says as she sits down and throws her head back. While she wasn't looking, I was looking at her. I wasn't just looking, I was admiring her. I couldn't help it, she was the most beautiful girl I had laid eyes on and she didn't even have to try!

"How long as he been crying?" I ask her, gaining my attention back to the troublesome boy.

"About 40 minuets." As she says this, I notice his ears, found the problem. I was kind of shocked that she didn't notice.

"He has an ear infection." I say to her with a head nod.

"Wh-what? How do you know that?" Her voice sounds kind of hurt that she didn't solve the problem herself, I liked that about her.

"Come here." I say and she stands right beside me, "Look at his ear. It's redder than this one, little swollen, and it's very sensitive, 100% classic ear infection.." I confirm my diagnosis.

"How did you know?" Again she looks hurt, but for the baby this time.

"My brother used to get them all of the time."

"So I should take him to the pediatrician?" Pediatrician-smition, I had just what she needed, a home remedy for an ear infection.

"Lucky for you this cowboy has his own home remedy that cures the infection." I say and then she finally looked into my eyes. She didn't do that much, so when she did I made sure to hold it as long as I could. She had drop-dead gorgeous hazel eyes, I bet most girls were jealous. I couldn't help but wonder why she didn't look me in the eyes, was she afraid?

Feeling the stare down she breaks, "Are you sure? Will it hurt him?" Then she rubs Nash's arms.

"No, my brother actually liked the way it felt." I say and then I start my journey looking for my supplies, "May I?" I forget to ask her.

"Go ahead." She confirms and then I get to work.

DAKOTA LAID NASH ON her bed, because she refused to do it on the couch because she didn't want me to spill or Nash to fall off. So here we are, in her room, which I'm pretty familiar with, ready to cure Nash of his infection. "Cooper you better be sure about this, my aunt can be a scary lady and I'd hate for her to kill you." DaKota stops me before I grab the glass.

This makes me smile a bit because it was a little hope for me that she cared about me, "Aw how sweet." I smirk and she rolls her eyes, "Don't worry, I've done this a thousand times!"

"Famous last words..." She mumbles but I still hear her, making me roll my eyes this time.

I grab the eye dropper and gather the fluid and then carefully drop a couple of drops into Nash's ears, and he immediately stops sobbing. "We just need to do that every half hour." I say as I screw the dropper back on the container.

"Okay," Her face softens as she looks at me, I take in her features. "Do you mind watching him for a bit? I really need a shower.." She says and then stands up.

"No problem, I'd love to." I say and can't resist to look her up and down, she sees me and then she blushes. Good, I like when she blushes. "Remember to wash behind your ears!" I yell to her as she opens her bathroom door after she gets clothes. I mentally slap myself for saying that to her, and she gives me an awkward smile.

Soon after she turns on the shower, I decide to wonder around her room. I have already see her room before, but it gave me something to do as Nash lied on the bed. I looked through all of her photos, but then something fired in my mind, the journal.. No I couldn't read her journal, that would be so across the line, I'm sure she'd kill me. I wondered if she wrote anything about me in there, I would actually know what she thought about me.

I wasn't looking where I was going, so I tripped over a box or something. I landed with a thud and then I noticed something slide under the bed. I pushed myself up and reached under the bed and grabbed the plastic thing. At first I thought it was her driver's licence, but as I studied it more, it wasn't her name, it belonged to a Cassidy Smith. It was a fake ID! I pulled out my wallet and looked at my fake ID, they were different. So I pulled out my real driver's licence and compared, exactly the same.. What would she need for a fake/real driver's licence, and why North Dakota one?

I put the licence back into the box and where the box was, I was flabbergasted about it. I heard the shower turn off and I quickly regained my position back on the bed with Nash and waited for "Cassidy" to come out.

Soon she came out with a light blue Go Rope shirt on and some black Nike shorts, and a towel wrapped around her head. She was looking down sorting her clothes, but I was taking in her natural face, I had never seen anything like her before.. I'm not a girl but she had long eyelashes already, and perfect cheek bones. She even seemed to glow without the help of the sun.

I was caught up in my thoughts I didn't even notice her climb onto the bed. She laid right beside me and in front of Nash. "How's he doing?" She asked while stroking his cheek.

"Better." I say looking down at her as she started to sit up.

"I really owe you one, Coop." She sighs and I smile a bit because she hasn't called me Coop in a very long time, it sounded good. "You can go home if you want, I'm sure you have better things to do." She says not looking at me.

"I was actually gonna ask you if I could help you, it seems like you need it." I say to her and she scoffs and looks at me.

"I do not!" She shoves my shoulder, making us both laugh.

DAKOTA AND I HAD MANAGED to make a fort out of blankets and pillows. DaKota and I were letting out our goofy sides and being little kids again. I even think we were having more fun than Nash was. Did I mention that Kota had a beautiful laugh?

In our fort, we were currently watching The Lion King. Nash was in the middle, I was on the left and DaKota on the right. It was towards the end of the movie and Nash was starting to go to sleep. I looked over at DaKota and she was smiling at the sleeping child. "Thank you Cooper." She says and then puts her head on the pillow and turns her body towards me.

"For what?" I ask her, copying her actions.

"Today, if you haven't noticed I'm not a class A babysitter." She said and closed her eyes.

"I'm surprised." I say to her and smile as her eyebrows furrow.

"Why?"

"You've seem to done everything in your life, but had never babysat once." I chuckle and so does she.

"I've done it before! Just once, I never had time to babysit." She chuckles once more, sounding sleepier by the word.

"It seemed like the only thing I did was babysit my brother." I speak soft to her.

"You're good at it, its charming." She said really soft, and then my heart started to beat faster.

I was going to say something but then I noticed her deep breathing, she had finally gone to sleep. "DaKota?" I say to make sure, and she didn't say anything, she was out like a light. "I wish you were mine."

I give myself credit for coming up with this idea, I needed space from everything. My wonderful idea was to take a trail ride in the mountains, with my Blue roan, Sir Lance. I haven't done this forever, and it was a beautiful day to do so. My parents hated it when I went into the mountains, but I made sure I had everything I needed: Carhartt Jacket, two pairs of sweats, gloves, med kit, flash light, matches, food, tin cups, and more. If something happened, I wasn't gonna let Nature kick my butt.

Why was I needing space from everyone? Every one was on my case, for no reason. River was the most mad at me, I understood him a little, but others, they could kiss off. It all started last night at the Berg's wedding.

I was starting to break a sweat from all of the line dancing we were doing. At least I was wearing a dress to vent some places. We all cheered and clapped for each other as "Watermelon Crawl" ended and we all separated to our friends. Tonight I was dateless, again. River said he didn't want to come because he didn't like my brother. Believe me, I was over it by the first dance of the night.

I needed some water so I went over to the bar and grabbed a cup, while I watched the couples dance with each other. I looked down at myself, wearing a black shoulder less flowy dress with some dark-buckskin-fringed sandals. My hair was in a low bun, with strands sticking out. My eyes landed on Caleb and Ashley slow dancing. In just a few weeks, they would be sharing their first dance as a married couple, I could not wait for the wedding.

"Hey Kota." A deep voice says beside me, and it's no other but the Cooper Blackwood. Things have been awkward between us since he helped me with Nash. That night I heard what he said, but he didn't know that I knew. But what made me mad was that I had found out that Cooper had stayed the night and slept beside me, the whole night!! I had a boyfriend! Have, I have a boyfriend. After I confronted him about the wrong thing he did, we got into an argument and I found out that he was dating Avery. What the hell? I was so confused when he said that, why would he date her? Also why would he said what he said to me while he's seeing someone! I was beyond mad.

"Hello Cooper." I side glance him, he's leaning his forearms against the bar, looking at me.

"Where's River?" He said and I cocked my jaw and turned to look at him. I wish I wouldn't of looked, because when I looked at him I instantly forgave him.. He looked incredible. He was wearing nice jeans and a Black pearl snap long sleeve, topped of with a charcoal American hat.

"Where's Avery?" I raise my eyebrow and he smirks, and then moves and now his back is against the bar and his left arm is against mine.

"I am sorry about the other day, I wanna be friends again DaKota." He says as he looks me in the eyes. I look hard and long and see the sincereness in his eyes.

"Okay." I sigh and his face lights up with happiness, making me smile.

"Okay?" He repeats me and I nod. "I think this deserves a dance!" He says in a matter-of-fact tone and then stands in front of me while I look away from him.

"Cooper, I don't think we shou-" He cuts me off.

"C'mon, you did say you owed me." He wiggles his eyebrows at me and I chuckle.

"Just one." I give in to him and he smiles more at me and turns to the side and motions his arm to the dance floor.

"Shall we?" He says and holds out his other hand and I grab it, him leading me to the floor.

We took position, his hand on my back, my left hand in his right, and my right hand on his shoulder. I hated to say it, I wasn't uncomfortable. Willie Nelson's song, "Blue Eyes Crying In the Rain" came on when we started dancing, I loved this song.

"I love this song." We both say at the same time, earning a chuckle from both of us, but I blushed.

"You're a good dancer." I say to him and he looks impressed by me and gives me a crooked smile.

"Thank you." He says almost proud, and then my eyes advert to Caleb and Ashley. Ashley looked like she was very happy with my brother, and my brother even looked happier. They were perfectly made for each other and every one knew it. "Give you hope don't it." Cooper's voice awakes me from my gaze.

"What hope?" I asked confused.

"Hope that you'll find that one person for you." Cooper says, call me cheesy but I could literally feel my heart strings tug.

"Yeah, they give me hope for that day." I say and look back at Caleb and his sweetheart.

"The guy who gets to call you his, is going to be one lucky son of a gun." Cooper's drawl swoons me. And I mean it, it literally made my knees wobble. I looked in Cooper's warm chocolate eyes and then to his light pink lips, then back to his eyes.

Before I knew it Cooper was slowly inching down, until I was ripped away from his hold. "Keep your distance, Blackwood." It was River who was holding me behind him, which I quickly got out of his grip.

"River, don't start.." I say beside him, and I don't dare to look at Cooper. "Let's just leave.." I say and grab right above his wrist and pull him in front of me. Before following River, I can't help but look at Cooper and he looks at me knowingly, we both knew it was a mistake.

So River's obviously pissed at me that I danced with Cooper. He said that I knew that Cooper liked me and that I was just teasing him, but I had no idea whether he liked me or not, or if I liked him or not. Both of us are in a relationship, but I couldn't like him. I couldn't let myself do it.

Then my family was mad because I was dancing with Cooper too. They thought it was wrong of me to dance with someone who wasn't my boyfriend or family. I disagreed because Cooper was just a friend, but they didn't think he was just a friend. Cooper is just a friend, and they needed to get that through their skulls.

I STOOD WITH MY HORSE on the highest ridge that we could get to. The sun had gone away, but the scene was still breathtaking. Conifer trees surrounded the mountains and it seemed every little creature was out and about, enjoying their home. I brought my binoculars to my eyes and scanned the scenery, being amazed with every little detail the Lord had blessed.

The summer had been good to the mountains. The rain and sunshine brought lots of nutrients to the plants and animals, making the plants a vibrant green and the animals alive and well. I breathed in the sweet smell of mountain air and the relaxing scent of summer.

Sir Lance put his head on my shoulder and I scratched his face and enjoyed his presence. "You're the only boy I like, and Pharaoh." I mumble to him and he knickers. The reason I didn't ride Pharaoh today is because he doesn't do well on trails, all he wants to do is run, and that was not good for the unpredictable trails.

I had made my decision about my wonderful situation. I was going to stay with River, and keep my distance from Cooper. What my family has been telling me about Cooper has finally clicked in my head, there was little chance I would pick him.

I noticed the skies were suddenly getting darker and darker by the minuet. I decided it was time to start the two and half hours journey home. I put Sir Lance's tack back on and grabbed my water bottle and drank a couple gulps of water. I mounted myself onto the saddle and steered my horse back onto the trail.

As we were walking down the trail from the lake to get some water, something caught my eye in the trees. It wasn't heavily forested, but some trees made it difficult to see some things. I was curious because I had never seen any one on this trail before, so I stopped my horse. From the corner of my eye I saw it move again, I looked and it was a horse! A saddled horse, where was it's rider?

I looked harder and then I saw something moving on the ground and then I realized it was a person. I looked harder and the person was having a hard time getting up, of course I pulled on the reins and cantered my horse over there.

As I got closer my stomach and my heart dropped, "Cooper?!" I yelled as I got off my horse and went to Cooper who was groaning. I knelled down beside Cooper and looked into his eyes.

"What are..you doing..here?" He said in painful breaths.

"I went on a trail ride. Cooper, what happened?" I ask him as I inspect his head and body for any cuts or bumps.

"We were coming from the lake and a rattlesnake came out in front of my horse and he got spooked and managed to throw me off.." He says and then he hisses as he moves a bit.

"Don't move! What hurts?" I ask him as I continue to inspect him. I notice that he is clutching his side and then he hesitantly moves his right arm that is holding his left side. I look at his hand and it's covered in blood, I gasp as I see the gash in Cooper's black shirt and in his skin.

"I'll be right back, keep pressure!" I say and then I jump up and grab my water and my med kit. I ran back to the bleeding Cooper, and opened the kit. "Take off your shirt." I order at him and then I hear him laugh.

I look up and he's smirking at me and then sends me a wink, "I knew you wanted me." He huskily said.

"Not the time Cooper." I almost growl at him as I start to examine the cut. It's oozing blood and it about six inches long, and it looks bad. It's not just some cut that I can put a band aid on, this cut needs stitches and we were no where near a hospital. I must say it was really hard to focus on the cut, because I had never seen Cooper shirtless, and I was in awe... And I never knew he had a tattoo, Faithfulness, it was sexy.. Gosh! What am I doing? Bleeding man here DaKota!

My face must of told Cooper it was not good, "What? What's wrong?" He asked me with a hiss at the end as he tried to look at it.

"You're gonna need stitches, and please don't try to move." I say and scan my brain for any of my smart and creative ways.

"Shit!" He exclaims as he lays back onto the ground.

"Cooper, do you trust me?" I ask in all seriousness and move up so we can have eye contact.

Cooper looked like he didn't even have to think about it, "Yes, I trust you." He says and I nod.

"Okay, this may or may not hurt. I don't know." I breathed hard. Internally I was panicking, I had to gather myself.

"I trust you DaKota, you can do it." The last part wasn't a confirmation, it was encouragement. I looked at him, just to see if he was going to change his mind. "Just do it already, I can handle the pain." He says and I nod quickly. I grab my water bottle and start to pour the water slowly on the cut, Cooper hisses with pain. Out of instinct I grab his hand for him to squeeze mine.

"I'm just cleaning it right now. Then I'll look for any pebbles or anything that you could of picked up." I say as I finish the cleaning. I look at my kit and then I grab the tweezers. I try to get at a good angle to do this, but it seems the only option is to get on top of him. "Cooper, I need to sit on your legs to do this right. Is it okay?"

"Go ahead." He says and I was glad there was no seduction in his voice. I sigh and then sit on top of him and then scoot up so I'm more on his waist. I cleaned out some little dirt pebbles and then some grass. I grabbed my kit and grabbed the surgeons needle and then threaded it.

You can do it. Deep breath DaKota, you got it. Take your time. I said to myself, trying to calm down.

"Okay, I'm going to start start suturing.. I may need two hands though.." I say and then he lets go of my hand and I examine how I am going to do this. "Slowly sit up, so I can correctly put the stitches in." I say and using his rock solid abs he sat up, inches away from my face. "Perfect." I say and then, "3..2..1." I say and then I enter the needle through the cut and Cooper hisses and then grabs my thigh for comfort.. And for once I didn't even flinch..

As I was stitching, I couldn't help but notice his breath hitting my skin. We were so close that I could see the dark iris in his eyes, they were beautiful. As I pulled the thread through the skin he hissed very loud and squeezed my leg. "I'm sorry Cooper, is it hurti-"

"No! I am fine, you're doing great. Maybe a little quicker, a storms coming real fast." He said and then I looked up and confirmed his statement, I needed to hurry.

I HAD SUCCESSFULLY stitched and patched Cooper's cut and now we were both heading back home. The weather was getting worse and worse. When I mean worse, I mean it. The skies were a dangerous gray, and it was thundering and lightning like crazy! The wind was whipping like hell, it was raining, and it was just, bad.

I was trying not to get scared because if I got scared, so would my horse. Cooper and I horse's were already starting to get antsy, and being unpredictable. Cooper and I looked at each other often to see if each other was okay, I was really worried about Cooper. He needed to stop putting stress on the stitches and the cut, he was going to be in pain for a while.

Then the whole sky went rogue. A huge crash of thunder and lightning combined, and then a tree crashed down right in front of us, both of our horses bucked, we both managed to stay on. Cooper and I looked at each other and he rode beside me, "Follow me! I know a place we can go!" He yelled over the loudness of the storm, and I just nodded and then we took off.

Cooper lead us through some trees to our safety, a cabin. The dark-logged-cabin was in good shape and was a decent size, just one level though, but it looked big. Although, I would of been good with any type of size of cabin, I was just glad to get out of this storm. Behind the cabin was a small barn just the right size for our horses. The horses were the biggest priority right now, so we quickly got them settled into the barn, and got some jackets on them and fed them. The whole time my heart was pounding, I was silently freaking out.

Cooper and I were drenched when we entered the cabin. My hair was soaking wet and so was Cooper's. "Don't worry about getting anything wet, just do what you gotta do. I'm gonna start a fire, and there's good reception up here to call your parents." Cooper says as he takes off his boots and goes to the fire.

I pulled everything from my saddle bags and decided what I needed right now. My first priority was calling my parents, so I grabbed my phone and went into another room. I could only imagine what this conversation was going to be like.

"DaKota Ann Jones! You scared me half to death! Where are you? Are you okay?" My mother's voice pierces my ears.

"I am okay mom." Is all I say to her and then she sighs in relief.

"Where are you?" She asks.

"Mom, is dad around you?" I ask her.

"No, he's at work, why? And answer my question!"

"I'm in a cabin, but I'm with Cooper. Do not tell Dad! He will just freak out for no reason! Long story how Cooper and I ran into each other, but we're both okay."

"DaKota you know-"

"Do you trust me mom?" I cut off my mom and she sighs.

"Okay, but you will tell your father when you return tomorrow. Please stay safe, and remember to say your prayers tonight. I love you and so does your dad." She says into the phone, and I knew I could trust my mom not to tell my dad. If my dad knew, he would march up here and take me home.

"I love you guys too, I'll keep you updated. Bye." I say and then I hang up the phone and go back into the living room, where Cooper was watching the fire in his soaked clothes. I didn't say anything to him, I just watched him.

There was one thing I knew for sure, this was not going to be easy..

"So is this your Cabin?" I speak up after watching Cooper for a couple minuets. Cooper's head whips towards me and then he stands up to speak.

"Uh yeah, my mom and I bought it when we first got here. We've only used it a couple of times though. I guess it was a good investment though." He says and then we both awkwardly laugh in the situation. "You call your parents?" He says, breaking the awkwardness.

"Yeah."

"How'd they feel about you staying the night with me?" He sadly snickers and it makes me feel blue inside. He returned his gaze on the crackling fire, he definitely looked conflicted about something.

"Cooper don't be like that." I say in a pleading voice and he shakes his head.

"There's a shower in that bedroom over there." He changed the subject and then walked away from the fire and then in front of me a few feet. "I think my cousin might of left some clothes here, but I'll show you to the master room." He said and then turned and walked down the hallway with me following him. Man, did I hate wet jeans, but on Cooper, they shaped him so well.

Cooper walked into a room and I was pleased with it. It had a king sized bed, it's own bathroom, and a small see-through-door to outside that had a view of the barn and more, it was perfect. "I'll be right back with the clothes." He said and then left me alone in the room.

While he was gone I busied myself with looking at the rustic decorations. Mustang drawings on the wall, along with other nature pictures. I found myself staring at the pictures of the lone wolf peaking behind a tree, it reminded me a lot of Luca. Luca was one of the wolf pups in the den of the night when I first became the Wolf Girl. Luca was a wolf you wouldn't forget. He was a black wolf with a very unique dark marking. The markings were like claw marks down his face, but they weren't battle scars, he had them ever since he was a pup. "These should fit you." Cooper's voice startled me and I looked at the clothes he had in his hands.

"Thanks Cooper." I say sincerely and he just nods.

"Everything you need should be in there. If you need anything when you're done I'll probably be in the living room. It's an one room cabin, so yeah." He says and then leaves, and I actually giggle at him, he was being shy, it was funny.

I STEPPED OUT OF THE bathroom and felt very refreshed. Thankfully during my shower, my bra and underwear had dried above the heated vent. The clothes that Cooper gave me where a baggy white gray shirt, and some running shorts, they were a little loose, but it was comfortable after being in drenched clothes.

I walked into the living room, where Cooper sat on the couch looking into the fire. "Um, where should I put my clothes?" I ask him and again he stands up right away and walks over to me.

"I'll take them, I just put my clothes in the washer." He said and then I looked him up and down. He was wearing baggy gray sweats and a navy blue shirt that the sleeves were cut off, and his hair was still wet from his shower.

"You do laundry?" I chuckle at him and he blushes a bit as he nods and takes my clothes from me. "My brother doesn't even do laundry, he has one thing coming for him living with Ashley."

"Single mom I guess." He says again being shy, why was he acting so weird tonight?

I shrugged it off and decided to go sit in front of the fire, Cooper did a good job starting it and keeping it alive. The fire felt great against my skin, and it smelt great too. I brought my knees to my chest and turned my head to the left and took a deep breath as I heard the thunder from the storm. Storms always gave me bad flashbacks from the most frighting night of my life.

I was awaken from my flashbacks when I felt his skin against mine. I looked to my right and he was right beside me, he sat criss-cross but his arms behind him supporting him up, his left arm against my right. When the thunder boomed, I felt safe because I had Cooper beside me. When he saw me look at our closeness he spoke up, "Are you hungry?" Then we make eye contact and I can see the image of the fire in his eyes, it was mesmerizing.

"No, are you? I'd be happy to make you something, it'd be the least thing I could do." I say to him and he shakes his head.

"I'm not either, but thank you." He says back.

"What time is it?" I ask him and then he leans back and I assume he was looking at the clock.

"Quarter to 10." He says and my eyes widen, that late already?! After he says it, a yawn escapes my lips.

"I think I'm gonna go to bed.. Um do you have any blankets I can use for the couch?" I ask him as I stand up and motion towards the couch.

"The blankets are on the bed, but that's where you'll be sleeping." He says and I shake my head and look up at him.

"Cooper, I couldn't take the bed. And that couch is too small for you!" I say and he shakes his head again at me.

"No, I'll take the couch." He says.

"No." I say stubbornly.

"Your sleeping in the bed and I'm sleeping on the damn couch, okay?" He says and then I decide to finally give up arguing with him.

"Okay, thank you. But if you feel uncomfortable, just come wake me up and we can switch." I say and then he shakes his head at me and then shoo's me to my room.

Once I'm in the room, I turn to him and say, "Actually could you get me a glass of water?" he nods and then leaves the doorway.

I go to the door where it looks at the barn and I see Lance stick out his tongue out their little window and it makes me laugh. Through all of the lightning and clouds, it was a full moon, it was beautiful in this gloominess. As I look down I notice something really embarrassing, I had my shirt on backwards. I groan and then take off my shirt, "I didn't know you had a tattoo." Cooper's voice scares me and then I quickly pull my shirt over my head.

"You weren't suppose to see that." I say to him as he walks over to me and hands me my glass of water.

"You saw mine." He smirks and I roll my eyes.

"Mines a secret." I say to him and he seems to perk up.

"So I'm the only one who has seen it?" He asks me.

"Yeah, and I'd appreciate it if you wouldn't tell anyone." I say pointedly at him.

"Why? That's an awesome tattoo, DaKota." He says, making me blush.

"Thanks, but my family isn't a big fan of tattoos." I say and he scoffs a little, making me raise an eyebrow.

"Caleb has like three." This shocks me.

"What?"

"You've never seen them? They're rank!" He says and it makes me roll my eyes.

"What does your tattoo mean?" I ask him, changing the subject.

"That's a story for another time." He smirks at me playfully. "What does yours mean?"

"That's a story for another time.. Good night Cooper." I say and then I go to the bed, but don't get under the covers yet.

"Good night DaKota, sweet dreams." He says softly and I nod and then he grabs the door knob and then closes the door, making him disappear. I climbed under the soft covers and then I said a quick thankful prayer and then I closed my eyes, letting myself go to sleep.

HE WAS ALL OVER ME. He liked being all over me. He liked being in control. He was always in control. I screamed for him to get off me, but he just slapped me and continue to rape me. He had no dignity for himself anymore, he just kept going and going, ignoring my cries for help. He cupped my cheeks with one hand and then spit on me, I shivered in disgust. "I know you like that my lovely.." I couldn't take it anymore, I felt myself giving up. The pain was unbearable, I just wanted it to stop, but it would never stop if I didn't do something about it.

I shot up from under the covers just as lightning struck and the thunder crashed. My breathing was heavy and I had to control it. It was my sixth night terror tonight, I wouldn't able to stop them without my pills. Then the worst thought came into my mind.

COOPER

WAS I CRAZY?! I COULDN'T have Cooper sleep in the same bed with me! But I did feel safe with him, I wasn't so crazy.. There was a blazing pain in my stomach, and I knew it was from the nightmares. I couldn't handle it anymore. I took a deep breath and threw the covers off me and started my long journey to the living room.

My mind was contradicting my actions, stay, go, stay, go, stay, go, stay. When I saw Cooper, my heart automatically felt sorry for him. He looked very uncomfortable. His feet were hanging off the edge, and his neck looked unnaturally positioned, I warned him. "Cooper." I say and he doesn't move. "Cooper, wake up." I say and then I push on his shoulder.

"DaKota?" He mumbles under his breath.

"Um, I was wondering if you could keep me company in my room. Thunder storms kind of scare me." I say and then he sat up and rubbed his eyes, he looked adorable.

River, you're dating river.

"Yeah sure." He said and then I gave a quiet thank you and walked back to my room and got back into bed. I didn't feel the bed sink down at all, so I popped my head up and looked around. Cooper was laying on the floor in front of the bed, making me smile at him.

"Get in the bed, you idiot." I chuckle and then back down and lay on my side, and then I feel the spot go down.

"Now, no crossing the line DaKota." Cooper says in a fake strict tone making me laugh as I close my eyes and try to go to sleep.

THERE WAS SOMETHING strange going on. Something against my skin, it felt good, but also it sent a warning sign to me. I opened my eyes and looked at the source, and I began to freak out when I saw Cooper was tracing the scar on my leg. What the hell was he doing?! My shorts must of bunched up from me moving around. Shit, double shit. I jumped out of the bed and Cooper sat up and worry consumed his face.

I made sure to pull down my shorts as low as they could go, and every cell in my body was starting to panic. I felt my whole body start to shake. "DaKota what's wrong?" He asks me getting out of the bed.

"Stay right there!" I yell and still try to comprehend what is happening right now. "What the hell were you doing?" I asked him.

"What's that scar from?" He asks me, and I scrunch my eyebrows at him in anger and confusion, mostly anger.

"Don't change the subject." I say to him as I turn away from him.

"Why not, Cassidy?" He says and I swear when he said that my heart stopped. How the hell did he know about that?

"What did you call me?" We both knew damn well what he said, and he gave me that face telling me to explain.

"Cassidy Smith, from North Dakota." That was the name the police gave me for my protection and for staying under the radar. Lord how did he find that?

"It's my fake ID." I shrug to him looking him in the eyes.

"That's bullshit and you know it," he throws in my face. "DaKota you better stop lying to me." He said angry.

"I don't know what you're talking about." I say quietly.

"You know you can trust me DaKota, please." He says softly taking a step towards me.

"I don't know why you care so much." I say looking away from him.

"Because I like you DaKota! Screw that!" He pauses, "Hell, I like you a lot DaKota! I like you so much that know things about you that no one else does. Like how you act around people. I can tell when you're comfortable and uncomfortable. And when you're with River I can tell it's both. Why are you with him if he makes you uncomfortable?" Cooper shouts right away, but then he relaxes with the truth is out.

He likes me?

159

"If you actually knew him you'd find out he is a really nice guy, and he's sweet."

"That's all?" Cooper chuckles.

"Well, he's.. handsome.. knows horses-"

"He doesn't know shit about horses. Tell me the real reason DaKota." He said to me like he already knew the answer.

"Why are you dating Avery?" I bring back at him, really wanting to avoid his question.

Cooper throws up one of his arms and takes a deep breath, "Shit," his southern drawl really comes out when he said this. "I'm not even dating her DaKota, I can't stand her! The only reason I told you that is because you're dating River and that made me hurt less." He said and I was shocked but relieved at the same time.

"Hurt?" I ask him and he slowly looks at me and takes another step towards me.

"It hurts me to see you with him.. You know how badly I just want to steal you away from him and wrap you in my arms? Or when I see him make you smile? That should be me. But what really hurts me is to see the way he treats you, which is complete crap! You would be so much better with me, and you know it." He confesses to me and all I could do was stand there and try to get all of this through my brain and comprehend it.

I knew he was right, but I didn't want him to be right. I couldn't let it happen.

"Do you remember that time we were sitting on your porch swing?" He said and I just nodded. "That was the first time I tried to kiss you, oh man I wanted to kiss you. Or last night, I knew you wanted to kiss me, I could see it in your eyes DaKota. I wanted to kiss you and you weren't going to stop me." He says confidently and I almost stomp my foot in anger. Why did he have to be right!

"What are you trying to prove?" I ask him.

"That you like me and you won't tell yourself that you do. You like the way I look at you. You like the way I make you smile. You like my humor, and you like that I am a really nice guy. But you know what you hate about me?" Again, I don't answer him. "That I'm perfect for you." Cooper didn't sound arrogant at all, he sounded genuine and real. But what shocked me was that I hadn't realized that he had grabbed my hands.

I looked down at them, it felt so good. It felt like nothing I had experienced before. My body felt safe, cherished, and comfortable. But the sparks that were running through me were indescribable. "Cooper, I can-" I could feel the tears clouding my eyes, and I was about to break.

"Do you see? You're denying it.. You didn't even flinch when I grabbed for you." He said and then I looked into his eyes, how did he know?

"What? What do you mean?" I ask him as I take a step away from him, separating our hands.

"When ever River tries to touch you, you flinch. In fact, I've seen you flinch to any man that isn't your father, brother, or me. Tell me why that is, DaKota."

"No, I don't know what you're talking about." I say and shake my head and run my fingers trough my hair.

"Please tell me, please." I shake my head. "Why won't you just tell me?!" He raises his voice at me.

"I was raped!! That's why I flinch when ever a man tries to touch me! I was stripped off my innocence! It was just rape, he stalked me. He took pictures of me doing everything, eating, changing, sleeping, everything! That story about going to visit my cousins for two years? Complete lie! Wade, my rapist, escaped from jail and we all knew he was coming for me. So my family planned for me to live on my own in Bismarck. That's where Cassidy Smith comes from, that was my secret identity. When I knew that Wade was no longer coming after me, I knew it was time to come home. And here I am, still afraid. My parents don't know that I have to take pills before I go to bed, because they keep me from having night terrors, but sometimes they don't work." I had no idea what came over me to spill my biggest secret, but I did. Once I got started, I couldn't stop myself.

No one said anything. But the next thing I knew I was threw into a sympathetic hug in Cooper's arms. Then it all came out, the tears. They were pouring out of my eyes. Cooper tightened his arms around me and for once, I felt protected and safe. I knew that I could trust Cooper, I knew everything he said to me earlier was true. I like Cooper, I liked him a lot, despite what every one says about him. Not many people would hug you after you tell them you were raped, but Cooper did. Cooper did about everything right when it came to me. "I am so sorry." He said after a while of us hugging. "DaKota I am so sorry.. There's is no reason why you deserved tha-"

"Stop, please stop.." I look into his eyes and then to his pink lips, "I don't deserve you Cooper." I say quietly as I step away from his arms, already missing his embrace.

"Don't say that." He says hurt.

"No! You need to hear this! I need to tell someone this." I wipe my eyes and take a breath, "When I was in Bismarck, Wade found me again." When I said this Cooper locked his jaw and balled his fists, "He found me and kept me in a basement for three days! No water, no food, no clothes, just the hope someone would find me or I would just die. Wa-"

"Don't tell me anymore." Cooper says protectively.

"No, I have to tell someone, it's eating me alive. Wade abused me so many times, he wouldn't stop, he couldn't stop himself, he lost control. That scar on my leg? That was from him sticking a knife into my jeans because I kept him from unbuttoning my pants. I had managed to survive the pain and after I escaped him, I stitched myself up. I tried to get him to stop, he was just so blind.. I hate myself because I felt bad for him. For him! Isn't that sick?" I stop and Cooper still looks pale and pissed off. "So when I knew he left, I found a way to escape and I did. I went back to my apartment and grabbed my gun and waited.."

"DaKota, do not go on!" Cooper looked very scared, or scared for my well-being.

"I planned it so perfectly. I drove my car to somewhere public and waited for him to see me, so I lead him to an alley. I hid behind a garbage can, and when he was far enough, I stood out from behind. He turned around and looked horrified when he saw the gun aimed at him, and I said to him, 'Do you feel that? That's called fear. That's what I feel everyday, only about 20 times worse. You deserved this so long ago, goodbye Wade.' and then I pulled the trigger, perfect shot to the heart. I had called the police and told them everything, there was no charges or no media.. I had told my parents not to worry anymore because he was gone for good. They thought he was locked in jail, but I know he is dead, and I killed him." I cried and I cried. Then what I had just said it me like a semi truck doing 80. "Oh my gosh, I had never said that out loud. Cooper what did I do? I killed someone!" I started to bawl and began to start hyperventilating.

Cooper's arms again brought me into another comforting hug. "DaKota, you did nothing wrong. You did what you did to survive." He said and then he kissed the top of my head. He pulled me away, but keeping his hands on my arms. "You are the strongest girl I know. I knew that before you even told me. I just can't believe you haven't told anyone." He said.

"I am Catholic, killing is a sin. I would be shammed by the Church and my family would be embarrassed because of me. Of course I couldn't tell any one." I say softly. I look in Cooper's eyes and I can tell he is furious, but when he realizes that I'm looking at him, his faces softens.

"You know what DaKota? Fuck them. Who ever judges you because of your past deserves to go to hell! They have no right to judge you, and if they want to they're gonna have to come talk to me, which will end up in them having a broken jaw." In all of this seriousness, Cooper had managed to make me laugh, and he smiled when he heard me laugh.

"Thank you, Cooper." I say and then I hug him.

"Doesn't this feel right?" Cooper said and then he just ruined the whole moment for me. I quickly took a step away from him and he looked confused.

"Cooper, I can't I'm dating River." I say to him.

"Give me a reason why not."

"Because I have a boyfriend, we've discussed this already." I say looking at the ground, avoiding his eye contact. "Please just drop it."

"No! I am not going to drop it, tell me why you're dating him." He exclaims at me.

"Because dating River, gives me an excuse to not have feelings for you!!" I shout and immediately turn around, man what a night of me expressing my thoughts. Way to go DaKota, way to go.

"So you do like me." I could hear the smirk in his voice. I don't say anything.

"I couldn't even date you if I wanted to." I sigh.

"And why not?"

"My father told me things about your father, and he doesn't want me to be around you." I confess and he groans and huffs.

"No offence, but your dad doesn't know shit! I hate my father, I haven't seen him in years. You know what? You're afraid. You're afraid of your father and your afraid of your feelings towards me. It isn't fair to me, DaKota. I wish you wou-" I couldn't take it anymore. I turned around to chew him out, but the next thing I knew was his lips were on mine.

Cooper was kissing me, and I was kissing back. Both of his hands were on both sides of my face and my hands found his wrists. This was good, no, this was right. I had never felt anything so right in my life, it was unbelievable. I had never been kissed like this, I never wanted it to end. We both wanted each other, like our lives depended on this kiss. I had butterflies in my stomach and my knees were starting to go weak.

Cooper was the one to pull back and I didn't want to open my eyes because I didn't want it to end, but it did. "Wow." I blushed and Cooper laughed and then tucked a piece of hair behind my ear.

I stepped back from him, "Cooper you better not do that again." He looked shocked and angry..

"Are you serious?" He threw up both his hands and turned in a circle.

"I'm serious, you better not do that until you ask me to be your girlfriend." I had a playful smirk on my face and his head snapped towards me and he smiled and walked over to me.

"Really?" He asked like a little boy.

"Really." I confirmed and then he picked me up and spun me around and kissed me on the cheek, but then he hissed and let me down. "Are you okay?" I ask him as he pulls his shirt up and the white gauze was starting to have red splotches. "I need to change it." I said and pulled him to the living room.

I HAD FIXED COOPER'S stitches, which just needed to rinsed and I changed the bandaged. So now him and I were on the couch, side by side, my head on his shoulder, our feet on the wooden furniture in front of us, and watching the fire burn. "Where did you learn how to suture?" He asked me.

"I used to wanna be a doctor-" He cuts me off.

"Of course you did." Cooper laughs.

"Anyways so I looked up videos how to do it and I would practice on my old stuffed dolls that I never played with." I say.

"You are something, darlin'." He said and then kissed the side of my head.

"I like that." I mumble and then stand up and grab his hand. "Let's go to bed."

"Oh and I like that." Cooper smirks and I roll my eyes at him and we go back to the bedroom. As we both get into the bed, Cooper automatically pulls me into him but I scoot away.

"Nuh huh." I giggle and he groans but then I feel a wet peck on my cheek.

"Night DaKota."

"Good night Cooper." I whispered to him as I closed my eyes.

The first thing I saw when I opened my sleepy eyes was a muscular back. Cooper must of taken his shirt off while we were sleeping. All at once, last night's events hit me. One of the most intense nights I've ever experiencs. Before Cooper could wake up, I quietly went into the bathroom and took a swig of mint mouth wash, since I didn't have my toothbrush with me.

I crawled back into bed, being as quiet as I could. Although I did peak over his shoulder to look at his sleeping face, he's so adorable. And this time I don't have to feel bad about it because I'm going to break up with River today, but what the hell are Cooper and I going to do about my dad?

Cooper starts to stir in his sleep and then he rolls on his left side, facing me. Then in a couple of seconds his eyes slowly open, and then he gives me a small smile. "Good morning." His incredibly sexy morning voice says, making me internally groan.

"Morning." I smile back.

"How long have you been up?" He asks me.

"Just a couple minuets." I shrug and he nods.

"Do you want breakfast, or to get going right away?" He asks me as he sits up in the bed, the covers coming down and covering his waists, and he rubs his eyes.

"Well, I was hoping we could talk."

"We can do that on the trail, I still gotta wake up." He says and then I nod. "I'll go get your clothes." He said and then places his hand on my leg through the covers and gets up and leaves. I get off the bed and look out the door, it looks beautiful outside, even after the storm. I see the horses peek their heads out the window of the small shelter. "Here you go, I'm gonna go get the horses fed and ready." Cooper's voice makes me turn towards him.

"I can help after I get dressed." I say to him and he shrugs.

"Alright, but don't forget your stuff in the living room." He says and then he gives me a small smile and then leaves the room.

AFTER UNTACKING AND cooling down Sir Lance, it was finally time to face my parents. During the ride back Cooper and I didn't exactly set in stone about what we were going to do, but the whole time Cooper seemed very satisfied. With what, I don't know. During our ride back, I would see Cooper smiling to himself, even when we weren't talking. I hope it was because of us, but who knows.

I walked into the house and was immediately consumed by my mother's arms, "Oh my sweet daughter!" She sighed with relief and tightened her arms around me. "Colby get in here!" She says as she lets me go and then my heart pace starts to quicken a little bit.

I hear footsteps around the corner, and then stepped out my father, dressed in dirty clothes as usual. "Oh honey, you're home." He said and and then hugged me shortly, he was acting weird.

"If you hadn't of found Cooper, I don't know what I would have done." My mom says and I look at my dad and he rolls his eyes.

"Yeah, what a coincidence. Did he take care of you and your horse?" My dad says sternly towards me.

"Yes, Cooper was very kind and put me first." I say to my dad in a mater-of-fact tone.

"How does River feel about this?" My dad says and I almost scoff, since when he did care about River?

"I haven't told River." I say quietly and look to the floor.

"What did you say?" His voice becomes louder and then I look up at him, "Why doesn't your boyfriend know that you spent the night with Cooper."

"Because he hasn't talked to me since the wedding, and nothing happened." I say back to my dad.

"Nothing happened?" My dad said back to me this time, making me raise my eyebrows at him.

"Yes, are we done talking about this?" I ask him as I folded my arms.

"Yes, but only if you remember our conversation from the other night." He says and then walks out the door, and then I walk upstairs to my room, remembering what my father told me the other night: I couldn't see Cooper anyone if I was dating River.

I GRABBED EACH FRONT piece of my hair and pulled them back around my head, combined the pieces and then I braided it all the way down. My hair looked really good today, the curls actually were tamed, I must say I look good. I stood up and went over to the full-length mirror.

I was dressed in a open-shoulder green top, and then I had on some light blue jean shorts, with some distressed spots. My working out payed off because my tan legs looked toned underneath my jeans. I slipped on some black fringed gladiator sandals, and then I went over to my dresser and put on my braided anklet, and then put my phone in my back pocket.

I didn't say anything to my dad as I walked out of house, heading to my pickup. It was a really nice day outside, sun was out and there wasn't a cloud in the sky. I lived for these days. I started the truck and then put 'er in reverse and headed out to my diner.

Once I pulled into the lot, it looked like a normal day of customers, about 20 or so. I parked in my usual spot, grabbed my keys and then I walked into the diner. When I walked into the diner, I automatically knew what the special was, duck poppers, the best. "Hey sweetheart!" Maybell calls, turning my attention to her.

"Hey Maybell, how's it going?" I ask her as I make my way around the counter to have a conversation with her.

"You know, nine to five." She says and then I chuckle at her comment.

"Seriously, how are you? How's it going with Mike?" I ask about her husband, Mike. I've heared they've been having trouble with their crops lately.

"He's been down lately, and I just do my best to try to help him, but a wife can't fix crops." She sighs and shrugs, I nod in response.

"Well, tell him hi from me, I haven't seen him in ages!" I say and she smiles at the gesture and nods. "Do you need any help?" I ask her as I see her messing with the cash register.

"I don't know about tables, but last night I fell behind on logging the receipts, so if you could do that." She says as she stuffs her notepad in her apron and walked around the counter.

"Sure!" I say and then I go to the cash register and pick up the basket full of receipts, log journal, and calculator.

As I was working on the receipts I saw a couple coming to the register, so I stopped writing and calculating and closed the book and turned my attention to the Silverton's, what a lovely old couple. "Hello DaKota!" They greet me with big smiles, and then I hear the door bells ring, but not paying attention to it.

"Hi! How was your food today?" I ask as I take their receipt from and start punching numbers into the register.

"Fantastic as always." Mr. Silverton says making me nod with satisfaction.

"DaKota, you must tell me your secrets on how you get prettier everyday!" Mrs. S compliments me making me blush.

Before I could answer, Mr. S says, "No need to tell her, there's no way she could get any prettier." He says to his wife and then kisses her on the top of her head, making my heart melt at the sight.

"Here ya go, $8.83. Have a nice day!" I say to them and they return a kind smile back to me and then walk away from me, hand-in-hand. One word, goals.

I opened the log book up again and then started on the next receipt, until I heard, "Hey DaKota!" I turned my head to a bunch of roughies sitting at the round booth. I scanned the table to see Rusty, Ryan, Jake, and to my pleasure, Cooper. When Cooper and I make eye contact, it takes everything inside me not to go over to him and hug him, but he gives me a crooked smile instead.

I walk over to their table and then I hear a playful cat whistle from Jake, "Lookin' good, wolf girl." I can't help but blush and look at the ground.

"Where's the girlfriend? Oh sorry, I meant River." Rusty laughs and makes the others laugh and I roll my eyes.

"Don't you mean soon-to-be-ex?" I say and from the corner of my eye, I see Cooper's face light up with excitement, but then he quickly covers it.

"Really?" Ryan asks and I nod my head.

"What made you change your mind?" Cooper said making me look at him and he's got on his sexy-devil-smirk on, making me smirk a little bit.

"Just not my type." I say and then return my attention to the other boys.

"Finally!"

"Thank God, I hated R-Hey River!!!" Rusty exclaims, making all of our heads snap to our right, seeing River walking towards us. Oh my, here we go. River wrapped his arm around my waist and kissed my head. "What's he doing here?" River says looking at Cooper and Cooper just laughs and looks at his friends knowlingly.

Before Cooper can answer I say, "Uh can we go talk somewhere else?" I say to River, stepping away from his arm.

"I'm sure the boys won't mind us talking in front of them." River says in a 'bro' voice.

"We don't mind." They all said at the same time, with smirks plastered on their faces, making me roll my eyes.

"Are you sure?" I say to River in a slow pace, making it clear that we shouldn't talk in front of them. River just nodded.

"River, I thi-"

"I think we should break up." River says, making me completely shocked but at the same time I was relieved. I start to act like I was sad, I moved my lips side to side, took a breath, and dropped my head.

"Well, I did not expect this at all." I saw in fake disbelief, making some of the guys giggle.

"Yeah, I just don't think it's working out. I had fun and stuff though!"

"What kind of fun?" Jake asks, making me roll my eyes.

"Well I have to be honest, DaKota is a great kisser." My eyes automatically landed on Cooper's and his smirk widened. "One last hug before I go?" River turns to me again and I sadly nod and open my arms and then we hug.

"Bye." We say at the same time as we pull away and then he walks away and out the door. When he's fully out of the Cafe, we all burst out laughing.

I'm still working on logging the receipts into the journal, but taking quick peaks around the diner, mostly at Cooper though. I couldn't stop thinking about our current status, but I knew I had to concentrate on logging. After River and I broke up I just felt a huge weight lift off my shoulders and I felt great. I felt like I was going to actually have fun, and do what I wanted with myself now. It was only two weeks, but being with his high maintenance butt, it made it feel like months.

"Hey wolf girl." A charming voice said from beside and I looked to my left to see Cooper sitting down on the counter stool, just the sight of him made me think of our kiss last night and I started to blush.

"Hey Coop." I say and then look back at the log.

"I'm taking you on a date tonight." Cooper says very confidently making my eyes widen, looking into his gorgeous eyes. The way he said it made me feel like I didn't have a choice, but there wasn't even a chance I would of said no.

"Really?!" I couldn't help but feel excited, this was like the sunshine to my rainy day.

"Yep!" He smiles brightly, "I'm going to pick you up at 7, sound good?" He says as he turns his body fully towards me. I was eager to go on the date with him, but I couldn't help but think of the darker side of going on a date, my dad.

"Cooper, that sounds really great, and I want to go, but what about my dad?" I say and I expected his smile to fade but it didn't, he looked mischievous.

"Don't you worry about that," He winked, "So what ya say?" He asked, hope full in his eyes, making my heart melt. I wonder what he planned with my father, but something inside me told me that everything would be fine and to trust Cooper.

"Okay, I'll go on the date." I say and he smiled triumphantly.

"Sweet, I'll see you at 7, sharp. Oh and you can stay dressed like that, you look beautiful." He says the last part quietly to me, making me blush hard.

"Do I need to bring anything?" I asked him as he stood up.

"Just your pretty self," He smirked and I rolled my eyes, "I'll see you later." He said and then took a couple steps back.

"Bye Cooper." I smile softly and then turn back to the log book.

"Oh and DaKota, I can't wait to kiss you again." He shocks me when he whispers in my ear. It sent chills down my body and I started to blush. Before I could say anything to him, he was already walking out the door. Not without giving me one last look, sending me a wink.

IF I TOLD YOU I WAS nervous, I'd be lying. I am over the moon nervous for my date with Cooper tonight. Screw butterflies in my stomach, I felt like I had a safari in there! I think I went through every possible way my dad would react to the news of me going on a date with

Cooper. That reminds me, I should probably go tell my dad that I'm not seeing River anymore.

I quickly ran downstairs and casually went to the fridge and grabbed a bottled water, "Just to let you know, I'm not dating River anymore." I say like it's not a big deal, and then I hear Caleb cheer from the living room, making me roll my eyes.

My eyes landed on my dad's expression, which I couldn't read. "Why?" He asks, squinting his eyes at me, telling me he was in deep thought.

"Just not my type, and we had nothing in common." I shrug and then he nods and then I start to walk back upstairs.

Laying in my bed my thoughts consumed me, I couldn't turn them off. I was thinking about everything. Anything to my horses to what Cooper had planned for this date. Then I started to think about what Cooper said to me at the diner, I can't wait to kiss you again, his words made me redden. I began to think about our first kiss, but I snapped out of it when I heard a truck door slam. My head snapped towards my clock, 7:00, dang he really meant sharp.

But wait. He's coming to the door to get me? I had thought he would just wait for me in the truck, but this meant my dad would be in the same room as Cooper and I. Crap. I shot out of my bed and headed towards the stairs that lead me to my date. As my right foot hit the wooden floor, I see my father had beaten me to the door and there stood Cooper in front of my dad.

I had stopped in my tracks because of shock. Not shock because of the confrontation, because of Cooper. He was wearing a royal blue button down shirt tucked into his probably nicest jeans, with a golden belt buckle, and wearing his nicest black felt cowboy hat. He looked irresistible. But his appearance wasn't the only thing that made my heart swoon, he was holding a bouquet of different colored lilies. I looked at my dad and he looked in shock, "You what?" My dad said in a deeper voice.

Cooper looked very calm and relaxed, "I wanted to ask you permission to take your daughter on a date." I have never heard anything more romantic in my life.

My dad looked dumbstruck as he looked between Cooper and I, it was the longest ten seconds of my life. "Well I am impressed that you have enough nerves to even come here and ask me that after everything I have heard about you, Blackwood." My dad said, making me very confused at what he was getting at. I looked at Cooper, and he was still looking into my father's eyes.

"Well Mr. Jones, it-" My dad rudely cuts off Cooper.

"Save it, I've told my daughter already, I don't want her being around you and your trouble. And I definitely do not want her dating you." My dad says very harshly and clear to Cooper.

"Dad!" I try to protest but he snaps his head towards me, making me cower like a little girl. My dad was being unfair to Cooper, he never gives him a chance.

"With all due respect, Mr. Jones I haven't caused any 'trouble' in a-"

"It doesn't matter, I'm saying to you with respect that you can not take my daughter on a date." My dad cruely mocks Cooper, and then Cooper's face drops a little, making me sad and angry at my father.

"Well I am sorry to have wasted your time," Cooper says in a respectful tone, but yet also sad. If we were in a cartoon I think the flowers would have sadly dropped dead. "Goodnight Mr. Jones, DaKota." He says tipping his hat, and then leaving our porch.

"Dad, it should be my choice if I want to go on a date with him!" I raise my voice at my dad and he looks angry.

"How many times do I have to tell you?! I do no want you around that kid, this is the last time we are discussing this! Go to your room." He says and then we have a deadly stare-off until I stomp my foot a little and turn and go to the stairs.

My dad was acting like a thirteen year old girl who didn't get front row tickets to Justin Bieber concert. Couldn't he just give Cooper one chance? Cooper has done nothing wrong to my father or any of our family. And now Cooper was just being very respectful and.. understanding? It was like he knew my father wasn't going to say yes, he was expecting to be turned down. Well he has another thing comin' for him.

"Mom!" I yell to my mother while I go downstairs into the kitchen.

"Yes?" She sticks her head out of the laundry room and then I walk over to her.

"I'm going for a ride, don't know how long I'll be gone." I say to her and then she stands from her knees.

"Well I'll come with you." She said and wiped her hands off.

"No- I mean I just kinda wanna be alone for a bit. Sorry." I say to my mother and her face softens and then she nods.

"No problem, next time." She said and I nodded and then slipped away and grabbed my sandals and headed for the barn.

I decided to ride Pharaoh bareback to Cooper's house, just because it wasn't far and I didn't want to take the time to saddle my horse. I've also decided that I am 18 years old and my dad didn't have the right anymore to tell me who I can and can not date. Cooper is the only boy I truly feel comfortable around, and why that is, amazes me. I was going with my gut feeling, which has never let me down.

Before I knew it, I was riding up to Cooper's barn, where I just saw him enter. I rode Pharaoh over to the old wooden hitching post, slid of him, and then tied him up. I quickly walked up the the entrance of the barn, my heart pounding faster with every step I took. My eyes quickly landed on Cooper's back, he was carrying a barley stack, still in his nice clothes. I'm going to have to teach him some new things. "Just because my dad said no, doesn't mean that I say no." I spoke and then he stopped in his tracks and then turned to me.

"Let's be real DaKota, he doesn't like me, so maybe I shou-"

"Cooper shut up and come here." I cut him off and demand him. All I wanted was to be with him. Cooper looked relieved and then he dropped the stack and got to me in a hurry. Soon his hands found my face and then after that our lips found each other's. The automatic feeling of Cooper's lips made me melt into him and just feel at home. I pulled back and opened my eyes to see Cooper looking down at me.

"Are you sure?" Cooper asked me and I rolled my eyes.

"Cooper, I wanna be with you. My dad has no choice in my decisions." I say confidently, making him flash off his beautiful smile.

"C'mon!" His smile widened as he grabbed my right hand and then pulled me in the direction I came from.

I LEANED BACK INTO Cooper, I found that I could hear him better as he talked. Currently, we are both on Pharaoh, me in the front and Cooper behind me. Cooper is showing me around his pasture and his property, which I actually find interesting, because he's telling me stories of each location. Cooper grabbed my hand on the reins and then pulled back, making Pharaoh stop. I watched Cooper slide off, "What are we doing?" I asked as he placed his hands on my hips and lifted me off the horse and beside him as he slipped his arm around my waist.

"Isn't it breath taking?" He says, making me look forward to sun setting around the hills of the great Montana landscape.

"I could never get used to it." I say putting my head on his right shoulder.

"This spot right here, is very special." Cooper said, making me lift my head off his shoulder and then looked at the side of his face, admiring his rugid features.

"Why?" I asked him.

Cooper turned his head to meet my gaze, looked at my lips, then back to my eyes. "Because this is the spot where I'm asking you to be my girlfriend." He says, making me blush. He turns his body, so he's fully facing me, and then he takes both of my hands into his. "DaKota, will you be my girlfriend?"

I don't say anything, I just pull him into me and kiss him. His arms wrap around my waist and pull me closer to him, but soon after he slides his arms lower and lifts me into the air and over his shoulder, catching me completely off guard. So now I'm facing his perfect butt covered by denim, "Cooper! Put me down!" I laughed as he started walking around.

"I'm pretty sure the creek is near here." He said in a mischievous voice making me gasp.

"C'mon Cooper!" I say, still laughing.

"It's alright darlin', I wouldn't do that." He says as he puts me down in front of him. "Yet." He adds smirking and making me roll my eyes at him.

"On a serious note.." I say and the stick my hands in my back pockets and look at the ground and then in his eyes. Cooper sighs and picks at the brush, and then looks around.

"Your dad doesn't want us to date, and if he finds out he's going to do everything in his power to keep us away from each other." Cooper says and I nod.

"So we just gotta keep him from knowing." I mumble.

"So like sneaking around?" Cooper says, with a little smirk on his face.

"Yeah, I guess so." I say to him, raising my eyebrow at him.

"So we get to have a secret meeting place, and then go places where no one else will be?" Cooper says, walking towards me.

"Pretty much." I confirm to him, looking up at him as he stands in front of me. "Are you okay with that? It's pretty much our only option."

"I'm perfectly fine with that, I get to have you all to myself." He smiles as he puts his hands around my lower back.

"Okay then," I smile and kiss his cheek, "But you do know that you can't kiss me whenever you want to in public, or even look at me too long."

"But I like doing those things!" He whines, making me giggle at him.

"It'll be hard for me too, but in the end it'll be worth it." I say quietly as I lean up and place a kiss onto his lips.

Cooper pulls back and says, "Definitely worth it." He smirks, making me shove his shoulder away from me.

"C'mon I should be getting home." I say and start walking back to Pharaoh who was grazing a few yards away from us.

"Okay." Cooper sadly sighs and then I grab onto Pharaoh's mane and hoist myself up, then Cooper holds up his hand and I grab it and help him up.

I SWEAR I WAS WALKING on clouds as I walked into my house from getting back from my "ride". I ignored the fact that my dad was at the kitchen table doing some paperwork, I was just too happy to let my father get in my head. I walked to the fridge and grabbed a pitcher of iced tea and pour myself a glass. "Hey, Kota. No hard feelings right?" My dad's voice awakes me from my daze.

"Yup, no hard feelings." I smile, but not for the reason he thinks I am.

I stepped out of the shower, wrapping a soft white towel around my body and then combing my hair out. Then I apply some facial treatments to my face, I use to have a really bad acne problem, so I do my best to try to keep it away. After that I start to brush my teeth, as I am doing so I hear my phone buzz and I look and it's Cooper, "Hey girly." His text made me smile.

"Hey, Coop." I send with a blushing emoji.

"Anything happen with your dad when you got home?" He replies back.

"Not really, I guess he kind of apologized."

"Well that's good.." He said and I started to type my response but then he sent, "Would it be weird if I said I missed you already? Cause I do."

"No it's not weird, I miss you too.." I send back, making put my phone down quickly. It was weird for me to be sentimental and romantic so fast into a relationship.

I threw my phone onto my bed, and then I changed into some shorts and a sports bra, officially ready to go to bed. I tucked myself in, under my unfortunately soft blankets. I picked up my phone and opened Cooper's text, "That's good to hear, darlin."

"I'm exhausted, good night boyfriend.. Thanks for a great day!" I say and then went for his reply before I get to get some shut eye.

"No problem ;) Goodnight my beautiful girlfriend." Words couldn't explain how reading that text before I went to bed made me extremely happy..

"That's my good boy." I say as I patted Pharaoh's croup and dropped his reins as he rode back to the barn. We just got done with our barrels practice and he did a wonderful job with his leads and his balance. I didn't see myself having a big career with barrel racing, I thought of it more of a hobby with my horse. I didn't see myself going to the NFR, although that would be pretty cool, but I just don't think it was for me.

Obviously, I would still compete at rodeos that are pretty close to home, I still love doing it, and Pharaoh and I are pretty good. I wanted to peruse my dream of being a farm vet and carrying on the diner.

Anyways, I'm not sure what I am going to do today. Maybe I'll hangout with Taylor, we haven't in a while and I missed her. I also haven't hung out with Cooper since Wednesday and it's Friday, I know not a big deal, but when you're in me and Cooper's situation, it's hard to find time to talk to each other with out someone noticing. Plus, Cooper and I are both really busy, especially Cooper. He either has to work at the sale barn, doing stuff around his ranch, or he is practicing, and he has to eat and rest in between. That's what I found attractive in him, hard working. Obviously that isn't the only thing I found attractive about him, I could go on forever about his attractiveness.

I got off of Pharaoh and tied him to a hitching post, just outside of the barn. I undid the flank cinch and then the front cinch, then slid the saddle of the beast and then took it to the tack shack. When I carefully put the saddle away, I walked over to the barn and turned the hose on and grabbed the necessities for bathing my horse.

SITTING ON THE COUCH, watching Reba, while Ashley is laying on the other couch, while having her calves on Caleb's lap. It was about 1 o'clock and I was becoming extremely bored, and it's too hot to do anything with my horses. So I grabbed my phone and pressed on Taylor's number. "Who ya calling? River's butler?" Caleb said and then laughed, amusing himself. After Ash saw me rolling my eyes, she kicked Caleb real close to his family jewels and he backed down.

"Hey Kota!" Taylor's bright voice came through the phone.

"Hey Tay, wanna do something?" I ask, and then getting up and walking to the kitchen.

"Yeah sure, what do you wanna do?" She asked me.

"Wanna go swimming or something, it's so dang hot out." I reply.

"Ya, you can come out to my pool if you want." She said.

"Okay! I'll be there in about 10." I inform her and then start heading to my room.

"Sounds great, bye girl." She said excitedly.

"Bye Tay." I said and then we both hang up at the same time.

I arrived at Taylor's house around 10 minuets later, just like I said, and I could not wait to dive into her cold pool. It was a blazin' 99 degrees outside, and I felt bad for whoever has to work outside today. I already had my swimsuit on, so I just parked my truck in her grass, and then went to her backyard and I could already hear the music. There Taylor was, already floating on her red-circular-crab floatie. I climbed the stairs of her back deck and stripped of my clothes, she still hasn't noticed I am here.

So I decided to have some fun with that. I quietly went back down the stairs and then silently climbed up the pool ladder, and then smoothly put my body in the cool water, hardly making any ripples. I can usually take cold water, but this was really cold, and it took all of my nerves to not just dive under and get used to it. Anyways, I reached Taylor's floatie and then in one swift move I lifted it up and tilted it so she ended up in the water, which I know she hated. I started to laugh, and I laughed even harder when she surfaced because she let out a loud gasp. "You know what this means!" She said and then lunged at me and tackled me into the water.

It didn't affect me because I don't mind getting my hair wet, and I wasn't wearing any makeup, so no harm to me. When we came back above the water, we came out laughing that's just how we were, happy as can be. "Let me go get your floatie, and I know you don't need sunscreen because you never burn." She rolled her eyes at me at the last part. It was true, I have never got sun-burned, I just always get dark, family genes.

Taylor threw the flat-dark blue floatie into the pool and then I grabbed onto the sides and hoisted myself up and then laid on my back, unhooking my swimsuit so I wouldn't get tan lines. "So Taylor, how's Beau?" I ask her as she get back on hers.

"Amazing, completely amazing." She said in a day-dream voice, and I could basically hear the smile in her voice.

"That's great, Tay. I'm really happy for you." I say in all honesty.

"What about you? I heard you dumped River, any new guys yet?" She asked me. I was dying to tell her about me and Cooper, but I just couldn't risk it. I knew even if I did tell her, she wouldn't tell anyone, actually sometimes she rambles and slips something, but it would probably only to Beau. Taylor is my best friend and I hated lying to her, but this was the only way.

"Nope, single as a pringle." I said with a smile, because that's what happens when I think of Cooper.

"I just don't get it." She said frustrated.

"What?" I ask her and then open my eyes and see her sitting up on her floatie and looking at me, with a thoughtful and distressed expression.

"Why you are single?! Let's face it, you are smokin' hot, girlfriend! You have the kindest heart, sweetest soul, greatest body, and the most gorgeous face! Also you can shoot a gun, shoot a bow, ride crazy fast horses, and rope a God-damn steer! And not to mention you own a diner! What man wouldn't want to date you?" She said, making me smile at her. I love her. I was very thankful to be able to call her my best friend.

"Thank you Tay, but you basically described yourself! I'm nothing that special, and I'm sure I'll meet the right guy someday. Heck, he'll might even come into the diner and that's how we meet!" I say, hinting that I'm talking about Cooper, but she doesn't know that.

"I know!" She perks up and throws up her hand in excitement.

"What?" I ask her.

"What about Cooper? I mean c'mon he is the definition of attractive! I could definitely see you guys together! Oh my, you guys would make beautiful children!" She says, making me go wide-eyed at her.

"Woah, hold your horses.. I couldn't date Cooper. My dad tells me he's nothing but trouble, and he flirts with Avery all the time!" I say like it's a big deal, even though I know all the truth behind it.

"Yeah, I guess you're right, but you guys still would make beautiful babies. I would proudly get to call them my God-children." She confidently says and I shake my head as she lays back down.

"Let's talk about you and Beau's babies, beautiful dirty-blonde hair and bright blue eyes?!" I say, trying to change the subject.

"Yeah, ours would kick your baby's ass!" She says, yup, she's back.

THE SUN AGAINST MY skin felt amazing, the warmth sent happy signals to my brain. I think I've been tanning about three hours, making sure to evenly turn onto my back and then on my stomach. I was confident that I was going to get some tan from today, and that alone made me happy. Laying on this floatie gave me a lot of time to think about things, mostly the reasons why I love summer: Sun, warm temperatures, lots of trail rides, rodeos, swimming, fairs, shorts and tanks, and lots of the outdoors. "Kota! You're phone is ringing!" Taylor's voice shakes me out of my happy thoughts.

I slide off the floatie and then quickly climb the pool ladder and then walk over to the small picnic table where my phone is indeed ringing. I pick it up and put it under some shade to be able to tell who it was, Cooper. "Hey." I answered the phone.

"Hey girly, what ya up to?" He said making me bite my lip, trying to contain a smile. I side eye Taylor and she's laying back on the floatie, but I decide to walk a distance just to be safe.

"I'm at Taylor's, what's up?" I ask him, crossing my one arm under my arm holding my phone.

"Well I just got off work, and I'm missing you a bit." He said and I already felt the butterflies in my stomach.

"A bit, huh?" I ask him, letting out a chuckle.

"Okay, maybe more than just a bit. But if you're at Taylor's we can just hang out later." He says, but I can tell in his voice that he doesn't mean it fully.

"No, I've been here most of the day. Give me a half an hour and I'll be there, okay?" I tell him, making my way back to the pool area.

"Great, by sweet thang." He said making me giggle.

"Bye, Coop." I say and then I hang up and walk over to the pool. "That was my mom, I gotta get home for supper." I say to Taylor as I put on my clothes and I watch her nod.

"Okay, well thanks for spending the day with me and letting me talk your ear off about Beau." She says and I laugh.

"No problem, thanks for letting me come over! Tell your parents hi from me, and I'll see you tomorrow!" I yell as I walk away from her and to my truck in their driveway.

Once I get into the truck, I hurry up and buckle, and then put 'er in reverse and then get the hell out of the drive way, because I needed to get home and take a shower and leave before my parents got home. So I didn't have to make up an excuse for leaving Taylor's and then going back to her house for supper. So I was going about 65 on the dirt road, while the speed limit is only 45, no cops around here though.

I finally got to my house and to my luck, there was no one home, just the dogs laying on the couch in the nice-air-conditioned house. They were the most energetic, but laziest dogs I know. I stopped from my hustling and gave each dog a nice scratch behind the ears, and then hustled to my bathroom. I quickly ripped off my clothes and hung up my swimsuit and them stepped into the shower, without turning music on, and that meant business.

I had showered, brushed my teeth, combed my hair, and put on mascara in 15 minuets, to say the least, I was proud of myself. Now came deciding what to wear.. I walked to my closet and pulled out jean shorts and loose dark gray Army tee. I grabbed my Holy Cow Couture Santa Fe moccasins and slipped them onto my feet and then put on perfume and deodorant and headed for my truck.

I slowed down when I pulled into Cooper's drive and I started to look around for him when I drove to where I usually parked. And as on cue my boy walked out of the barn, both us smile at each other. I turned off my truck and then I turned to grab my phone from the passenger seat, as well as opening the door. When I turned to jump out of the truck, Cooper was standing in front me already. "Hi boyfriend." I smiled like a fool.

"I like when you say that." He smirked and then pulled me out of my truck and up in his arms, my feet not touching the ground, and I wrapped my arms around his neck. He planted a sweet kiss on my cheek and then put me down, leaving an arm around my shoulder. "You eaten?" He asked me as we stepped onto his porch steps.

"I'm starving." I say to him as he opens the door for me to enter into his cozy home.

"Good, I made lots." He said and then I raised my eyebrows at him, "Okay fine I didn't, but I gotta bag of 100 pizza rolls that can be ready in 15 minuets." He said and I laughed as we separated as he went to the fridge.

"I can make something, too." I say to him, sitting down at the table, putting my left calf under my right thigh.

"Nah, I don't want ya to do worry 'bout it." He said, still looking for food.

"Let me cook for you!" I whined and his head popped up and raised his eyebrows, "Please! It'll be fun! Plus, I'm a great cook!" I said and put my hands together and begged him.

"Okay, but only 'cause you're so dang cute." He smirked, making me blush. I mentally threw up my hands in victory, but kept cool on the outside.

"Okay, let's see what ya got." I said as he stepped aside for me as I entered their regular sized kitchen and open their fridge and pantry, searching for ingredients to combine together.

I LOOKED AT COOPER from across the table and he looked exhausted, not from lack of sleep, from eating so darn much of my hamburger hot dish, and fruit and vegetables. I had to say, my hot dish was quite delicious and I was full myself, but Cooper ate most of it. "Did you even eat today?" I asked him as I took his dish from him and carried it to the dish washer and loaded it in there.

"Yeah, I had eggs and bacon in the morning, but I only had one PB&J at lunch." He said with a yawn at the end of his sentence, and then he ran his hands through his hair, now looking tired from lack of sleep. "What ya wanna do now?" Cooper asked me as I returned to the table and stood in front of him.

"Don't matter to me." I shrugged and then he stood up and he grabbed my hand and turned around and pulled me with him. "Where are we going?" I asked him, then I realized we were going towards the stairs.

"My lair." He says in a evil-but-cute voice making me laugh as we quickly glide up the stairs and then his room.

Cooper's room was very much like him, charcoal gray walls with red rustic decor, cowboy figures, all of his buckles hanging in a display case, pictures of Reese and his mom, but only one picture of him. His bed was my favorite item of the room, it was seriously the most comfortable bed I had ever slept in, and his comforters were so warm and cuddly!

As I walked over to his bed, something caught my eye, a new picture frame on his night stand. I was awe-struck when I saw the picture was of me and him. Cooper took the picture while I was on his back, with my arms wrapped around his shoulders and smiling. Cooper had a crooked smile, that fit him perfectly. I picked up the frame and ran my finger across the precious picture, and then I looked up at Cooper who looked nervous/scared. "When did you do this?" I asked him in a soft tone. The frame to me meant that Cooper really cared about our relationship, it made me fall deeper for him just like that.

"Right after we took that picture." He said and then came in front of me. "It's not weird is it?" He asked, as if scared of my reaction.

"No, Cooper. I love it." I smile at him and then he cracks a smile at me. "Thank you." I say and then I lean up and plant a kiss on his soft lips. Cooper wraps his right arm around my waist, bringing me closer, and I take my left hand and put it right under where his hair stops.

After a long couple of moments, I pull back and then a though erupts in my mind, "Where's Reese?" I ask him and then he perks up an eyebrow and laughs, making me confused.

"That's what you though after we kissed?" He said and then lays down on his bed and then lifts the covers, inviting me in.

I carefully put the frame back where it was and then I lay next to Cooper, putting my head on his chest and tangling our legs together, and wrapping my left arm around his stomach, my favorite position. "He's at my aunts house in Billings." He sighed and I nodded against him. Laying with Cooper was so warm and relaxing, but yet intimate, I loved it. I felt safe in his arms.

COOPER

"DID YOU EVEN EAT TODAY?" DaKota's soft voice wakes me out of my food coma. Seriously, I am having a bad case of food brain. She just made me the best hot dish I had ever had, but I wouldn't tell my grandma that. I looked up at my beautiful girl, she barely wore any makeup, which she didn't even need. Her hair was natural, pieces curly waves framed her face, and her hazel eyes seem to pop out even more wearing that loose gray shirt. Every time I looked at her I felt like my heart skipped a beat.

"Yeah, I had eggs and bacon in the morning, but I only had one PB&J at lunch." I yawned, answering her. "What ya wanna do now?" I asked her as I looked up to her as she stood in front of me.

"Don't matter to me." She says, making me stand up and grab her hand. "Where are we going?"

"My lair." I say in a fictional voice, enjoying her laugh after I say it. She was the cutest person ever.

When we walk into my room I saw her evaluating it, like she wanted to memorize it. I just let her do her thing, because I could watch her all day. After she was done looking around she found the picture I set up next to my side of the bed, I started to become nervous. She picked it up and blushed and smiled romantically, seeing her smile made me smile. "When did you do this?" She sounded shocked, but in a happy way.

"Right after we took that picture." I told her, "It's not weird is it?" I asked her, maybe it was going to fast for her, but I knew it wasn't for me.

"No, Cooper. I love it." She widens her smile and then I feel my heart beat decline. "Thank you." She then leans up and puts her lips against mine. I immediately wrap my arm around her and bring her closer to me, and then her hand goes to the back of my head, her fingers in my hair, it felt so good.

She pulled back after a while and then asked, "Where's Reese?"

I was stunned that she asked me that, "That's what you though after we kissed?" I joke with her and then lay in my bed, inviting her to join me.

She puts the frame back in it's place, and then comes under the covers and automatically puts her head on my chest and arm around me, she was so cuddly! "He's at my aunts house in Billings." I sigh, closing my eyes and then I feel her nod against me. If someone asked me what I wanted to do for the rest of my life, it'd be this: Kota lying right next to me, the sound of the wind through the window, soft music in the back round, and knowing that she was safe with me, it's perfect.

I FELT POKING ON MY shoulder as I was sleeping. I just murmured, "Kota stop." and furred my eyebrows and buried my left check on top of her head, getting closer. I didn't want to wake up, it was too soon.

"I will not stop until you explain to me what this is." My eyes shot open when my brain recognized what voice that was, my mother's. I cranked my head towards her and she was standing almost above me with her arms crossed, reading for an explanation. I mentally cursed as I threw back my head. "Don't look so scared, I'm just mad you didn't tell me sooner!" Her expression softened and shocked me a bit.

I looked down at DaKota and she was still sleeping, her head still on my chest. If she were a princess, she would be Sleeping Beauty. I used my left arm to shake her shoulder and she moved a bit, but moved closer to me. "Wake up girly." I softly say to her and then she opens one eye and in a moment she sees my mom and then she moves and sits up and looks at me.

"It's okay dear, I've been waiting for this day for a long time. I'm just glad you guys have your clothes on. I'm just kidding! I'm so glad you are with him, now maybe he will learn some manners! Maybe if you could teach him-"

"Mom..." I drag out and she laughs and throws up her hands.

"Okay, I get the hint. I'll see you soon, okay Kota?" She says as she walks to me door. DaKota just shyly smiles and nods at her and then my mom closes the door.

DaKota whips her head at me, and she gives me the are-you-serious-we-just-got-caught look. I smile at her and then she says, "What the hell Cooper!"

"Whoops." I start laughing. When I look back she looks confused and pissed at the same time, so I take my right hand and bring her cheeks to face mine and then I kiss her. I'd hope the kiss would tell her not to worry and that everything would be okay.

"You can trust my mom, she won't tell anyone. I'll talk to her after you leave, trust me." I say and then plant a kiss on her nose.

"Okay, I should probably get going." She sighs and then moves from underneath the covers and off my bed.

"Just a bit longer! Pleeaasssee!" I pout my lips and she looks hesitant, and then a small smile forms on her lips.

"Fine, but only if we watch Friends." She pointed her finger and I nodded and then she returned her to her spot and I grabbed the remote and turned on my TV and then went to Netflix. I loved watching Friends with her, because it was a funny show, and laughing with her was the best thing ever.

As we rolled into town, I rolled down the window and began looking around the great town of Helena. Helena was one of my favorite places to compete, it had a great atmosphere and the set up was amazing. Plus, I've won every time I've entered here, knock on wood though. Also I got to see my friends from the Eastern part of the state, I was really excited to be here.

Every one in the family is here, dad, mom, Caleb, Ashley, and our corgi-blue heeler mix, Jade. We always brought Jade with us, it was good entertainment when there was nothing to do. Jade may be small, but she is one of the best cattle dog there is, also she is really cute! Our other two dogs are at Taylor's house, where her parents are watching them because Taylor is also coming down with Beau.

We all gaped at the huge Cathedral, we've all seen it before, but it seemed each time we all noticed something different about it. Like this time, I noticed how the mountains reflected off the glass of the huge windows, it was amazing. "Hurry up, we're behind schedule!" My mom said to my dad and I scrunched my eyebrows in confusion.

"We're just fine, stop you're worryin'." He says back to her and she just roll her eyes and looks back at the window. My mom always said that kind of stuff, but he was always so laid back, I guess that's how most guys are.

"What schedule?" I asked them, peaking my head around my mom's seat.

"We're having a cookout for anyone who wants to join, we've invited the usual people we hang around and told them to spread the word." My mom says, turning her head to look at me through her peripheral vision.

"Okay, sounds fun. What ya cookin' dad?" I ask him.

"Your brother and I are making hot dogs, burgers, and pork chops." He really emphasized the part about Caleb, and then Caleb groaned.

"Why do I have to help? I'm sure other guys will be more than willing to help you out!" I always loved to listen to Caleb talk because he sounded like he had a Canadian accent, with a couple of long 'o's.

"Because the Jones' are hosting it, so the Jones cook. And you will not talk to me like that, young man." My dad says, his tone of voice tells all of us that it's the end of discussion and no one dares to speak of anything until we get to the grounds.

So that's what we did, no one spoke, you could only hear Jade panting and the sounds of vehicles we passed. But now, my dad was backing up the trailer into a spot and I couldn't wait to get out of this crowded truck and stretch my legs and walk around.

I TUCKED MY PHONE IN my back pocket of my Miss Me jeans as I looked around the grounds. I was looking for a black and red goose neck trailer, with some odd detailing on the side of it. Why was I looking for this trailer? Well to answer, I was looking for my boyfriend. Cooper told me to meet him there when I got here.

My eyes finally landed on the trailer, and then I saw Cooper brushing his horse, what a beautiful sight to see. A smile crept on my face when I saw him and I couldn't wait to talk to him. But I was stopped when I heard my name being screamed, "DAKOTA!!" I stopped walking and I turned around and saw my old friend Dallas running towards me. Dallas had beautiful long black hair, and she always curled it, she was a rodeo queen. She also had a pair of blue and green eyes, that showed off her dark skin. People said we looked like sisters, I could see it, but she had a more rounder face than I did.

Before I could say my hello, she jumped on me and gave me a big ol' hug. I tightly wrapped my arms around her, balancing myself from her explosiveness. "Hey girl." I laughed as we let each other girl.

"I didn't know you were competing today!" She said stepping in front of me, blocking my vision of Cooper. But I leaned on my right leg, so I could see him and I saw him looking at us.

"I always compete here." I chuckled and she gave me a confused look.

"You haven't for the last two years, where ya been?" She playfully shoved my shoulder.

"Oh yeah I forgot," I cocked my head and started to think of an excuse, "I was focusing on school for a bit, you know me." I laughed off.

"You and your schoolin'. I heard you guys are having a BBQ tonight, I am invited?" She said, and while she was talking I was looking at Cooper, who had his back turned to us.

"Well of course, we have a lot to catch up on." I said to her and smiled more.

"Where were you headin' just now?" She asked me and then looked behind her.

"I was just walking around, hoping to get some me time before every one and their brother comes over." I said to her, even though the cook out was starting soon.

"Well I hope I didn't interrupt." She kindly said and I heard the sincerness in her voice.

"Oh no you didn't." I replied back to her, kind of getting antsy now.

"Well good! I just saw a bunch of cowboys heading towards your trailer, you single?!" She asked me. I didn't want to lie to her, but she has been know to let stuff slip out to my mom before.

"Yes ma'am, but I think I'm gonna walk a bit more. We're where we usually are, you can't miss it." I said to her, feeling bad I was skipping out on her. "But when I get there, I'm all yours." I offered her a smile, trying to let her know I was truly sorry.

"Don't sweat it, more boys for me!" She stuck out her tongue at me and slapped my butt as she walked past me. I laughed at her and then started walking towards Cooper, who was no longer beside his horse.

As I reached his trailer, I made sure no was looking at me or around this area. "Cooper?" I said aloud.

"In here." His drawl said towards the back of the trailer. I ran my fingers across the trailer until I reached the back, and saw him sitting down in the middle of the stall. "Close the gate." He said and I reached back and closed the door, making it a little darker in the trailer.

When I turned back around, I ran into a chest, and then felt arms being wrapped around my waist. I saw him start to lean in but I pulled my head back and laughed, "Don't I get a 'hi' first?"

"Hi." He said quickly and then planted a wet one on me, making me relax in his arms. I put my hands on his chest, enjoying our proximity. I was the one to pull back, making him loosen his grip on me. "Who was that?" He asked me.

"My friend Dallas, we always see each other at this rodeo." I say and he drops his arms from my waist and takes a step back.

"Did you wanna go finish your conversation?" He asked me as he put his back against the trailer, and I turned to face him.

"No, we'll catch up later. This is probably the only time we're gonna be alone." I say to him and nods.

"You guys are having a BBQ?" He asked me and I nodded. "Why am I not shocked that I wasn't invited?" He muttered in a sad voice, making me feel sorry for him.

"There really isn't an invitation, more of just a 'hey did you hear..' type of thing. We always have one here." I said to him and then he finally looked at me.

"Not last year, and come to think of it, I don't think they had it the year before." Cooper said and I scrunched my eyebrows in confusion. "Maybe they didn't, because they didn't feel right without you there." Cooper added, seeing my expression.

Why did that anger me? Maybe because they stopped doing what they enjoyed because of my situation. I hated when people stopped doing something because of me. "Is it weird that I hate that they did that? Lately they have been driving me crazy! My brother is rebelling against my dad, causing them to fight. And Caleb does his chores poorly just to piss my dad off, so I have to fix them. Like my chores aren't as hard as his! My dad is treating me like a fragile little girl, and is keeping me on a tight leash. Plus, he doesn't like you and then he can't stand your family name. The biggest problem is that him and me are too much a like, so we get into arguments. And my mom my mom just stands there and watches! Doesn't defend her children when they are obviously right, ugh! And I just spent five hours with them in one vehicle, I'm all out of patience!" I complained to Cooper, feeling good to get off my chest.

"Can I tell you something?" Cooper asked, totally avoiding my rant. I looked up and Cooper was off the wall and a few feet in front of me. He had a smirk on face, one that said I-shouldn't-be-laughing-but-I-find-it-humorous.

"What?" I crossed my arms because I don't think I'm gonna like his answer.

Cooper's height towered over mine, making me look up to him. His hands raised and uncrossed my arms and held each hand in his warm and comforting hands, and he ran his thumb across the top of my hand. "You're really cute when you rant."

I rolled my eyes at him and I started to back away from him, but our hands were still connected and his strong arms pulled me back into him. "Whatever, you're just saying that." I say and looked at the ground, to hide my blushing.

"I'm serious, Kota." He laughed, and bending down to get to my eye-level. "It's cute because you never do it. You're always so humble and quiet, it's fun to see you talk and talk, I love it." He said and I couldn't help but smile at him.

"I'm serious, Cooper. They drive me insane!" I started to laugh because I realized he was right. I rarely complained like that, especially to him. I finally looked up at him, because he went back to his normal height.

"I know they do, hun. But they're your family, and you know you don't know what you'd do without them. Right now Caleb is just going through   that I'm-going-to-be-a-married-man-so-I'm-gonna-start-acting-like-it   stage, challenging your dad because he's old enough to do things on his own now. You're like your mom, humble and likes to stay out of drama. And your dad, well he's just an asshole." He laughed at the last part, and I couldn't help but agree with him. But what Cooper said made sense to me and I really appreciated he actually cared to help.

"You're right, this isn't unusual for my family. Enough about me! What's up with you?" I gave him a soft smile, and quickly glancing at his soft lips, then back to his captivating eyes.

"I don't wanna talk about me." He said, and he caught me looking at his lips. "Right now, I just wanna kiss my girl." He slowly leaned down, and I stood on my tip-toes to reach his lips quicker. He placed his hands on both sides of my face, his touch sending warm sparks through out my body. I reached for his tee shirt and clutched the fabric in my hands and pulled him closer to me, making my body go against the trailer wall.

The kiss wasn't slow, but it wasn't aggressive either. It was, in simple words, perfect. Cooper definitely knew how to kiss a girl and make her feel like the girl in the world. Yup, it was that good.

Cooper's lips left mine, and softly placed little kisses beside my lips and on my jaw line, and then returned to my lips. This time, the kiss began to slow, and then I pulled away from him. Neither of us spoke, just looked at each other. Cooper's soft pink lips were now a darker shade of red and more plump, and he looked amazed. I only wonder how I looked. "We should probably get back to the cook out.." I said softly, and looked toward the trailer door. I looked back at Cooper and caught him looking at my lips, but then he returned to my eyes. "I'll go one way and you'll go the other?" I say to him and his facial expression softens and he sadly nods.

I go and push the trailer back open, exposing the setting sun and the warm wind. I was about to step out of the trailer, but my arm was yanked back and my body thrown into Cooper's. "One more." He said in cute-seductive voice, making me smile and then we quickly kissed. "It's gonna be hard to resist doing that tonight." He said as we both stepped out of the trailer, and we looked around for wandering eyes.

"Just try not to look at me." I shrug and he chuckles.

"That's hard, too." I roll my eyes at him.

"Well then I guess, we'll both be screwed. We'll both agree to stay a safe distance from each other." I say as I start to walk away from him, going in the opposite direction.

"No promises." He smirked and then he winked and turned his back to me and started walking back to my trailer. I couldn't help but stare at him, I mean he's just.. Cooper.

My Cooper

"I ROPED HIM FASTER than a speeding ticket and you know it!" I laughed at my brother as I put down my rope as I sat down in a lawn chair next to my mom. I reached down with my left hand and pulled out a Gatorade from the cooler and took a sip of the refreshing drink.

"Dude, just admit your sister beat you." Rusty said as he sat down on the chair on the other side of my mother, "Mrs. Jones, how are ya?" He said and tipped his cowboy hat at her.

"Well, and yourself?" She asked with a polite nod.

"Well not as bad as your son here." Rusty cracks out a laugh, and I looked at Caleb and Caleb gave Rusty a death glare.

"You, me, again." Caleb suddenly turned his attention to me, giving me a stern finger point and looking angrier than a bull.

I scoff and laugh at him, "Caleb, sort yourself out. That is the only time I have beaten you, go get a beer and calm down." I say to him and throw him a beer and he only pops the can and stomps away.

"So Rusty, how was your food?" My mom sweetly to Rusty and he puts down his beer.

"Just how I like it, ma'am. Where is that husband of yours?" As he said that, I looked around for my dad. When it came to rodeos, my dad was a very social man, every one knows him around him. I wouldn't be surprised if he was at a completely different trailer on the other side of the grounds.

"Last I saw him he was talking to Cooper." I think I got whiplash when my mom said this. My heart began to race and questions filled my head, why would he talk to Cooper?

"Why was he talking to-" I whispered to my mom, but I was cut of by a very excited Rusty.

"Stetson Aimes!!" My heart skipped a beat when Rusty announced the name. Kill me now. My eyes slowly traveled from my mom, the grass, the boots, and then the face of Stetson.

CHAPTER 4

Stetson Aimes and I were very complicated. Key word: were. I haven't seen him since the last time I was at this rodeo, and that was a very long time ago. We met at a rodeo when we were 14 and were on the same circuit, so we saw each other a lot. He liked me and I sorta liked him. Looking back, I know now that I liked his good looks and his charm, and to be honest he doesn't have much of a personality. As we got older and went to bigger rodeos, I saw him flirting with a lot of other girls, but he claimed that he was only talked to me. Being naive back then, I believed him.

"DaKota." He said with his famous smirk, and with a greeting nod.

"Stetson." I tried to say with a polite voice. "If you'll excuse me, I'm going to find Dallas." I say, mostly to my mom as I stand up from my lawn chair. As I walked past Stetson, we both glanced at each other, he still had that stupid smirk on his face, it took everything not to roll my eyes at him.

I walked pass small groups of people and greeted them as they greeted me. I found Dallas and my other friend Lauren standing by Lauren's trailer. They both saw me at the same time and both gave me kind smiles. "Hey Laur." I smiled and hugged her and she returned the hug. "You won't believe who I just saw." I say in a monotone voice.

"Who?" Dallas said eagerly, she loved drama like this.

"Stetson Aimes." I say like it was some type of miracle, and both of their jaws dropped.

"Did he say anything?" Lauren asked me and I shook my head.

"I got the hell out of there before he could, Rusty was there so that helped." I shrugged. "But if I must say, he still looks good. But remember how awful we were?" I laughed at myself.

"Amen to that." Lauren said and I laughed at her.

"You know who else looks good?" Dallas said and I saw her looking at something other than Lauren or me, but I didn't look.

"Who?" I asked her.

"Cooper Blackwood, that boy is one fine piece of cowboy." I looked into her eyes and followed where she was looking, and there he was walking in our direction, but not coming towards us. Him and I locked eyes, he gave me a small smile, nothing too obvious. We held eye contact until we couldn't anymore. "Did he just smile at you?!" Dallas said in disbelief.

I had to contain my smile, "We're friends, he's a pretty cool guy." I say to them and they both laugh.

"Have you guys kissed?" Lauren asked me.

"No!" I exclaimed and they both looked at each other suspiciously.

"Oh c'mon! A boy doesn't give you that kind of smile because you guys are just friends!" Dallas said and put air quotations when said 'just friends'.

"I swear on my grave!" I playfully shoved Dallas, "But seriously, remember how bad Stetson and I were?"

"Looks like he wants to remember again, Stetson 6 o'clock." She said in a lower voice and dipped her head to hide her voice. Ugh, I just want a peaceful night!

"Ladies." His deep voice said behind me and Lauren and Dallas both picked up their heads and greeted Stetson. I still hadn't turned around to look at him, "DaKota, can we take a walk?" He said hesitant, and I slowly turned around.

"Sure, I'll see you guys tomorrow?" I said to them as I took a step towards Stetson.

"Yeah, bye." They said with a hint of humor in their voice and I rolled my eyes.

Stetson and I stopped at a trailer, which I assumed was his, and my back was facing the trailer door. I stood in front of him and I saw him look me up and down, yup, still hasn't changed. "What do you need Stetson?" I asked him and crossed my arms.

"Why do you think I need something?" He asked with a boyish smirk, making me glare at him.

"Because you always do." I return to him and he chuckles.

"I just wanted to talk to you." He said taking a step toward me, making me take a step back, and hitting the trailer. "I've missed seeing your pretty face around here." He said and closed the distance between us, putting his forearm above my head, making me look up at him. I only allowed this, because I didn't want to make a scene.

"Ya, well I've been busy." I said plainly, not up for his games.

"I heard that you ran away with that Jeffery kid." He said, his face in confusion and I began to laugh. He couldn't be serious, who would tell him that?

"No, I was visiting my cousins in North Dakota. Who told you that?" I continued to laugh.

"Avery did." He said like Avery was a very reliable person to talk to. This made me laugh even harder.

"No shit." I laughed, "There's no way I did that."

"Seriously, I missed you." He said and then he looked at my lips, then back to my eyes.

"Oh really? What did you miss about me?" I questioned him. I didn't mean it come out flirty, I made sure my voice sounded uninterested.

"Everything, you're different from all the other girls." He said and then he placed his hand on my upper leg, close to my hip. But my heart stopped when he did it, because it was right on my scar. I immediately pushed his hand off my leg, my heart was starting to beat faster and faster, as the flashbacks filled my mind.

"I'm sure you would know about every girl, and don't touch me." I said in an angry voice, but the last part came out fragile. I don't know how many time I had said that line in the last two years.

I don't know why I stayed where I did, maybe I was in shock from all the flashbacks, but I just stood there. "Oh c'mon." He chuckled and put his damn hand back on my leg, and this time I couldn't move. I felt paralyzed under his touch. I looked to where his hand was and the flashback of when the scar originated came and consumed me.

"I'm not kidding Stetson, p-please take your hand o-off me.." My voice was very shaky, and almost unrecognizable.

Then Stetson's other hand found my waist and pulled me closer to him, making sure that hand on my scar tightened and ran up and down. "What's the matter, Kota? I miss the time we used to spend with each other, please let me-"

"She said no." A deeper voice said from behind us and I knew it was Cooper, but I was too in shock to move away from him.. I should of became calm that Cooper was here, but that flashback is still playing over and over.

My scar was beginning to burn under his touch, and I still couldn't move. "She's just being stubborn, why don't you go somewhere else, bud." Stetson said to Cooper and then grabbed onto my arms and pulled me to the side of him, because I began to stumble backwards.

"Why don't you let go of her and I'll leave ya alone." I think Cooper said, but everything was starting to get hazy.

"Is that a threat, because I know you have a history of fighting. You and that daddy of yours are sure some tag team." Stetson finally let go of me, but I stood in place.

"You don't know when to quit do ya? First off, don't ever touch a girl when she don't wanna be touched. Second, don't ever talk about my family." Cooper's voice became angrier, and stepped towards Stetson.

"I'll save you the trouble." Stetson said and threw a punch at Cooper, but Cooper easily dodged it and shoved him. "Oh c'mon, daddy would be disappointed!" Stetson said and flicked Cooper in the head.

I tried to focus on Cooper and Stetson, but the image of Wade consumed me. Wade holding a knife. The knife in my skin. The burning of the skin. The bloody knife being waved in front of him. My screams and protests. Wade's moans and groans. Wade's laughter. It all became too much for me when I saw Cooper punch Stetson in the face, and then I felt myself fall to the ground and pass out..

I WOKE UP WITH A POUNDING headache while Dallas, Lauren, and my mother stood above me, all with panicked looks on their faces. They all looked relieved though when I opened both eyes. My mom started to speak but I turned my attention to the groans and yelling of men. I turned my head to see Cooper being pulled off Stetson's body, Cooper with a bloody nose and eyebrow, but Stetson was worse. Stetson also had a bloody nose and eyebrow, but had a bloody lip, and cuts and scrapes all over his face. "Help me up." I said, ignoring whatever they said to me.

Rusty and Caleb were holding Cooper and Stetson was held by his friends, "Why am I being punished! He's the one who doesn't know how to respect a woman, he had it coming for him. Where is she?" Cooper said frantically and his eyes landed on mine, and I saw him relax.

I was still in shock, but this time it was because of the fight. It just looked horrible, and I felt, angry. Angry at Cooper for doing it. Why did it always come down to fighting for him? Why couldn't he just walk away?

I felt myself moving, because my mom was guiding me to our trailer, avoiding the fighting scene, where the two boys were still raging. As I stepped onto the trailer steps, I stopped and looked at Cooper, who was free of Rusty and Caleb's hold. I made sure to send him a message that I didn't agree with his method, and he looked hurt, really hurt. I was disappointed. Everything was going great, and he had to go mess it up again.

I stirred on the couch, trying to find the right position to fall asleep. Oh who was I kidding, it wasn't the discomfort that was keeping me awake, it was Cooper. After everything that happened, he tried calling me half an hour later, but I ignored it. Cooper texted me, and I replied back to him that I needed some time to think, and he texted me back, I didn't respond, and then he called me again.

Cooper knows that I don't like when he gets into fights, but I'm not saying that to control his life. It's just I don't want him getting into trouble, it just gets him even more pissed off. I know Cooper can resist fighting, he just needs help, and I am going to be the one to help him.

But as I lay here and think about tonight more, I realized the real reason I was like that, is because of Wade. He'd be the one who made me angry. Thinking of what he did to me really got me on edge, and it didn't help that Stetson was making it worse. I don't know what happened to

Stetson after, but I'm sure he ran off to get "comforted" by the first girl he saw.

I threw the covers off me and I sat up on the couch, I needed to go talk to Cooper and apologize. I looked at the time, 12:13, maybe he was still up. I grabbed my sweatshirt off the coat rack and pulled it over my head, and slipped on my moccasins and quietly went outside and headed for Cooper's trailer.

When I got closer, I saw a tiny light on in his trailer, he was still up. Maybe he had the same problem as me. I played with the hems of my arm sleeves and walked up to the door of the trailer, and then I knocked on the door. As I was waiting, I realized it was really cold outside, and I was just wearing a sports bra under my loose sweatshirt, and wearing running shorts. The door finally opened and Cooper looked very confused until he saw it was me.

Neither of us said anything, just stared at each other, "Come in, it's cold out here." He spoke first and grabbed my hand and pulled me in. Cooper switched on a light, and then I saw his face clearly, he had a tiny scrap above his eye and there was still some blood on his nose and looked a little bruised.

"You missed some blood." I said to him and he gave me an are-we-really-doing-this look. He just looked at me, so I got up and grabbed a wash cloth, ran some cold water on it, and then turned to him. He relaxed his shoulders once he realized I wasn't so pissed not to help him. I took a couple of steps to him, reached up and gently cleaned the blood off his face.

"I'm sorry." He said after I pulled down my hand, so we were still close. "But that jackass deserved it. I saw him talking to you and how he was so close to you, and I was mad but I calmed myself down. But when I saw him put his hand on your hip, I knew it made you feel uncomfortable, so it made me uncomfortable. When he didn't accept no, that's when the anger set in. I saw the look on your face and that's when I walked up to him and said something. But he was the one the throw the first punch. I just saw-" I cut him off with a hug, my head was turned against his chest, and I wrapped my arms around his mid-back. He was quick to hug me back, he even let out a sigh of relief. "Are you okay?" He asked me and I pulled away.

"Yeah, it's just that when he kept touching me on my scar, flashbacks of Wade took over. I blacked out because it was just too much for me." I said as I climbed the stairs to his bed and lied there until he came up with me. We laid next to each other, turning our heads took look at each other. "I have to apologize too. I think the main reason I was mad is because of Wade. It makes me angry because he's gone and he still has control of me, I'm sick of it."

"I'm sorry, is there any way I can help?" He asks.

"I just don't wanna talk about it.." I sigh and then he nods. "Can I ask you a question?" He just 'mhm's to me. "Is there any way you can stop your need to fight?"

"I don't feel the need to fight, Kota.." He sighed and turned his head and looked up at the ceiling. I still looked at Cooper, and I started to admire his features. I wonder what his dad looks like, was he just as handsome as Cooper? "I just don't like it when people disrespect someone or me.."

"So it's more of a pride thing?" I asked him, he still hadn't turned his head to look at me.

"I guess you could say that. It's just I grew up around that stuff, I saw my dad do it all the time. I know it's not right, but I guess I do it because I'm not good with words. I'd rather use my fists to make my point, rather than try to talk it out." He said, and I could tell in his voice that he was getting frustrated and some what disappointed with himself.

"Well a lot of guys think that, but I could see how your background influences you more than others. You know what I think?" I asked him and my question got him to turn his head back to meet my eyes. "I think you just need something to keep you from getting the urge to punch."

"How so?" He scrunched his eyebrows at me.

"Oh I don't know," I turned my head this time, "When you wanna punch someone, you just gotta think of what could calm you down." I sighed and the silence between us told me that we were both thinking. "Like a happy place."

"I can't think of anything." He said and I saw him look at me.

"Well what is the one thing that makes you forget about everything else going on?" I said to him, while I was still thinking.

"You." He said and then I turned my head to meet his eyes. His eyes were serious, but also displayed a pretty light brown color that spelled out 'love'. Hearing him say that made the butterflies go off in my stomach, I couldn't help but be happy. We didn't look away from each other, the moment was too perfect to spoil with words. "You're the one that makes me feel that everything will be okay. Just the thought of you, Kota, strengthens me." He said then ran his finger over my arm, just for second but it meant everything.

"Okay, so what do you like doing with me the most?" I asked him in a whisper, because quite frankly, he took my breath away.

I followed his eyes down my hand at my side, and then his thumb traced the back of my hand and then stopped. "I like when you hold my hand," I returned stroking the back of his hand and then I intertwined our fingers together, both our gazes looked at our hands. "Holding your small hand in mine symbolizes that we're a couple, and no one else matters but us. I like feeling your enticing soft hand against my calloused hand. Holding your hand is holding a small part of you, and to me, that is the only thing that matters." I realized I was still looking at our hands, so I looked back up to Cooper, who was already looking at me with those loving eyes. Right now I was feeling that feeling you get when you want to cry, but there's no tears in your eyes.

I rolled over so my chest was against his side and I put my left hand on the other side of him and I didn't waste any time to kiss him. His right hand tucked a piece of loose hair behind my hair, the warm touch of his finger gliding against my skin made me melt inside. Then he cupped my face with that free hand. This kiss was just, wow. Very romantic and passionate. I gave his hand a squeeze and then I pulled back from our sweet kiss. "You were wrong." I said to him and he gave me a confused look.

"About what?" He asked me and I smiled at him.

"You're very good at words." A laugh escapes my lips, but then I become serious as I lied down beside him again, but closer to him this time. "That means a lot, Coop. Thank you." I say and lean my head against his shoulder, and rub my thumb across his hand.

"I like this." He said after a while of silence. His voice was quiet, like he didn't want anyone to hear us.

"Like what?" I asked him.

"Talking to you when it's 1 o'clock in the morning, everything seems so simple and it makes it feel like we aren't hiding from everyone."

"Yeah," I mumble as I disconnect our hands and I turn my body and drape my arm across his stomach and put my head in the crook of his neck. His left hand started drawing circles on my back, "Well everyone except for your mom." I chuckle and his chest lets one out too. "But I like being with you, I wish I could do it all the time. But for now, I just wanna go to sleep." I say and finally close my eyes.

"What about your parents, won't they notice you gone in the morning?"

"I've already set my alarm clock for four, they aren't up by then. Good night, Cooper." I say and snuggle into him more.

"Good night, pretty girl." He said and then kissed the top of my forehead.

"C'MON! RUN!" I SAY to Pharaoh as we run home in our run. Once he finishes the run I pull back and turn him to the left and he comes to a slow lope and then we exit the arena, "The time for DaKota and Pharaoh is 16.31! This time puts her in second, and there is only one run left!" I give Pharaoh a nice pat on the neck and a good job. Also a nice pat on the butt, because he enjoys that.

I get off Pharaoh and pulled the reins over his head and immediately loosened his cinch, to let him know he did a good job and let him relax. I pull the reins over his head and begin walking him our trailer. I look down as I walk and I fix my purple cinch shirt, and I admire my Cowgirl Tuff Jeans, my Ariat square toes, and my gold oval belt buckle from a Jackpot in Wyoming. That was most of my outfit, but my hair was down in my natural curls, and I had the classic barrel racer ear-rings in, big silver crosses.

I reached the trailer and tied him to it, and then I took off his sport and bell boots and threw them to the side, and then I removed all of his tack, and then put it in the tack compartment neatly. After that I went up to Pharaoh, who was currently submerging his head into the portable water trough and playing with the water, making me laugh at him. Pharaoh had two sides to him: serious and seriously goofy! I went up to him and felt his skin, to my luck it wasn't hot, so it meant I didn't have to spray him, just brush him.

I grabbed the pick from the grooming box and went to his front leg and bent down and pulled it up, so I was able to pick out his hooves. I did that to the other three legs and then I grabbed the curry comb and starting going over his beautiful coat. "Great run sis." I heard from behind me and I stopped grooming Phar and looked behind me at my brother.

"Thanks Caleb, congrats on the check." I smiled at him and he shrugs at me, making me frown.

"I barely even got a check." He mutters and I roll my eyes at him.

"You still got a check and the other 20 guys didn't, so stop that." I scolded him and returned my attention to my horse.

"How are you the wise one?" He asks me and then I hear him grab the other curry comb and then he goes to Pharaoh's left side and starts combing.

"Because I'm your little sister and it's my job, but I think Ashley's doing a good job of that, don't you think?" I say to him and look at him and he scoffs at me.

"Maybe a little too much."

"Oh shut up Caleb, you know she's always right when it comes to your decision making." I point my finger at him and then I reach down and grab the dandy brush and throw it at him and then grab one for me.

"Oh yeah? What about that one time," He cuts himself off as if thinking about it more, "Yeah nevermind, you're right." He says and then I roll my eyes in an obvious way. "So how ya feeling about last night?"

Last night with Stetson and Cooper or last night in Cooper's bed?

"I'm fine, Cooper came up to me and apologized earlier, even though I wasn't mad at him." I shrug and continue to brush.

"Well I sure as hell wouldn't of apologized, I'd be damned if I didn't do the same thing." Cooper says in a matter-of-fact tone.

"What do you mean?" I ask him.

"Don't take this the wrong way, but in your situation, if I saw someone doing that to you, I'd make sure they couldn't touch anyone like that for the rest of their lives." He says in a very confident tone. "Plus your my little sis, I'm actually a little sad I didn't see the bastard first. But Cooper saved my ass from getting an ass chewing from dad if I got into another fight."

"Yeah, thank God for Cooper." I muttered in a somber tone.

"Can I ask you something?" Caleb asks me in a serious tone, which automatically makes my heart beat faster. Does he know about me and Cooper? Did he realize that Cooper fought Stetson because we're dating? Did he see me get into Cooper's trailer?

"Yeah." I mumble, scared to say anything else.

"Is it true?"

"Is what true?" I ask him in a curious voice, really paying attention to my horse's well-being.

"Is it true Cooper came to our house with flowers and asked dad's permission to take you on a date?" Relief came over me as I realized I didn't have to lie to Caleb.

"Yeah, why?" I asked him and he handed me the dandy brush and then I handed him the soft brush, and got myself one, and continued.

Caleb chuckles and he looks impressed and that he can't believe it, "That takes a lot of balls, especially how much dad has expressed to Cooper that he doesn't like him. It's a shame that it didn't work out."

Too bad I didn't listen..

"Yeah, a shame." I muttered again and took a deep breath and watched the dust fly off my horse's coat.

"Would of you said yes if dad let you?" Caleb asked me and I automatically stopped brushing.

Crappers.

What do I say to that?

205

"I would of sa-"

"Hey DaKota, come with me to get our checks!" A familiar voice said behind us, and I turned around to see my savior, Dallas. She literally saved me from answering the question I didn't know how to answer.

"Thanks bro!" I say to Caleb and then run towards Dallas, leaving my brother to finish up my horse, he probably hates me right now...

"Hey Dall." I greeted her and joined her as we walked to the office to receive our checks.

"Hey girly!" She says in her sweet voice, and she goes on about talking about her run, but all I can think of is how Cooper calls me 'girly' in his sweet and charming voice that I've come to admire, I admire everything about him.

IT WAS A WHOLE BUNCH of us girls sitting in the bleachers just for the competitors, they were pretty good seats, right by the chutes and close up. It was now night time and the last event of the night, bull riding. I looked up around the arena and admired how the big stadium lights illuminated the arena and you could see the moths and other insects flying around.

"And now in the Montana State Bank chute is the hometown guy, Stetson Aimes!!" The crowd cheers for him. I look at Dallas beside me and she rolls her eyes at him, "He will be riding Kaw-Liga!"

The bull jumps out of the chutes and busts to the right and Stetson throws his arm, and looks very in control of the bucking bull, it was a very rank bull, but Stetson was handling it. As much as I hated to see it, he made the ride, and it was good. People cheered, but none of us girls for various reasons. "How about 85 points on the ride!?" People cheered loudly and I rolled my eyes.

"And now, for the last rider of the night in the Grizz Chute we have Cooper Blackwood of hometown Little Rock, Arkansas! And to your luck ladies and gentlemen, we saved the best for last, Cooper will being riding the rankest bull provided by Rinell Bucking Bulls, Your

Mama's Hoss!" People cheered and clapped, while my heart race started to quicken.

I watched intently as Cooper nodded his head and the raging bull exploded out of the chute, jumping maybe four feet in the air, but Cooper stayed balanced. The bull had wicked sharp turns and unexpected jumps, he was truly rank. But Cooper made it look easy, super easy. Cooper threw his arm like a pro, and looked like he was on a practice barrel! The buzzer went off and the bull bucked and Cooper went into the air, but barely landed on his feet, running away from the still-bucking bull.

All of us girls cheered for him, it was one hell of a ride! "I told you folks that we saved the best for last! And I think his score proves that! 87.5 points for the young cowboy! That'll get him a paycheck and a buckle! Great ride Cooper!" I hollered after this, Dallas joining me, making me not feel so embarrassed after I did it.

Dallas and I were walking back to our trailers, talking about Dallas' worst memory of high school. I mostly laughed at her and listened, because she really enjoyed telling stories, so I didn't want to ruin it for her. "Huh-oh, 12 o'clock." Dallas said while ducking her head and I looked up and Stetson was walking straight for us, and soon enough he was a couple of feet in front of us.

I looked up at him and the street lamps barely illuminated his face just enough to see the bruises Cooper caused. I didn't feel one ounce bad for him. "I just wanted to apologize for last night, and I hope that one day you'll look at me the same way you once day. I really am sorry.." He said, and I could tell in his voice he meant it.

"I appreciate it, Stetson.." I shivered, but I looked at him for a bit, and then he walked away from us, leaving us both in shock from his sudden apology.

"Well that was.." Dallas said.

"Awkward." I finished for her and then I looked up again and realized we were at my trailer. "Well I'll see you tomorrow Dallas, good night!" I said to her and she waved, "Night." She smiled too.

I opened the door to my trailer and my mom and dad were already in there, both having a glass of water. "Good job tonight kiddo." My dad says to me, making me smile.

"Up for a game of Uno?" My mom says and I nod at her and then they both sit down at the couch-booth seat and I go to the fridge to grab a bottle of water. As I close the fridge door, I feel a buzz in my back pocket. I pull out my phone and see a text from Cooper, "Meet me at the weird street light." I knew exactly where he was talking about.

I turned to my parents, "Dallas just texted me and asked me to help her find her wallet, do you mind?" I asked and they both shrugged, indicating I could go.

Cooper was leaning against the wooden light, his black cowboy hat shielding his face. People called this the weird street light because it was lop-sided, it was just.. weird. When Cooper heard my boots on the dirt, he looked up and smiled. "Hey." And then he snaked an arm around my waist, took off his hat and kissed me, slightly dipping me, making it extremely romantic.

Cooper let me up and took his arm back to his side. "Good ridin' tonight Cowboy." I smirked at him and he did to.

"Wish I could say the same to you. Second? Really DaKota? I'm disappointed." He says in a serious voice but I know he's joking, but I still shove his shoulder, making him laugh. "Can I tell you something?" He said as his laughter died down, and I nodded for him to go on. "I couldn't stop looking at you today, you look absolutely stunning, like always." When he says the last part he grabs both of my hands and swings them a bit.

As we come in from a swing I lean up and kiss his cheek, "Thank you." After I kiss his cheek, I take a step closer to him. "Can I tell you something?" He nods, "It was pretty hot seeing you ride that bull." I was shocked I said that to him, my cheeks began to furiously blush.

"Really?" I nod in response, "Then you should see me when I'm practicing at home without my shirt on." He smirks and wraps his arms around my back.

"Can't wait." I smirked and then we both started laughing, but in my head I couldn't stop imagining him without a shirt on, being all sweaty, stop it DaKota! You can't wait to go to Church.

Nope, definitely can't wait to see him shirtless.

I watched as people stood up and started to exit their pew, as I continued to sing the closing song. I was singing with some older ladies, they were around my mom's age, so I knew them pretty well. But who didn't I know in this town. I couldn't help but look around one last time, looking for a certain brown-eyed cowboy, but he wasn't here, just his mom in the back. I was sad that Cooper wasn't at church, he used to come, but he didn't today.

I felt bad for his mom sometime, sometimes the other moms would talk harshly about her and her so called "husband". Saying that it was a disgrace that she could marry such a man, who was supposedly the devil. This is before I knew about Cooper's family, or I would of said something to them about it. Because Desiree is a very lovely woman, and one of the nicest people I know in this town.

After the song ended, we closed our books, thanked the lovely pianist and guitar players for doing a good job today, and then we stepped off the little stage near the altar. I said goodbyes to to women in the small choir and then I joined my family who was waiting for me. "Hey." I said as I stood next to Ashley.

"Nice job, and by the way, I love your dress." Ashley said and playfully tugged at my dress, making me smile as I looked down at my dress.

"Thanks."

I don't mean to sound conceited but I thought I looked pretty cute today. Going along with my dress, my hair was straightened with a waterfall braid in on one side, my hair reached down to my tail-bone, and then I was wearing a pair of Holy Cow Couture cream-colored moccasins. Always have to look good when you go to church.

Standing outside with my mom, I look at other groups of people conversing with each other, not really caring what the current group is talking about. I look up at the beaming sun, as it already feels too hot, it's only 11 o'clock! "I bet she hasn't seen her husband in years, if you even call him that." Suddenly this sentence gets through to my brain and

I'm able to process what Mrs. Hewitt said to the other girls. Then I look where she is looking, and I see Desiree talking to Father Matthew.

"I've warned Father about her and her family, I wonder if he's tellin' her to go to confession." She snickers and then some follow her, laughing along. I look back at them, then to my mom, who just stands there quietly, then I look back at them. What Catholic's they are, judging someone without know the whole picture.

"What's so bad about her family?" I question Mrs. Hewitt and the others, my tone is innocent and unharmful.

"Haven't you heard about her husband? Her-"

"But why does marrying her husband make her a bad person? Maybe there's something more to that, maybe she's trying to get out of it, maybe you guys shouldn't be so quick to judge." I cut her off, earning a glare from my mother, but I don't mind her.

Mrs. Hewitt is baffled at my words, and her moth opens, hoping words will come out, but they don't. "Well her son is a prime example of her actions, gettin' in all of those fights." Oh, she did not.

"So Cooper's a bad person for standing up to people who talk the same way you're talking right now? Is that the only thing you know about him? I see the way you judge people in church. I saw you even look at Mrs. May here, and then turn around and stick your finger in your mouth.-"

"DaKota." My mother warns me, but I don't loose eye contact with Mrs. Hewitt as Mrs. May gasps in disbelief.

"If you think that makes her a bad mother, you should check under your son's bed and see all the adult magazines and pot pipes under there." She dramatically gasps at me, and I just smile sweetly at her, "Y'all have a nice day now." I say with the best-prettiest smile I can give them and then I walk away from them, my mother apologizing behind me.

COFFEE POT IN HAND, I laugh at the table full of story-tellin'-cowboys, they sure could make any one's day. I fill each of their cups, giving them a smile and then left to go make other rounds at booths and tables. Sunday's were my favorite, because of church, then the church crowd at the diner, and they are usually my craft days also.

I looked at my family, sitting along the island counter, deciding not to go over to them because I didn't want to get scolded, again. Oh, you betcha I got scolded after the Mrs. Hewitt incident, but I really didn't care, because I knew I was right. "DaKota, come here." I hear my father's voice behind me and I mentally curse and turn around and go towards them.

"Yes?" I ask them going around the counter, putting down the coffee back onto the hot plate.

"We're going to Missoula after this, to go sort out stuff for the wedding, you need anything before we leave?" I smile at this because maybe I could get Cooper to come over for bit, since we haven't had some time together in days.

"No I'm good." I have to bite my lip to keep my smile from growing.

"Why are you smiling?" My brother raises his eyebrow at me. "You're not thinking of having a boy over are you?" He jokes and I roll my eyes, even though it's what I exactly plan to do.

"I'm just excited for the wedding." I play off and they all nod once and then I'm off back running around the diner, helping or serving people.

I rip the order ticket out of the pad and then place it on the order 'merry-go-round' yelling, "Gotta a new one." and then Maybell comes from the kitchen, balancing plates in her hands. "Let me help ya." I say and literally take plates from her hands.

"Thank you honey." She says and then I follow her to her table and give the correct plates to the correct customers. As we turn to leave the table she says, "Cutie at table six." I roll my eyes, but it turns into a smile once I see the cutie she's talking about. I can only see the backside of him, but I knew it was him. He was wearing his National High School rodeo jacket, that jacket looked so good on him.

"Maybell said there was a cutie over here, but I wasn't expecting you." I tease him as I stand in front of the booth. His eyes light up when he sees me and his pink lips turn into a smirk and then he chuckles.

"Well hi to you too. I ran into your parents on the way in, your dad actually said hi to me." He says, surprising me in a way.

"Well that's surprising. So did you just come here to see me, or get food?" I say to him, having a hard time hiding my smile.

"Of course I came here to see you, I missed my girl." His smile could make someone rob a bank and then make them turn themselves in after just because he told them to flashing them his smile.

I lowered my voice a bit, "My parents are leaving for the day, wanna come to my house after you're done eating?" His smile widens at my invitation.

"Only if I get to spend some time with Pocahontas." He says making me laugh. Pocahontas is a crazy-buckskin miniature horse that we have, and she's a real show. Cooper absolutely loves her.

"Okay, what do you want to eat?" I ask him, pulling my note pad out and clicking my pen.

"Chocolate chip pancakes, bacon, and chocolate milk." He says and then hands me his menu.

"Okay, that should be out in about 10 minuets." I start to turn towards the kitchen, but he catches my hand and pulls me close to him, close enough I can smell his cologne. "And for dessert I want a kiss from my girlfriend." He softly whispers in my ear.

I pull away, my cheeks getting red, "That might take a little longer than the pancakes." I say and start to back away from him.

"I'll wait." He calls out to me as I smirk back at him and go into the kitchen.

I looked down at Cooper's plates in my hands, and my smile faded when I looked up and saw someone sitting next to him in the booth. You guessed it, that someone would have to be Miss Avery Johnson, she has some nerve. Cooper looks up and meets my eyes, he looks sorry and has a look that says that he couldn't do anything about it.

She still hasn't noticed me yet, until I forcefully slide the plates down onto the table and then she looks up shocked and she smiles. "Hello DaKota." Oh please. Then I notice how close she actually is to Cooper, her arm pressed against his.

"I'm surprised to see you here." I cross my arms over my chest, letting her know my attitude towards her.

"Oh you mean after you attacked me?" She says and I scoff at her. "I'm not surprised you did though."

"What does that mean?" I noticed Cooper shift uncomfortably.

"I've heard that dogs like to fight." She says with a smug look on her face as she stands up, getting closer to me. "You're just jealous." She says and then I laugh, then I see Cooper stand up, almost in the middle of us.

"I'm jealous? Please tell me why." I laugh again, waiting for her to answer.

"Because every one knows I'm better than you. After you decided to go on a little vacation, this town was all over me, Avery this, Avery that. Not once did anyone mention something about pathetic DaKota." I clenched my fists at my sides, resisting the urge to knock her out.

"Avery that's enough." Cooper's deep voice says and she just smirks.

"Weird, never heard you say that to me before Cooper." She smirks, making my blood boil. Cooper's face turns hard and he doesn't even look at me.

"I think it's time for you to leave." I say to her and she stands in her place.

"You know I'd slap you but I don't want to get whore all over my hand." She smirks like that's the best comeback she's ever had, bitch try me.

"Why not? You already have it all over you're body." Cooper lets out a laugh, earning a death glare from Avery.

Avery squeals and then she raises her hand to slap me, but in a flash I'm pulled behind Cooper and then I hear the impact, but Cooper doesn't looked phased at all. "Oh Cooper, baby, I'm so sorry." She apologizes and then reaches up to touch his face. Cooper steps back, making my chest hit his back, and I'm ready to pounce again. She ain't touching my man.

"Avery you need to leave, now!" Cooper said, his hand still wrapped around my lower arm, me peaking around his shoulder. Avery stomps her little pedicured feet and leaves the diner, Cooper and I watching her go to her Slug-Bug and struggling to back out of her spot, what a little bitch.

I PARKED MY PICKUP in my usual spot, while Cooper's pickup parked beside mine. I shut off the engine and jumped out and slammed my door, I'm obviously still fuming over the whole Avery encounter ten minuets ago. I didn't turn around to look at Cooper but I knew he was out of his truck by the sound of his door closing. "DaKota." He calls for my stomping self as I head for the porch of my house.

I turn around to face him, "Why didn't you let me at her?" I crossed my arms and clenched my jaw at him. He stood in front of me with a look on his face that I didn't like, one that said you-know-I'm-right.

"If she would have slapped you, I'm afraid you would have done more than just break her nose. And you could have been possibly sued, so you should be thanking me for saving you some money." He says with a straight face for most of it, but at the end he adds a playful smirk.

"Yeah well it would have been worth it." I stubbornly say with a grumble and look away from him, and then he wraps his arms around my waist, me still with crossed arms.

"Did I tell you that you look real pretty today?" He says with a gorgeous smile as he leans down more to get my attention.

I look at him for a second and then I roll my eyes and return my gaze at the barn, "You're just saying that to make me feel better." I shift weight onto my other leg and he takes that opportunity to pull me closer.

"I bet it worked, though." He said as he pressed his forehead against mine, making me look him in the eyes. I couldn't help but smile when I saw his glimmering eyes and the way he had to bend down to get to my eye-level.

"I guess.." I give into him and his smile widens, making me smile more, too. His face leans down and his lips capture mine, and we share a nice, romantic kiss for a couple of moments, automatically my day 10 times better..

COOPER

AFTER PULLING AWAY from her delicious lips, I gave her a soft smile and then unwrapped my arms from her, put pulling her into my side and wrapped an arm around her shoulder and we started walking towards the porch. "But she was way too close to you." DaKota mumbles under her breath but its loud enough for me to hear. I look down at her and shes looking down at her moving feet.

"Never would of thought you as the jealous type." I smirk a little bit and she looks up, but not up at me.

"I-I not really, but at the same time I- I don't know.." She kicks at the ground in frustration making me laugh, and then I give her shoulder a comforting squeeze.

"It's okay, if I had a super-hot boyfriend like me, I'd get jealous too." She smiles and then she smacks me in the stomach, making me laugh with her. If I could have anything in the world, I would ask to see that smile for the rest of my life.

"Race you to my room!" She says and then she takes off in front of me and I watch her long hair move along with her quick movements, and watch her dress come up higher, showing off her amazing legs. Being caught in my staring, I start to race after her.

I clearly let her beat me to her room, but I was right behind her the whole time. If it was one of my buddies, I would shoved him into the wall and I would of been the victor of the race. Once we both get into the room she turns around with a victorious smile, "HA HA! I beat you!" Then she claps her hands and does a little dance, making me laugh. "Maybe next time." She shrugs to me and goes towards her bed.

But I catch her arm and pull her back into my chest, and lean down so my mouth is close to her ear. "Maybe next time I won't be nice." Then I attack her neck with playful kisses and she giggles and squirms in my arms, and then I let her go. My eyes go from her to the obvious sewing machine in the corner of her room, she must of put in a while ago. "What's this?" I ask her and then I walk over to it and touch the fabric lying across the table.

"Nothing!" She says and then tries to block it by standing in front the machine, it makes me laugh.

"You sew?" I ask her in slight disbelief. Her shoulders relax and she nods and then steps away, almost as she's embarrassed or ashamed she does. "Can you show me?" I ask her and then she looks up at me and her eyes light up with excitement.

"Really?"

"Yeah! Show me what your workin' on." I nudge her on and she smiles a bit.

"Okay, go grab that chair." She says as she takes a seat on the plumped-cushioned burgundy swivel chair. I do as she tells me and then I grab the wooden chair from her other desk and pull it and settle it down to her left side. I watched her turn on the machine, making the needle light turn on and the needle adjusts, awakening.

"You seem excited." I laugh at her because her smile hasn't worn off like it usually does.

"I actually like sewing a lot, and I've never shown someone how to sew! Okay first, I'll show you the parts of the machine and explain how it works.. So the first thing is the bobbin, this is your bottom thread..."

I couldn't help but let out a small smiling as she continued to explain to basics of sewing to me, it was just too cute. I loved to see her talking about something so passionate to her, and seeing her eyes light up because she was excited to teach me. I would often find myself staring at her lips at time and she would catch me, and then would tuck a piece of hair behind her ear and then blush, I loved when she did that. That little action told me that I was doing something right, I was making her feel good about herself. She deserves to feel good about herself, there isn't one thing I can think of that makes her a bad person. Not one. DaKota is everything and more I could ever want in a girl, and I know that I am in love with her.

I was in love with her even before we starting dating. Strange enough, the moment I knew I was in love with her was the first time she punched Avery. When she punched Avery in the face, that showed me her strong, angry, and protective side, which she never shows. I'm not sure why I haven't told her yet..

Okay that's a lie.

I'm scared. I'm scared that she's not there yet in our relationship. I'm scared she'll be freaked out because of her past. I don't want to scare her, that's the last thing I want in the world. Plus we've only been dating for a few weeks, so it's probably too fast. "Cooper, did you hear what I said?" She asked me, leaning her neck down to look into my eyes that are on the bottom of the machine.

"No, sorry darlin'." Then I leaned over and gave her a kiss on the cheek.

"What was that for?" She smiled and looked back down at my lips.

Because I love you.

"Just cause." I smirked and she nodded and then she continued to instruct me.

Tomorrow.

Tomorrow I am telling DaKota Annie Jones that I am in love with her.

I watched as Taylor pulled the shifter up and put the pickup into park and she unbuckled. However I didn't unbuckle, I was too busy thinking. I can trust her, I know I can trust her with my biggest secret, she is my best friend. "Tay wait.." I said as she put her hand on the door handle.

"What is it?" She asked, noticing my facial expression. I turned my body towards her more and take a deep breath.

"You can not tell anyone else this.. You got it? And so help me God if you do.." I warn her and she rolls her eyes.

"Who am I going to tell?" She questions me.

"Just pinky promise." I say and hold out my pinky. She wraps her pinky around mine and we both say, "Pow pow." What we've always said when we've made promises with each other.

"Okay, spill."

"I've been going out with Cooper Blackwood, and no one knows except for you, Cooper, and his mom." I say quickly and her jaw dropped but then she squealed with excitement and leaned over the center counsel and hugged me.

"Oh my gosh!! You guys are perfect for each other! But why keep it a secret?" She asks me as she pulls back, relief coming off my shoulders.

"Because my dad doesn't like him. Cooper even asked him permission to take me on a date, and my dad said no! Oh my gosh Tay I wish you were there, it was so romantic. Every cowgirl's dream."

"Hell I'd do the same thing if I was you, that's too bad that your dad don't like him though. Is he a good kisser?" She asks me, getting off on the details of my secret relationship.

"The best." I smile, remembering the way his lips felt on mine. "He's got this bad-boy reputation to him, but he's such a sweet and romantic guy. It's like he does everything right, he never stops amazing me. When I'm with him, I feel.. free.. He makes me feel like I'm on top of the world." I realize my rambling, but it feels good to have someone to talk to about this, not just my journal.

"I'm happy for you, Kota. I'm glad you told me!" She said and we nodded at each other and then she slipped out of the truck. Before I did the same, I texted Cooper to let him know that Taylor knows, and then I slipped out of the pickup and followed Taylor to the market.

Inspecting the vegetables, I was deciding if they were ripe enough to put in my basket. Taylor and I were the youngest people in the market, much older people surrounding us and helping us out. Normally, I would just go to my garden to get vegetables and my fruits, but the market has what we don't grow.

I grabbed the ripest watermelons and placed them in my basket, full of other fruit and vegies for my mother. I looked at Taylor as her phone started to ring, and she looked at it and looked confused, "Don't know who it is." She said and then answered it, moving away to get some privacy from other ears.

I looked down at my color-filled basket and decided I had everything I needed, so I went to the check out line. "That'll be $15.93." She smiled sweetly at me and then I handed her a 20 dollar bill, and then she returned me the four dollars and seven cents. By the time I had my groceries, Tay was returning from her phone call.

She came up to me and grabbed me by the forearm and started to drag me back towards her pickup. "Where are we going? Don't you need yours?" I asked her, looking back at her basket, which others were already taking from.

"No time for that, I've just been ordered to get you ready for a date." She said as we got into her pickup and closed our doors. A date? I didn't know I had a date with Cooper tonight, especially one that Taylor needed to help me prepare.

"What kind of date is this?" I asked her, suddenly getting nervous as she starts driving.

"I can not share that information, but I will tell you that it'll be the best night of your life." She smirked, okay, now I am really worried.

"Lord help me.." I muttered under my breath.

I SUNK DOWN A LITTLE bit in the tub as the bubbles touch the underside of my chin, tickling my skin. The once hot water was now turning into a soothing warm temperature. I was ordered to take a calming bath, with lots of scents added. My hair was in a bun because I was also ordered not to get it wet. I rarely took baths, I never have time to, and now I know why people do it so often, it feels great. My relaxation was ruined when Taylor knocked on the door, "Okay I'm back! Get out of that tub and put on a robe and then come out." She instructed me and I rolled my eyes, she was taking this job serious.

I stood up and stepped out of Taylor's bath and dried myself with a towel and then wrapped her black fleece robe around me and then tied the belt around my waist. I'm at Taylor's house because my parents are in town, but they could come home anytime. So Taylor ran to my house and grabbed what ever she needed and now she's back. My skin was already aching from missing the warm water, and I was getting goosebumps from the cool air.

I opened the door and it looked like a salon in her room. Makeup was neatly scattered across her vanity, curler and a straightener on, and extra hair things in different places. I walked over and sat down in her chair and then she turned the chair so I wasn't facing the mirror. "You are not allowed to see anything until the time comes." She said in a wised-tone voice making me roll my eyes.

"Just please, don't make me look like a barbie doll like you did in seventh grade." I groan to her, remembering the heavy blue eye shadow and thick eyeliner and teased hair.

"I can't believe you still hold me to that, and I promise that I'll make you look like a super-model." She said and then she tilted my head and started to do her thing, I just hoped she would do a good job.

I gasped at when I saw my hair, it was beautiful and very elegant. The curls where just the way I liked them, big, loose, and real curls. The way the curls framed my face had a glowing affect to my facial structure, and made my eyes pop more than they already did. I was also pleased at my makeup, my normal foundation and eyelash length, but she added some blush and a light coat of a darker shade of eye shadow, I liked it a lot. I looked stunning in my opinion. "Oh my." I breathed out to her as I looked from the mirror to my best friend.

"I told you, only took my two hours. Okay, now time for the outfit! Now here's the deal, I can't let you see what you are wearing because it will give up the surprise. So I'm gonna put it on for you and then you're gonna put the robe back on."

"This seems so silly, can't you just tell me?" I said to her as I stood up.

"No, now close your eyes." She demands and before I close my eyes, I roll them. I untie the belt and reveal my black lace strapless bra and matching pair of underwear. "Oh good choice." She snickers and I roll my eyes into the back of my head.

Through much struggle, Taylor manages to get the garment on my body, and then she puts the robe back around my body. I can tell the garment is a dress, but it's not a typical sundress, it's a two piece. I look down and all I can see is the bottom of the dress and the color is a deep burgundy. "Okay, now what?" I ask her as I see her going to her bag of goodies.

"Now we get the heels, and then I take you to your special date." She smiles and then she pulls out a pair of black heels that I recognize as mine. I haven't worn these in forever..

I sit down on her bed and put on the heels, and then stand up and walk around, getting used to them. "Ready?" She asked me and then I nodded. "Okie dokie." She smiled brightly and then she leaded me out of her room and towards outside.

My nerves were starting to build up inside me as Taylor was driving. I had so many questions about this date: why was I getting so dressed up, why am I being blindfolded, why can't I see my dress, why can't I know anything? All I know is that we are driving on a road full of pot-holes so that means that we are out quite away. I felt the pickup slowing down and then coming to a slow stop, "We are here, just a second." She said and then I heard her shut her door and then she opened mine and helped me out.

She took my arm and held up my dress as she helped me walk to wherever I was going. Then we came to a stop and she took off my robe and then she said, "When the music plays you can take off your blindfold, have fun." She said and then I heard her walk away, and then the tires of her truck going away.

Instantly I recognized the song, "I cross my heart" by George Strait as it started playing and then I took my blindfold off and my eyes looked at my dress first. Oh my gosh, it's so beautiful. The color matched perfectly with my dark skin. It is way too much of a formal dress to wear on an ordinary date.

Then my eyes averted to the twinkling lights hanging from the side of the old-wooden barn doors, and then the lights continued all around the interior of the barn. The twinkling lights made the wooden rustic color of the barn feel like soft, romantic, magical heaven. As the lights traveled further, my eyes shifted from the ceiling to the best part of the set-up, Cooper standing in the middle of the wide open spread of the barn. The way he looked in the tuxedo took my breath away, even though I've seen him in a tux before, this time was different, he took more time getting ready. As our gazes met he took off his black felt cowboy hat and I noticed his slightly slicked back hair, making him look very handsome and attractive.

I walked towards him and I noticed his eyes traveling up and down my outfit, admiring myself. Words couldn't even explain how amazed I was at all of this, it was incredible. "What is all of this?" I said, looking at all of the lights above us.

Cooper's face turned into a proud smile and then pulled out a single white rose corsage and placed it on my left wrist, "DaKota Jones, welcome to your very first prom." When he said prom I melted into a puddle inside.

I couldn't believe it, he actually remembered? I was never able to go because of my leave of absence, and I remember telling him that I wish I could of gone because it was one of my dreams as a little girl. My heart was going to explode of pure happiness and affection. This was just too much to believe right now, it seemed like a dream.

"You remembered?" I asked with a shaky voice and then I noticed the tears in my eyes, clouding my vision of my perfect boyfriend. I took a deep breath and then a tear slipped down from my eye and then Cooper reached up and wiped it away.

"Of course I did," He gave me a soft smile, almost laughing at my tears. "When you told me that my first thought was 'you are going to give her that prom, whether or not she is yours.'"

"This is the best thing anyone has done for me, thank you Cooper. I love it." I say and plant a kiss on his cheek.

"C'mon I'll give you a tour." He said and then held out his arm for me and then I wrapped my right hand around his elbow and then he started walking. "As you see, this is the dance floor, where I plan to show you my moves." I laugh at his cockiness, "Over here is the snack table, with your favorite snacks, cheddar jack cheese-its, cookies, cheetos, swiss-rolls, and cool-ranch Doritos. Then we have the punch, but what kind of prom would it be if the punch wasn't spiked? But if you don't want the spiked punch, there's just regular punch." While he was saying this, I couldn't help but just stare at him. How his lips tugged up as he talked, and the way his mouth went into a crooked smile when he explained the cliche spiked-punch.

"You're such a goof." I giggled at him and then he smiled down at me.

"Next stop is the picture station, with a camera on a tripod and a new memory card so we can take as many pictures as we want. But the deal is that there has to be at least one kissing picture." I looked at the camera on the tripod in front of the neatest looking wood of the entire barn. "And now it's time to go to the dance floor."

MY HEAD WAS LEANING against Cooper's as his arm around my waist, and my right hand in his left, as we slowly danced to the music. This was our sixth song we danced to, and every song Cooper indeed did surprise me with his different moves. This night has just been so perfect, I don't want it to end. "Hold on for a sec." He said, stopping our romantic dance.

Cooper left me in the middle of the dance floor and then he jogged over to the stack of hay bales, and then cleared his voice and looked around. "If I could get everyone's attention," He said in a formal way, making me laugh at his joke. "It is now time to announce this year's King and Queen." He said and then his eyes landed on me for a second, making my lips turn into a smile.

Cooper pulled out an envelope from the inside pocket of his tux jacket. He opened the envelope and said, "The votes are in, and this year's prom king is Cooper Blackwood!" And then he tossed the piece of paper behind him and then jumped off the stage and then back on, pretending to be the announcer and then himself.

Deciding to play along, I started to clap for him and then Cooper straightened out his tux, "Thank you, thank you. Really, there's no need for the applause." He said with a joking shrug and then I stopped clapping for him.

Then from behind a bale he pulled out a crown, making me laugh as he put it on himself. "Now, it would be my honor to announce this year's prom queen!" He again pulled out an envelope and opened it, his eyes dramatically widened and he said, "By the looks of the votes, this years prom queen has won by a long shot! Cowboys and cowgirls, your 2016 prom queen is DaKota Jones!"

I faked like I was surprised, by holding my hand over my mouth and pretending to look around me in disbelief. Cooper helped me up onto the stage and then he pulled out a gold tiara and then I bent down and he placed it on top of my head. "What an honor." I whispered to him and he smirked, grabbed my waist and pulled me in for a kiss and dipped me in his arms.

After our "coronation" we went over to the picture station and took lots and lots of pictures. Cooper and I doing almost every pose we could think off, and of course doing the kissing picture. After the pictures we returned to the dance floor.

The song, "Amazed" by Lonestar was playing, and I sang the lyrics in my head, really starting to understand what they meant all this time. Cooper stopped my thinking when he stepped back and he looked down at me, "What's wrong?" I asked him in confusion because he looked like he was trying to decide whether to do something or not.

"Nothing. Nothing is wrong at all, everything is perfect." He said confidently and then he pulled me back to continue to dance.

"I love you."

At first, my ears didn't comprehend what Cooper had just said, but then I realized what he really said. My feet stopped swaying with his and I looked at his chest, unable to look him in the eyes. Did he really just say that? "I am in love with you, and I have been since the first time my eyes landed on you."

He's in love with me?

Cooper Blackwood, in love with me? This night could not get any better, it's not possible. I looked deep into Cooper's eyes and all I saw was adoration and love, my heart skipped a beat. Then I knew, I knew I loved him. I loved that he did all of this, just for me. I love the way he works so hard, the way he scratches the back of his neck when he's embarrassed, the way his lips look after he kissed me, and the way he is so strong mentally and physically.

"I love you Cooper." I say, again with tears in my eyes, why am I being so emotional tonight? Cooper was the first to make a move by leaning down and capturing my lips with his and cupping my cheeks with his hands. My hands go to the back of his neck, playing with the ends of his hair. This kiss was just, beyond perfect. A perfect balance between love, passion, and desire.

We both pulled back at the same time, our lips slowing coming apart and then we look into each other's eyes. I bite my lip, trying to hide a smile when I get an idea, "I wanna show you something."

CHAPTER 5

Hand in hand, Cooper and I walked in the forest going to my favorite spot in all time. Good thing I traded my heels for a pair of Holy Cow Couture moccasins, and Cooper lent me his leather rodeo jacket to protect me from the chilly summer night. I looked up at the full moon, giving us the necessary light to find our way around. I knew they would be here tonight, they always come on the full moon. "Where are we going?" Cooper asked me as we both dodged a tree branch.

"You'll see, we're almost there." I said as I guided him through the trees and over the rocks and fallen branches.

I looked to my left and recognized the hole in the ground, the wolf's den. The memories made me smile, but I continued to walk. "Was that a wolf's den?" Cooper's voice came from beside me.

"Yup." I reply plainly, like it's no big deal. Then we reached the opening, out of the trees. This area was the only clear opening for miles, it was surrounded by trees in a circle, like something had wiped out all the tress before. The unique thing was there was a huge rock or boulder in the middle. It wasn't shaped like a boulder, it had slants and flat spots, perfect for climbing. "We're here."

"Okay, now what?" He asks me and then I smiled.

"You howl." I said to him and he looked confused but then he did, and we waited, and then nothing, proving my secret point. "Now watch this." I said and turned towards the rock and using my diaphragm I let out a strong and confident howl. After my howl ended, it was silent, only hearing the crickets and slight wind in the distance.

Then he emerged from the crevasse of the rock, his piercing yellow eyes looking at me, recognizing me. The moonlight helped see the outline of the black wolf more clearly, showing his above average size and dark color. But I don't need that, I know it's Luca, the once pup who had the courage to walk over to me in the den. But now he is the Alpha of his pack, battling his father to take his rank. "Sit down." I instructed Cooper, and then we sat down on the cool grass.

After Luca truly knew it was me, he howled to the others, letting them know it was okay for them to come out. Then six other wolves came out from hiding and went to different spots on the rock and laid down. Luca still stood and then he lowered his head, in greeting, and then went over to his Alpha female and laid next to her. "That's why they call me wolf girl." I whispered to Cooper.

Cooper looked at me in disbelief and his jaw was dropped, "That is the most amazing thing I've ever seen in my life."

"I know, I've never shown any one that before." I confessed to Cooper and then he smiled.

"Well I'm honored." And then he kissed the side of my head, and I leaned into him. "I love you." He said softly.

"I love you too." I said back, and smiled. Taylor was right, this is the best night of my life..

I thought today would be a very happy and peaceful day, but so far, it's been the complete opposite. Ashley, my mother, and I are running around the house and around town to get everything ready for the wedding today. I can't believe that it's finally here! I am so excited for my brother and Ash, I know it's going to be great and be the best day of their lives.

"Dad! Do not touch that!" I order my father, who is poking the centerpieces, which I did all by myself. The centerpieces were old cowboy hats that I had collected, and I cut out the top of the hat and placed perfectly arranged flowers.

My dad threw up his hands in a surrender type and then backed away, "Man, do I love being controlled by a bunch of women." He jokes and then he walks out of the house and into the nice fresh air. Today was a perfect day to have an outdoor wedding, not too warm, not too windy, nor too cold, it was superb.

I carefully put the centerpieces into wooden crates and then I carry each of them to the box of my pickup. After I loaded the last crate, my phone was buzzing in the band of my running shorts and I pulled it out and saw that Taylor was calling me. "Hey Tay." I greeted her as I walked towards my porch to get more stuff.

"Hey, what are you doing?" She asked me.

"Just getting stuff ready for the wedding, you know, sweating my ass off." I joked with her and she let out a small laugh.

"Do you want help? I feel bad because I am a bridesmaid too and I'm not even helping." She sighed and I did too.

"You can if you want, just bring all of your supplies and stuff over and then we can ride together." I say to her as I enter the house and I see my mom getting the table assignment cards.

"Okay! Be there in a few!" She said and then she hung up and I did too, and looked around for things to pack up.

ONCE AGAIN, I WAS RUNNING around the ceremony venue, fixing anything that was out of place. I made sure the chairs were perfectly in place, and the decorations were hung nicely. After I was done with this, it would be time to get all dolled up with the other girls. I walked to the spot were Ash and Caleb would get married and looked at the chairs, prefect.

I ran into the building that the other girls were in, and walked to the designated room for us. When I walked in the room, I noticed the girls getting their hair done while sitting in the chairs, and soft country music playing in the background. "There she is!" My mother's voice said from the other side of the room, talking to who I presume was another makeup artist.

"I just had to another check on everything." I say and then I grab a red robe and my bridesmaid dress then go behind the privacy screen and strip of my clothes, except for my strapless bra and underwear and then put on my dress carefully, then put my robe over it.

Once I'm back out into the open, I sit down in my spot, in the middle of Taylor and Ashley. Both of them currently getting their makeup done, so it's my turn now. The lady that my mom was talking to comes over to me, "Hi I'm Julie." She sticks out her hand for me to shake.

"DaKota, nice to meet you." I smile at her and she smiles back and then she starts digging into her makeup box and occasionally examines my face. Then she pulls out a mascara tube and stands in front of me and starts to do her job.

"You excited, Ash?" I ask Ashley as Julie continues on my eyelashes.

"I don't think excited is the right word right now." She nervously chuckles.

"Then what is?" I ask her and then she sighs.

"I'm very nervous." She sighs.

All of us girls say at the same time, "Why?!"

"What if I trip in front of everyone? Or if I mess up on my vows." She then tips her head back in frustration and then my mother walks in front of her and grabs Ashley's hands and that gets Ash's attention as she looks up at my mom.

"I remember this moment on my wedding day," Mom sighs, "I was starting to get cold feet too. I was scared that when I got up there in front of the whole church I'd have a big smile on my face when I said 'I do', and then when it was Colby's turn he would say 'I don't'. I would of looked like a fool."

"How did you get through it?" Ashley pleaded with eager.

"I told my mother and she asked me, 'If you really think that's going to happen, why did you ever agree to this day?' and I took a deep breath and knew that she was right. If I would of ever thought he would of said no, then why was I at that church? Then I imagined our life after the wedding, because he was going to say 'yes'. We would go on our honeymoon in Cancun and we would never keep our hands off each other because we were going to be so happy and so in love. We'd tell everyone that we were Mr. and Mrs. Jones, and I'd flash off my ring to other women. Then after we come home, we'd come back to the ranch and begin our life together. I'd actually looked forwards towards the arguing and then the making-up, Colby's great at that part," I cringe at that part as my mom chuckles, "Then I imagined Colby panicking when it was time to go the hospital to deliver our first child, and him holding our baby. So Ashley, right now I want you to imagine you and Caleb's future together, and when you do that you'll realize that nothing even matters at the ceremony, because in the end, you'll have Caleb."

I was so mesmerized by my mom's words, I was speechless, I couldn't imagine what Ashley was feeling right now. I looked over at Ashley and her eyes were glossy, but she had a soft smile towards my mom. She squeezed my mom's hands and then she took a deep breath. "Thank you Chey, that really helped. Now I'm feeling the feeling when he asked me to marry him." She leaned forward and hugged my mother carefully not mess up her makeup.

"You are welcome, sweetie." My mom hugs her back and then she walks over back to her chair, her makeup artist continuing her work. I also reposition myself on my chair and then Julie continues to do my makeup.

We all stood in front of the mirror, fixing and adjusting ourselves as we waited for Ashley to get on her dress and present her beautiful self to us. As I looked down at my shoes, my mind traveled to Cooper, who hasn't seen in me in heels before and won't today because he won't be coming. I haven't seen him in a week and I missed him a lot more than I thought I would. I felt a hand on my shoulder and I looked up at my mom, "Are you alright?" She asked me and I gave her a soft smile and nodded.

"Yeah, I'm good." I tried to put on a strong voice and she nodded at me and then I saw Ashley step out of her dressing room and I was amazed on how great she looked. Her dress was a simple looking Goddess style v-neck with beautiful floral embroidery on the sides. Her hair was done similar to mine, but more elegant with flower pins in her hair.

"Oh my gosh!" We all said at the same time as we crowded around her and she laughed and looked at us nervously.

"Do I look alright?" She asked with a sheepish smile.

"Honey, I wouldn't be surprised if Caleb saw you and swept you off your feet even before you say I do!" Taylor said and we all laughed and I couldn't wipe the smile off my face as I looked at Ashley and glowing-ness.

Jake stood beside me as we watched Taylor and Rusty walk down the aisle and then he held out his arm for me and then I looped my arm through and he asked, "Ready?" I gave him a soft smile and nodded and then we walked down the aisle as we smiled at the guests. As we reached the front, Caleb and Jake shook hands, and then Caleb gave me a proud smile and then the music started playing and then everyone stood up and turned around.

Ashley was looking down and then she looked up and I heard lots of whispers among the guest saying how beautiful she looked. Her father took her hand and kissed it, making her smile along others. I turned my head to look at Caleb and his toothless smile turned into the happiest smile I ever saw from him. I hope one day when I get married that my soon-to-be-husband will look at me that way.

I SAT AT THE WEDDING party table in the barn where the reception was taking place, watching people dancing, but mostly watching Caleb and Ashley. They couldn't keep their eyes off each other, I am so happy for them. When my eyes left them, I caught my own parents laughing at each other, it made my smile increase. They were dancing a two-step, which they have mastered, looking flawless and effortless. I wonder if Cooper knew how to two-step.

I looked down at my phone to see if I had any new messages, especially from Cooper. I had a couple of snap-chats, but nothing from him. I sigh and then turn my phone back over and look at the dancing crowd. While looking, my eyes caught something by the open barn door. A man with a cowboy hat, looking at the ground with one foot at a 45 degree angle against the wall. He had a white dress shirt with charcoal blue vest and jeans and black boots on. Something looked very familiar about the cowboy, but when he looked up the tiniest bit, I knew who it was.

I watched him keep his head down and then walk outside slowly. A smile crept on my face as I stood out of my chair and made my way through the dance floor. I finally reached the barn door, feeling the warm breeze hit me and then I looked around for him, scrunching my eyebrows together when I couldn't find him. I walked towards my left and reached the side of the barn, and then out of nowhere my arm was snatched and I was pulled roughly into a chest.

I giggled as I looked up to his warm brown eyes and he smiled as I put my arms against his chest. "Hi." I smiled lovingly at him.

"Oh how I missed that beautiful smile of yours." He said desperately and then took off his hat and swooped down and laid a big fat one on me, not that I was complaining.

I pulled back in realization and looked around us, "What if someone sees us?" I ask the smiling fool in front of me. Cooper leaned towards me, looking around to, and then he grabbed my hand and started to jog towards somewhere. "Cooper, I can't run in heels!" I laughed as I struggled.

"Cm'ere darlin'." He said and in one motion he bent down and carried me bridal style and I gasped when he did it. I wrapped my arm around the back of his neck as he walked over to a door in the back and then went up some steps.

"Where are we going?" I asked him and he just smiled and didn't say anything. Then I looked around and saw that we were going to the attic. Cooper let me down as we reached the attic door and then he opened it and we walked in, "How did you know about this?" I asked him as I looked around the small room.

"Lucky guess." He said and I scoffed and I turned around and shoved him in the shoulder. "Can I tell you something?" He asked me as I stood in front of him.

"Yep." I said and then I fixed his vest, making it straighter.

"You look hot in heels." He said and grabbed both of my hands then planting a kiss on my cheek. "But then again, you look hot in everything, even your muck boots and shorts." Then he kissed my other cheek.

"Thank you. I thought you weren't suppose to be home for another two days?" I asked him and he sighed.

"I skipped Bedford, because I wanted to come to the wedding and see you of course." He shrugged it off.

"Cooper you didn't have to do that." I squeezed his hands.

"What, aren't you happy I'm here?" He scrunched his eyebrows and I rolled my eyes at him and stepped closer to him.

"Of course I am, Coop. It's just that you didn't have to give up that rodeo for me, you could of won some more money." I looked down at our hands and then he pulled them apart and wrapped his arms around my lower back and pulled me closer, making me look up at him.

"I already won $4,000, and no amount of money compares to my girl." He smiled proudly, making my knees weak.

"Right answer." I smirked and then I kissed him.

"I'LL MISS YOU GUYS!" I said as I gave Caleb and Ashley a hug before they got into Caleb's pickup. "But I hope you guys have lots of fun!"

"Thanks, Kods. Love ya lil' sis." Caleb kissed me on the side of my head. "Well, we'll see ya guys in a couple of weeks!" They waved to our family and then Caleb helped Ashley into his pickup and then ran to his side and got in, and then the diesel came alive and he took off, probably couldn't wait to get her alone.

"Never thought I'd miss that slob." I said as my father wrapped his arm my shoulder, giving it a squeeze.

"Me too, honey." He chuckled.

"Do you mind if I go over to Taylor's house?" I asked him and he shook his head. "Okay, I'll see you tomorrow then." I smirked to myself that I knew I wasn't going to Taylor's house, rather going to spend some time with my boy. I hated lying to him, but he did this to himself, he just doesn't know it.

I threw my keys into the air and caught them and carefully jogged over to my pickup and then I opened the door and hopped in and started the diesel engine. I put on my seatbelt and then I put my foot on the brake and shifted into drive and then started for Cooper's house.

I parked right next to Cooper's powerstroke, quickly cutting the engine and jumping out, well attempting to with my heels. For some reason, I was so excited to see Cooper, even though we hung out a little bit at the wedding. I just wanted to stare into his brown eyes and look at his gorgeous smile, he was perfect to me!

Cooper met me on the porch and he had an annoyed look on his face, but then he wrapped his around around my waist and kissed the top of my head, standing next to me as we walked inside his house. "My mother wants to take pictures." He groaned quietly to me, so that's why he was still all dressed up.

I was going to say something but then Desiree's voice entered the room, "Oh DaKota! You look absolutely stunning, like you should be on the cover of a magazine!" She gasped, making me blush and smile at the same time.

"Thank you Desiree." I smile brightly at her and Cooper's grip tightens around me.

"Mom, do we really have to take pictures?" Cooper groaned and slightly threw his head back, while his mother stood there with her camera giving him the death glare.

"Cooper Blue Blackwood, we are going to take these pictures even if you have to fake the smile." She sternly says making me smirk, because she was going to get her way no matter what. Cooper quickly pulled me closer to him and then I put my hand on my hip and started smiling as she held up the camera. "Cooper stand straighter!" She ordered and Cooper didn't dare to disobey.

After about thirty pictures, Cooper lead me into his room and once we were safely in he said, "Stubborn women, I tell you." Then he sat on the edge of his bed, then I walked in between his legs.

He put his hands on the back of my thighs and then I hummed, "Yes, please tell me about stubborn women." I cocked an eyebrow at him and then he gulped looking like a little boy who just got caught doing something he knows he should't be.

"I love 'em." He smiled nervously making me chuckle and roll my eyes at him, "I'm gonna go change quick." He said and then I stepped out from his legs and he passed me and went to his dresser and got some clothes and went into his bathroom.

I laid on his bed, taking off my heels, enjoying the automatic relief that I felt. I threw the shoes towards the bedroom door and dug my heels into his covers. "Hey babe?" Cooper called from the bathroom. Huh oh, usually when he called me babe he asks me to do him a favor.

"Yes?" I closed my eyes, waiting for his offer.

"Can you rub out my back and shoulder?" He asked and I opened my eyes and saw him leaning against the bathroom door frame, wearing a navy blue cotton shirt and some black basketball shorts.

I sighed, "Take off your shirt and get the lotion." He silently said 'yes' to himself and did low fist bumps close to his chest, making my shake my head and close my eyes again. I opened them back up when I felt his weight make the bed sink, "Where does it hurt?" I ask him sitting up and focus on his muscular back, with some cute freckles that I adored. Cooper showed me where it hurt on his shoulder and lower back and I pumped some lotion into my hand and then spread it around his back.

To make it easier, I sat on his butt, firstly massaging his lower back. "I never knew your middle name was Blue." I said and he groaned softly. "What?" I asked him.

"It's embarrassing." He mumbled into the sheets.

"No it's not! I think it is very attractive, Cooper Blue." I smiled to myself and pressed harder into his skin, noticing how tight he was. "Jesus, Cooper. Do you ever stretch?"

"Well I didn't after today, because I had to hurry to get to a weddin'."

"Oh sure, blame it on me." I rolled my eyes and he chuckled. "Am I getting the spot?" I asked him.

"Oh yeah." He said deeply. After a couple of moments of silence he said, "I'm so glad I have you." I stopped massaging for a moment, thinking about what he just said, and then I continued.

"Why?" I smiled to myself, biting my lip to quit it.

"If I didn't have you, my mom would still be rubbing my back, and you just do it soo much better." Well that wasn't what I was expecting..

"Thanks." I said monotonously and then he started laughing at me.

"I'm just kiddin', darlin'." The left side of his face was turned towards me and I looked at him, admiring his smile and the way his slightly-curly-and-shaggy laid on his face. He could be identical to the guy who plays Lane Frost in the movie, "8 Seconds". As I moved my hand on his shoulder, I found his knots, slightly moving them around in their place, making him groan as I put more pressure.

I've been doing this for a bit and I'm starting to get a little bored and tired. I looked at Cooper and I started to smile for an unknown reason. I felt so comfortable around him and I wanted to show him that. So I stopped rubbing his back and softly placed a kiss on his shoulder, and then another on the spot where his neck and shoulder met. Then one just below his ear, and then I moved to the other side, copying the same spots, but adding one upon his jaw, getting closer to his lips. Once my lips found his cheek, he quickly turned his body, so now I was sitting on his stomach. His hands found my back and pulled me closer to him, my hands going to the bottom on his neck, playing with his hair.

He pressed his lips against mine, our lips falling perfectly in sync with each others. The way my body was feeling was amazing, I felt aroused and relaxed, something that I have never felt before and I loved it. I moaned when he licked my bottom lip, making me open wider as his tongue found mine. His hands pressed more firmly into my hips and I tugged on his hair, making him groan, giving me pleasure.

His sweet lips left mine and trailed down my chin and jaw to my neck, sweetly sucking on different spots, well knowing which were my favorite. Deciding to take it to a next step, I grabbed his hand and put it on the zipper of my dress. He pulled away from my neck, making me look down at him, and he put his forehead against mine, both of us heavily breathing. "You sure?" His voice was soft and concerned.

I nodded against him and then he wrapped an arm around me, standing both of us up, and his left hand unzipping my dress as we kissed. Once the zipper reached the bottom, his hands found my shoulders, slipping off the dress, making it fall to the ground. I slowly looked up from the ground and looked at Cooper as I stood there in my white lace strapless bra and underwear. "You okay?" He asked me, cupping my face with his hand.

I didn't say anything, but I smashed my lips against his, making us fall back on the bed. After kissing Cooper for a while, I let my lips travel down his neck and kissing more towards under his jaw. Cooper's hands traveled around my body making me shiver in pleasure, and then returning back to his lips. Not long after, his hands go on top of my butt and he lightly grabs it and I gasp and he then takes the opportunity to maneuver his tongue inside my mouth, which I didn't mind.

After that, Cooper sat up and then flipped us over, making my head fall against the pillows. He laid in between my legs and his hands found mine, intertwining our fingers making me smile. His lips went between my breasts, and slowly down my stomach, sometimes nipping, making me moan with pleasure. His hands left mine and ran up and down the sides of my thighs as he continued to place kisses random places on my body. Continuing his soft kisses, "I'm. So. Obsessed. With. You." He said in between kisses.

I moaned as he kissed my hip, right on the bone. I love how his warm lips felt against my goose-bumped skin from his traveling fingertips. He came back up, putting his body weight on me and we didn't waste anytime to find each other's lips. He tasted so sweet, like strawberries, I couldn't get enough. Cooper's right hand traveled from my cheek, going to the left side of my ribs, running his finger over the band of my bra, and then lingered on my hip, him feeling the lace of my underwear. I tugged on the ends of his head and he groaned, making me smile underneath our kiss and then he pressed his lips harder against me, hungry for more.

I was sad when he pulled away from my lips, going to the corner of my mouth, kissing, and then to the corner of my jaw, kissing more, and then he pressed a lingering kiss under my ear. I ran my hand over his shoulder, onto his back pressing him more into me. He slowly went down my neck, not missing one inch of skin. "Cooper." I said as I opened my eyes, looking down at him.

"Yes baby?" He softly said, still kissing my skin. My insides lit up when he called me baby, he sounded so sexy when he said that.

"Can we take a break?" I asked him, biting my lip.

He quickly returned his face in front of me, concern all over his face. "I didn't do anything did I?" I couldn't help but laugh at him, his face was just too cute! Now, he looked even more confused at me.

"No, Coop." I smiled and then kissed him again, "I just think we should take a break." I said and he nodded and then smirked.

"A break huh?" Implying that we would go for round two soon.

"You know what I mean." I giggled as I shoved his chest. Cooper smiled at me and then he sat up and moved to my left side, supporting himself on his elbow looking at me. "Can I wear your shirt?" I said as I moved off the bed, towards his dresser.

"I recommend the Montana Oil one, you look sexy in that one. Even though you look good already." He winked at me, looking me up and down, me still in my undergarments. I blushed furiously and looked away from him and quickly grabbed the navy blue shirt from the drawer, putting it over my head. Then I went into his bathroom, took out my wedding hair and then carefully combed it out. After I was done, I set down the brush and then smiled to myself, remembering how Cooper's lips felt against mine.

I walked back into Cooper's room and saw him lying on his back with his eyes closed, his arm covering his eyes, he was probably exhausted. I went over to the bed and sat on the edge and gathered my hair into a high ponytail and secured it with a ponytail, pulling some strands to make it messy. "If you wanna get some sleep, I can just go over to Taylor's house." I say as I fix my hair.

Then, out of nowhere, I feel the bed dip from behind me and then Cooper's arms wrap around me and I feel his breath against my neck. "I sleep better with you though." He cutely whined into my ear, and then he softly nibbled on my ear lobe. Then gripping tighter on my chest, he falls back making my back fall against his chest.

"You're acting like we've been away from each other for a long time." I chuckled.

"A week is too long being away from you." Then he placed a kiss on the top of my head. He lets go of me and then I roll off him and go to the top of his bed and get under the covers, him doing the same as me. Before I could lay on a side, Cooper puts his head on my chest and wraps his arm loosely around my stomach. I loved this side of Cooper, cuddly. It was seriously the cutest thing in the world. My right hand started making circles in the middle of his back, while he settled in. "Good night DaKota, I love you." He mumbled, his fatigue settling in.

"G'night, I love you." I replied, closing my eyes soon after and then falling to sleep with my Cooper in my arms.

Soft sheets tangled across my legs as I stirred in my sleep, finally waking up after a good nights sleep. I opened my eyes slowly, letting them get used to the morning sun, and then I turned my head to the left, expecting to see a sleeping Cooper, but nope. I was surprised, but then I remembered I have a hard-workin' boyfriend, so I just rolled over onto his pillow. I looked over at the clock and saw it was already eight o'clock! No alarm clock this morning, no wonder it felt amazing waking up just now.

After gathering my thoughts, I grabbed the comforters and pulled them off me and got out of Cooper's bed, and into his bathroom to get some mouth wash. I cringed when I saw my reflection in the mirror, my hair was a mess! After spitting out my mouth wash, I took out my mess of a bun and redid it.

I walked back into Cooper's room and then grabbed some sweat pants, so I didn't have to change back into my dress or go with out pants in front of Desiree. I grabbed my phone and shoved it into my pocket and then I decided to go downstairs to the kitchen, maybe Desiree was in there. As I was walking down the stairs, I saw Reese and Desiree already at the kitchen table eating some cereal and watching one of Reese's TV shows. As soon as my foot hit the cool wooden floor, Desiree looked up and smiled, "Good mornin', DaKota."

I smiled back at them, "Good morning, mind if I eat some cereal with you guys?" I asked as I walked towards them.

"Sure thing!" Desiree said as I walked past her.

"Not Lucky Charms! Those are mine! Eat Captain Crunch, those are Cooper's!" Reese's little voice boomed as I walked into the pantry and was reaching for a box, which I now grabbed Captain Crunch. Desiree and I both laughed at his concern, he was just so cute!

After breakfast, I decided I should go out to see Cooper before I leave. So after putting my dress and heels into my pickup I went over to the gate to the pasture and there was Cooper, fixing the barbed wire fence about 30 yards away. I climbed on to the top of the gate and sat there. He didn't notice me, and I sure as heck didn't mind. It was a hot and muggy morning, which lead to a shirtless and sweaty Cooper. Which then lead to a happy DaKota.

I watched as he worked his tools and the wire, all of his muscles moving along with him, it was mesmerizing to me. He wasn't wearing his usual American straw cowboy hat, he just had a King Ropes truckers hat on backwards. "Hey cowboy!" I said and then he gave the wire one last twist and then looked over in my direction and squinted his eyes because of the sun, and then smiled and stood up and started walking over to me.

My eyes couldn't help but look at him from head to toe, mainly focusing on his six pack abs that were covered in sweat and some dirt. My eyes found his gleaming brown eyes and he smirked, "Like what you see, darlin'?" He then held out his arms, pretending to be cocky.

"I don't know turn around," I smirked and he chuckled and then turned around and popped his hip at me, trying to make his butt look good. He turned back around and walked closer, "I sure do." I winked at him and he laughed.

He came in between my legs and smiled up at me, "Good morning pretty girl." I leaned down and made sure to hold onto the gate so I didn't fall on him. His lips tasted like coffee and sweat, but I sure as hell didn't mind, it was surprisingly sweet to me.

"Mmm, good morning cowboy." I said as our lips left each others and then Cooper backed away and then climbed the gate and sat right next to me so our legs were touching.

"You headin' out?" He asked me, looking forwards.

"Yeah, I just came out here to say goodbye." I said and looked at him and then he looked back at me.

"I'm sorry that we couldn't wake up together this morning, but you sure are cute as hell when you sleep." He said and nudge my shoulder, making me blush.

"It's okay, I know you have more important things to do out here." I said softly playing with my hands.

"DaKota, they're not important things." He said getting my attention, making my eyes to go back to him.

"What do you mean?" I said and then he reached out and tucked a piece of hair behind my ear and gave me a soft smile.

"These things are things that I just have to do. Sure they are important," He paused and looked over his land, "But to me, nothing is more important than you." He looked back at me, and I felt my lips tugging into a smile and blushing as always.

"You seem to always have the right thing to say." I giggled and he did to.

"Yeah but I mean 'em." He placed his hand over my knee and I put my hand over his and then looked at him and leaned in to give him a sweet chaste kiss. Every time we kissed, it sent shivers down my spine and fireworks across my lips.

"I love you." I said as we pulled back and rested our foreheads together.

"I love ya, too." He said and then hoped off the gate. "I'll see you later, yeah?"

"Yeah, bye Cooper." I said as I hopped on the other side of the gate.

"Bye, darlin'." He left me with a wink, making me shake my head at him.

I COILED MY ROPE AS I loosened the slack and pulled the loop of the dummy's head, another day, another catch. I looked at the pink dummy and remembered the day that my dad bought it for me, even though I hate the color pink. We were all at a rodeo, supporting my uncle and my dad and I remember complaining about not having my own dummy because my dummy of a brother wasn't letting me use his. I think I was seven or six, but even then I knew how my missing tooth smile could melt my dad's heart. So after the go round, he went to Runnings and bought his little daughter her own dummy, and I've been using it since.

I wish Caleb was here, so I could kick his butt and make fun of him for his slow swing. Caleb was known for taking his time on swinging and aiming for the two feet catch, everyone knew me as the better heeler. Although, Caleb and I were about the same level at heading, depending on our horses. "DaKota!" I heard my name being yelled and I stepped outside of the barn and looked at the porch. There stood my dad looking around for me and he saw me, "Supper!" I gave him a small nod and then I took off my roping glove and put it on top of my rope and left the barn.

The screen door slammed behind me as I entered my house, the delicious smell of grilled chicken and salsa filled my senses. I looked at the table and saw the quesadilla on my plate, I internally moaned with satisfaction. I love quesadillas! "Smells good, mama." I said and kissed the side of her head as she walked with the pitcher of iced tea.

"I forgot your pig of a brother is gone on his honeymoon, so there is lots, eat up!" She said, pointing at the multiple quesadillas on the plate.

"With pleasure." I licked my lips and sat down next to my dad, and then my mom sat across from me. She reached across for my hand and I grabbed hers and then my dad's right hand.

"Dear Almighty father in heaven, thank you for blessing us with this mighty fine food and allowing us to be together for dinner. We thank you for the rain, good crops, healthy stock, and our ability to continue to do what we love. In your name we pray, amen." I raised my head and smiled at my dad who lead the prayer.

I took a bite of my delicious quesadilla, and loved the way the cheese melted in my mouth and the chicken had a spicy kick to it. As I finished chewing my dad spoke, "How'd the practicing go?"

I looked at him while he was cleaning his face with a napkin, "Pretty good, but I'll admit I missed Caleb and his annoying comments. I don't ever think I've practiced without him." I chuckled at the last part.

"I'm so glad that wedding is over, now that boy can focus on helping around here." Classic dad. I looked at my dad, literally biting my tongue deciding if I was going to speak up for my brother. I hated how much my dad put pressure on Caleb to help, Caleb works his ass off everyday. I looked at my mother and she had a despaired look on her face, keeping to herself as usual. I knew she wanted to say something, but she didn't want to get into an argument with my dad. Well I'm sick of that.

After long awkward moment of silence, I took a silent breath and said, "He's not a boy, dad." Both of my parents heads snapped up to look at me. My dad looked at me, waiting for me to go on. "He's a married man now. He's gonna be focusing on getting a place to call home for his wife, and starting his own family there. There's no doubt he'll be out here helping us when he can. In his life now, it isn't just about CJ ranch, it's about him now." I think my dad had just watched someone burn a million dollars from the expression on his face. My mother, she looked worried for me.

"Where did that come from?" Dad asked me, putting is napkin in his lap and turning his body toward me. There was no turning back now.

I felt my hands start to clam up, so I rubbed them on my jeans. But then I remembered who I am. I am someone that stands up for something they believe in. Here goes nothing. "Well you're always yankin' on his chain about pulling his weight around here, and calling him distracted by Ashley and wanting to out to hang out with his friends at the bar. It's not fair to him." My dad looked amused at me, which really worried me.

"And how's that?" Now he had crossed his leg over his leg, looking forward to hearing me answer.

"Caleb works his ass around here, all morning and all evening, just like you. But you've got to realize that he's been doing that all of his life and he's young, all he wants to do is have fun. But instead of do-"

"He has fun at rodeos." My dad interrupts me, scrunching his eyebrows.

"Yeah, the two days out of a month," I rolled my eyes at him. "Dad, can't you see? All he wants to do is impress you, because he thinks that you think he isn't a good rancher."

"I think he is a very good rancher." My dad says, trying to prove me wrong.

"Yeah well you sure do a good job at expressing it." I say crossing my arms.

"Watch your tone, DaKota." He says, he always pulls that one on me when he's the one who needs the tone check.

"Do you get what I'm saying though?" I say to him, ignoring his useless comment.

"I hear you loud and clear, but that still doesn't change that he needs to help us."

"Dad," I paused looking him straight in the eye, "Ever since I got back from my..you know what.. you've never asked me to help. I've been doing all the ten year old chores."

"Well to be honest, after your situation it's all you can do." Well damn, I was not expecting that. I started to glare at him, all I can do? I was baffled at him, I looked at my mom who looked like she knew this was coming.

I stood from my chair, "What the hell does that mean?" I asked with a whole lot of fire.

"DaKota!" My parents said in unison, warning me not to swear at them again. I shook them off, this was not the time.

"Well I want an answer!" I said to them and my father sighed and looked at the ground.

"Well after you came back I decided that you weren't ready to take responsibilities. You weren't as up to speed and you seemed a bit off, not your usual self. The DaKota before was up and giddy to go spend the day out in the field, but now you're just an extra hand."

That hurt. Screw that. That hurt so fucking bad, I couldn't help but tear up. My dad was mentally insane for saying that stuff. An extra hand? That meant I was only good for making sandwiches and doing kid stuff for him. Where did he get off on even thinking that? He was throwing me a pity party and I had about 'nough of it.

It didn't help that I was getting flashbacks of my initial rape and picturing Wade's face in my head. God, I just wanted to go upstairs and take a shower because I felt so disgusting remembering his touch on my skin. I had to think of Cooper's soft and gentle touch to calm me down, holding my hand, running his thumb over the back of my hand.

I finally opened my eyes, a tear escaping my eye, I didn't bother to wipe it off. "I'm sorry." I hissed at him and I saw the remorse on his face, but it didn't phase me. "I'm sorry I was stalked. I'm sorry I was stalked until the point of rape. I'm sorry I was raped by a mentally insane man, who wouldn't leave me alone. I'm sorry it came down to the point that I had to leave my home because my life was in danger. I'm sorry th-"

"That's enough, DaKota!" My mom cried for me, I looked at me and I saw the tears in her eyes, her blue eyes becoming glassy.

I looked back at my dad, who was hanging his head in disappointment. "I'm sorry daddy that I'm not the perfect little girl anymore." With that, I turned on my heal and began walking to the stairs.

"DaKota, wait now." He tried but I stopped and turned to him.

"Save it, I'll see you in the morning when I'm mucking the stalls and combing the horses." I threw at him and then ran up the stairs and slammed my door back into the frame as hard as I could. I went to my balcony doors and opened them, hoping that fresh air would do me some good. I paced around my room, walking in and out to my balcony. I needed to calm myself down and the only way I could think of was talking to Cooper. But I didn't want to do that right now, I would just fall apart and I didn't want to do that to him.

I eventually cooled myself off, but when I heard a knock on my door, I didn't answer it. I replied back to it by grabbing my blanket, phone, and book and then slamming my balcony door. Okay, maybe I hadn't cooled off yet. Whoever was at the door, I hope they got the message.

I startled in my chair as I heard my phone ringing on the table next to me. When the hell did I fall asleep? I reached for my phone, along with a quick yawn. I looked down at my hand and saw it was Cooper, thank God. "Hey." I said quietly, resting my head back down on the chair, watching the sun go down on the mountain horizon.

"What's wrong, Kota?" He asked me so soft I swear he was in front of me.

"I just had a fight with my parents, nothing new. But whats up?" I changed the subject while sitting up in my chair, bringing my blanket with me.

"I have an idea to cheer you up." He said and it made me smile, because I could imagine him smirking. I loved when he smirked, it was incredibly sexy.

"And what would that be?" I asked him, suddenly my mood lightening.

"All I'm gonna say is honey, put on your dancin' boots. I'll be there in 15."

I LOOKED DOWN AT MY outfit, Wrangler cut offs, a Willie Nelson graphic tee, concho belt, and my Ariat pointed toe boots. I had to admit, I looked good. I stuffed my phone into my pocket as I saw Cooper's pickup coming down the road. I grabbed onto the side of my balcony railing and carefully put myself on the other side of it. My feet landed on the tiles of the roof and then I sat down and scooted down, until I was near the gutter. Trust me, this isn't my first time sneaking out. A long time ago, I had stuffed an old plastic ladder in the gutter. I'm surprised my dad hasn't found it yet.

I jumped off the ladder and then turned around and looked at Cooper, parked at where I told him to. I started running towards the pickup. I looked back at the house in case anyone was standing on the porch. All clear. As I reached the truck, the passenger window rolled down and there was Beau, Taylor's boyfriend. "Sorry, I called shotgun." He smirked and I playfully rolled my eyes at him and I grabbed the back door handle and opened it and climbed inside, where Taylor sat on the other side.

"Hey DaK-hot damn girlfriend!" She cheered looking me up and down making me blush as I saw Cooper turn his head to look at me. "Cooper doesn't she look hot?" She said as I sat down and buckled myself.

I looked at Cooper, who had a straw hat on and a Hooey cotton tee, looking damn good himself. "Very." He winked at me which drew a giggle and blush from me.

"So, where are we going?" I asked them as Cooper made a quick U-turn down my drive.

"Reza's." They all replied together, all of us looked at each other with excitement. Reza's was a honkytonk bar our neighboring city called Bowman. I had never been there, but I've heard that it is a hoot and a holler. People said that if you didn't leave that place with a smile, you were probably in a fight or someone spilled beer on your shirt.

I looked over at Taylor and softly smiled, "Hey," I said making her look at me, "You look very pretty, too." She just rolled her eyes at me and I chuckled at her, returning my look out the window.

The parking lot of Reza's was packed, lots of pickup trucks and other vehicles, I was getting so excited! Cooper managed to find a parking spot in the back of the lot, backing the large truck with skill into the spot. I unbuckled and jumped out of the truck, already walking for the entrance. "Slow down, DaKota!" Taylor yelled behind me.

I turned around, walking backwards with a huge smile on my face, "I'm so excited!" Then I stopped and reached for Cooper's hand and then started to drag him with me. We weren't even in the bar and you could hear the music playing and then I thought of something. "Cooper, I don't have my fake ID."

We stopped in front of the door, him gripping the handle of the door. He looked relaxed, "Don't worry, I know some guys." Then he opened the door, where neon lights and loud music came into vision, making me smile.

We all entered the bar, there wasn't as many people as I thought, but still a lot. I looked at the dance floor and it was calling mine and Cooper's name. I felt Cooper's hands on my waist, pulling me into him. "Ready?" He said into my ear because it was really loud in here.

"Yes!" I nod and just like that, Boot Scootin' Boogie by Brooks and Dun comes on and I lead Cooper over to the dance floor. People around us line up in rows, and we wait to see what dance they're doing and then we quickly pick up on it and start with them. I looked around me and saw a bunch of older cowgirls and cowboys dancing around me, the four of us were only of the few younger people here. Everyone looked like they were having a great time, faces that were full of smiles and sweat. This was only the first dance and I was having a great time.

AFTER THE ELEVENTH song ended, I was out of breath and I could feel the beads of sweat on my forehead. I felt buzzed and high on dancing right now, I never wanted to stop! I crashed into Cooper's chest and gave him a hug and kiss on the cheek. "What was that for?" He chuckled and I looked up at him, he was also sweating, but it was attractive on him.

"It was a thank you for tonight. I'm having so much fun."

"Well I'm glad you are, you deserve it." He smirked and then leaned down and planted one on me, and I melted into him, I loved his kisses. "I'm gonna get a beer, is that alright?" He asked me after I pulled away.

"Only if you get me one." I smirked and he looked shocked, frankly I was too. I rarely drank, but tonight was about having fun and forgetting about everything else. I'm young and I'm going to act like it!

"Alright." Cooper said and left me to go over to the bar. I leaned against a wooden pole and watched the dance going on right now, watching Beau and Taylor dancing together. I smiled at them because Taylor was smiling and laughing, I hope they stay together forever. I looked over to the bar at Cooper and saw him waiting for our beers, man he was one fine piece of cowboy, and he's mine.

I was distracted from looking at Cooper that I didn't see the figure standing in front of me. I jumped back a bit from the stranger, he chuckled. "I didn't mean to scare you." I eyed him up and down. He was wearing a tight black tee, with some jeans and boots, and a backwards ball cap. I didn't know what to say to him and he noticed so he spoke again, "I wanted to ask you to dance." Again, my tongue tied itself. "I mean, a pretty girl like you deserves to be danced with."

"I'm actually here with my boyfriend, sorry." I say and I looked around him, looking for Cooper. Then I realized that was the first time I had admitted I had a boyfriend to someone, and I felt proud.

"Yeah, like I haven't heard that one before. No guy would leave someone like you alone." He laughed, "C'mon just one dance." He stepped closer to me.

"Really, I came here with someone else. I'm flattered, but no thank you." I tried my best to be polite to him.

"At least until he comes back from wherever." He begged, now grabbing my hand, putting me in shock.

"Well he's here now." Cooper's deep voice comes from behind the stranger, making me relax. "And I suggest you drop her hand before I drop you." Cooper walks over to stand beside me, holding our beers.

"Alright, I get it." The stranger drops my hand and holds up his hand and begins to walk away.

"Thanks." I say as I grab my beer and take three big gulps and so does Cooper.

"I'm not leaving you alone again." He said, still looking at the stranger. I roll my eyes at him as I take his hand and we go sit a table and continue to drink our beers.

I finished my beer, and Cooper basically chugged his, and now we're just talking at the table and waiting for a good song to come on. Every time I asked Cooper to dance he would turn me down, he's still in a mood from that stranger. "C'mon, let's dance!" I say to him and I see him looking up over me.

"He's still staring at you." Is all he says to me and I roll my eyes at him. I stand up and reach out and grab his cowboy hat and I put it on me.

"If you want it, come get it." Then I go out to the dance floor and start dancing to "Fake I.D" by Big and Rich by myself. I made sure to move my hips dramatically and keeping eye contact with Cooper. I could tell Cooper was fighting with himself on whether or not to come out here and dance with me. I loved watching him watch my hips and my butt when I turned around.

The song ended and the song "Yeah" by Usher came on, and then once I started dancing again Cooper finally started towards me. I looked around me and I saw couples began to dance with other. "We're here to have fun." I say to Cooper and grab the collar of his shirt and slam my lips on his. "And I wanna dance." I breath after our kiss and then put his hat back on his head.

Cooper smirked, "You look hot with my hat on." Now I know he loosened up. So I decided to go out of my comfort zone and turned around and started to dance against him. He was shocked from my movements, but he quickly caught on and put his hands on my hips. He pulled me even closer against me, and leaned down so he was breathing against my neck. I had never really grinded with someone before, but I'm pretty sure I got the hang of it because Cooper sure as hell wasn't complaining.

I LOOKED DOWN AT ME and Cooper's conjoined hands and smiled softly. We were currently walking towards my ladder on the side of my house, using our phones for lights because it was 2:30 in the morning. We had truly danced the night away, one of the best nights of my life. Also I was slightly buzzed, so it was even more fun. "You have fun tonight?" Cooper asked me as we reached the side of the house.

"The most fun I've had in a long time." I smiled at him. "Did you?" I asked him and he nodded.

"Any time I'm with you, I have fun." He sounded cheesy, making me smile. He pulled his hand away from him, making me fall into him and then he dipped me down and kissed me. The kiss was soft, very romantic and loving, the best kind. Once I was upright, I chuckled and blushed.

"I probably should get to bed, thanks for tonight Coop." I say as he wraps his around me, but then his face gets hard.

"Can I ask you a question?" He sounded serious, making me stop and scrunch my eyebrows together, waiting for him to continue. "Do you think you can do that dance again, but in private?"

"Cooper!" My eyes went wide and I bet that was the reaction he was expecting because he started laughing. I smacked his chest and backed away from him and then I started to climb up to my balcony.

"So is that a no?" He said while laughing as I landed my feet on my balcony.

"It's a maybe." I blushed as I stood against the railing, he nodded and stuck his hands in his pockets.

"I'll take a maybe." He smirked and winked.

"Good night Cooper, try not to dream of me tonight." I smirked and started backing up to my door.

"Oh, I know I'll be taking a cold shower now and in the morning." Cooper was so confident while flirting, while my face turned into a fire hydrant every time. "Good night, Kods." He softly said making me smile as I turned and opened the door into my bedroom and entered.

I didn't bother to go into my bathroom and take off my makeup and wash my face. I just slumped into my bed with a goofy smile on my face because of Cooper. I grabbed my phone and went to my photos and opened the picture Taylor took of me and Cooper tonight, I smiled and I set it as my home screen so I could look at it all the time.

I am so in love with Cooper Blue Blackwood, it's insane.

I screwed my mascara brush back into the tube and looked at myself in the mirror and decided I was finally satisfied with my eyelashes. I ran my fingers through my freshly washed hair and combed over how I liked it. There was something about taking showers in the morning that made me ready to take the on the day head first. Also, I was exhausted from last night so it also gave me a nice wake up.

As I walked into the kitchen, the sweet smell of warm strawberry juice and waffles filled my senses making my glands salivate. "Good morning, sweetie." My mother said to me as she was cooking eggs at the stove.

"Morning." I said quietly as I saw my dad come and sit down at the table, him looking at me. We both gave each other a look that said "don't wanna talk about it" I guess we came to an understanding, but not forgiveness, for me anyway.

I took my seat unwillingly next to my father as my mother brought the tray of Belgium waffles that looked mouth watering. As always, my dad got first pick, then me, and then my mom. We passed what we wanted around the table. I added the warm strawberries to my waffles, with some grapes and pineapples on the side, and some eggs and bacon. As always, orange juice was my drink.

My dad stuck out his hand and so did my mother, I hesitated with my dads, but I quickly took his in mine. I bowed my head and closed my eyes as my father started the morning fast prayer. "Dear Lord, we thank you for letting us wake up to another beautiful Monday morning. Also, thank you for letting us be fortunate enough to have this meal this morning, and as a family. We ask you to protect us from any harm that may come to us throughout the week as we work hard in your name. We ask that you bless our family, friends, and neighbors. Please continue to help us go down the right path in our journey in your greatest gift of life. Amen."

I don't understand how my father could be so sentimental during a prayer, but yet be so rough with his word usage any other time. I guess the power of Lord works in mysterious ways, especially on my dad.

Washing the dishes, I looked up at the window and watched my father drive down our dirt road. He didn't say where he was going, which he never usually does. He probably doesn't want me coming in case I wasn't "ready" for it. I rolled my eyes to myself at the thought. Whatever, I'll just have to get over it and prove myself to him, even though I shouldn't have to. "Where is he going?" I asked my mother who was cleaning the kitchen.

"An auction in Bowman." She says and I nod to myself as I continue watch him drive. I feel myself glaring at him as my mind goes deeper and deeper on what all my father has said to me since I got back from Bismarck. I did nothing to make him say these things, I was so confused. He's treating me like such a young and clueless little girl, it's pissing me off. "DaKota!" My mother's voice breaks through my thinking.

"Hm?" I say blankly to her.

"Are you alright?" She asks from beside me, when did she get there?

"Huh-yeah." I say and look down at the dish I'm holding, or should I say death gripping. One squeeze of my hand and I'm sure the dish would shatter into a million pieces. I loosened my hold and looked at my mother who looked concerned.

"Do you want to go for a ride? It's a beautiful morning, and you could use a hair cut." My mom says calmly and runs her fingers through my hair, focusing on the ends.

"Sure, sounds great." I say with a small smile and then put the dish into the drying side and wipe my hands dry.

I SLID OFF MY MARE Scarlet's left side and I grabbed her reins and tied them to a branch on the tree, making sure she had enough room to be comfortable. My mom and I didn't say much on our ride up to our hair cutting spot, on top of a hill that overlooks the barn and our ranch. All she said during the ride was, "You know you can tell me anything." I found it weird and suspicious of her to say that. It was a beautiful spot and very relaxing to just sit up here. We had managed to keep a chair up here, because mom would always cut Caleb and I's hair ever sense we were kids.

So I took off my flannel, so I was just wearing a black tank top in case my mom poured water on my shirt. I looked over at my mother who was gathering her tools from her backpack, and then I took a seat on the old rustic chair that faced the barn. "Okay, I'm ready! Are you?" Her voice said from behind me.

"Yep." I sat up straighter and she grabbed my hair and started to do her thing. I looked down at the pasture to see the horses playing with each other, drawing a smile from me. I watched as Pharaoh played with Caleb's mare, they were best friends and often inseparable. They acted like brother and sister, like me and Caleb. Pharaoh hasn't had any incidents after the night were my bull headed dad threatened to take him away from me. He's been acting the same from when I left two years ago. He and I had a bond like no other, by far my favorite horse I've owned.

"So are you going to tell me what you were doing with Cooper Blackwood last night?" My eyes went wide from my mom's sudden comment.

Shit.

"I don't know what you're talking about." I said, making me voice sound like she was crazy for thinking so.

"So that wasn't Cooper's Powerstroke in the drive?" Damn. Caught..

"Fine," I sighed giving in, because there was no getting around her. "Wait, how did you know?" I asked her.

"I happened to walk on the porch when you were running out to him, I ducked back in when you turned around to look. You're lucky you're father was still sulking over your argument, or it would of got real serious up in there." I couldn't help but chuckle at my mom's phrasing.

"Are you going to tell him?" I said hoping she would say no.

"No," A huge breath of relief released from me as she answered me. "I know what it's like to be young and in love." She calmly said like it was no big deal.

In love?

Was she talking about me and Cooper? There was no way that she could know about us. Is there?

"In love? Mom what are you talking about?" I chuckle at her, hoping she would fall for it.

"It's okay, sweetie." She didn't sound disappointed, almost a happy and relieved sound. I felt her drop my hair, telling me that I was okay to move.

I turned in my chair to face her, and with a hard swallow I looked up and nodded at her. "Are you gonna tell dad?" I asked her and she laughed.

"No." She laughed and I sighed in relief again.

"Oh my gosh mom, you have no idea how bad I wanted to tell you. Wait-how did you figure it out?" I asked her standing up to fully face her.

"I know you Dakota, it took a wile to figure out, but I did." She looks into my eyes knowingly, "You stand up for him when you're father spits out unnecessary comments about him, even though you do it for other people too, but him, you have this look on your face. Your face looks like your father isn't just insulting Cooper, but you also. It became personal to you when you knew Cooper more, which I assume is when you developed feelings for him. Also the way you stand up for his family, that's when I started to think about everything. Then I noticed when he's in the diner, you always have this goofy smile on your face even when you're not talking with him. Plus, there's always the side glances you guys sneak to each other."

"I thought we were keeping it pretty low." I mumbled.

"You guys are, I'm just more observant than most. And lately you've been asking to go Taylor's, when usually you just tell us you're going over. You mask it pretty well, but I could always see that you were hoping for a yes. And when you got it, your eyes lit up in excitement. I could tell there was something more than just going to Taylor's, but I never knew what is was. In church, I always see you looking for him, hoping he'll show up with his mom, because you always stop looking when you see Desiree.

Then there's the way you guys dance with each other. Others might not feel it, but I could see and feel the intensity from you guys. But what sparked the idea in my mind is the way he looks at you, and only at you. I will admit, when you weren't here I'd see him talk to other girls, but never had I seen his eyes sparkle the way they do with you. He loves you, doesn't he?"

"He really does, and I love him too." I say with adoration, very happy with my mom's piecing of the puzzle. It made me feel all giddy inside because I can just imagine Cooper looking at me the way my mom just described.

"Oh DaKota, I'm so happy!" She says and then she hugs me tight and I hug her right back. "I know how happy you are with him, because when you come home from something that I now realize is usually with Cooper, you look like you are on cloud nine. You're happy right?" She pulls back and holds my shoulders, looking into my eyes.

"The happiest, he's really the best. Oh mom, you wouldn't believe how romantic he is for his charming-bad-cowboy reputation!" I say as I sit back down in my chair, ready for her to continue my haircut.

"Like what? I want to know!" She says, making me laugh.

"You know how I never went to prom?"

"Yes." She says, her voice hinting that she knows where I'm going with this.

"He threw me my own prom! I'll have to show you pictures later. Mom, it was the best night of my life!"

"Oh honey that's so great-" She cuts herself off with a huge gasp, making me worried. "DaKota Annie Jones! When did you get this tattoo?!"

Double shit.

"In Bismarck, it's not a big deal mom. Please don't ruin a good moment." I sigh and then I hear her take a deep breath in and out.

"I won't tell your father about that either." She pauses, "So is he a good kisser?" She says and my face reddens from her question.

"Mom!"

"What? I don't a repeat of Mason again." She says and I chuckle at her. She's right, Mason was not the best kisser. I shivered at the thought of Mason kissing me, but it quickly changed as I thought of Cooper's soft and warm kiss.

"Yes, he's very good." I blushed even more.

"Does his mother know?" She asked me like it was some kind of trick question.

"Well she kind of caught of sleeping together." I instantly regretted my word choice as my mother almost screamed of the thought of Cooper and I having sex, which we haven't. "Not like that, mom! I mean that I fell asleep on Cooper's chest in his bed, and she walked in."

"Oh thank you, Jesus! You guys haven't though, right?" I could tell it was hard for her to ask me by the sound of her voice.

"No, you know me mom."

"Yes, I'm being silly. Just tell me more romantic things about your cowboy." She recovered and I felt a lot better talking to my mom about me and Cooper. I just hope she wouldn't slip to dad about it, that would really had gas to the fire.

I PUNCHED IN THE NUMBERS in the cash register as I rung up two customers. I gave them their change with a smile, "Have a great rest of your evening, come back soon you guys."

"Oh, we'll definitely come back again." One of the boys said, eyeing me up and down. I just shook it off, I got those comments all the time. I looked to my left where Cooper was sitting on the stool at the counter, making sure to watch those two boys all the way out the door and into their pickups. "I'm impressed." I say to him as I begin to wipe off the counter around him.

"What, that I didn't say anything to them? That doesn't sound like me at all." He dragged out the last part making me laugh. "Trust me, it was a lot harder than it looked."

"Well thank you." I said to him and I desperately wanted to thank him with a kiss, but there was other customers so we couldn't.

"Do you need help closing up? I noticed Maybell isn't here."

"No, it's alright, but thank you."

"You sure? Because I was hoping we could finish that dance." He said in a low voice, so I could barely hear it.

I smacked his shoulder again, "Cooper Blackwood." I pointed my finger at him and then he stood up while laughing and grabbed his jacket.

"Alright, I'm gonna head out. Good night, DaKota." Cooper did a quick look around the diner and then placed a quick kiss on my cheek, making me gasp. Cooper displayed his famous crooked smirk, making me blush.

"You're asking for trouble, Blackwood." I say as he walks to the door.

"I like trouble." He winks as he opens the door and walks out. I couldn't help but smile at my boy as I continued to wipe the counter top and tables.

Five minuets until closing time, I look around the diner to see a couple of different tables with old men still talking with coffee. They're usually here until this late, I don't know how they could have coffee this late. It made me wonder what they did when they got home, I cringed just thinking about it.

As I came back from the kitchen, I saw a new customer at the back corner booth. All I could see was a dirty brown, beat up, gus style cowboy hat and a dirty black coat. I started walking to the man and when I got to him, something didn't sit well with me.

He noticed me, and then he slowly lifted his head, revealing his face to me. There was something about this man's face that intrigued me, but I couldn't put my finger on it. He had deep brown eyes, black flowy hair with some streaks of gray, and a rough and rugid face. He looked like he just came out of a western.

"I saw that you're closing pretty soon, am I troubling you for a cup of coffee?" He had one of the lowest voices I had ever heard, it reminded me of Sam Elliot's.

"No, not at all. Is that all?" I asked him, trying to put on my best polite smile.

"Yes." I nodded at him and as I walking towards the kitchen the older men who I talked about earlier were walking out.

"Moneys on the table, DaKota!" They said and I smile.

"As always, have a good night guys." I reply back to them as they walk out. As I'm pouring a cup for the stranger, I'm regretting not having Cooper help me close out. There was just something unsettling with this guy.

I carefully walked with the hot cup of coffee, watching as the steam rolled off the liquid and into the air. The stranger looked up as I sat the cup down, "Thank you darlin'." He rumbled off his tongue, and that pet name made my suspicion grow even more. I gave him a curt nod and turned on my heel and started to walk away. I only got a few feet away when he spoke again, "How's my son doing?"

I stopped in my tracks as all the clues came together like a jigsaw puzzle. I knew that those deep, brown mesmerizing eyes looked familiar, and now I realize that Cooper had gotten them from his father. His father, that was in my diner. Whose father he hasn't seen in years. What was he doing here? What did that mean for Cooper, Desiree, and Reese?

I turned back to him to see his back turned to me, making me walk back over to him. As I studied him more the more I realized he looked like a true outlaw from an old western movie, he fit his part perfectly. But how did he know I was involved with Cooper?

Gathering courage, I stood up straighter. "Wouldn't you like to know?" I crossed my arms, and he must of got a kick out of my actions because his smirk widened.

"He's always liked the feisty ones, just like his mother." He paused, as if he was remembering his wife. "How's she doing?"

"Why do you care? Why are you even here?" I asked him and then he stood up, making me take a step back for precaution.

"Protective, are we?" He chuckled. I didn't want to answer him, I'm sure he'll make into something humorous . "What? I can't check on my family?"

"I wouldn't exactly call it a family, and after how many years?" His smirk turned into a dangerous frown and he looked all business now.

"Hasn't anyone taught you to mind your own business about someone else's business?"

"As much as they taught you to be a father to your sons." His face softened as I mentioned his sons, but he covered it up quickly. "It isn't fair to Cooper to have act like a father to Reese, and not even lawful to your wife to have to raise Reese all by herself." I must of hit a soft spot because in a flash, Cooper's dad had grabbed me and spun me into his chest and into a choke hold.

"You better shut that pretty little mouth of yours girl, you can get into a whole lot of trouble with that thing." He tightened his grip on my neck, making me gasp for air. He made sure to do this for another twenty seconds, tightening every five seconds, to get a bigger reaction from me. "Don't mess with me girl." He says and then releases me from his grip, making me fall onto the ground at his feet. He begins to walk away and then stops, "Thanks for the coffee." He tips his hat at me, making me glare at him. "Oh and tell my boy that my offer still stands if he knows what's good for him." And with that, Cooper's dad walks out of my diner and I'm still on the floor trying to get my breathing steady.

I DON'T WASTE ANYTIME getting out to Cooper's place. I was hoping that I wouldn't find his dad's vehicle out there, which I didn't even know what it looked like. Would his dad pay them a little visit, or was visiting me a warning for them? It was about 10 o'clock when I pulled up by the porch. I slammed my truck door and ran to the porch and quickly knocked on the door.

Cooper came to the door and when he saw me he looked very confused. "DaKota? What are you doing here?" He said as he cocked his head and let me in.

I saw that Desiree was sitting at their kitchen table and I looked around for Reese. "Where's Reese?" I asked them.

"He's in bed, what's wrong Kota?" Cooper asked more worried and I looked at Desiree and gave her a serious look and she sat up straighter, realizing something serious was happening.

"Your dad just gave me a little visit at the diner." Desiree put her head in her hands while her elbows rested on the table, and she rubbed her temples.

"Jesus Christ." They both blew out.

I looked at Cooper and his jaw was locked so hard, I thought it was going to break any second. "Did he say anything?" Cooper looked at me and then his eyes widened. "Did he touch you?!" His voice boomed as if he already knew the answer.

"No." I lied, I didn't want to make the situation worse.

"Don't lie to me." He growled, making me cower into my socks. I slowly looked up at him and nodded. "What did he do? Tell me." His voice wasn't as threatening anymore, but still louder than usual.

"I was telling him how he's a piece-of-a-shit father and then he put me in a choke hold. After that he dropped me to the floor and told me to tell you that his offer still stands if you know what's good for you."

"Are you okay, DaKota?" Desiree says like a typical mom.

"I'll be fine. But Cooper, what's his offer?" I asked him. Cooper's eyes went from mine, to the floor, to his mother.

"To go with him."

"That's crazy." I laugh, but they didn't think it was funny. "So what does that mean now?" I ask them.

"There's no way to tell with Bill, he could come back tomorrow, or come back in five years. I'm sorry that he involved you in this." Desiree says.

"I'm staying with you until closing time from now on." Cooper suddenly pulls me into a hug and I hug him just as tight. "I'm so sorry, baby."

"No, I'm just worried about you guys. What do you think he wants?" I pull away from Cooper, but he keeps one arm wrapped around my waist, holding me like he was never letting go.

"What he always wants, the satisfaction of controling our lives." Desiree says, making all of our faces turn more gloomy than before.

AFTER MORE DISCUSSION about Cooper's dad, I decided I should head home because I could barely stay awake. Cooper walked me to my truck, closing my door after I climbed in. The window was down and Cooper leaned against my door. "Please text me when you get home. I need to know that you're safe." Before I buckled myself, I leaned over and placed my lips on his.

I kissed him with so much love and appreciation, and he returned it, his more of protection and love. None the less, it was an amazing kiss. I pulled back and whispered, "I love you."

"I love you, too. See you tomorrow?"

"Yes," I started my truck and buckled, "And you can count on that dance tomorrow." I said as I backed up, trying to lighten Cooper's mood. Which I succeeded because he smiled.

"It's a date." He said and I laughed as I turned the wheel and started down the drive.

When I got out of my pickup and started walking to the porch, I texted Cooper I was home and then I tucked my phone into my pocket. I opened our porch door and walked in to see the lights were off, good, I didn't feel like talking to anyone right now. I jogged up the stairs to my room, and then kicked off my boots and threw on some shorts and took off my shirt and jumped into bed.

I looked at my phone and saw that Cooper had texted, "Thanks for letting me know. I am sorry for what happened tonight, I hate that it did."

I frowned as I read it, and I replied: "It's not your fault Cooper, please stop beating yourself up. I'm just happy nothing happened to you guys."

He replied: "I love you so much DaKota Annie Jones.

My heart skipped about three beats while reading his text, "Every time you say that, you make me the happiest girl in the world."

Cooper replied: "Good, you deserve it.. Sweet dreams, my angel." That was the last thing I saw before the darkness overtook my eyes and I fell asleep with a smile on my face.

I stirred in my sleep as I thought my covers moved. I turned my head, trying to return to sleep because I was having such a good dream and it was too early to wake up. Soon I felt weight being pressed down on me, and felt a near presence. Then without me moving, my hair moved off my shoulder and then I felt hot breath against my shoulder. I opened my eyes, and saw a denim covered body, and brown hair. As the kisses started on my neck, I decided to fake being asleep.

His kisses were slow and soft, going from my collarbone, to the base of my neck, up the side of my neck, then a lingering kiss below my ear. "I know you're awake." He whispered huskily as he began to nibble on my ear. The sound of his voice sent my insides on fire, damn this boy.

"Doesn't mean you should stop." I shrug a little and then he chuckles lowly and then his lips find my jawline, slightly nipping at the skin. He trailed his lips across all the way across my jaw, then going to the other side of my neck, man he was an expert at this.

His left hand touched my bare shoulder, sending shivers down my skin from the contact. His hand traveled down, taking my covers lower, revealing my sports bra. He had managed to slip himself under the covers with me, his hand finding my bare waist. His lips nibble all the way up my chin and they finally find my lips, which we then devoured each others lips. I wrapped my hands around his neck pulling him closer to me, and then running my fingers through his hair.

The kiss was becoming heated when he licked my bottom lip for entrance and I opened wider for him, and then he laid fully in between my legs. We both moaned into each others mouth when Cooper grinded himself on me. My left hand left his hair and ran down his back as far as it could, scratching his back.

I pulled back breathlessly as I realized this was going to far for the morning, and I hadn't even brushed my teeth! My hand covered my mouth and Cooper laughed at me. "Don't be self conscious, I love kissing you in the morning." He said like he was in a dream as he leaned back down and tried to kiss me again, but I turned my head so he got my cheek.

"Cooper, I need to shower." I said, trying to pry himself off me.

"I'm not letting you up until you kiss me." He said, his words making me look at him realizing he was serious. I leaned up and pulled his head down to mine and connected our lips and we kissed for a couple moments and then pulled back. "Have I ever told you how beautiful you look in the morning?" I rolled my eyes at him as I pushed him off me finally.

"Thank you," I blushed as I got out of my bed. "When did you get here?" I asked him.

"Just a few minuets ago, your mom told me to come wake you up, I gladly accepted." He smirked.

"She really likes you." I smile softly and he doesn't looked shocked.

"Ladies love cowboys." I pick up my shirt and throw it at him making him laugh and look at the tee shirt from years ago.

AFTER MY SHOWER, I combed my hair and then I applied lotion to my legs to make them soft. Plus, after I shaved my legs they get itchy, so the lotion helped with that. I took off my towel and put it on again tighter because I forgot my clothes in my room, and I'm betting Cooper is still in there because he loves seeing me in a towel. His words not mine.

I opened the door slowly and peeked my head around the door and sure enough he was laying on my bed on his phone. He was laying on his side, with his elbow holding up his head. When he saw me he smirked. Then he let out a long whistle and then held his chest and fell back onto the chest, like he had been hit with something. "God damn, my girl is beautiful."

My lips pulled into a huge smile as my face reddened. "You're such a dork." I giggled going over to my drawers to get my clothes.

"Only for you girly. Now hurry up, everyone is waiting on you." He said, making my eyes go wide.

"Why didn't you tell me that earlier? I would of took a shorter shower!" I say and then I run back into my bathroom and quickly change into a Dale Brisby Rodeo Time shirt and a pair of black Nike shorts.

Today, Taylor, Beau, Caleb, Ashley, Cooper and I are heading out to go to Mandan, North Dakota for the Mandan Rodeo days. All couples were taking their own vehicles, but my mother wanted to take a picture off all of us before we went. She insisted on it, she was not going to be denied her picture.

I quickly hung up my towel and then went back into my room and started to search for my rodeo riggin bag, my boots, and cowboy hats.

"Where's my stuff?" I mumbled to myself as I looked under my bed and frantically searched my room.

"Honey." I hear Cooper's voice but I ignored it because I was too busy looking in my closet. Where the heck did I put it! How could I loose a riggin bag! I know I put it beside my bed yesterday! As I turned to walk to the other side of my room, Cooper grabbed my shoulders and stopped me. "Honey, I put all of your stuff in my pickup already."

"Oh," I chuckled and then looked into his eyes and smiled, "Thank you." I leaned up and kissed his cheek.

"That's all I get?" He says as I start to walk away from him.

"Yep," I smirk evilly. "They're waiting for us down there." I say as I open my door and then walk outside into the hallway.

We all gather into one line in front of my porch as my mom holds up her phone, trying to take a picture of us. Beau was on the far right, then Tay, then Cooper, then me, then Ash, and lastly Caleb. All of us girls had our heads leaned towards our men, showing that we were proud and happy. "Alright you guys! Go on and kick ass and take some names! Have lots of fun! Love you guys!" She said as she gave us each a hug before we went to our pickups and trailers.

I walked over to my girl, Scarlet, who was poking her head out Cooper's trailer window. "Hey girlfriend." I say grabbing her nose and giving it a kiss and then a scratch, her favorite. I was bringing Scarlet this weekend because I was team roping with Taylor, not barrel racing.

I grabbed the handle to Cooper's truck and opened it and jumped in, literally this pickup was hard for me to get in. "I laugh every time I see you try to get up." He says from the drivers seat with an amused face.

"I have little legs!" I say as I close the door and buckle myself.

"I beg to differ, you have incredible long sexy legs." He said, putting his arm on the back of my chair, looking backwards as he backs the trailer so he can make a u-turn.

"You're awful flirty this morning." I say with a bit of disbelief and I angle my body towards him.

"Better get use to it darlin'." He said plainly, focusing on not jack-knifing the trailer into his truck.

I return to my original position in the passenger seat, as Cooper makes his u-turn and starts our way down my drive. I was hesitant about agreeing to enter the Mandan Rodeo. I was indecisive because Mandan is a city right next to Bismarck, the city where everything ended for good. I know nothing is going to happen, but I'm just scared that I will be paranoid the whole time. Or that I will be having flashbacks whenever, I don't want it to ruin the time with my friends. Hopefully being with Cooper will help relax me and we can spend quality time together, not worrying that we're going to get caught.

MY THOUGHTS WOKE ME from my nap in the passenger seat, but I kept my eyes closed once I heard Cooper singing along with a Miranda Lambert song which I recognized as "Me and Charlie Talking". I really wished I had my phone in my hands to record this, he was so confident singing this song. He had to lighten his voice to match Miranda's which I found hilarious because he didn't sound half bad at it, I only wondered how he sounded in the shower.

I heard him tapping the stearing wheel and I could only imagine him bobbing his head up and down to the beat of the song. A wide smile crept on my lips, I was struggling on holding back a giggle from my lips. This was a song that I would never imagine him listening to, ever. He knew every word to it!

Once the song ended and an George Strait song came on, I decided to turn my head to face him, gaining his attention. I had the chair lied all the way back, so I was practically lying down. "Well good afternoon sleepy beauty." He smirked and than raised his eyebrows at me. "Why are you smiling like a fool?"

The smile stayed on my face, possibly smiling even more. "You're a great singer." I giggled and he ducked his head back and groaned.

"How much did you hear?" He asked me and then I reached down the side of the chair and pulled the level and returned my seat back to normal.

"Just the last song, I enjoyed waking up to you singing your little heart out to Miranda." I teased him a bit.

He looked at me and very sarcastically said, "Ha-ha." with a fake smile on his face making me laugh.

I sat up straighter and looked out the windshield, "Where are we?" It looked like we were in the middle of no where.

"Little outside of Beach." He says looking out his window.

"Okay, so just a couple of hours left?" I asked him, looking over at him and he nodded looking at me and smirking.

"My girl is so smart!" Again with the sarcasm. It was me this time to respond with a fake-sarcastic smile and laugh.

"Have you ever been to North Dakota before?" I asked him and he nodded.

"Just to Medora, not to any of the bigger cities. Medora is actually pretty fun, I wouldn't mind going there again sometime." Hmm, I'll have to remember that one.

"We used to go to the Musical all the time as kids, it would be our special vacation for good behavior." I said smiling down at my hands in my lap as I remembered sitting in the front row, and then being called up to dance with other kids.

"I can't imagine that you have ever been bad in your life." Cooper said in a matter-of-fact tone, making me roll my eyes at him.

"I can be bad!" I scoffed turning towards him with my jaw dropped.

"Okay, DaKota." He chuckled like he was letting me win the argument.

"I can!"

"Like what?" He amused himself with this question.

"Well, right now! My dad doesn't know we're dating. Oh, and I snuck out the other night! There's plenty of stuff like that!" I crossed my arms, proud that I proved myself to him.

"Okay, that stuff is cliche though." He stumped me with that. I huffed in my seat, going into deep thought trying to find something. A smirk came on my face when I found one particular memory that I was slightly embarrassed about, but it proved I went out of my comfort zone.

"Okay, how 'bout that dance I did for you." My smirk got bigger once, I saw Cooper's slight squirm at the thought of it, but then he started to smirk.

"I don't remember, you'll have to explain it to me." Classic Cooper, always getting me to blush. I playfully shoved his shoulder as my face turned beet red.

"Cooper!"

He laughed at me, and I couldn't help but admire his super sexy smile that drove me insane. Once he calmed his laughter he said, "Oh I remember." He smirked at me, making eye contact. "That was bad." I'm sure my face was as red as a freaking fire hydrant by now. Cooper added on to it, "I think I'm ready for round two." Oh my lord!

"Cooper, stop!" I groaned as I put my face in my hands. "You won't get another one of those if you keep laughing at me!" I say pulling my face away from my hands as I felt my cheeks get lighter.

"I'm not laughing at you, DaKota. I'm laughing because you're just so damn cute!!" He says and then he reaches for my hand and brings it to his lips, planting a small kiss on my knuckles. The small gesture instantly lightens my mood, damn him.

"Whatever you say, Cooper." I say and pull my hand back from him, but he just grabs it again and intertwines our fingers together as he continues to drive. I look at our hands and then at him he smugly smirks. Without looking at me, Cooper gives my hand a squeeze and then I rub the back of his hand with my thumb, returning his gesture.

WE FINALLY MADE IT to the rodeo camp grounds at 7:30 and Cooper backed in next to Ashley and Caleb's trailer. I was tired, but it was too early just to sit around and do nothing. Maybe we could go out on the town and explore, I vaguely remember some good bars around this town. But right now, we had to get settled in. Walking back to the trailer, I went to the trailer door and stepped into the trailer and smiled at the horses who both turned to look at me. "Hello, pretty ponies!" I baby talked them, grabbing Scarlet first and then tying her to a rope hook on the trailer. I then grabbed Cooper's gelding, Gator, and did the same.

Cooper appeared and then he offered me a small smile, "Should we give them a small stretch?" He said to me, stretching himself.

"Sure, lets go over to the arena." I say as I untie Scarlet and then walk next to Cooper as we lead our horses to the stadium.

"Are you tired?" I asked him as we continued walking, getting our horses used to their surroundings.

"I've had longer drives, why?" He asked me, looking over at me.

"Well I was thinking that maybe all of us could go find a bar to go chill out for bit, maybe get some food?" I ask him and he slightly nods to my offer.

"Yeah, I'm good with whatever we do." He says and I just nod. "Does your neck hurt?" He asks me, sparking confusion in me.

"What kind of question is that?" I chuckle.

"You didn't even use your pillow while your slept on the way here. You looked so uncomfortable, but yet, you slept for so long." He laughs.

"Trust me, I can sleep wherever and whenever. When I was a kid, I took a nap on a law mower. My chiropractor says I have strong neck muscles." I laughed and he did too.

"Weirdo."

"Okay, whatever." I playfully scoff at him and roll my eyes at him.

"What? You think I'm weird?" He asks me and I confirm by giving him a nod of my head, "Like what?" He challenges me.

"You!..you..." I stop and try to think of something that makes him weird, but Cooper's such a laid back guy! He notices my stumble and he smirks, "You have weird feet!" I tell him confidently, but he just raises his eyebrows at me. Okay, I admit, it was weird of me to just say that.

"Okay," He sounds disbelieving, "What's wrong about my feet?" He debates with me, knowing that I'll have a hard time trying to prove to him why they are weird.

"Well the toe next to your big toe is in fact bigger than your big toe! Then the other ones are smaller than that one!" Cooper starts to laugh at me, and I can feel my cheeks start to heat up.

"A lot of people's toes do that, DaKota. But good try." I roll my eyes at him, not ready to give up yet.

"Well, they're hairy!" I argue again, now just making a fool of myself.

"Like any other guy's." He says and then he reaches out for me and wraps his arm around my shoulder, giving me a petty squeeze. "Just admit it, DaKota. I don't have anything weird about me, hell, I'm perfect." He says in a fake peppy tone, telling me he's joking, but I still roll my eyes at him.

"Yeah, keep tellin yourself that, pretty boy." After I say this, he kisses my cheek and then unwraps his arm from my shoulder as we enter the arena where other people are running their horses. "Will you give me a leg up?" I ask him as I throw Scarlet's lead rope around, and grab into her mane. Scarlet is 16 hands, so it's pretty hard to get on her with no stirrup. Cooper leans down and cups his hands and I put my foot on his hands and he easily lifts me up and I swing my right leg over.

Still on our horses, we ride back to Cooper's trailer and see that another trailer had parked next to ours. I thought it was Taylor and Beau, but they are on the other side of Caleb and Ash. As we get closer to the truck I can hear voices getting closer and then two people come out from behind the mystery trailer, and as if Scarlet was reading my mind, we stopped in our tracks.

Stetson Aimes.

I threw my head back and asked God why he would do this to me. When I returned my head back and made eye contact with him, he actually had the nerve to smirk at me. He looked surprised, but also amused, like it was a delighted surprise to see me. But then his eyes traveled over to Cooper and his lips turned into a frown, and Cooper's face was as hard as stone. Great.

"DaKota! What an great-unexpected coincidence!" He awkwardly smiles looking away from Cooper's death stare.

"Yes it is Stetson, how are you?" I try to put on my best fake-polite smile to him.

"Oh I'm doing okay." He says and then looks over at his friend, "Oh! This is my travelin' partner, Jamison Dodge." I give the guy a small toothless smile. "Cooper, nice to see you." Stetson says, but Cooper remains the exact same as before, silent.

"Cooper, be nice." I whispered under my breath looking at him.

Cooper looked at me and gave me a look that said 'do-I-really-have-to'? I nodded to him and he sighed and said, "Same to you." I rolled my eyes at that.

"Well! We better go feed our horses, see you guys around! Nice to meet you, Jamison." I say as I tap Scarlet in the right direction. That Jamison dude tips his hat at me and then Cooper and I go around to the other side of the trailer and slide off our horses. "You could of at least smiled at him." I mumbled at tough ol' Cooper as I tied Scarlet to the trailer.

"Why should I be nice to him? He assaulted my girlfriend!!" He said in a firm voice, not afraid if Stetson heard us, which I'm pretty sure he heard Cooper.

"Keep your voice down!" I whispered-yelled at him as I got the horses feed ready.

"I don't give a rat's ass if that jackass hears me." Cooper says as he starts to help me with the feed.

"He did apologize." I point out to him, trying to give Stetson the benefit of the doubt.

"An apology isn't enough for what he did to you." Cooper says as he takes his bucket to his horse and I follow and do the same.

"So beating the shit out of him wasn't enough, either?" I cross my arms at him and he stands straighter and sends me a knowing look.

"Okay fine," He sighed and leaned his right arm against the trailer looking at me, "But it doesn't change that I don't like him." He added, and then looked to his right as if he was staring at Stetson.

"Well that's fine if you don't like him, but you don't have to make it obvious." I say taking a couple of steps forward towards him.

"I'm just trying to help the message be clear to him." Cooper shrugs and I scrunch my eyebrows.

"What message?" I ask him.

"That if he tries anything with you or me, he's gonna wish he hadn't." Cooper said seriously and I restrained myself from rolling my eyes at him.

"Oh Cooper, you're such a tough guy." I playfully say as I wrap my arms around his waist and look up at him. Cooper just needed to relax because Stetson isn't going to do anything to us, I'm sure of it. Cooper looked down at me and kind of glared, not liking my teasing. "Oh c'mon Coop! Lighten up!" Still nothing. "If you don't smile, I won't kiss you for the whole entire weekend!"

"You wouldn't." Cooper says weary, raising an eyebrow suspiciously.

"You know how stubborn I can be." I say plainly as I back away from. This whole thing was a bluff, there was no way I could resist myself from Cooper when this was the only time we could actually act like a couple in front of people. Cooper looks me up and down, thinking over my ultimatum. I cross my arms and give him a serious bitch face, proving my stubbornness.

"Alright," He laughs and his smile shows, making me smile and uncross my arms. "Now come here and give me a kiss." He reaches out for me and pulls me into his chest and leans down and places his heavenly lips on mine and I instantly melt into him.

I woke up to what I thought was my alarm clock, but the sound was definitely not "Kerosene" by Miranda Lambert. Instead the sound was a snoring Cooper right beside my face. I was currently laying directly on my back, my right arm at a 90 degree with my hand under a pillow. My left arm was around Cooper's shoulders. Coopers head was resting on my shoulder, while his left arm was sprawled against my chest while his left hand was resting on my upper arm.

I looked down at him and couldn't help but smile. It was usually me who was "spooning" Cooper, but to be honest, I liked this a lot better. Being like this made me feel appreciated. I didn't get to see this side of Cooper often, he almost seemed like a low-key baby. The way he was so snuggled into me have me a strong sense of something, like I was precious to him. Sure, he does a lot of romantic things for me and that's his soft side but this was different. He looked almost, vulnerable. Not weak, but if he were to let me go right now, he would lose me.

Cherishing this moment, I brought my left hand up and I started to run my fingers through his soft hair, careful not to wake him up. I didn't care that his snores woke me up, I'm glad I was lucky enough to witness this. His eyebrows were lightly scrunched, as if he was focusing on dreaming, hopefully about me. His lips were slightly parted as he breathed. When Cooper was sleeping he looked adorably innocent and youthful.

Okay, I had to get a picture of this. Carefully, I untangled my fingers from his locks and reached over for my phone, slightly moving causing me to stop to see if he woke. Once I saw he was still soundly asleep, I grabbed my phone and opened my camera and took a couple of pictures from my view and then one above us, just getting his position in the picture. Then I looked over them and decided that they were perfect and made my heart happy and warm.

I put my phone back, noticing the time was almost seven o'clock. Tonight we had to be warming up by 7:00 because the rodeo started at 7:30, so we had time to waste during the day. I sighed and started to run my fingers through his hair and then he snuggled more into me, making me smile with adoration. I ran my fingers to the nape of his neck, my fingers tingling when they contacted his soft tan skin. Cooper was shirtless, so I ran my nails across the middle of his back and made circular patterns.

"That feels amazing." His incredibly sexy rough morning voice grumbled out, sending chills through out my body.

"Good morning." I hummed and smiled even though he wasn't looking at me.

Cooper took his arm off mine, and then made his hand into a fist, pushing himself up and doing the same to the other arm, so he was looking down at me. Cooper lips turn into a goofy smile once he looked at me, making me smile more. I watched his eyes as they inspected my face. I'd usually be insecure about someone doing this, but with him I absolutely loved it. "Gall, have I ever told you how freakin' beautiful you are?" His voice was still rough, but yet so smooth. It wasn't fair to me.

"Only about a thousand times." I chuckle and roll my eyes playfully at him.

272

His eyes almost sparkled what I assumed was happiness as he leaned down lower to me, "Well that's it's not enough." Then what we've both been waiting for since we've woken up happened when his lips connected with mine. My hands automatically went to his stubby cheeks, loving the way his unshaven face felt under my touch.

The kiss didn't last long, but for once I was okay with it because it was morning and we both needed to freshen up. "I call the sink first." I pushed him away from me, making him land on his back. I crawled to the end of the bed and walked down the steps until he stopped me.

"Wait," He said and then I turned to him and he had his phone in front of his face. "Smile pretty girl." I sighed and tilted my head back and to the side and then bringing my hands to under my chine and popped my foot, trying to be cute. He gave me a thumbs up, telling me I could continue. So I went to the sink and looked at myself in the mirror. My hair was pulled into a slightly messy high ponytail, curls falling to frame my face. I had on a navy over sized Carhartt shirt, that almost reached my knees.

From my makeup bag, I grabbed my headband and put it over my ears and pushed it up until it reached my hairline and then I started the water, gathering it in my hands and then splashing my face. I turned off the water and then pumped my face wash into my hands and then smothered it on my face. While that was descending in my pores, I began to brush my teeth.

"Okay I'm done." I say as I hang up my wash cloth and then lay on the couch, resting my back against the wood. I checked my social media, occasionally liking some pictures on Instagram and Facebook. When I went on Snapchat I had a ton of stories to watch but there was one that intrigued me the most. Cooper's. I clicked on it and it was the picture he just took of me and the caption was "#NaturalBeauty" Ugh! My heart is going to explode!!

I looked at Cooper who was brushing his teeth, slightly smirking at me through the mirror. I stood up and placed my hands on his shoulder and kissed his cheek, "I love you." I say and then go back to my original position.

"I love you too, baby." He said in a deep funny voice because his mouth was full of toothpaste, making me laugh and shake my head.

COOPER HELD THE DOOR open for me as we walked into the restaurant Dakota Farms. There was a sign that said to seat yourselves, so Cooper and I took a booth next to a window. There were mostly older people in here, enjoying some coffee and the newspaper. "I've been here a couple of times, they have really good food. You'll like anything." I tell Cooper as I look around.

"Alright, then you can pick for me." Cooper said gaining my attention.

"Really?" I asked him and he smiled and shrugged.

"Yup, if you say I'll like anything. Let's so how well you know me." He said putting his arms on the table trying to be somewhat intimidating.

I cocked an eyebrow at him as a young waitress came to us with menus, "Good morning. I'm Lucy and I'll be serving you today, what can I get you to drink?" She smiled brightly at us.

"I'll take an orange juice." I said to her.

"I'll just have a water." Cooper said with a toothless smile.

"Okay, I'll be back with those." She nodded and walked off and I opened the menu, decided what to get for me and Cooper.

"How hungry are you?" I ask him so I know how much he wants.

"Very." He said and I nodded as I decided on what he was going to get. It wasn't anything special.

The waitress came back right on time as I made up my mind, she carefully put our drinks in front of us and pulled out her notepad and clicked her pen. "You guys ready?" She asked and I nodded.

"I'm going to have a caramel roll with a cup of kneophla soup. And then he is going to do the number eight, pancakes, hash browns, sour dough bread, and sunny side up!" I say her and she smiles, writing down the information.

"Well that makes my job easy! Okay, I'll put that in for your guys." She says as she takes our menus.

"Thanks." Cooper and I say in unison.

"So, how'd I do?" I ask him as he cocks his eyebrow, impressed.

"You even got the eggs right, sunny side up is my-"

"Favorite." I finish for him and he smiles at me. I take a sip of my orange juice and I look around again, but once I spot a familiar face walking through the door, I advert my eyes immediately. "Shit." I mumbled under my breath, ducking my head down.

"What's wrong?" Cooper leans forwards.

"Don't look, but that's my old boss from when I lived in Bismarck." I say quietly as I slowly lift my head back into original position, trying to act normal.

"What's wrong with him?" Cooper asked me.

"He's always been a little suspicious of me. He always asked me why I was always so silent, and when I missed three days because of you know who, he came to my apartment to check up on me. That day, I was a mess and he caught me in my worst while I was packing my bags, I was a sobering wreck. I was so embarrassed and right there I told him I was leaving and didn't tell him why."

"I'm sorry, honey." He softly said and the grabbed my hand and gave me a reassuring squeeze.

I sighed and returned my focus on my wonderful boyfriend, "I'll be fine, but thanks." I say forcing myself to suck it up. He probably didn't even remember me. I mean he's probably had lots of people work for him, a girl like me wouldn't be any thing special to him.

"Cassidy?"

Man, do I have the shittiest luck in the world.

Then I began to laugh, Cooper went wide-eyed at me. "Just start to laugh, make up a conversation." I say through gritted teeth, still trying to fake a laugh. Cooper followed me and gave me his best fake laugh, which wasn't too bad.

"Oh man! That was the funniest moment in my life when he fell into the water!" Cooper made up while he was laughing. But from the corner of my eye, I could still see Nick, my old boss, coming in our direction. My heart was pounding in my chest, and by now I think I was hysterically laughing.

"Cassidy-Cassidy Smith?" He said once again now reaching our booth. Well there was no getting out of this one.

I did my best trying to look surprised to see him, "Mr. Sullivan!" He looked very skeptical of me, probably wondering what I was doing back in this area.

"Nick, how are you?" He asked in what I could understand was a concerned voice.

"I'm doing just fine! How are you?" I ask him with a smile, as if that day never happened.

"Um, Cassidy may I talk-"

"Oh, how rude of me! Mr. Sullivan, or sorry, Nick this is my boyfriend Cooper. Cooper this is my old boss Nick." I had to cut off Nick before he could ask me to talk in private, this is the only thing I could think of.

Cooper slid out of the booth and stood up to shake Nick's hand, "Nice to meet you, sir." Cooper said and then slid back down.

"Same to you. But Cassidy would you mind if we-"

"Excuse me, sir." Lucy, our waitress, said as her and another girl came with our food. Okay, maybe my luck was turning on me. Lucy placed our delicious looking food in front of us and I could see Nick still looking at me.

"Well, I guess I'll leave you guys to your meal. It was nice to see you again, Cassidy." Nick said very confused about what just happened. I would be too if I were in his shoes.

"Have a nice day." I smiled to him as he turned around and walked to the other side of the restaurant, to a booth where we couldn't see each other. I looked at Cooper and sighed, "Thanks for playing along."

"I could of just told him to leave you alone. Guys like that are scared of jealous-handsome-rugid-cowboy boyfriends." Cooper was joking, well about the handsome part. But I had no doubt that Cooper would do that for me. I had even thought about it, but I didn't need more attention drawn to us. Who knows how Nick would react to Cooper and vice versa.

"I know, but it all worked out." I say as I take a bite of my warm caramel roll. This was a little piece of heaven as it melted in my mouth. "Do you wanna try this?" I asked Cooper after I wiped my mouth.

Cooper nodded and then I cut a piece, stuck it on my fork, and feed the caramel roll to Cooper. Once the food entered his mouth, his eyes rolled to back of his head and he moaned. "Oh, that's good." He said with a mouth full. "We're getting some to go." He said looking at the counter making me laugh.

I TIGHTENED THE CINCH around Cooper's bull dogging horse, Gator, giving him a pat on the stomach after I was finished. "You're such a good boy." I then kissed his muzzle and scratched behind his ear. I had to tack Cooper's horse because Cooper was getting our back numbers and he running a bit late. I didn't mind because soon I had to start warming up Scarlet.

Looking around me, I looked for Cooper, but he was no where to be seen. So I grabbed a couple of cinnamon apple treats for Gator, along with his supplements. I grabbed the hoof pic and walked back into the trailer and looked at the time, 7:15, Cooper was running really late. What could be holding him up? But when I stepped out of the trailer I saw Cooper coming over in a golf cart with what looked like a security guard. I waved at the driver once Cooper got off and jogged over to me. Relief washed over his face once he saw that Gator was tacked and ready to go. "Oh thank you so much, Kods. You're the best." He said and quickly hooked an arm around my waist and plated a big kiss on my lips and then handed me our back numbers. He turned around and I pinned his number on, 119.

Then he grabbed the reins and put his boot in the stirrup and hauled himself up onto the saddle. "Why were you so late?" I asked him.

"Apparently I have a fan group here," He said and then he kicked Gator forward, walking away from me. My jaw dropped a bit, Cooper had groupies? "Don't worry honey, don't need to be jealous!" He turned his body towards me, still riding forward. He had a cocky smile on my face and I still realized my jaw was dropped, making me clamp my jaws shut.

"Hey girly are you ready yet?" Taylor's voice came from the front of their pickup.

I looked at her and shook my head, "I still have to tack Scarlet." I say as I walk up to her and hand her my back number and pins. "Please?" I turn around and I feel her adjust my shirt and then she pins it on. I was number 120. Today was I was wearing a vintage stripped shirt with some dark blue Kimes Ranch Jeans. After she was done pinning it on, I jog to the tack room and grab her saddle pad and saddle.

I stuck my left foot into the stirrup and grabbed the saddle horn and hoisted myself up into my saddle and laid my rope around the horn. I stood up in both of my stirrups and moved around a bit to see if everything was cinched the right amount, and everything seemed fine.

As we rode up to the racing track behind the arena the security guards opened the gate for us and we looked around at the other competitors. As I was looking around, I saw Cooper warming up with a couple of buddies of his. I pulled my phone from my front pocket and checked the time, 7:29. I looked at the arena and the rodeo queens were riding out the sponsor flags, so they would be doing the National Anthem soon. "Let's go over by the chutes." I say to Taylor and then kick Scarlet into that direction and Taylor and her horse follow.

We went right next to the bucking chutes and then I dropped my reins around the saddle horn and slouched in my saddle. "Hey cowgirls!" A male voice said from the top of the chutes.

Taylor and I both looked up and saw a rough looking cowboy sitting on the gate of chute with a couple other boys, who were smiling at us. Taylor and I just gave him a polite smile and nod and returned to watching the rodeo queens. "Y'all going to the Lonesome Dove tonight?" He spoke again.

"No, sir." Taylor said in a tone that hinted to leave us alone.

"Oh come on! It'll be fun! Especially if you hang out with us!" He tried to persuade us.

"Knock it off, Elliot. They both have boyfriends that could kick your ass without lifting a finger." My brother's voice came from the walkway of the chutes. My chest released a relieved sigh and I could see Taylor lighten up too.

"Damn!" Elliot hissed making me laugh. The boys scooted down the chute more and Caleb stood at the railing looking down at us.

"Thanks Caleb." I said.

"No problem little sis. Even if you guys didn't have Beau or Cooper I still wouldn't let him hit on you."

"Why?" Taylor asks before me.

"Did you look at him? The dude is straight up creepy." Caleb said and we both started to laugh, even though Elliot wasn't that bad looking.

I shook my head at my brother, "Well not everyone can be as handsome as you, Caleb." I joke with him. Caleb straightens his posture and smirks.

"Damn straight, little sister. Glad you finally came to your senses." Well I just boosted his ego about twenty times.

"GOOD JOB GIRLS." THE lady smiled at us as we grabbed our checks for $873. Tonight we took the top time in the first go with 6.1 seconds and we are sitting second in the average. Caleb took second score in the first go with a score of 84.5 and Cooper had a no score because his calf got away from them. The steers weren't the best tonight so I think Tay and I got lucky with our pick because we got the best steer.

"Thank you." We both said and smiled at the lady and then started making our way to our trailers with our horses.

"We kicked the boys' asses tonight!" Taylor says as we put the horses in the stables after we untacked them.

"You bet, girlfriend! I hope that Cooper rides tonight, or he's gonna be grumpy in the trailer." I say as I grab the brush out of the bucket and start brushing Scarlet down.

"Oh yeah and that doesn't mix well with making out." Taylor said and I scoffed at her and she started to laugh.

"Whatever, Taylor." I laugh at her and shake my head.

"Oh c'mon! This is the only time where you guys won't get caught and you're telling me that you guys aren't all over each other?" She said in disbelief as she bent down to brush the under belly of her horse.

"Well we're more lovey-dovey than usual but it's not like we're kissing more than breathing. In our relationship we don't need that kind of intimacy. Not that that's a bad thing, though. I mean sure from time to time we have our heated moments, like yesterday morning he woke me up with a very heated kiss. But with us," I stopped talking and couldn't help but smile, "its so easy to talk with each other. I like to listen to his problems or his passions and he likes to do the same. For me, being comfortable with him is just as intimate as any make-out session." I could feel my cheeks start to heat up so I bent down and brushed Scarlet's under belly.

"That's pretty amazing." Taylor said and I nodded to myself, "What did you mean by comfortable? Did something happen in a past relationship to make you be more careful?" Taylor caught onto me.

"You could say something like that," I sighed, "I don't wanna talk about it, it happened a long time ago. And we should get going, bulls should be starting soon." I change the subject as I put my brush into the bucket and close Scarlet's stable door.

We stood right by the gates as we waited for Cooper to ride his bull and I was getting antsy. What rodeo girlfriend wouldn't? So far the top scores are 84 and 86 and Cooper was up soon. What Taylor said earlier really got me thinking, was I enough for Cooper? This is so weird to think about, but did I please him enough? I'm probably just over thinking it, am I?

I get knocked out of my thoughts when I hear, "Now in the Dakota Community Bank and Trust chute is Arkansas native, Cooper Blackwood riding 'Bad Dog Alpha'! This bull hasn't been rode for seven consecutive times! Can Cooper make the eight seconds? Cowboys and cowgirls put your hands together if you think this cowboy can conquer this bull!"

Being the supportive girlfriend I am, I whooped and hollered for Cooper. The crowd also roared to life, them wanting to see this rank bull get rode and probably get their money's worth. I watched Cooper scoot up closer to his rope and then a second later he nodded his head and the gate flew open.

The gate wasn't the only thing that flew, 'Bad Dog Alpha' jumped four feet off the ground making the crowd scream with excitement. After that huge jump the bull landed and bucked so hard and spun so fast that I think I got whiplash from just watching. "Ride! Ride Cooper!!! Spur!! C'mon!! Ride!!" I yelled so loud that my throat longed for water.

Cooper's arm looked sharp and his spurring looked effortless, making it look as if anyone could do this. My heart pounded the whole eight seconds and Cooper barely made it to the last second but he still made it! That ride was awesome!! I cheered again and fist pumped in the air and gave Taylor a proud high five. I looked into the crowd and they were cheering a storm.

Cooper scrambled away from the bull, making my heart slow down a little. He looked out of breath and he was looking at the judges, waiting to hear his score. "Alright the score is in," The announcer said, "Okay Mandan, North Dakota, you are going to like this!" He stopped again making us wait with suspension. "90.5 points for the young cowboy! Well done, Cooper!" I cheered louder and Cooper fist pumped and then he took off his hat and tipped it to the crowd and then gave a bull fighter a bro hug and walked back towards the chutes.

CURRENTLY ASHLEY, TAYLOR, Beau and I are waiting for Caleb and Cooper in Cooper's trailer. We are playing Uno and other card games and just hanging out. "Didn't Caleb say they'd be here in a couple of minutes?" I asked as I laid down a card.

"Yeah and that was twenty minutes ago, I wonder what trouble they got into." Ashley says as she intensely looks at her cards, then laying down a card that made Taylor pick up two extra cards, earning a snicker from all of us. Then as if on cue, the door opens and it's Caleb, alone.

"Where's Cooper?" I ask.

"Well we were on our way back and then a bunch of people surrounded us, or Cooper should I say. They all wanted pictures with him, I think he called them his groupies." Caleb says and then kisses Ashley on the cheek as he sits down next to her at the table.

"I got to see this!" I said and basically kicked Beau out of my way as he sat at the end of the table booth. "Move!" I ordered and he got out of my way and I ran out of the trailer.

Sure enough about 60 yards away from the trailer was about 15 people, or should I say girls, surrounding Cooper. Like Caleb said, they were taking pictures with him, which didn't bother me, just pictures. "Your boyfriend is famous with the women, little sis." Caleb chuckles and then grunts which I can assume was an elbow to the ribs from Ashley.

"Jealous much?" I say not looking at him.

"I wouldn't answer that." Ashley warns him because we all know he was going to say yes. I look back at them to laugh, but as I look back I just catch a buckle bunny laying her lips on my man! Cooper instantly steps back and he laughs nervously and even from here I can see how red his cheeks are.

"Excuse me?!" I gasp and then I immediately take off for the circle of girls.

"Get her, girl!" I hear Taylor's voice from behind me.

As soon as I reach the circle Cooper's eyes land on mine and he looks guilty even though he shouldn't be. I make my way through the wave of girls and stand next to Cooper. "Alright girls! Picture time is over!" I say and they all groan and turn away, all except for one. The tramp who kissed Cooper. "You too, honey." I then "shoo" her off and then she leaves with the others.

I turn to Cooper and he looks like he just shit his pants and he's waiting for an ass chewing from me. His face makes me burst with laughter, making his eyebrows furrow. "You're not mad?" He hesitantly says testing if its a trap.

"No, I saw you pull back right away." I say and then take both of his hands in mine and let them hang in front of us.

"What if I told you that it wasn't the first time it happened tonight?" He says and then I step back and disconnect our hands and then his lips turn up in a smile to spill that he's joking.

"You're so funny." I sarcastically smile and he reconnects our hands and swings them out so we get closer.

"I love ya girly." He smiles more, making me smile and then lean up for a kiss. Once mine hit his, my heart melts into a gigantic puddle, no exaggeration there.

"Hey! That's my sister!!" Caleb's voice comes from the distance. We don't pull away, instead, I grab Cooper's cowboy hat and hold it in front of us so Caleb can't see us.

After we're done with our romantic kiss, I put Cooper's hat back on and then he wraps his arm around my shoulder and we start to walk back to the trailer. I wrap my arm around his waist and clutch his shirt in my hand so it's more comfortable. "Really dude? I just saw you shove your tongue down my sister's throat." Caleb exaggerated, making us groan with disgust.

"Oh shut up, Caleb!" We all say together.

"Well we're going to bed, good night guys." Taylor said as they drifted towards their trailer.

"Same here." Ashley said as she dragged Caleb away from Cooper.

"Night!" We said in unison as we watched them go to their trailers.

Cooper closed the door behind me and then he slumped down into the table booth seat and then began unbuttoning his pearl snap shirt, revealing his tanned chest. I opened the fridge and grabbed him a water and put it in front of him. "Cm'here." He chuckled as I turned away he grabbed my waist and pulled me into his lap. My legs went under the table as his went to the side.

I wrapped my left arm around his neck and my fingers went to the base of his neck, feeling the ends of his hair. "Congrats on the ride tonight, cowboy." I smile down at him.

"Thanks," He says and then plants a chaste kiss on my lips. "And way to kick ass tonight, I'm happy I got to watch you."

"Thanks, and I guess we're a pretty kick ass couple." I shrug my shoulders playfully.

"Hell yeah girl," He says making me laugh, "C'mon lets get ready for bed." He said and then I scooted off his lap and over to my duffle bag of clothes.

After I washed my face and brushed my teeth, I climbed up to the bed and got under the covers, waiting for a following Cooper. Cooper reached up and turned on our mini fan and then slipped into next to me and pulled the covers up more. I rested my head on his chest and tangled our legs together. "You didn't even ask how much money I got." Cooper suddenly says, making me scrunch my eyebrows.

"I don't care how much you make." I say leaving my head on his chest.

"God, you're perfect. Good night, Kods."

"Night, love ya." I say and then I kiss his cheek and return my head on his chest, where I can here his perfect heartbeat. I could get used to this.

Waking up to the sound of kitchen pans clashing wasn't what I was expecting to be woken up by. "Shit." I moved the hair out of my face and put my hands behind my back to hold myself up and then I looked down by the sink and table and there stood a guilty looking Cooper. He stood there looking at me shirtless and still in his shorts, he looked apologetic as he held the pans.

"What are you doing?" I said as I looked at the time on my phone, 6:45. We'd usually be waking up around 8 or so, so what was he doing up?

"I'm sorry, I didn't mean to wake you up." Cooper says as he puts the pans back on the burner, "I was going to make you breakfast." He sounded so sad it was so adorable and it managed to put a smile on my face.

I threw the covers off me and made my way down to where he stood and I went up behind him and crossed my arms around his shoulders and rested my hands on his pecs. I had to stand on my tip toes to be able to do this. His skin felt warm and soft under my touch and then I rested my chin on his shoulder, "It's okay, Cooper." I tried to cheer him up as I placed a kiss on his collarbone. "But you can still make that breakfast." I smiled as he turned his head smiling down at me. He unwrapped my hands from his chest and turned into me as he put my hands on the back on his neck and put his hands on my waist.

"Yes ma'am." He slightly drawled with a smirk on his pink lips. "I know what I'm hungry for." He said as he started to lean down. I smiled as I slowly leaned up and pulled him closer to me. My lips found his first and he tasted like mint and coffee, although I didn't mind.

The kiss didn't last long, but it was still a sweet kiss. I looked up at Cooper and gave him some gentle pats on his cheek and said, "Now get to work." Then I stuck my tongue at him and he copied me, gosh he was such a cutie!

After brushing my teeth and washing my face I climbed back into bed and grabbed my phone and started going through social media like everyday. On Instagram I saw a post by Hyo Silver and then an idea popped in my mind as I looked at Cooper through my peripheral. I went to Hyo Silver's website to browse through their unique and beautiful creations. Some were too big. Some were too flashy. Some were too simple. But then as I clicked to the next page, my jaw slightly dropped. As soon as I saw it, I knew it was the one.

Without hesitation, I added this cross pendent to the cart and headed to buy it. I put in all of my information and the other mumbo-jumbo and then I clicked the big, "Place Order". I know Cooper would love it as much as I do. Now, I was excited for it to come in and to give Cooper as a present to show him how much he means to me. I mean he does all these great things for me and I really haven't gave him anything back! It was about time I do.

"What ya doin'?" Cooper says after he jumps on the mattress making me rise like we were on a trampoline.

I quickly put the phone screen on my chest and turn my head to look at him, "Just on Facebook." Cooper looks suspiciously at me as he raises his eyebrows, so I decide to change the subject, "Shouldn't you be cooking?" He gives me a mock smile.

"It's done and made with lots of love." He smiled cheekily as we both scooted down to the couple of steps and then the smell of pancakes comes to me and I smile.

I grab four plastic plates from the cabinet and hand two to Cooper who stands behind me. I then take two perfect looking pancakes, but then I notice something. M&M'S in my pancakes, my favorite! "Okay, you win boyfriend of the year." I admit to him as I drool over my pancakes.

"I just know what my girl likes." He softly smiles as he grabs three pancakes. Next I dish up some sausage, and the fruit selection that included strawberries, pineapples, and grapes. Grabbing my plates I sat down at the table and popped a grape in my mouth as I poured my orange juice and a glass for Cooper.

"I wonder if the others are up." I say as Cooper sits across from me.

"Probably not, but I wouldn't be surprised if Caleb caught wind of our food and woke up and joined us.. No offence, but your brother is the biggest pig I've ever seen." I laughed at this because it was true.

When Cooper said brother my mind crazily thought of how Caleb could be his future brother in-law, it was stupid and it was too early to even think about Cooper and I possibly getting married. Although, so far in our relationship I wouldn't complain about marrying him. "Really?" I looked up at Cooper and his eyes were wide and I was confused on what he was saying.

"What?" I asked him equally as confused at him.

"You just mumbled about future-"

"Oh my gosh, I said that out loud?" I groaned and put my head in my hands. Seriously DaKota? Smooth, real smooth. Ugh! I could just hit myself right now! Cooper probably thinks I'm psychotic now for thinking this.

"You don't have to be embarrassed, sweetie." Cooper said and grabbed my hands and set them down on the table, making me reveal my reddened face to look at him. He picked up his fork and cut his pancake and just before he took a bite he said, "I plan on marrying you one day."

My heart beat quickly picked up speed and my jaw dropped a little, absolutely stunned at his intention. Cooper looked as cool as a cucumber enjoying his breakfast, that smooth son of a bitch. I gave him once last skeptical glance and then as I looked down at my pancakes a smile formed on my face as I thought about becoming Mrs. Blackwood. DaKota Blackwood, wow, I liked the sound of that. Actually, I really freaking loved it.

US THREE GIRLS SAT on some lawn chairs in front of Caleb's trailer enjoying some iced tea as we waited for our guys to come back with some supper. It was around five o'clock, and we won't be eating again until the rodeo is over which is a long time away from now. "Don't be such a wimp!" I laughed at Taylor as she explained something to us about how she was scared about telling Beau that she was now on birth control.

"I just don't want him to get the wrong idea! Just because I'm on it doesn't mean that we're gonna have sex 24/7, and I know he'll think that." Taylor sighed at the end, but then she looked back at me. "And don't be telling me about being a wimp! You're keeping your boyfriend a secret because your scared your daddy ain't going to let you see him."

It went dead silent between us three as we all tried to comprehend what Taylor just said. I was shocked at her words, but I knew deep down she wasn't wrong. I tried to speak but nothing came out, "I didn't mean that, DaKota. I really didn't. The birth control has some major side affects on me, and you just saw the bipolar part." I knew Taylor was sincere so I didn't take to heart, but what she said did make me start thinking about Cooper and I's relationship.

"It's okay Tay, I know you didn't. But it is true, I am scared that when my dad finds out that he'll do everything in his power to keep us apart. And when Cooper asked to take me out on a date my dad made it very clear that us dating was not going to happen in a million years. I'm scared that my dad will be so disappointed in me and he'll basically disown me as his daughter." I confess to them because it was all true. The thought of losing Cooper and losing the trust and respect from my father is absolutely terrifying.

"DaKota, your dad loves you very much and I don't think you and Cooper's relationship will come in between you guys." Ashley says as she puts a comforting hand on top of mine.

"I don't know, Ash. My dad is very strong headed man, you've seen the way he is with Caleb."

"So you're just never going to tell your father? Ha, good luck with that." Taylor says, slightly being sarcastic and serious at the same time.

"I believe the sooner you tell your father about this, the better." Ashley says as she sits back in her chair and I slowly nod to myself, knowing she is right.

"I know I need to do it soon-"

"I don't mean to interrupt-" A male voice says from behind us and we all turn around to see Stetson standing there with his hands moving back and forth as if he was antsy. "But DaKota, you're a vet student right?" He looked so hopeful in my answer.

I looked at the girls before answer and they encouraged me to answer, "Yeah, why? What's up?"

"Can you take a look at my mare for me?" He sounded desperate but I was hesitant on saying yes to him.

"Yeah sure, just give me a minuet and I'll be right over." I say as I stand up from my chair and head over towards Cooper's trailer.

Stetson was hot on my heels the whole time as I get my vet kit, and then I follow him to his trailer. "What seems to be the problem?" I ask him as he opens the trailer door and there stands a buckskin horse and another horse behind her.

"Well her appetite has gone down a bit, she won't touch her hay, but she'll sometimes eat her feed. Lately she's been distancing herself from the other horses, and I've noticed a color change in her. She used to be lighter but now her coat has became darker." He explains to me as I put on my gloves and take out my stethoscope and check out her lungs. "She lost a foal a couple of weeks ago. If I didn't know any better, I'd say she's suffering from a broken heart." He slightly chuckles, but this catches my attention.

"Well it wouldn't be the first case. Did she loose it at birth or did it pass from something else?"

"Mountain lion, damn thing came out in clear day light and took advantage of Missy's distraction. Missy put up a good fight and got the lion to go away but she watched her filly bleed to death.. Poor gal.." He said as he patted her neck with affection. "She ate some before you came, but she'll only take two bites and then she's done."

"And you said she doesn't eat hay?" I say as I listen to her stomach, I could hear a low grumbling. "Only seen her eat it once since the accident and since then, nothing."

I stood up and gave the mare a couple of scratches and pats on her withers and then she whinnied and then my suspicion become a possibility. "Has she been sensitive on her withers?" I ask Stetson.

"Yeah, won't let me touch them. Do you know what it is?" He asked me quickly.

"Well I think she has gastric ulcers which are small erosions in the lining of the stomach. Symptoms are usually lose of appetite, color change, and change of demeanor. And I guess when she ate that hay that it hurt her stomach so bad that she won't do it again until the ulcers are gone. But we won't know for sure until we can see inside her stomach, so I'd get her to a vet and get her checked out." I say to Stetson, "But other than that her lungs sound good and she has a good heart beat." I say as I put my stethoscope away and take off my gloves.

"Do you think it's my fault?" Stetson says dejectedly as he holds his horse's head in his hands and stares at her in her eyes. I had never seen this side of Stetson so I just stared at them for a couple of moments before he looked at me, waking me out of my daze.

"Gastric ulcers are usually caused by stress, so my guess that seeing her filly in that kind of state after the attack really did give her a broken heart. Horses are one of the best mothers of all mammals, it can take them months to get over something like that. So don't beat yourself up about it Stetson. The best thing you can do for her is to take her to a vet and then do what the vet tells you to do." I say as I clip the latches of my kit.

"Okay, thanks a lot DaKota." He says as we step out of the trailer, "I know I probably didn't deserve the help, but I really appreciate it." He says sadly as he looks at the ground and then meets my eyes.

"You're forgiven for that little altercation, I don't hold anything against you." I say in a soft voice to him because I felt a little bad for him. People make mistakes, and I'm sure it won't happen again. Stetson's face turns into a slight smirk as he looks at me, but then he quickly wipes it off.

"Thanks again, DaKota. I've had that horse since I was a kid, and you could of possibly saved her life. Can I hug you?" He says making me chuckle at his shyness, which I had also never seen him like that.

"Yes." I laugh and open my arms and we hug for a brief moment as I pull away but then he just holds tighter. "Okay, Stetson you can let go now." I awkwardly laugh and then he lets go and I look at his eyes and they're looking behind me.

I take a step back and then grab my kit and turn around and start to walk away. As my eyes travel from the ground they meet a special pair of deep brown eyes, ah crap... Cooper did not look one bit of happy, but his glare wasn't directed at me but at what was behind me. "I told you to stay away, Aimes." Cooper's voice was low and I ducked my head at his tone.

"I was just looking at his horse, it was nothing. C'mon Coop." I say and I put a hand on his chest, trying to direct him back to our trailer. But Cooper steps further into my hand, looking more threatening.

"I don't know about you, but I usually don't hug my vet, especially like that." Cooper says, still giving Stetson the death glare.

"It was a harmless hug, now let's go." I beg as I grab his arm and pull back but he stands there like a stubborn mule.

"If it was harmless then why does he have that stupid ass smirk on his face?" Cooper says finally looking at me, his eyes were ice cold.

"Because of the way you're acting like. You're letting him get his way. Now c'mon!" I grumbled to him as I finally pulled him with all my strength and finally got him to move.

I drug him all the way to our trailer, not caring that the others were watching the whole thing go down. I opened the door to the trailer and Cooper shut it behind me, and then I dropped his arm. I walked a couple steps in front of him and turned on my heel and crossed my arms and he copied me.

We stood there and looked at each other, waiting for the other to speak first. After a while I cocked an eyebrow at him, daring him to wait any longer. "You know I don't like him." Cooper says making me scoff.

"So I can't talk to him?" I question him, raising my eyebrows even more.

"Well why would you? After what he-"

"I don't give a shit what he did to me, it was a mistake! I'm so far over that I don't even care! And if I don't care, neither should you!" I closed my eyes after this and took a deep breath, trying to recollect myself. "Don't you trust me?" I asked him slightly softening my voice from before.

"Of course I do, but sometimes you don't see the bad in people and one day it's gonna bite you in the ass!" He said and then ran his fingers through his hair and took a deep breath.

"So I'm just gonna let you decide who is good and who is bad for the rest of my life? You're not fucking Santa, Cooper." Cooper clenches his jaw at my sarcasm, but I could rather care less right now.

"I'm just trying to protect you, Kota." He takes a step towards me, trying to relieve the unbearable tension between us.

"Well I'm a big girl and I can take care of myself and make my own decisions." I defend and then take a small breath deciding I should go easier on him. "I admit that when I see you talking to Avery I get wary about her, but I don't worry about you, because I trust you."

"But that's Avery." Cooper makes a solid point to me and I shake him off and step closer to him.

"Not the point," I say and then add, "I'm just saying that you don't need to be this big-macho-manly-man in front of other guys." Then I reach out and place my hands on his elbows and then he wraps his arms softly around my back.

"But those guys have history with you." I take a step back in his hold to fully look at him.

"So what?"

"Anything can happen." He drags out, and tightens his hold, trying to bring me closer to him.

"Anything from them? Or anything from me? I'm going to need you to be more specific." I say, slightly testing him, but now is the time to do it.

"Anything from them, but I'm just worried that you won't be able to handle the situation." He looks defeated by finally confessing to what he was really thinking.

I scoff at him, unbelievable. I push at his chest making us separate. "You know what?! I've had it about to here," I raise my arm above my head, "with guys telling me what I can do and what I can't! You're just like my dad!" I say and then I stomp past him, but not without his attempt to stop me by grabbing my arm. "Please don't follow me." I lower my voice as I open the door and storm out of the trailer.

The others are standing outside the door and when they see me they act like they weren't eavesdropping. I don't look at them as I head to Caleb's trailer. "DaKota!" Cooper's yell comes from behind me so I quicken my pace.

Once I get into the trailer I go sit at the table and put my head in my hands and rest my elbows on the table and run my fingers trough my hair. I let out a frustrated sigh and my brain starts to begin overthinking. Tonight is going to be freaking awesome.

IN ORDER TO SUCCEED tonight, I needed to get my mind clear and just think about roping. Tonight I was heeling for Taylor, as last night she heeled. Last night we didn't make the top three because I had an illegal head catch, so tonight we need to make up for it to be in the top three in the average. Today is the Fourth of July so there is going to be a lot more people and lots going on around the arena.

I made Taylor bring Scarlet over to Caleb's trailer so I could tack her up over here because I still didn't feel like talking to Cooper. I was being serious, he can't keep thinking that I will do anything he tells me to. Doesn't he know how stubborn I can be?

As soon as I mounted on Scarlet I realized that Taylor forgot my roping glove, probably did it on purpose. "I'll be right back." I said to Taylor as our horses were in front of all three trailers. I kicked Scarlet into Cooper's trailers direction. I quickly unmounted and jogged to the tack room and grabbed my glove, but as I turned around Cooper was coming out of the trailer.

"DaKota." I blew him off buy quickly getting mounted on Scarlet and then loping right past him, clearly sending him a message.

"C'mon." I say to Taylor as she stares at me because of my actions.

I backed Scarlet into the right side box and got myself situated and made sure Scarlet was ready also. Once done, I nod to Taylor and then she takes a deep breath and nods her head. The chute bursts open and Taylor makes sure not to break the barrier as I follow the steers hindquarters. When Taylor throws and catches the steer and turns him, Scarlet does an excellent job getting close to the steer and with a few swings from me I throw the loop and make the catch and dally. Once the steer is stretched I let the slack go and looked at the time board, 7.0 We'll see where that gets us tonight.

All of this clearing my mind stuff really let me see Cooper's side of things and I curse at myself for being so hard on him. I know he means for the best, but he's not completely innocent and neither am I. "Way to go, sis." I say as we ride out of the arena.

"You too, sista!" She says making me laugh. While looking around, my eye catches Cooper walking towards the bucking chutes and I decide to go over there. Tonight he didn't get a time with bull dogging because his feet got caught up.

"Just wait here." I say to Taylor as I lope Scarlet over to Cooper. He doesn't look right away but the more I cut him off from walking he finally looks up. His look is hesitant but he stops.

"Just clear your mind, and spur the hell out of that goddamn bull." I add a small flirtatious smile at the end to let him know that I'm not pissed anymore. He gives me small hopeful toothless smile but before he can say anything I decide to make an exit by pulling on my mare's reins and she backs up and quickly makes a getaway.

And spur the bull he did. Cooper made an 87 point ride on another rank bull, putting him first in the overall! That's a big paycheck for him! Taylor and I ended up fourth in the average with an okay paycheck. Caleb took the W for broncs, great weekend for the sqaud. Since Scarlet is in the stables, I walked back to the bucking chutes, waiting for Cooper to be done with his interviews.

Right now the rodeo is putting on a mounted shooting demonstration before they put on the firework display. I think mounted shooting is pretty fun to watch, but I never have time to go watch! My grandpa used to do it and I used to watch him as a little girl.

I spotted Cooper walking away from the cameraman with his gear bag slung over his shoulder. I walked over to him and I quickly caught his attention. I began walking along with him as I stuck my thumbs in my belt loops. "So you're not mad anymore?" He hesitantly asked me, making me laugh.

"No, I think I let my stubbornness get the best of me. Sorry 'bout that." I chuckled and he did too.

"I think we both outdid ourselves, I'm sorry too." He said and then I ducked under his left arm and locked my arms around his waist, giving him a side hug. He put his left arm around my shoulders, keeping me glued to his side.

"Good ride, Coop." I say to him looking at the ground.

"I had some pretty good advice from someone." He said and I smiled, knowing it was me.

"They must be pretty cool."

"The coolest." He confirmed. "C'mon I have a surprise." He said making me wonder what he could be up to.

Cooper drove through the competitors area where everyone would warm up their horse or just hangout, making me curious to where we were going. He then drove onto the race track and I noticed them getting ready to light the fireworks. He parked the pickup and got out with me following him to the box of the truck.

I saw multiple quilts, blankets, and pillows situated neatly, waiting to be used. I looked at Cooper as he put the tailgate down and held out his arm, waiting for me. "When did you do this?" I asked him.

"Between events." He said as we both got situated under the covers.

"How did you know I was going to forgive you?"

"I didn't, but I did it just in case it was one of my groupie's lucky day." Cooper joked and then I slapped his chest.

"Not funny." I said as I laughed and then I laid my head on his shoulder.

"You know I love ya." He kissed the top of my head.

"Love you, too." I said and then the boom of the fireworks made us both look up at the colorful sparks in the air. As I was admiring the different fireworks, I turned my head to look at Cooper and we both smiled at each other and simultaneously leaned in. On cue, another big boom of fireworks sounded as we kissed. The kiss felt like we hadn't kissed in ages. Cooper and I were hungry for each other.

When we pulled back, desperate for air, I moved closer to Cooper, resting my head in the crook of his neck. We continued to watch the big and wonderful fireworks, loving the way they lit up the black sky. The fireworks were great, but I have to say the fireworks from our kiss outdid the them, by a long shot.

COOPER

I ROLLED OVER IN MY bed, my legs taking the sheets with them making a tangled mess. I was face down in my pillow, so I turned so I could actually breath and then I forced myself to open my groggy eyes. First my eyes landed on my alarm clock, the time reading 6:50, second, my eyes then happily drifted over to the picture frame of me and DaKota. My lips instantly turned into a foolish grin at the thought of the love of my life.

Love of my life?

Could DaKota be the love of my life already? We've only been dating for little over a month and a half, but man, does it feel like I've known her a lot longer than that. It's crazy to feel like this in that amount of time, but I can't deny the feelings I have for her. I literally can not imagine my life without DaKota. Not only is she smoking hot, but very intelligent, unique, caring, stubborn, and independent, the list goes on forever and forever. I wish I could show her off to everyone I know, even to people I don't! But I understand why she doesn't want to tell her father, that man has it out for me, and I can blame my awesome father for that.

DaKota's dad thinks I'm the one who still the money from the sale barn, but in reality, it was Bill. He set me up by stealing my jacket and then going in the sale barn and purposely turning to the camera, my dad knows better than letting the cameras catch you. When I confronted him about it he said it was a warning, a warning for the next time he asks me to come with him and do his dirty work.

That was the last time I heard from him, until that night he paid Kota a visit at the diner. Without him telling us, my mother and I both knew that was the last warning, and the next time he comes back, he was not going without a fight. Of course, I didn't tell DaKota that because she would worry herself to death. DaKota doesn't deserve that kind of danger, she deserves to be worry-free and happy. She shouldn't even have to question her safety around me, and while my dads still around, safety is not promised.

Maybe her dad is right about me.. DaKota is too good for me, she deserves only the best. But could I really let her go so easy? I knew I had to keep DaKota if I wanted to keep my sanity, I wouldn't let go of her without a fight.

Shaking my head and sighing to myself, I just tell myself that everything will be okay in the end. I grab my phone off the nightstand and quickly text DaKota, "Good morning beautiful." with a heart and heart eyes emoji and send it. I know she's still sleeping, she'll be awake by eight o'clock. I wonder what shes going to do today, I know I won't be able to see her later because I'm busy all morning and afternoon.

I GRABBED THE FIVE bags of Total Equine Feed and then put it onto my shopping cart, and then steered it over to the cattle feed. I scanned the brands and then spotted the bags of Total Bull Feed and grabbed ten bags of it. All I hear in my head is the sound of a cash register making the "chah-ching" sound, because I was breaking the bank today. Not only did I need more feed, I had to get supplies for fencing, and dewormer for the horses and cattle. Just another day in the life of a cowboy.

While I was pushing my cart out to my pickup a unwanted voice called my name, "Cooper! Cooper!" I dropped my head back and groaned to myself. There was no avoiding her now.

"Hi Avery." I put on my best fake smile for her.

"Haven't seen you around much, stranger." She says and then puts her finger on my bicep and drags it down my arm, trying to be seductive.

"I've been busy, like right now." I say as I grab a bag of feed and toss it into the bed of my pickup.

"You've always been a hard-working man, Cooper Blackwood."

"Quit acting like you know everything about me, Avery." I unintentionally snap at her, she looks taken back by my harsh tone. "I didn't mean to snap, sorry." I apologize sincerely.

"It's okay," She says as she starts to back away from me, "Well if you ever want to come over or something, you know where to find me." She winks at me and turns away in time to miss me cringing at her.

"Yeah, in hell." I mutter to myself as I continue loading the bags into the box. As I drop another bag into the box, I notice some guy leaning against my pickup. He had his head hung with a brown cowboy hat hiding his face. When he looked up, I recognized him as Colby Jones, DaKota's dad. What does he want?

"One of your girlfriends, Blackwood?" He says and motions his head where Avery was still walking to her smart car.

"No, sir. I only have one girlfriend." Well my compulsive mouth just dug my grave for me, way to go Cooper.

"Oh? And who may that be?" He says with a sarcastic and curious smirk.

"If you came over just to harass me, you're wasting your time." I tell him as I continue load my bags.

"Oh son," He laughs, "You haven't even heard harassing from me, yet."

"Then what do you want?" I said aggravated.

"Oh I just wanted to check if you paid for the feed. Or if you just stole 'em. Cause I know ya like to do that." He says casually as he inspects the bags.

"You know what?" I ask him and then I pull out my wallet and hand him $350, the same amount that my father stole from him. "Here. Now we're even, okay?" I said agitated by his cocky smile on his face.

He gladly took the money from my hands and tucked it into his pocket, "If you think that changes what you did,-"

"I don't care what you have to say. You were robbed of 350 dollars and now you have that 350 back, if I were you, I'd forget about it and move on. Now, if you'll excuse me, I have some adult problems to figure out." I emphasized the adult, to tell him that he's acting like a child in this argument.

I pushed the cart out of the way and opened the door to my pickup and as I put my foot on the running board he spoke again, "You wanna know why I won't let you near my daughter?" I don't know why I didn't just continue to get into my pickup, but his words sparked something in me to make me listen. With my jaw clenched, I turned towards him, ready to listen to his answer.

"My daughter is a strong, smart, and independent girl and she doesn't need some cocky-playboy-thief-rodeo cowboy to drag her down into the dumps. DaKota has a lot of potential in front of her, I can see it. And I'd be damned if I see her with Bill Blackwood's son, ruining her future by putting her in danger and living life on the run. Someday she deserves to come home to a stable house after leaving her own vet clinic and to someone who isn't a threat to her well-being like you are." Colby sounds like he is sugar coating the whole thing, as if he's taking it easy on me.

Pissed, I get into my seat and grab the door and slam it into the door frame. I turned over the engine, hearing the diesel come to life and I saw Colby stand back from me. As I drove past him, we both gave each other looks. His look to me was a warning look, and I gave him an angry glare. The worst part is that I believed him, everything he said. I have no idea how many enemies my father has made over the years, or how many can be looking for revenge. There is always that possibility they will use DaKota as a target to get back at my dad, but my heartless father wouldn't do anything for a girl who meant nothing to him. Even, if that girl was the love of son's life.

I PLACED THE PICNIC basket on the ground where I placed the denim quilt over the sage grass. I sat down and crossed my legs as I took out the champagne glasses, even though we were going to be drinking DaKota's favorite, orange juice. My mom had made some kind of subs, and I packed some fruit and some chips. I hope DaKota will like it.

Speaking of, I heard some sage grass crunching and then I saw her walking over the small ridge of the rolling hill. My God. She looked like she just came down from heaven and then went to a vogue photo shoot. She was wearing a white sun dress with her tan vintage corral boots, her legs looked so smooth I couldn't wait to touch her skin. Her hair was braided, but the pieces she left out were flying gracefully in the wind, perfecting the moment.

When she saw me stand up she smiled brightly making my heart skip a beat, and then she quickened her pace to a jog to come wrap herself around my neck in a hug. I wrapped my arms around her and lifted her up and spun her around. "Hey girly." I said into her neck, placing a kiss under her ear.

I placed her feet on the ground, but neither of us let go of each other. She took a slight step back to look at me. I looked into her gorgeous hazel eyes and instantly fell for her again, "I know I saw you two days ago, but I missed you so damn much." She said like she didn't believe herself, but I did because I felt the exact same.

Then without hesitation she pulled my neck down and smashed her lips on mine and my body instantly reacted to her actions. I pulled her against me more and moved my lips with hers. The kiss wasn't long nor short, just right. I pulled back and smirked when I saw her lips slightly swollen and a little darker than her usual light pink ones. "C'mon, I hope your hungry." I said and grabbed her hand and lead her over to the blanket.

Before we sat down, Kota took off her boots and then we both sat down right next to each other, and then I reached into the basket and pulled out a sub for her and for me. Then I pulled out the container of mixed fruits, and bag of Cool Ranch Doritos. I grabbed her glass and poured her orange juice, she smiled once she saw the drink. "Just for you." I cheekily said and then she placed a kiss on my cheek.

"You know me so well." She joked and I raised my eyebrows at her.

"I do." I smiled, she still looked at me like I didn't.

"I bet I know you better." She challenged me and I raised my eyebrows in interest.

"Wanna bet?" I asked her as she took a bite of her sub and I copied.

As she finished swallowing she nodded and said, "Okay, lets play a game." She says competitively.

"What does the loser have to do?" I asked her and she slightly rolled her eyes at me.

"No one has to do anything." The soft side of her comes out and I decide to test her.

"Why? You scared?" That got her attention as she looked back at me.

"No," She said quickly and then I could tell she was thinking of a consequence of the loser. I notice her cheeks redden as she was thinking, what is going on inside that little pretty head of hers? She nervously looks at me and says confidently, "For each question a person gets wrong, they have to take off an article of clothing."

Holy crap, I was not expecting that from my girl, but I'm not complaining. This game just got a whole lot more interesting. "Okay, you go first." I say as I move to sit across from her and we both cross our legs. DaKota sat slightly different so I couldn't see up her dress.

"Okay," She said and then asked, "We'll start off easy, favorite color?"

"Turquoise." I say in a 'duh' tone making her chuckle. "What's mine?" I could see her smile fading as she began to question herself.

"Blue." She's confident in herself, but she has no idea.

"Oo, not off to a good start, darlin'." I say to her in a disappointed voice and her jaw drops.

"What?! Blues not your favorite color?" Absolutely flabbergasted, it makes me laugh.

"Nope, it's hazel, just like your eyes." I say as I pop a grape into my mouth and then she glares at me.

"Oh c'mon-!"

"Sorry girl, you know what has to happen.." I shrug carelessly at her. DaKota looks at me with challenge as her finger tips travel up her arm and to the strap of her dress, and I freeze realizing what she's about to do. She pulls the strap down, but then stops and reaches down her leg and

300

takes off her sock. She starts to laugh and I let out a frustrated breath, this girl is going to be the death of me.

"Okay, since you decided to go the hard route, what was my first word?"

"Horse." I confidently say. When she says nothing, I know I got it right and so I ask my question, "What was the first buckle I won?"

"You won the Arkansas State buckle for calf riding in the year of 2007." She surely says and it's correct.

"Impressive." I smirk.

"What was my first pet?" She asks me and I do take some time to answer it, you wouldn't believe how many animals this girl has had.

But then it comes to me, "A palomino pony by the name of Girlfriend."

"Impressive." She copies me.

"Who was my first kiss?" I ask her and her jaw drops in disbelief.

"You've never told me this!" I laugh and shake my head at her.

"On the contrary, we played 20 questions on the drive to Mandan and I told you!" She looks at the ground and I can tell she remembers asking me now.

"Well shit, I don't know." She says throwing her hands angrily, but it was adorable to me.

"Missy Gonzalez, in the first grade.. Now take something off, honey." She mocks me with a laugh and takes off her other sock. Sometime she's gonna have to take off that dress.

"Okay fine, you wanna play dirty? From that wolf pack I ran into when I was younger, what was the wolf's name that first came to me in the den?" She raised an eyebrow at me, knowing that she got me.

I was stumped, but I wasn't going to give up.. Jax? Zeek? "Jax?"

She claps her hands together and smiles, "Nope! Luca! Now shed some clothes, boy." Well I already had my boots off, but I didn't want to take my socks off, I needed a distraction of some sort. So with a cocky smirk on my face, I grab the bottom of my shirt and lift it over my head. Her eyes follow my every movement and then land on my bare stomach, got her now.

"Okay miss smartie pants," I say and she sticks her tongue at me. "What do I like best about myself?"

"Like physically? What kind of question is that?!"

"A hard one apparently and yes." I retort and she rolls her eyes. She then studies me and I watch her eyes move to different parts of my body.

"You're favorite characteristic about yourself is." She puts a finger under her chin, "Your hair." She nods confidently but as I start to smirk, she quints her eyes and then they go wide before I can speak. "NO!! It's not your hair, it's your damn smirk!" Bingo.

"Nice save, what made you change your mind?" I ask as I pop another grape into my mouth and so does she.

"Because you do it all the time to me!"

"So it works?" I smirk at her and then she blushes red, already telling me the answer.

"I'm just surprised you didn't say your face." She shrugs and then takes a sip of her orange juice.

"Why do you say that?" I curiously ask her.

"You look in the mirror more than me." I can tell she's trying not to smile. "You always gotta make sure you look pretty.."

"Pretty?" I say offended. "I do not look pretty."

"Oh no, you're definitely a pretty boy.. Okay next question." She says making me laugh and then she looks at me, but it's not the expected cutthroat expression. She looks more curious and shy. "When you first saw me, what went through your mind?"

I was a little shocked but I was not going to hold back, "Well I saw you come into the diner my first reaction was that an angel had just walked out of heaven and straight through those doors. I thought to myself that you were a real show stopper and when I heard Maybell say your name I was captivated right away. I had this weird feeling in my stomach that I've never had before, I think it was my heart was telling me that I had to get to know this girl no matter what." I paused, "I get that same feeling in my stomach every time I see you." I didn't realize I was looking at the ground, but when I looked up DaKota was much closer to me, our knees almost touching.

I looked into her eyes and she was staring at my lips and then they looked back at mine. I noticed her eyes were glazed, was she going to cry? "Okay you win for that." She said breathlessly and wasted no time connecting our lips together for a sweet romantic kiss.

Using her knees and hands, she crawled more towards me, making my back softly land on the ground and she crawled over me. I cupped her soft cheeks, softly moving my thumbs back and forth. She slowly lowered herself on half of my body, so only one leg was tangled with mine. Her hands played with the ends of my hair, making my body go crazy. My fingertips traveled softly down her neck and down her bare arms and I felt her shiver under my touch, making me smile into our kiss.

We both needed air, so I broke the kiss and moved my lips to the corner of hers and down to her jaw and slowly made my down her neck. She lifted her neck so it was easier for me. As I kissed her randomly, my fingers ran down her sides and then finally found the back of her thighs. Good gravy they were softer than I thought.. I riskily traveled up her thighs and went under her dress and reached her spandex covered butt, momentarily stopping and softly grabbing, and then she moaned making me relax. God she is so perfect in every way. My hands rested on her back under her dress, my thumbs making circles.

Then I grabbed her a little tighter and flipped us over, making us roll over a couple of times. DaKota giggled under me making me smile with happiness. When we landed in one spot, I leaned down and started to kiss her again. She ran her hands over my shoulders and ran across and connected them in my hair making me moan into her mouth.

She wrapped her legs around my waist and pushed me down impossibly closer to her. She moved her hands out of my hair and then to my biceps that were supporting me, she grabbed onto me like I was going to disappear any second. The way her chest felt against mine was so arousing, I could feel my jeans get a little snug. I moved up on her and there may have been a little more touching, but she moaned as I did so.

I broke our kiss and I started to kiss her neck, "I" another kiss on the base of her throat, "love" making my way up. "you." then I placed one right under her jaw. I lifted my head above hers and we just stared into each other's eyes for what seemed for the longest time, but in reality it was only a couple of moments. "C'mon, lets watch the sun set." I say and then roll off of her so she can sit up.

I comfortably sat up while she sat in between my legs as we watched the sun set over the mountains and hills. She leaned against my chest and rested her head on my shoulder looking forward. I couldn't help but admire the way the setting sun light made her tan skin glow even more than it already did. She looked at peace with everything, like there was nothing wrong with this unfair word that we live in. Her eyes may see the world in front of us, but in my eyes, she is my world. "I could stay like this forever." She softly says, barely enough for me to hear it.

"Me too.. So what did you tell your parents you were doing?" I broke the comfortable silence between us.

"I told my dad that Ash and I were going shopping, so Ash dropped me off and she went shopping by herself."

"Speaking of your dad." I say dreadfully because I didn't want to ruin this perfect moment.

"What happened?" She groaned picking her head of my shoulder that now was cold, missing her warmth.

So I explained our conversation which did not impress her at all. "I am so sick of him! Sometimes I could just knock him in the head a couple of times! That's it!" She frustratingly stood up with me following her.

"What do you mean?" I ask her.

"I'm gonna tell him, tomorrow." She baffled me with her statement, but then I came to terms with it. It was time we tell her father about us, I've wanted to for a long time.

"We're going to tell him." She looked shocked at my words, but then I grabbed both of her hands and she relaxed some.

"You're going to do it with me?"

"Of course I am, baby." I say and kiss the top of her head and she sighs gratefully.

"You might need to wear a bulletproof vest though." She laughs softly and plays with my now clothed chest. I can't see her eyes but then I hear her hiccup a bit, was she crying?

"DaKota, look at me." I say softly and she slowly looks at me with her teary eyes, "Sweetie, what's wrong?" I bring her closer to me, and her fists are against my chest.

"I'm so scared, Cooper." She says and then a tear rolls down her face and I'm quick to wipe it away.

"DaKota, I don't know what is going to happen, but whatever does, I am going to be right by your side the whole time." I say and use my thumb to wipe off more tears.

"Promise?" She looks up at me with big, hopeful eyes.

"I promise, now come here and let me hold ya." I say and then she drops her hands and wraps them around my back and I wrap my arms around her shoulders and hold her tight because I'm never letting her go.

"I love you Cooper Blue Blackwood." She sniffles and hugs me tighter.

I kiss the top of her head, "I love you more than you'll ever know."

Last night was the worst sleep I've had in a long, long time. Not only did I have more of the attack night terrors, but I couldn't stop thinking of different scenarios of how today is going to go. I honestly don't know why I am so freaked out about what will happen, I mean if we hid this for this long, we can find another way to get around my father.

I secured the halter on Pharaoh and I grabbed the lead rope and walked him over to the hitching post and tied him off here. I didn't feel like saddling him, so I just grabbed a saddle blanket and a bridle. I undid his halter and then put it around his neck, and then got him to get his bridle on. I flipped his reins over his head and then adjusted his saddle blanket evenly and then hauled myself up.

I gave him a nice pat on the neck for standing nice while I got on and then I directed him to the road. I decided I could treat him into seeing his other horse friends from the other houses around here.

Even from my ride, I still didn't have an idea for the upcoming argument with me and my father. I'm not so worried about my dad yelling at Cooper, because in the end its going to be me and my father at each others throats, that, I know for sure. Maybe if I go to the diner, it will take my mind of things and help me relax. After letting Pharaoh into the pasture, I walked over to the porch where I saw a package on the steps. I looked closer and it was addressed to me, what could it be? Oh! Its Cooper's necklace! I'm so excited to see it!! I grabbed the package and jogged up to my room and grabbed a scissors and opened it.

The necklace already came in a black velvet box so I didn't have to wrap it or anything. I opened the box and there it was, it was so beautiful! I put the box on my desk and then went to my closet to change into some Rock and Roll Revival jeans, my hand tooled belt with buckle, and a plain dark gray tee shirt, and just put my hair into my natural wave ponytail.

Cooper should be here in about ten minuets to receive his gift that he doesn't know of, but in the mean time, I'm helping wait tables. It was somewhat busy being one o'clock, but it was manageable. I took an order ticket to the kitchen and put it on the order wheel deal thingy. When I did that, I took two orders to the right table. "Here you guys go, two cheese burgers with sweat potato fries. Anything else I can get you?" I asked them with a kind smile.

"No dear, thank you." Mrs. Stevens says to me and then I walk away. Mr. and Mrs. Stevens are the cutest old couple here! Every time they come here they order the exact same as each other, and almost always get something different every time. They say they still like to try new things together, how cute is that?

As I came back from the kitchen I heard the bell call ring a couple of times and I went behind the counter and I saw Cooper there with his famous smirk plastered on his face. He was wearing a maroon Hooey hat that had quite a few dirty spots on it, but it still looked good on him. Then he was wearing a loose black tee and some jeans. "Oh Cooper, your orders in the back, follow me." I say as people were around us.

Cooper follows me around the counter and comes to the break room without a soul seeing us. I closed the door behind us and turned towards him, "What's up?" He asked me.

"I just wanted to give you something." I cheekily said as I pulled the box out from my pocket and handed him the box.

"Shouldn't you be on one knee?" He joked with me, earning a light push in the arm. "And you shouldn't of got anything for me, I don't need anything."

"I know, but you're always giving me nice things, I thought you deserve it too. Now open it!" I say excitedly looking at the box.

He hesitantly looks at me and then looks at the box and opens it and he smiles when he sees the necklace, "DaKota, this is too expensive-"

"Oh hush it! Do you like it?" I ask him.

By the look on his face, I can tell he doesn't want to, but he does, "Yes, thank you so much, babe." He said and leaned down and gave me a quick peck on the lips.

"C'mon put it on!" I say and then he pics up the necklace and secures it around his neck. I am so glad the chain length is correct, right on his sternum. "Okay, you look really good with that on." I say as I look him up and down.

"Oh really?" He says as he grabs my belt loops and brings me closer and we share a romantic but too short of a kiss. "I'll wear it everyday."

"You better." I give him a pointed look. "So I was thinking that you could come over around 7?"

"I'm free whenever, but seven is good. Just shoot me a text when to come over."

"Okay." I say and then turn to go to the door, but his hand stops me.

"One more." He said and pulled me into him and planted one on me, it was sweet. We pull back at the same time, and give each other a soft smile and head for the door.

When I open the door, Maybell is standing there and Cooper and I are standing there like deer in the headlights. "Oh um we were just-"

"Since when do we do take out?" She smirks knowingly as she holds up a plastic bag filled with wrapped up food and hands it to Cooper. She gives me a I-know-whats-going-on look making me blush a deep red.

I step out with Cooper following me and we go back into the dinning area and I walk Cooper to the door, "I hope you enjoy your meal."

"Oh I will." He winks at me as he opens the door and walks out to his pickup, leaving me with a smile on my face.

AFTER MY DAD SAID GRACE at the dinner table, we dished up the food my mother made for us. It was spaghetti with garlic toast, it looked delicious to my empty stomach. I looked at my father who was the only one eating at this moment and then I looked at everyone else to see them watching him also. I told my mother, Ashley, and Caleb that I would be telling dad after supper, so we were all on the antsy side.

But I took a deep breath, picked up my shaking fork and began eating. Seeing my actions, the rest followed me and began eating. But still, no one spoke, it was deathly silent and my father noticed. "Why is everyone quiet, I'm sure you have something to say, Caleb." My dad jokes at Caleb's big mouth that he is known for never closing once he starts going.

Caleb looks singled out and he looks at me and then to my dad, way to make it obvious Caleb. "Nope, it was a normal day for me."

"Is Ashley pregnant?" My dad says as Ashley drinks her water and Caleb chews his food, causing them both to choke.

Ashley coughs and covers her chest and wipes her mouth, "Excuse me?" She looks astonished by my dad's accusation.

"Well there must be something going on because no one is talking." He says casually, no hint of anger in his voice. He sounded normal, like he was actually relaxed and not a ticking time bomb waiting to go off.

"You're not, right?" Caleb says nervously at Ashley and she looks offended at him.

"No you dummy, I'd think you'd know if I was." Ashley says and Caleb lets out a big sigh of relief, I swear he started to sweat at the thought of Ashley being pregnant.

"So, what did you do today D?" D? My dad hasn't called me that since I was a little girl, why was he so happy all of a sudden?

"Oh I just went on a ride with Pharaoh this morning and then worked at the diner, the usual." I shrugged playing with my spaghetti, mostly avoiding his eye contact.

As my mother and I were cleaning off the dinner table, I saw my dad was watching the news and he usually has a beer while doing so, but this time he didn't. But with certain things happening soon, I know he needed a beer before it. So I went to the fridge and grabbed him a Coors and brought it to him, "Oh thank you sweetie." I just gave him a slight nod as I continued with my mom. She gave me a knowing look and I gave her the same look back.

My heart started to pound as I saw Cooper's pickup coming down the drive, and from beside me, my mother gave my hand a slight comforting squeeze. I looked at the table where my dad was still siting and was slightly relieved when I saw he had finished his beer. My dad turned his head to outside as Cooper's truck turned off and I walked out the door, "Who's that?" Of course, no one answered him.

From the kitchen, you couldn't see Cooper's pickup, so when Cooper came out of his truck, I gave him a huge hug. "Ready?" He asked me as I let go of him.

"As I'll ever be." I sigh and then he grabs my hand and brings it to his lips, making me softly smile. The gesture made me think of the time we were in his trailer and he told me that holding my hand is what can make him forget all about his problems, and for me, it did the same thing.

"I'm going to be right beside you the whole time." He said as we started walking towards the porch.

As we traveled up the steps of the porch, I kept my eyes down, knowing that my father was looking at us now. I grabbed the handle of the door and we both stepped into the house, which now became silent at the sight of us. I finally looked at my father and he was staring at our conjoined hands. "DaKota, you better start explaining what I am seeing right now. " His voice was dark and sounded dangerous as we finally made eye contact.

CHAPTER 6

"**D**ad, Cooper and I have been seeing each other-"
"Behind my back?!" I shrunk into my socks from the volume of his voice, I lowered my head in disappointment. "Alright, so how long has this joke been going on?" My dad grasps the concept but still sounds as if Cooper and I dating was something that was something temporary.

"Dad, this isn't joke. Cooper and I have been dating for over a month and half now and I do not regret one single moment of it. Cooper treats me so well, he makes me the happiest when I'm with him-"

"I told you I didn't want you near this kid and you go ahead and do it anyways! DaKota you're just blinded by his tricks and games, but soon you'll find out who he really is." He says frustrated and continues to raise his voice.

"Sir, I am not playing any games with DaKota. I would never do anything to hurt her-"

"You're hurting her by just being with her! I told you that you're going to ruin her future and I am not going to just sit by and watch it happen!" My dad yells at Cooper, but Cooper stands his ground, not flinching one bit.

"You don't know anything about him! Why won't you just listen to me!" I say, finding some courage and strength in me enough to raise my voice at him.

"Because you're young and naive! You don't know what you want right now. You're just fantasizing the thought of being in a committed relationship-"

"No dad! I have been through hell and back these past few years, making me grow stronger and wiser. I know what I want, and it's him. You can't make my own decisions for me, I am not a little girl anymore!"

"You weren't here when he first came here-"

"I don't care what has happened in his past! You know, you and mom have always told me to never judge a book by its cover, so why are you doing it to someone I love!" I yelled at the top of my lungs by the time I ended my rant, and it went dead silent when I confessed I loved him in front of my father.

"You love him?" He laughed hysterically making me scowl at him, "Well isn't that just the cutest fucking thing in the world!" He then looked at Cooper who stood straighter, "Oh and I bet you told her you loved her right before you jumped into her panties."

I heard my mother gasp from behind the island counter at my dad's accusation, but me, I was speechless. Tears started to form in my eyes at my father's hurtful words, how could he think I would let Cooper do that?

Cooper took a defensive step towards my father, making our hands separate. "How dare you talk about your daughter like that!" His voice was thunderous.

"So you're not denying it?" My dad said cocking his head at Cooper.

"Dad!" Caleb's voice piped in, I could tell he was hurt for me.

"Colby!" My mother's gasp was heard and I was shocked she interjected in our argument.

"What?" He turned towards my mother disgusted, "Can't you see that this kid has changed our daughter? The DaKota I know would never lie to her parents about something like this! She has changed, Sheyenne." He paused to look at me, "I don't even know her anymore." That stung like hell, letting the tears come out.

"Dad, I haven't changed." I said as I wiped my eyes. "This isn't some fling that's been going behind your back. I know that Cooper is the love of my life, I can feel it. Dad, you just have trust me on this."

"Trust you?" He laughs and puts his hands on his hips. "How can I trust you when all you've done is lied to me? This is already the beginning of him ruining your future, him ruining your relationship with your family!"

"Cooper isn't like that!!" I scream at him. "Haven't you seen how happy I've been lately? Why do you think I come home with a smile on my face every day? It's because of him! I don't give a shit what you say about him, I know who he really is and that's all that matters!" My dad just gives me a disgusted look, making me cry even more.

"Colby, can't you see how concerned she is about this? If this wasn't the real deal, why would she be fighting you about this?" My mother says, shocking me that she is actually standing up for me and not just standing there.

"Why are you defending this?!" He yells at her.

"Because I can see they are in love, I see the way Cooper looks at her and it's the same way you used to look at me. I have never seen my daughter this happy before, why are you trying to ruin this?" She softly says to my dad.

My dad looks very confused, but then it turns back into his usual angry self. "You knew didn't you?" When she doesn't say anything, it confirms it for him, "Why didn't you tell me?!"

"It wasn't mine to tell, and I knew this would happen if I did. Colby if you only heard the way DaKota talks about him, you wouldn't doubt how they were meant to be together. Don't you think she deserves the best?" My mother's words made me cry even more, but I wish I could say the same for my dad.

"I know she deserves the best, that's why I am going to break this up!" He yells, now turning his attention back to Cooper and I. "Now, how many times do I have to tell you that I don't want you near my daughter! I don't want you to think about her, look at her, and sure as hell don't want you touching her! And I don't want you seeing him either! From now on, I forbid you to see him! And don't think you can just sneak around like before. If I catch you trying to see him, I will literally hand cuff you to me and throw away the key! Do you understand?" There is no room for misunderstanding in his voice, he meant it all.

"You can't do that!!" I scream at him.

"Just watch me." He says as he grabs my wrist in a threatening way.

"Sir, there is nothing that will stop me from seeing her." Cooper speaks up again.

"Oh I know one thing that could, one buckshot to the chest. That'll definitely do it, unless you don't think so? We could try it right now if you'd like." My father says as he starts to walk over to the closet to get the shotgun, but I dig my heels into the floor, stopping him.

"You're just mad that Caleb and I are getting older so we don't have to obey your every order, and it pisses you off knowing that there is nothing you can do to stop it!" I spit at him with all the venom I have inside of me. He looks at me with so much anger and dissatisfaction of a daughter.

"You shut your mouth!" He barks in my face but I don't flinch as he brings my wrist closer to him, being more threatening.

"You hate it," I pause, "You hate not having control over people because it makes you feel-"

I hear my mother and Ashley scream when I fall to the ground from the impact of my father's slap. I hold my cheek to tame the stinging, then I look up at my father who just stares down at me with a unreadable face. I look up at my father with tears slowly rolling down my face, trying to comprehend what he just did.

Caleb yells, "What the hell dad!" Cooper rushes over to me and comforts me, I look at him and cry into his chest.

"You're not my daughter anymore." My dad's dark voice speaks up again making me look at him through my blurry vision. My heart breaks into a million pieces after hearing his hurtful words.

"Dad." I sobbed towards him.

"Get the hell out of my house." He demanded with so much hurt and betray in his voice, it was devastating. Cooper helped me up and wrapped one arm around me trying to help as my legs were unstable and weak. We started to walk towards the door, but before we reached it, I stopped and turned around.

"I hate you." I hissed at him and then Cooper and I quickly left the house and towards his truck.

"DaKota!" My mother chased after me, but it was too late. Cooper was already tearing up the dirt road beneath the truck.

I put my elbows on my thighs and cried into my hands as Cooper drove to God knows where, "I hate him so much." I cried to Cooper, he didn't say anything he just started to rub my back hoping to make me calm down.

AFTER DRIVING AROUND for some time, Cooper and I decided just to go back to his house and I would stay the night. I had finally stopped crying as we stepped out of the truck and Cooper immediately engulfed me a warm hug. "I love you so much, no matter what."

"I love you too." I say and then he unwraps himself from me and grabs my hand as we walk into his house.

But what we see when we enter makes us stop in our tracks, Desiree and Reese are tied to the table chairs, facing us. What the hell is going on?! Little Reese looks so scared and Desiree looks worried, not for herself, but for her sons. "Hello son." A deep voice says from the corner of the room.

Bill comes walking over towards us and Cooper automatically stands in front of me. Cooper looks fearless towards his father, "Oh hello DaKota! What a pleasure to see your pretty face again! I wasn't expecting you to be here, this makes it so much more interesting!" He says in a sick manor.

"What the hell do you want? Why are they tied up?" Cooper says to Bill, who smirks at his youngest son and wife.

"Well I had to get your attention somehow." He says and then his look turns serious. "You know what I want, Cooper."

"I am not going with you, get that through you sick-twisted mind of yours."

"Wrong answer." His dad deeply frowns and then steps towards Desiree and then pulls out a knife and holds it on her neck.

"Stop!" Cooper, Reese, and I both yell at the man.

"You have ten seconds to make a decision, or your mother finally gets her wish of being free of me." He says pushing the knife closer, finally on her skin. Bill starts to count down slowly and psychotically. Cooper looks conflicted with himself, which worries me because I know he would sacrifice himself over his family any day. "Nine..T-"

"Fine! But I'll only go if you beat me." Cooper blurts out making my very confused at what he was talking about.

Bill's eyes light up with what looks like pride once he knows what Cooper means. He lowers the knife from Desiree and stands up. "Son, I never knew you had the balls."

"What are you doing?!" I whisper-yell to Cooper.

"What I have to do." He turns his head to me as Bill walks past us and through the door. I look into his eyes and he looks determined but also heartbroken.

"Cooper don't!" Desiree screams as Cooper turns to walk out the door. When I see Bill is gone, I run to the kitchen and grab a knife and cut them free of the ropes.

"What's happening?" I say to Desiree as she hugs Reese.

"They're going to have a standoff." She says frightened. Are we in a fucking western movie!? Who the fuck has Mexican standoffs!

I stand at the door of their house and I see the two standing across from each other, Cooper now armed with a .45 single action colt revolver by his side. I looked at Bill and he had the same gun as his son. Was Cooper crazy?! I ran down the steps and by his side and grabbed his non shooting arm, "Cooper what are you doing?!"

He still continues to stare at his father and then turns to look at me, "I know what I'm doing, now get out of here." He whispers to me and I stand my ground. "DaKota, I'll be fine, I love you, okay?"

A tear slips from my eye as I whisper, "I love you too." and then reluctantly leave his side and go inside with Reese and Desiree.

"All we can do is watch." Desiree says beside me as we stare at the window. My heart is pounding so hard, I think Desiree can hear it. I have to cross my arms to keep them from shaking. My fingers grab onto my cross necklace and I send a quick prayer to help protect Cooper. I mean this can't be real? Cooper can't just be be here and then not in the next minuet, can he? This whole day just has to be some crazy-messed-up dream, it has to be.

And then, I see Bill make the first move to shoot, and then Cooper, but before both shots are about to fired, one sounds out. I shut my eyes and then open them to see Bill laying on the ground with blood coming out if his shoulder.

I immediately run to outside and run to Cooper who is by his father's side, "You missed son." His father laughs at him, but Cooper takes the butt of the gun and pushes on the gunshot and he cries with pain.

"You know damn well I could of shot you right between your eyes if I wanted to, but unlike you," Cooper says, "I am not a murderer. Now pick your ass up, get in your truck and never come back here again. And if you do, I'll make sure to put that bullet where it belongs." Bill realizes Cooper's seriousness and painfully sits up and stands up and gets in his truck and drives away.

Cooper finally turns to me and gives me a look of despair as I run to him and hug him, "You jerk! You could of got killed!!"

"I know, it must of been this." He says and grabs his necklace from under his shirt.

"Don't do that again!" I poke a finger into his chest and he smiles down at me.

"Yes ma'am, c'mon lets go inside." Cooper says as we walk side by side into his house, safe and sound.

I jolted awake when I heard, "Police! Put your hands where I can see them!" I turned over so I was resting my back against the head board, and put my hands in the air. Their flashlights blinded my awaking eyes, but it still didn't blind out the guns they pointed at us. I looked at Cooper and he did the same thing as me.

"What the hell is going on?" Cooper yelled as two police officers came to his side of the bed.

I was scared out of my mind watching all of the officers with their guns pointing them at us, "Ma'am, are you hurt?" One comes to me and I shake my head.

"What's going on?" I asked frustrated, still keeping my hands in the air.

They grabbed Cooper's hands and put them behind his back hand cuffing him, "Cooper Blackwood you are under arrest for attempted murder. You have the right to remain silent. Anything you say can be and will..-" They read him the Miranda Rights as they walked him out of his room.

"Attempted murder?! " Cooper says to them like they're crazy, because they are!

"Cooper!" I yelled to him and he gave me one last look as he left the room. He didn't look scared, but sorry that I had to see this.

Bill must of went to the police after Cooper shot him, that son of a bitch. But how come they didn't arrest Bill, he's a wanted criminal around the country!! Something is not right here. "Ma'am, we're going to need to you come down to the station to answer some questions." An officer said to me as I followed them out of the room.

The blue and red flashing lights were all over his yard, but I managed to find Desiree by the police car they put Cooper in, she was crying, begging them to stop. I ran over to her and wrapped her in a hug, "It's going to be okay, he'll be fine." I say to her, but really I was just trying to convince myself.

WE'VE BEEN HERE FOR three hours, and we still haven't seen Cooper, and we probably won't until his trial, if he is tried. All we know is that he is being charged with second-degree attempted homicide against Bill Blackwood. After they found out who he really is, they arrested him in the hospital where he is getting stitched up.

I checked the time on my phone, 5:36. I checked my missed calls, four from my mother, two from Caleb, one from Ashley, and one from Taylor. Was I going to return the calls? Nope. I had no interest in talking to them right now, I needed to be alone. I had already gone through my interrogation and that was tough, they really messed with my head, but I just told truth about what happened.

"Here you go." A voice woke me out of my train of thought. I looked up and it was Cooper's lawyer with an iced caramel macchiato for me and Desiree.

"Thanks." We both said at the same time.

"Any news?" Desiree asked with big hopeful eyes.

"Yes, Cooper will be tried against a jury tomorrow at noon." I saw a tear slip from Desiree's eyes and I wrapped my arm around her trying to comfort her.

"Does it look good for him?" Desiree asked through her sniffles.

"It's hard to tell due to the circumstances on both sides, but I promise you I will do my best to protect your son." Lacy said and placed her hand on Desiree's knee.

"Can we see him?" I ask her.

"Yes, but only one at a time. Desiree would you like to go first?" She asked softly and Des nodded and stood up slowly. Lacy showed her to the room and then she wandered off somewhere. I took a sip of my coffee drink and savored the flavor.

Cooper just can't go to jail. He doesn't deserve to go to jail. His fucked up father deserves to die in jail, him, not Cooper. Who's going to help Desiree with the ranch? Who's Reese going to look up to? Who's ever going to make me feel the way Cooper does?

"Your turn." Someone poked me and I opened my eyes from my slight cat nap. I looked up at Des was looking down with a sad smile on her face.

I stood up and Lacy showed me the room, and I took a deep breath before I entered. I only made it one step into the room when the tears came. Cooper was handcuffed to the table and already dressed in an orange jumpsuit, "Don't cry, baby." He tried to smile but he failed miserably.

I took the chair and placed it beside him and he turned his head to look at me, "How are you doing?" I ask him.

"Better now." He grinned at me, making my lips tug up into a smile. "How are you?"

"I'm fine." I sigh.

"You suck at lying," He chuckled, "You need to go home and sleep."

"I don't have a home to go, remember?"

"My home is your home." His words forced me to look at him. I couldn't hold the tear back, so a few more cascaded my cheeks. "I wish I could wipe those tears away, please don't cry, Kods."

"I know," I sniffled, "I'm so sick of crying.." I chuckled. "Cooper, I can't do it without you."

"Don't talk like that, DaKota." He said sternly, but I knew he was right.

"Cooper-"

"I'm not going to jail. We're going to be together. One day I'll get to marry you. We'll have our own home. Then you'll have our children. And then we'll grow old together and laugh about how silly you're being right now." Cooper sounded so confident in his promises that it made me feel ten times better.

I leaned in and we kissed each other with so much passion and love it was knee weakening. After our kiss, we rested our foreheads together, "I love you." I whispered to him.

"I love you more."

Then the door busted in with the detectives who interrogated me earlier, "I'm sorry, Ms. Jones, but your time is up."

I looked at Cooper and ran my fingers through his hair and then kissed his cheek. "I'll see you soon, okay?" I say to him and he nods back to me.

"You should go back home now, Ms. Jones." The one detective says to me.

"Okay." Is all I say and then head back to where Desiree was sitting. "Do you mind if I stay with you for a couple of days?" I ask her as we head out of the precinct and to her pickup.

"No problem, we both shouldn't be alone until what the future holds."

NEXT DAY

I WALKED BEHIND DESIREE as we walked into the court room, the trial starting in about five minuets. Lacy, the lawyer, said that today was mostly going to be about trying to get the jury too see the shot was self defense because of Bill's dangerous history. It's trying to get the jury to realize that he was protecting his family and his own life by shooting Bill in the arm. Lacy was sure that the case was leaning in Cooper's favor, but we can never be sure.

I slid into the court rows, sitting in between Desiree and my mother, who came to support Cooper. I ended up calling her last night and we talked things through, even though she wasn't the one who I am mad at. She told me that she supports every decision I make and that she's giving my father the silent treatment. I have no intentions to talk to my father until Cooper's trial is done and we have some time just to get away.

As I play with the hem of my baby blue dress, I hear the judge say, "Enter the defendant." Desiree and I both sat up straighter, looking for our boy. The wooden door opened and Cooper walked out in his orange jumpsuit, handcuffed and walked over to the defendant table by a police officer. Cooper scanned the room for us and when he saw us, his hardened look softened, my heart broke for him as he sat down in the chair, turning away from us. My hand ached to hold his larger one, missing the warm feeling of it. "All rise." The judge said and all of us followed her orders as the trial began.

I felt the need to get up and walk around the court room as the jury left to go make the decision that would decide Cooper's fate. I held Desiree's shaking hand in mine, which was also shaking. My whole body was shaking in anticipation for the verdict. I couldn't tell you how many times I have prayed in the last two days, so much that I'm pretty sure God was getting annoyed with me. The whole trial was a haze to me, I barely remember what was said because my mind was constantly talking over the lawyers and judges. I thought of every possible situation that could happen now and in the future. I was trying to keep positive, but at this point, no one knows what will and can happen.

I looked at Cooper who was already looking at me, we didn't do anything but just hold each other's gaze. I couldn't read his face, and that was hard, I knew every one of his emotions. I had never seen this one before and that worried me, more than I already was. I crank my head in the direction of a door opening, revealing the jury coming back to their seats. From my peripheral, I can still see Cooper looking at me. What is he doing?

"Will the jury foreperson please stand? Has the jury reached an unanimous verdict?" The judge says turning towards the jury.

"Yes." Someone says and then they hand a piece of paper to the judge, she reads it and then hands it back. Of course, you couldn't read her emotion, it was her job not to.

"The jury finds the defendant guilty."

Everything around me goes blurry, I couldn't hear anything or concentrate on one thing. Guilty? How could they find my Cooper guilty? I do not understand how this even possible. Thinking of all the scenarios that could happen, I never actually believe that he would be found guilty. I don't have a solution to this! There's nothing I can do.. Absolutely nothing.

"Due to the circumstances of this trial, the sentence has already been set. Cooper Blackwood is here by sentenced three years in the Jefferson County jail on the account of second degree attempted murder. Thank you, jury, for your service today. Court is adjourned."

Desiree and I both stand up as Cooper stands up and turns to us one last time before he has to be detained. Desiree is already crying, and I'm trying to be strong for her and for myself. Cooper gives me a look that reads that he doesn't want to go, but he is not scared either. But his eyes hold something more, a wordless I love you.

After Cooper leaves the court room, Desiree turns into my arms looking for a hug which I wrap my arms around her, "It's not fair!" She cries out, gaining attention from others.

A hand on my shoulder, makes me look back at my mother and she gives me a 'lets-go' look and I nod. "C'mon, lets go home." I say as I only wrap one arm around her shoulder, guiding her in the right direction.

"Mrs. Blackwood!" Lacy's voice calls out as we exit the row. I stop walking and wait for her to get to us. Her face is sorrowful and she looks guilty, "I am so sorry, I tried everything."

"We know, thank you for everything." I say as Desiree can not find the words to speak as she is still crying. "When can we see him?" I ask.

"Unfortunately you guys will not get to see him tonight, but tomorrow you can definitely see him. Visiting hours start at nine a.m through five." She says in a defeated tone, making me hurt for her instead of myself.

"Thank you." I give her a great full nod as I guide Desiree in the direction to walk out of the room

As we walk to our pickups I say to Desiree, "Are you sure you don't want me to drive you home?"

"No, no.. I think we should both be alone for a bit. I've decided to take Reese to his aunts house and stay there for a couple of days, but you're welcome to stay at the house. I understand how much you are hurting right now." She says and puts a hand on my shoulder.

"But what about visiting him?" I ask her, isn't she dying to see him? Have a full conversation with him? Say a good-bye?

"I'm not ready to see him in there yet. I'll see you soon dear, call if you need anything." She says as we give each other one last hug and then we both get into our pickups.

AS I'M DRIVING I TURN my music all the way up, trying to block out my thoughts running through my mind. I was driving myself crazy. All I could think about was him. Every single memory that we have shared, good and bad. How am I going to going to keep myself sane without him?

I pull up to Cooper's house and park in my usual spot, turn off the engine, and step out of the pickup and decide to go to the stables, where Cooper's horses are. Sliding open the door, all of the horses heads poke out of their door and look at me, "Hey guys." I softly say looking at all of them.

I walk over to Cooper's favorite horse, JW, named after John Wayne. JW was Cooper's all around horse, did everything Cooper asked him to do, whenever and wherever. They had a special bond between them, and even in this moment JW knows there's something wrong. I walk to his stall and start to scratch between his eyes. "I just came to tell you that you might not be seeing your best pal for a while, but don't worry, you'll have Desiree, Reese, and I to take good care of you. It'll be tough, but we can get through it. It's not like he's gone forever, it's just a few years. If I waited 18 years for him, a few won't hurt, right?"JW just stared at me while I blabbered on, slightly sniffling from my oncoming tears. Who was I kidding? These three years are going to suck, suck some major donkey ass.

Walking through Cooper's house, I walked up the stairs and made my way to his bedroom. I lean against his door frame and take in everything I see. As usual his bed is unmade, despite the million times I've told him to do it in the morning. There is a pair of jeans by the side of his bed, covered in dirt and oil. There's a water bottle on his night stand, hardly filled with his damn Copenhagen spit. There's a few of his shirts scattered around the room, but I walk over to his black Cinch sweatshirt and grab it and just hold it into my arms. Then I fall back onto his bed and stare at the ceiling, and without my consent, the tears start flowing like the Rio Grande. I turn over, so I'm crying into his pillow that smells just like him, which makes me cry even more.

God, it hasn't even been three hours and I already miss him like hell.

I turned off my curling iron and then grabbed my hairspray and added another heavy layer of spray onto my hair, hoping the curls will last. I looked at myself in the mirror, making slight adjustments to my outfit. I am wearing a maroon T-shirt dress, a turquoise squash blossom necklace, and my buckskin coconut Lambert fringed heels. My hair is styled in big bouncy-romantic curls, I am wearing foundation and mascara.

I wanted to look good for him, to cover up how much of a mess I have been lately. All I've been doing is wearing his shirt around his house and watching sad movies. I've been avoiding calls and texts from friends and family. I needed to talk to Cooper before I could talk to anyone else. I needed to know he will be okay. The only two people I have been talking to is God and Desiree. Desiree and I check up on each other from time to time and we talk about what is currently on our minds, it somewhat helps. As for God, I ask him for guidance and ask him to look over Cooper as he is without his friends and family.

I grab my fringe satchel off the counter, as it holds money, my keys, and my wallet with all of my information. As I walk out of the door, I lock it and then let it close into its frame and walk to my pickup. I throw my satchel into the passenger seat as I climb into the drivers seat and then start my pickup and begin to make my way to the Jefferson County Jail.

I SIGNED MY NAME, DATE, time and the person who I was visiting, and then I pushed the sheet under the window to the girl. She gave me a nod and then I put the pen down and went to go take a seat with the other visitors. I looked for an open spot and spotted one in the third row, so walking in front of people, I sat in the chair, no body beside me. I couldn't help but look at the other people waiting, I wonder who they were visiting. Were some people like me? Visiting innocent people who don't deserve to be here, or consciously visiting guilty people because they don't care what they did. Mothers visiting their sons or daughters? Or vice versa? I know one thing we all had in common, we were all nervous about being here.

I stared at the picture of Cooper and I on my lock screen. It was the same picture as the one that Cooper has beside his bed, the one where I was on his back smiling happily and he had an adorable toothless grin. Then I opened my phone to my home screen, which was Cooper sleeping on my chest when we were in Mandan. My heart tugged at the thought, remembering the warm feeling of his arm across my chest and his warm breath against my neck. I'd do anything to go back to that moment right now.

As I was flipping back and fourth between the two screens a feminine voice called, "DaKota Jones." I tucked my phone back into my satchel and then stood up and walked over to the police officer. "The bag ma'am." She said and then I took off my satchel and put it in the plastic bin and walked through the metal detector.

No beeps sounded as I walked through, and then the lady walked me towards the visiting room. She opened the door and I followed her in the crowded room full of visitors and inmates. My heart beat increased with each step as I took to my seat, "He'll be out in a minuet." She said and I gave her a soft smile and nod as she walked away.

I began to play with the hem of my dress as I waited for him to come, other people's conversations started to consume my thoughts. Then the sound of a chair scooting back caught my attention. I looked up and saw him.

Our eyes met and something in me just wanted to break down and cry for him. He was in a charcoal jumpsuit, with a white shirt under. Over his shirt I saw his necklace , at least he had a part of me with him. He had grown a 12 o'clock shadow, making him look older, more suited for jail. "Hey." He tried to give me a happy smile, but it turned out sad.

I pressed the phone against my ear, "Hey." I barely spoke, wondering if he even heard me.

"You look beautiful, hot date later?" He jokes, earning him an angry/sad glare from me. "Okay, not funny." He says sadly as I stare at him.

"Is everything okay here? Do you need me to bring something from your house? Cause I can do anything you-"

"I'm okay, Kods." He cuts me off, slightly surprising me from his abruptness. "Have you figured anything out with your parents?"

"No, I haven't said much to them. I haven't seen or spoken to my father since that day, and I don't plan to for a while."

"Talk to them," Cooper's words confused me, causing me to furrow my eyebrows, "Don't waste your time hating your father, DaKota. He just wants what's best for you-"

"You're what's best for me." I angrily cut him off, is he deciding with my father? Why now?

Cooper gives me a look and he sighs, "I'm not going to be there anymore, Kota, just take the time to do it. The more time you don't talk to him, the worse it's going to get. Please.."

"I'll think about it." I say to him, "I miss you, Cooper." I suddenly say and I feel the tears start to build up inside me.

"I miss you too, darlin.'" He looks as if saying that hurt him, he was acting so strange. We didn't say anything to each other for a long time. I just stared at him, while he stared at the table, thinking of something. Then he finally broke it, "If you could only remember one memory of us

325

or me, what would it be?" His voice gave away that he unsure of himself asking me this.

What was going on?

Why was he telling me to make up with my father? Why is his asking me this ridiculous question? "Cooper, what are you doing?" I ask him as he finally looks me in the eyes.

"Just answer the question." His avoiding makes me even more afraid of his reasoning.

"No." A tear slipped from my left eye as I figured out where he was going with this.

Cooper's eyes were heart broken, apologetic, stressed, determined, and full of emotion. "Mine would have to be the day where you helped me moved my cattle to the different pasture." I remember that day, "I think that's where I started falling for you. You were showing those cows who was the boss, and if one challenged you, you laughed in their face. I just watched you and your horse take over the whole thing, not even caring that I was supposed to be the one doing all the work. By the smile on your face I knew you loved the kind of life we lived, and I remember thinking to myself, 'I'm going to marry this girl.'" He chuckled to himself. Why is he telling me this?

"Seeing you riding in the sage grass reminded me of your wild and free spirit, probably what I love most about you. When we got back to my house, you offered to make me lunch without me asking, showing your caring characteristic, and you made me the best damn BLT I ever had." He chuckled again. "Then we watched '8 Seconds' together and you cried at the end, even though you've watched that movie 20 times before. Even though we were laughing about it, I held you tighter in my arms, kissing away your silly tears. I was lucky because I got to see your soft side that no one else gets to see because you disguise it so well. That day I was lucky enough to see every side of the real DaKota Jones, that day I will never forget." There was a sad smile on Cooper's face and I could tell he was fighting back more emotions.

I shake my head at him, holding back my tears, "I'm not going to say it." I say stubbornly.

"Please, baby." He sounded desperate for my answer.

I took a deep breath, "I don't know why you're making me do this," I try to calm my shaky voice, "But if I have to, I'll never forget when we were driving one time and the song 'Cowboy Take Me Away' came on. In that moment I realized that I wished the song was about us. That'd you would steal me away from everyone and it'd just be you and me. I started to see a future with you, it was clear as day to me. I saw a house on top of a hill, no surrounding buildings, no street lights, nobody. I saw me in your arms as we stood out in a field watching the sunset." I took a deep breath, "I knew if you asked me to run away with you right then I'd drop everything and do it. No questions asked, just get in the truck and go, because I'd be with you. I thought I was going crazy, because I had never wanted something so bad with someone before. That burning desire in my stomach had me questioning every decision I ever made, I'll never forget what that felt like." By the time I was finished, another damn tear broke the barrier. That day was just a couple of weeks ago, but I'll never forget the way I felt after I realized what I had wanted with him.

Cooper leaned his arms against the table, gaining my attention. "DaKota, you deserve no less than the best." I shake my head at him, trying to get him to stop. "You deserve to have that feeling every day of your life, but I can't give that to you anymore." Through my glossy eyes, I saw his eyes start to water.

"Cooper, don't do this." My heart couldn't handle anymore loss, especially him. "Please, don't." But the look in his eyes tells me he's going to do it anyways.

He slowly tears his eyes off mine and puts the phone back, hesitating to stand up and leave. As he stands up he looks me dead in the eye and mouths, I love you.

"Cooper!" I yell at him as a guard comes and takes Cooper's arm and pulls him away. I stand up and yell again, "Cooper!!" He still doesn't look at me. I follow him, passing other visitors, all of them staring at me. "You promised me!" I yell at the top of my lungs, then he finally looks at me, a look of seriousness. His eyes only met mine for a split second before he walked through the doors with the guard, out of my sight.

I hear voices beside me, but my brain is currently still running through the motions of what just happened. Did he just- No.

I won't let him give up that easily.

I felt a hand on my shoulder, knocking me out of my confusion. I look over my left shoulder and the lady from the desk was standing beside me, "Ms. Jones, you can't be in here anymore." She kindly says and I nod slowly and follow her out of the visitation room and back to the waiting room, she returns my satchel and I make my way out of the parking lot.

I THOUGHT ABOUT GOING back to Cooper's, but I couldn't. I wasn't even sure what Cooper meant by the "only one memory" speech. The only thing I was sure of was that I'll stop going there when I know my damn answer. Why didn't he just tell me? Give it to me straight. That's all he had to do.

I felt a little better when I only saw my mom's pickup in the grass, I did not want my father to see what I'm about to do with my mom. I spot my mom walking from the garden, holding the watering pot in her hands. She looks up at my truck and her expression softens as she recognizes her daughter. Once I'm parked, I waste no time in jumping out and running to her and engulfing her in a hug as my tears pour out like a waterfall.

Her hands run through my hair, trying to comfort me. "Oh my baby." She whispers sadly as she kisses the side of my head. "C'mon lets go inside." She says and steps back from our hug. I look at her and sniffle and wrap my arm around her side and walk with her into the house.

She leads us into the living room and we crash on the couch and I continue my crying fest. I cry into her shoulder as she just sits there, not knowing why I am crying. I'm sure she has some idea, because she's a mom. "I don't understand." I say in horrific crying voice.

Her soft fingertips wipe away my tears, different from Cooper's calloused ones. "What happened, honey?" She genuinely asks me as she searches my face for an answer.

After I finished explaining to her, which was extremely difficult when I don't fully understand either, I cried into her shoulder once again.

My mom was quiet as she comforted me, not knowing what to say to me. I don't blame her. I wouldn't know what to say either.

"Like you said, you just have to keep going there until he gives you an answer. Maybe give it some time, so both of you can really think about it." She says, pulling me away from her shoulder. She takes my shoulders in her warm hands, and then looks me deep in her eyes. "You think he's the one, right?" She carefully says, making sure that I was sure.

"I am so sure that it makes my stomach hurt." I say confidently through my sniffling mess.

"You think that boy is worth questioning every decision in your life? You can't think of another boy making you smile or laugh? You see him in your future? You can't imagine life without him? You're happiest with him?" My mom strongly asks me and I nod back to her, my tears choking back my words. "Then you fight for him." I look into her brown eyes, seeing nothing but experience and sanity.

"How though?" I ask her taking a deep breath, trying to stop my tears.

"Like you said, you just have to keep going until he tells you or what you guys decide. I know Cooper, he'll just need some time, and so do you. Now, go take a nice bubble bath and try to relax. It's not the end of the world, baby girl." She says as she brushes the hair out of my face.

I nod, knowing she is right. I give her one last hug on the couch, and then I walk the familiar route to the upstairs bathroom. As I walk across the dinning room floor, I stop at the spot where my father slapped me. I stare at the dark wood, replaying the scene from a third person view, it disgusts me. From both sides, neither of us are innocent.

After my somewhat relaxing bath, I decided I needed a good vent to my journal, some where were I could really let my emotions out. Letting the towel drop from my wet hair, I walk over to my chair and pull out my journal, last written in two days ago. I flip to my last page and read my last paragraph.

"I don't know how he does it. Always manages to put a smile on my face. Even when I try to pretend to be mad at him(which I can do pretty well) he'll crack a joke, pull a joke on someone, or put on an incredibly sexy smirk , forcing me to smile. It's so frustrating!!! Then he'll wrap me in a warm hug and tell me I'm cute when I'm mad, which gets me mad again. Boy, I love this man."

I can see Cooper with a big victory smile on his face after achieving the mission to get me to smile and then pulling my waist into him and giving me a big bear hug and kissing me on the cheek. After the vision blurs, I realize I'm smiling, that son of a bitch did it even when he's not here! I take this as a sign, a sign not to give up yet. There's hope for him and I, I know it.

I woke up to something licking my face, Micah. My face scrunches when my senses takes in her bad morning breath, or just bad breath in general. I force myself to open my eyes to her sweet face right in front of mine. "Hi my sweet girl.." I barely say, still in a sleeping state. She continues to stare at me and I stare back at her, she wines and reaches her paw up towards me. "What do you want?" I ask her in that weird baby voice everyone does to their pet.

Micah pushes herself off me, earning a grunt from me and then she makes her way towards my balcony door. She wants to go outside for a walk, something we haven't done since we got into the rain incident. She pants as she looks back at me with hopeful and playful eyes. "Alright, just give me five minuets." I say as I roll out of bed and towards my bathroom.

The other dogs are already waiting for me on the porch when Micah and I walk out of the door. They already know what is going on like they planned it, making me laugh. They lead me down our dirt drive, already knowing the route we are taking.

It's a beautiful morning, the sun alone in the sky, shining above the dancing sage grass. The dogs stay close me as we turn onto the road and they start to follow different scents in the ditch. I on the other hand, try not to follow the depressing thoughts and images over these past few days. Instead, I try to focus on the sights around me. The golden dirt beneath my feet, the way the grass smells, the neighbor mares and their babies coming over the hills, and the free feeling I feel in my stomach right now.

If only Cooper was sharing this with me.

Dammit, don't think about it! I shook my head and then I started to quicken my pace, the dogs easily catching up with me.

Walking towards the diner, I straightened my shirt and took in a deep breath. This would be the first time in the diner since Cooper got arrested, I haven't been around this many people in a while. I only hope they would just ignore me and carry on with their lunch.

The bells rang and all heads turn to look at me, whispers and stares were very noticeable in everybody in the cafe. I was glued in my spot, I didn't know what to do in that moment. "DaKota!" I heard to my left and then I felt two embracing arms around me in a flash.

Taylor, the person who I needed the most right now.

"I'm so glad to see you." I sigh into her shoulder and then we pull away from each other.

"C'mon, let's go talk." Taylor said as she wrapped an arm around my shoulders and led me over to the farthest booth in the corner, away from everybody.

"THAT MAKES NO SENSE to me." Taylor scrunches her eyebrows with anger when I tell her what Cooper asked me yesterday when I visited him.

"I know, he totally shocked me when he said it. I'm not sure if he wanted to or not, he was pretty torn up about it."

"I wouldn't of answered." Taylor shrugged nonchalantly.

"I told him I didn't want to, but you should of saw his eyes. He could of sold the cops marijuana with those eyes. Damn him."

"So are you seeing him today?" She asks me as she sticks a spoonful of ice cream in her mouth.

"Yep, I'll probably go after we're done talking." I shrugged looking around us. "Everyone is looking at us." I sighed as I turned back to look at her.

"They're just curious." Taylor says slightly positive.

"No, they just want to see if I am a wreck or not." I sigh again and cross my arms.

"Is that a bad thing? To check up on you?"

"I wouldn't call gossiping "checking up" on me. If they cared, they'd come to my house or something." Neither Taylor or me say anything after that, we just just stare at the people trying to look at us without us noticing. Typical small town. "But what's up with you?" I ask her, trying to lighten the mood.

"Well Beau, just surprised me with a trip to California." She says hesitantly.

"That's great, Tay!" I give her my best smile I could pull off.

"No, it's not," She frowns and I furrow my eyebrows at her, "It's not the right time to leave." She says sympathetically.

"Tay, don't worry about me. I'll be fine. I want you to go because I know you've always wanted to go to Cali." I say softly to her. Taylor deserved to go have some fun with Beau, she didn't need to babysit me. I have plenty of people already doing that.

"Are you sure?" She asks, and I can she's getting excited.

"Yes." I laugh at her and then hearing my answer, she jumps in her chair and claps her hands and has a huge Texas smile on her lips.

"Thank you, I'm gonna go call Beau!"

When I parked my pickup in my usual spot, I noticed some other pickups here. One I recognized as Rusty's dad's, but the other's I didn't know. I left the keys in the ignition and climbed out and started walking to the porch of my house. Before I opened the screen door, men's laughter filled my ears. When I opened the door, all eyes landed on me. I'm kind of sick of everyone doing that lately.

Sitting at the table was my dad, Rusty's dad Rick, Kurt Schaff, Brad Storm, and William Beard. "Hey DaKota." They say as they come off their high of laughter.

"Hi, where's mom?" I turn my attention to my father who I have barely spoken to.

"She's on a call," He says as I start to walk towards the stairs. "DaKota, could you make us lunch before we head out?" Oh my freaking Lord. Does this man think I am a food-making-machine? Does he think all is forgiven all of a sudden? He is unbelievable and oblivious to the current situation.

I stop in my tracks and turn on my heels, "Make your own damn food." I say with my best bitch face to make my point. My dad's eyes lightly widen and he is definitely taken back, but his expression softens, realizing my reasoning for my attitude.

I don't care what the other guys think, I turn right back and head up to my room to get ready to go see Cooper.

I straighten my hair into a high ponytail and wear some ripped boyfriend jeans and a western graphic tee. I slipped on some buckskin fringe moccasins and my wallet as I walked out of my house. I hear the horses make some noise, so I look up and see my dad and his friends riding off like classic westerns, fast and never looking back.

I SMOOTHED OUT MY HAIR before I entered the visitor section of the jail, an uneasy feeling settled over me as I entered. It's just a jail, police officers every where in case something happens. I guess it reminded me of Wade, the man I hate the most. It was this prison where he escaped, and now I see that they have doubled their guards since then. Isn't that nice of them.

I offered the lady at the desk a polite smile as she handed me the sign in information. I filled in all the information and double checked if I missed anything and then handed it back to her, "If you could please take a seat while we get... Mr. Blackwood." She said and looked down at my scribbles. I gave her a curt nod and sat down in the first row of the waiting area.

My foot tapped on the plain carpet as I waited for them to call my name. From the corner of my eye I could see the lady get up and every time I thought she would call my name, but nothing yet. It was taking longer than it did yesterday, maybe there's more people here, I wasn't paying that close of attention.

I looked at the time on my phone and it was 3:32, I've been waiting for half an hour now. Maybe Cooper was busy. With what? Whatever they do in jail I guess.

"Miss Jones." Finally.

For some reason my heart started to pound when I stood up from my seat to go to the desk. I'm just excited to see Cooper, to hear him, to know how he's doing, and tell him that I miss him. I started to hand her my things but then she said, "I'm sorry Miss Jones, he doesn't want to see you."

Was my mind playing tricks on me?

"I'm sorry, what did you say?" I ask her politely and very confused.

"Mr. Blackwood said he's not taking any visitors today." She says to me and it takes me back.

"Oh, okay.." Is all I can say as I grab my things and walk away from the desk. Maybe he's already seen his mom today and needs to take a break, yeah, that makes sense.

But as I sit in my pickup and stare at the steering wheel, it dawns on me that I never saw his mother's name on the visitors list. My heart and stomach sink, making me want to throw up. Cooper didn't want to see me.

As I start to think more into it a tear slips from my eye without my consent. I wish I would run out of damn tears, I'm sick of them. I'm sick and tired of being let down. Right now there is nothing I wanted more than to march into Cooper's cell and slap him upside the head and ask him why.

Why

Why didn't want to see me? Why didn't he want to talk to me? Why didn't he care?

I DON'T KNOW HOW I managed to get home without getting into an accident. I don't even remember blinking at all. I was in a confused and angry daze the whole way.Pulling into my drive I'm glad to see my dad's friends gone because I could break down any second now.

When I opened the screen door, my mom already knew it was me, "Hey sweetie, how'd it-" Once she looked at me, she got her answer. "Oh honey, come here." She said with wide open arms.

Once in her arms I let the tears come out as they wanted, I didn't care anymore. I had a damn good reason to be crying. I felt my mom lead us over to the living room and she sat us down on the couch, breaking our hug. "Mom-he didn't want to see me." I said through my weakened tears and I managed to see her scrunch her eyebrows in confusion.

"What do you mean?" She said as she brushed my hair out of my face.

"He told the guards he didn't want to see me. He's giving up isn't he?" I cried, even though I tried calming myself down.

"DaKota, you don't know that." My mother says in her normal voice.

"But how will I know if he won't even talk to me?" I say as I take a deep breath and wipe the smudged makeup from my eyes.

"DaKota, do what you've always done," My mom grabs my hand in comfort, "don't stop until you you get what you want."

She was right, I wouldn't go down without a fight. If Cooper wants to ends things with us, he's going to give me a face-to-face answer. I'm not going to spend my time wondering if things are over. I'm going to find out, and if the answer is not what I'm hoping it is, I'm going to cowgirl up and continue with my life.

"Thanks mom," I say and lean in for a hug and she hugs me tight, "I love you."

"I love you to, my sweet girl." She kisses my forehead and makes me feel a little bit better. I don't know what I would do without my mom.

It's been six months. Six months since I've seen him. Six months since I've heard him. Six months since I've felt him. Six months too long without him. During the first two months I went every other day, each time with more hope. Then the next two months, I went twice a week. These last two months I've been going once in two weeks, whenever I had the motivation to get out of bed.

It's been hard. So damn hard. If you would of asked me a year ago if I would of let a relationship destroy me like this, I would of laughed in your face. But that's what happens when you fall in love. I payed the price for it.

Lately my typical day is waking up in the morning with a headache, because of my nightmares, take medication for it, and then I decide if I'm going to get dressed. Sometimes I do, sometimes I don't. If I do get dressed, I'll sit down for breakfast and then take Pharaoh for a ride, or just hang out with him. If I don't, I'll eat breakfast, barely talk, and then I'll go back into my room and stare outside my window.

Some days are just like normal DaKota, ready to take on anything thrown at me and very busy. I'll start to think that I'm healing, but then one little thing makes me think of him, and just like that, I'm back to sad DaKota.

I've also been helping Desiree and Reese out on their ranch. Over there it is the same as my mood, gloomy and depressed. Desiree has to be strong for Reese, but I can tell she is struggling. I don't mind going over there, because there I don't feel like I am constantly being watched and monitored.

When I'm with my family, they just stare at me. Waiting for me to do something out of the ordinary. I'd usually tell them to back off, but lately, I just don't care anymore. They know why I'm like this, they don't know how to help me. And frankly, I don't either.

Today, well is an in between moods day. After I'm done helping Desiree with the horses, I'm going to go visit him, well if he decides to come out from the dark. I mean for gosh's sake I just wanna know how he is doing, is that so hard for him?

I tucked my phone in the back pocket of my Kimes Ranch Jeans as I walked down the stairs into the kitchen, where my dad was sitting having a cup of coffee. "Where are you going?" His voice wasn't interrogating, but just making conversation.

"To help Desiree with her yearlings, and then go to Jefferson." I say as I swipe my keys from the counter.

"Wait," He says as I grab the handle to the door. I turn back to face him, "Would you like to help tag the Baker's calves tomorrow?"

"Are you serious?" I ask him suspiciously, because he hasn't involved me in anything lately.

"Yeah, why do you ask?" He asks me like it's nothing out of the blue for him.

"Well lately you don't include me in ranchin' anymore." I cross my arms.

"Well I just thought that if you got back at it, your spirits could be lifted." For once in a long time, I didn't disagree with him. He was right. Getting back on the saddle on my ranch horse, battling the cold, and working cattle with family could really do something for me. It was a great idea.

"Yeah, I'd love to. I'll see you later." I offer him a small smile as I walk out the door. I zipped up my Carhartt jacket when I felt the temperature of a February day in Montana. My boots crunched on the hard snow the covered the ground.

I didn't mind winter, but it definitely wasn't my favorite season. I love when the snow falls, drinking hot chocolate, wild rags, sledding, ice skating, and snowmobiling. I hate the crisp cold of it all. But I've been around it my whole entire life so it wasn't a big deal to me.

I also hate driving during the winter. People are just so clueless when it comes to ice on the roads! When it's snowing, take it slow. When it's not snowing, it's okay to go the speed limit. Don't text and drive when it's close traffic, or in general. Break early, you can never be too careful.

I pulled into Desiree's drive and parked in my usual spot. When I turned off the engine, I saw Reese's head pop up in the window, making me laugh. Him and I have grown close these past few months, I consider him and Desiree family now. I smiled as I walked up the steps he opened the door, fully clothed in snow pants, a Carhartt jacket, snow boots, and gloves and a hat. "States!" His nickname made me smile more.

"Hey Reese, are you gonna help today?" I ask him as I hug him.

"No, mama said I couldn't." He says with a frown but quickly cheers up, "But I'm gonna make a snowman!" He says flashing me his broken smile.

"Cool, maybe I can help you after I'm done with the horses!" I said and he nodded and crutched away from me and down the steps and into the yard. I watched him as he went to his knees and went to work.

I noticed Desiree walking the yearlings out of the paddock and into the arena. We were currently working on two, two year olds. A chestnut filly by the name of Daisy, and a black colt by the name of Ranger. They both showed promise of great ranch horses, already growing muscle in all the right places and are very responsive to Desiree and I. The only thing

337

they don't like is the sound of spurs, they kick out every time they hear or see me wearing them. And if they're going to be working ranch horses, they need to be sensitized to spurs.

I always try to lunge them first, and then try the spurs, and then move onto something different. The reason I don't so spurs last is because I don't want them to end on a bad note and ruin their confidence. I have seen so many yearlings being ruined by that type of training, and it is very avoidable. The last thing I want to happen is wasting months of training these horses and ending up to start all from the beginning because of one little mistake.

I UNTIED THE HALTER off of Ranger and gave his face a nice scratch before I waved him off. Ranger was a very friendly horse, very eager to learn and likes to play with the other horses. He always comes to the gate when he sees me, unlike Daisy who is timid until she checks me out from a distance. Ranger also had a beautiful black coat that highly contrasted with the bright white snow on the ground. Sometimes I think he wants to become a Paint, because he loves to roll on the snow.

As I walk back from the paddock, I notice Reese still building his snowmen. I take my phone out of my pocket at check the time, 11:45, I have time. "Need some help?" I ask him as I walk up behind him.

"You wanna make snowmen?" He asked me as he rolled the snow into a ball.

"Yes! Why do you ask?" I ask as I kneel in the snow.

"My daddy said big people don't do this." He sadly says as he stares at his snowball.

"Well Reese, your dad is a big poopy-head. So who cares what he thinks, you should never care what people think about you." I say as I start making my base ball. Reese giggles at me as he continues.

"States, you're awesome!" He laughs and it makes me smile.

In total, Reese created a snowman version of himself, Cooper, and his mom, and I just made myself. But I made one behind them all, representing their father, which would be a gift for Desiree and Reese later. As I looked at them all with Reese by my side and Desiree standing on the porch, I noticed that their is a chunk of snow missing from Reese's bottom ball. "Why is there a missing piece from your's sweetie?" Desiree called out.

"It's my nub!" He says and I look down at him and his lips form into a frown, "It's the ugliest of them." That broke my heart when he said that.

I sadly look up at Desiree and we both give each other the same look, and an idea pops into my head. I leave his side and go up to Cooper's snowman and kick out a chunk, and repeat to Desiree's and mine. "Now we are all like you, so that makes them all awesome." I stand in front of them and Reese's sad face turns into a happy smile, making my heart warm.

"What's with the extra one?" Desiree calls out.

"I'm gonna need you to come here for that one." I smirked at her and she raised an eyebrow at me. Once she was standing by us I started to explain, "That represents your father, you can either throw snowballs or tackle him, whatever you want."

"Snowballs!" Reese says as he grabs the already made snowballs and gets closer to the snowman and starts to hurl them at the face and body. Watching Reese put everything into it and making the best comments Desiree and I start to break out in laughing. Laughing so hard it hurts.

"I'll be back." Desiree says and I nod as I watch Reese pretend to hurt the man, punching it with all his might, but not so much that it hurts him.

I hear her walking behind me and then she says, "Reese, get behind me and cover your ears." My jaw drops when I see she's carrying a shotgun in her hands. Reese quickly gets behind his mom and then she puts the 12 gauge to her shoulder and seconds later pulls the trigger three times. The snowman no longer in existence, but merely snowflakes in the air.

"Damn, that felt good." She smiles once she lowers the gun.

Reese giggles from behind her and goes back to making another snowman. I folded my arms across my chest as the wind blew across us as we watched Reese. "He looks up to you." Desiree says in an inspired voice.

"Really?" I ask her, curious in what way I could be a role model to him.

"Yes, ever since Cooper left he only talks about you. 'DaKota this, DaKota that, DaKota said, she's the coolest girl ever'! Your're his best friend." A smile tugged at my lips when Des told me Reese's feelings. He is the sweetest and nicest little boy I have ever met.

"With Cooper being gone, he's the one who makes my day. He knows when I'm sad and he'll try to cheer me up, which he usually succeeds. I think of him as my little brother." I say and she smiles to herself while she looks down. "You did a great job raising your boys." I say as I wrap my arm around her shoulder.

"Thank you," She says genuinely, and then she chuckles, "He also calls you his girlfriend but don't tell him I told you." We both laugh together and Reese stops playing to see what we are laughing about. He smiles with us, seeing that his girls are actually happy.

Melissa, the officer at the Jefferson County Jail visiting desk, recognizes me, but realizes that I am not alone today. Desiree thought she would come with me today, because she had nothing else today. She also recognizes Desiree, she comes a lot but not nearly as much as I do. For the first few weeks, Desiree had only seen Cooper two times, other than that, she's in the same boat as me.

"How are you guys today?" She greets us as she slides the sign in sheet under the window.

"Same as always." I shrug as I sign the blanks on the sheet.

"Same as any mother visiting her son in jail." Desiree says as she takes the book from me and signs her information.

"Maybe today will be the day." Melissa says with a toothless smile and sounded hopeful but sad at the same time. Desiree and I return the soft smile and head over to the waiting area.

It's always the same when I come here. As I wait, I watch people get called and go visit their person. When they come back they either come out crying, with a huge hopeful smile on their face, or come out angry at the world. But nonetheless, they get to see who they come for. However, for me, my name only gets called so I can hear the same thing every time, "he doesn't want to see you". But yet, I still come.

As we're waiting, Desiree puts her hand over mine and squeezes, "I have a feeling in my stomach about today." She seems excited, so I take it as a good feeling.

"How do you know?" I ask her as she releases my hand.

"I'm a mom." She says in a "duh" and confident voice as she looks away as someone else gets called.

My hands begin to sweat and my heartbeat's pace starts to quicken at the thought I might get to see him today. It feels like a first date, but only in jail.

I wonder what he looks like. Does he have a beard? Some kind of facial hair? Did he get a hair cut? Are his eyes darker than usual? What ever he looks like, I'm sure he's still hot as hell.

"DaKota." They never call me by my first name, always 'Miss Jones'. What does this mean? I looked at Desiree and we both had a curious and eager look on our faces as I stood up to walk over to the desk.

I knew everyone was looking at me. They know me as the 'girl who just doesn't give up'. Every time they would tell me that he didn't want to see me, I always heard them whisper behind me. I couldn't care less what they said, that's not on the top of my worry list.

I wiped my sweaty hands on my dirty jeans as I walked up to the desk. For being police officers, they didn't hide their expressions well. They all had harsh and gloomy looks, not one making eye contact with me. Something wasn't right.

I looked at Melissa who finally had the guts to look at me. "He told me to give this to you." She spoke so soft, I knew that she didn't want to hurt me by her words. She slid a white box under the window, and I was too nervous to open it myself. I took the box with shaky hands and I stepped back from the window and opened the box slowly.

I was wondering when my heart would finally break into a million pieces.

Inside the box was the cross necklace I gave him. He was giving it back to me. I didn't think twice on what it meant. The necklace was a symbol of faith. Not his Faith in God. His faith in us. This was the answer I had been waiting for six months.

My body instantly reacted. My stomach started to twist and turn, making me clutch my stomach. The tears slowly fell down my already puffy cheeks. My mind was spinning out of control, I could barely stand with my trembling legs. I would of fell down if it wasn't for Desiree who wrapped me in the tightest hug I had ever received.

"He's done. He doesn't love me anymore." I said in shock as I just stood there.

"Shhh, let's just go home." She said quietly as I pulled back, but left one arm around my shoulder to guide me towards the exit. I tried to fight against her, but my muscles and bones were too numb to even bulge. As we were walking, I looked behind my shoulder for him. Hoping he would break lose from the officers and take back his necklace and me, and everything would be okay again.

THE DRIVE BACK TO HUDSON was extremely agonizing, no words were exchanged between Desiree and I. I couldn't stop staring at his necklace. I thought of every second we shared together, even when we weren't dating. I remember it all. I hated that I did, because I know I won't be forgetting the memories anytime soon. I didn't want to forget them, they were too precious to let go.

Is this why he only wanted me to remember one memory? Because he knew it would be too hard? What a coward. Still, it doesn't make me stop loving him. Honestly, I don't know if I'll ever stop.

Once we got back to Desiree's, I didn't go inside. I couldn't. There was pictures of him in there. Pictures of me and him in there. His clothes were in there. Reese was in there, the boy who had reminded me of his damned brother, and who had become my happiness. I knew if I looked at Reese, I would break down and he could not see that. Especially after what Desiree told me today.

So instead, I got into my pickup and drove away while Reese looked at me through their living room window. I usually don't drive with two hands, but right now I needed to so I don't swerve into the ditch and get seriously hurt, more than I already am.

My shaky hand grabs the handle of the door and slowly pulls it open, revealing my parents sitting and Caleb in the dinning room. They both looked up from their work and restricted their jaws from dropping at the sight of me. I finally let it all out.

I would of fell on the ground if it wasn't for Caleb's fast reaction time. He caught me on my way down and cradled me on the floor, hugging me tightly as my parents surrounded us. They all put their hand on me, but none of their touches could comfort me. "What happened honey?" My mom's sweet voice was heard through my tears.

I didn't say anything but hand her the white box containing the necklace. I knew she opened it when I heard my brother say, "What does that mean?" I sniffled, trying to get myself ready to explain to him.

"DaKota gave this to him," She says somberly, her heart breaking for me. "And now he's given her a gift back, her answer." Caleb's arms wrapped around me tighter when he realized how much I am hurting. Whatever the amount of hurt he thought, wasn't even close.

"Caleb, bring your sister to her room. Chey will you bring her some water?" As usual, my dad took charge and told my family what to do with me.

Caleb lifted me up and started walking towards the stairs and up to my bedroom. I saw my dad open my door and lift the covers for me and the Caleb gently laid me down and then squeezed in with me. He wrapped an arm around my shoulder and I buried my head in his chest. "Cal-"

"Shhh, just go to sleep.. It'll help, trust me." Caleb said and then kissed the top of my head. I didn't argue with him, sleep sounded so good right now. It'll help me escape my living nightmare.

Little did Caleb know, I didn't sleep a wink when he was laying with me. I couldn't sleep without my pills, or I'd be screaming the whole night. So when he slowly got out of my bed, I had to put on my best acting. I heard him open the door and then I heard my dad's voice, "I'm going to kill that boy for what he's doing to my little girl."

"Not before I do." Caleb's voice was heard after my dad's. I had never heard Caleb so serious in my life, I'm sure there's nothing more he wanted to do right now.

Then my door closed and I opened my eyes and turned to lay on my back and stare at my ceiling. My eyes were so swollen I could barely see through them. I threw off my covers and reached under my bed and grabbed my pills. I had a third of the bottle left, who even knows if I should use them anymore. If they can't work with my nightmares with Wade, they definitely won't work with my terrors with Cooper.

I can't imagine him not being able to hold me, comfort me, talk to me, make me laugh, inspire me, touch me, or kiss me again. Lord, he did so much damage in such a short amount of time, it's bewildering.

I successfully got two hours of sleep last night. However it was a productive seven hours of thinking. Through my severe heartbreak, I grasped the concept that what is done, is done. There is nothing I can do about it. I can't fight for him because he won't talk to me. And I can't spend two years waiting for him and waste the whole time by being sad and depressed.

That isn't me.

I forgot the real DaKota Annie Jones is one tough mother fucker. When she gets knocked down, she gets right back up and does it again until she does it right. She is thick skinned and patient. She doesn't tolerate ignorance and bullshit. She runs with wolves. She's barbed wire tough. She stands up for she believes in. She stands up for those in need. She has been abused and tormented and yet she still carries a smile on her face. When someone tell her she can't, she proves them she can. She laughs in the face of danger, she even welcomes it. And when life hits hard, she pulls on her worn out cowgirl boots by the boot straps and pulls down her faded family generation cowboy hat and she faces the test of life. And she sure as hell doesn't let some boy get in her way.

I wrote who I am in my journal, so when the feeling of suffering and heartache rolls back around, I'll just read that and go on as usual. I won't let myself fall into that pit of despair. I can't, because if I do, I know it will never let me escape.

After washing my face and putting on mascara, I walked down the stairs, already dressed in my jeans and couple of layers of shirts and a sweatshirt. My mom's cooking filled my nose and it made my stomach growl. I can't remember the last time I had food in the last two days.

All eyes were on me when they heard my feet land on the wooden floor. I could tell they were expecting to see a puffy-depressed-faced-girl, not a girl who was fully alive and ordinary. "Morning." I said to them as I grabbed a plate and started to dish up.

They watch me like a parent would watch their baby try to walk by itself, scared and cautious. I take my plate and sit down in front of my brother and next to my father. "You're not taking the day off?" My dad asks me as I finish chewing my first bite of my ham and cheese omelet.

"Why would I? I'm tired of doing that for the past six months." I say like it's not a big deal.

"So just like that you're over it?" Caleb interjected and my eyes met his. I couldn't tell what they read, which interested me.

"Yep." I said as I shoved a fork full of food in my mouth. I look at everyone at the table and their expressions were clear as day: they didn't believe me. Even I didn't believe myself.

"We'll start as soon as they call." My dad broke the awkward silence.

He was referring to the Baker's, a real nice family that just lived down the road about a mile away. They didn't have any daughters, just two sons that are around 24 and another around 21. Ryder and Walker are their names, Walker the oldest. In high school, I never really hung around them, for what reason, I don't know. They were always gone for a rodeo every weekend. I don't know how they managed to even graduate.

IT WASN'T TOO COLD outside, probably around 30 degrees. I'm dressed in a sweatshirt, shirt underneath that, my brown Carharrtt jacket, and my blue wild rag. As I walked Scarlet around the road, I noticed there wasn't any ice, so that was nice for us.

I swung my leg over Scarlet as I settled in the saddle I pulled my hat down low and started to turn her in circles. Once I let her know who's boss, I stopped turning and directing. I gave her a nice pat on the neck and dropped the reins. "Ready?" My father asked as we all waited for him to get mounted. We all nodded and then he turned his horse, Rosco, and we all followed him to the road.

The Baker's had a very nice ranch home and ranch in general. They were a very traditional family, with a Victorian and ranch styled home. They were very humble and often kept to themselves, but their boys kind of rebel against that. They like to sneak out and go to parties and dance with any girl they can get. They're not man whores, but just like to impress girls. I really didn't have a problem with them.

They greeted us at their gate to the pasture, which they had kindly opened it already for us to get our horses through. "Hey guys, thanks for coming." The Baker dad, Richard, happily smiled at us.

"No problem, neighbor." My dad greeted back.

"All right let's get started shall we?" Richard says, as we all walk our horses into the pasture. "So I was thinking that Colby, Cheyenne, and myself will take the north pasture, Caleb and Walker will take the west, and Ryder and DaKota will take the east."

I look at Ryder and he offers me a small smile as I lead my horse to him, man this is gonna be awkward. "Hey Ryder." I say to him as I reach him.

"Hey DaKota, long time no see." He says with a chuckle.

"Yeah, I guess we've been pretty busy." I'm sure we both know I'm lying about being busy these months, but he plays along with me. "How are you?" I ask him.

"Can't complain, I'm sitting second in my circuit right now with my big old dumb brother ahead of me." I laugh at this. Ryder and Walker competed in saddle broncs.

"Well congrats on that." I say as I look ahead of me, the cattle starting to be in my vision.

"What about you? You still compete?" He asked me, looking at me.

"Eh, from time to time, not as much as I used to." I look back at him and he nods. "I'm real busy with the diner and school."

"A vet right?" He cocks his head curiously.

"Right." I smiled surprisingly, how could of he remembered that?

"I don't know if I've ever told you, but your diner is one of the best."

"I appreciate that, thank you." I smiled genuinely, it felt good to smile like that.

346

The calf 'merred' in Ryder's grasp as I punched the tag through it's ear, and then I released the clamp and Ryder let the calf go. After it went back to its luring mama, I charted the information on the chart and slid it back into Ryder's saddle bag. Despite the cold temperature, I was having a lot of fun tagging with Ryder. We were joking around the whole time and doing stupid things, it really took my mind off everything.

"Okay, we have one more." He said as we looked around at the mamas and babies. "And lets make it fast, because it's freaking cold!" I let out a laugh and agreed with him.

I mounted on Scarlet and loped to find the last untagged calf, hiding with all the other tagged calves and their moms. I found it and Scarlet did her job cutting it off from the others and then Ryder hopped off and tackled it to the ground. I grabbed the kit and quickly wrapped the halter around the calf and got the scale and Ryder held up the calf and I wrote down the weight and sex. I grabbed the tag and applied it to the clamp, found the spot on it's ear, and then I used all of my strength to tag the calf.

As the calf was 'merring' from the corner of my eye I saw the mother getting closer and closer, and I still wasn't done with the clamp. It still hadn't clicked. "DaKota watch out!" Ryder yelled as I looked up at saw the cow charging at me.

Then Ryder's body flung over mine and safely pulled me away from the calf. His body was now over mine as we were both looking at the spot we were just at, where the cow was licking it's baby. "I guess I should of warned you we call her Mama Bull." Ryder chuckles and I look at him and start to laugh.

We laugh together for a couple of moments until I realize my hands are on his biceps and just how close we are. He seems to realize it because we gulp at the same time. And then the son of a gun starts to lean down and what do I do? Freeze.

His lips almost touch mine until I move my face away from his and shove his shoulders the other directions and then he pulls back, "Um, I just got out of a relationship." I say awkwardly.

"Yeah your dad told me."

I immediately shoved him off me and jumped to my feet after he said that, "He what?!"

"Well last night he called my dad's cell, but I ended up picking up his phone. So he and I got to talking and he knew that I'm single and so are you, so-"

"He told you to hit on me?" I say disgusted and angry. If my dad did tell Ryder to, why would Ryder go along with it? Just when I think my dad is actually changing.

"Not exactly, he was just hinting that it was an opportunity for me."

"Same thing! I can't believe this." I shake my head at him and turn to go to my pony.

"Now DaKota just wait." I heard him walking towards me, but it didn't change my mind. I mounted in my saddle, grabbed the reins and rode away.

I RODE ALL THE WAY back home, I couldn't tell if the steam in the air was from my horse or from me. Cooper literally just broke up with me yesterday and my dad is already trying to set me up? That is a bunch of bullshit.

After putting a jacket on Scarlet and cooling her down, I marched my way into my house to find my whole family waiting for me. I don't know when Caleb and my dad got back, but I'm glad they were here. My fiery eyes find my dad's confused and sad ones. "Are you serious dad?" I ask him, already raising my voice.

"What are you talking about?" He asked me as my mother gave him a confused look.

"It hasn't even been a full 24 hours since Cooper broke up with me and you're already trying to set me up with someone?"

"Colby!" My mother hisses in disbelief at him.

"Oh c'mon! I thought it'd be good for her to realize that there are other boys than Blackwood." My dad says as he verbally and physically rolls his eyes at me.

"He isn't just some kid, dad!" I yell at him, shaking the whole house. "He's the love of my life and now he's gone!" I take a deep breath, deepening my glare at my father, "Do me a favor dad, the next time you think something is good for me don't do it. Because chances are, it's just gonna make things worse."

My dad takes a deep breath in, like a bull who is ready to charge. "Why don't you do us a favor and tell us the truth instead of writing it in some diary." Everything in my body stopped functioning. I didn't know what to say, do, or even think. Everyone in the room is in the same kind of comatose as me, until my father marches behind my mom and opens a drawer and sure as hell pulls out my secret journal.

The diary that holds every thought, memory, emotion, tear, and most importantly, the truth. The truth about everything. No sugar coating, not even a slight misconception, the straight-honest-to-God-truth.

"Where did you find that?" My voice trembled as I stared a the diary in my father's hands.

"I was cleaning your bed sheets and it fell out of the covers," My mom said softly and walked over to me, "Honey, why didn't you tell us?"

"How much did you read?" I ask her, not wanting to give up any untold information.

"The first day you went to Bismarck until last night." She put a hand on my shoulder, with a mournful and somber expression on her face is what made me break. The tears busted through the seams, seams even the best seamstresses couldn't even fix.

"I was so scared, I didn't know what do anymore. I didn't want to kill him, I just couldn't handle it anymore." I sobbed in my mother's arms. "I am so sorry."

"Shhh-don't be sorry sweetie, I wish it was me who had done it." She said and then pulled me away from our hug and looked me in the eyes, "But sweetie, you can't hide things that like from us."

"I know, I just didn't know how to tell you guys."

"We should of never let you go to Bismarck by yourself.." My dad grimaces to himself, "That son of a bitch found you and tortu-"

My dad's words reminded me of the first time Wade found me in Bismarck, the way he smiled at my body, the way he smelt my hair, they way he touched me. My body started to shake in my mother's arms. "Colby that's enough!" My mother barked at him when she saw the reaction from me.

"I'm sorry." He says in a disappointed voice.

"Honey, you need to go see a therapist." My mom says in a worried voice.

"No! I'm okay, I really am. I know he's gone. He's never coming back. I know that I won in the end. I beat him in his own game."

My parents looked at each other for guidance, I could tell by their expressions that they weren't okay with me being "okay". "Okay, but if you ever need to talk about something, we're always here for you." My mom said as she hugged me once more and then let go.

I looked at my dad to see if he would say anything, but all I got was a apologetic look. I guess I wasn't all that shocked, that's how he is. I guess you could say, we had an understanding. When I was looking at my dad, Caleb's rough arms wrapped around me. "You are one tough son of a bitch, sister." Caleb's voice was no where near joking, this is how he hid is emotion. But his hug, that showed me how sorry and heartbroken he was for me. "I love you." He said as he kissed the top of my head.

"I love you too, big brother." I hugged him tighter than I ever have before.

CHEYENNE

AS I LAY IN BED, I stared at the diary lying in between my legs. I was still in shock by that book. My little girl poured so much of her heart and soul into it. It was a beautiful disaster. I can't believe how much she has gone through and hasn't even told me half of it. It breaks my heart.

Yet, I am so proud of her. I don't know if any girl her age could handle the things she's been through. She is only 19 and has already experienced things that people in their 50's haven't! She is so strong and in powering, it's inspiring.

And the things she wrote about her and Cooper were so romantic but so heart breaking. I was really hoping that those two would make it, but never say never I guess. Cooper was such a gentleman to her and treated her with the utmost respect she deserved. I wonder why he decided to call it off after six months? "Cheyenne." My husband's voice interrupts my thoughts.

"Hmm?" I say as I watch him get into bed with me.

"I asked you what you were thinking about?"

"Our daughter and how great she is." I smile to myself as I grab the cross necklace around my neck, DaKota and I had matching necklaces.

"Cheyenne, how do I make it up to her?" His words surprised me, causing me to look at him for more explanation. "I have been failing with her lately."

"She's not a little girl anymore Colbs. She has her own mind now, she knows what she wants and no one is going to stop her. Isn't that what we have always wanted for her?"

"Yes, but how do I-"

"You need to read this," I say and pick up the book and hand it to him, "This will help you."

"What would I do without you?" He says as he kisses my cheek.

"Fail miserably." I chuckle and so does he as we lay down and close our eyes to go to sleep.

Looking in the mirror, running my fingers through my hair, I decided to straighten my hair for church this morning. I had plenty of time, so why not. After I was done, I sat down at my desk and pulled my mirror closer to me and started to do my makeup. It didn't take me long to do my lashes because of their natural length, so next was my foundation and powder. As I apply my foundation, I start to hum my favorite song, Traveler by Chris Stapleton. As I look at myself through the mirror, I decided to add some blush, which I rarely put on.

When I'm happy with the outcome, I walk over my closet and start to pick out my outfit. It was too cold to wear a dress, so jeans it was. Then I picked out a shirt and then took off my PJ's and changed into my outfit. But as I looked at myself in the mirror, I decided to spice it up and add a boho headband.

Before I went downstairs, I put on two of my smaller turquoise rings on each hand and applied deodorant and perfume. I tucked my phone in my pocket as I closed my bedroom door and headed for downstairs where my family was waiting for me. "Okay, I'm ready." I say as they all look at me as my feet touch the cold floor.

The boys were already heading out the door, my dad grabbing his keys and Caleb following him out the door. "Cute outfit!" Ashley says as she grabs her coat.

"Thanks." I smile at her and look down at myself and walk out of the door and to my dad's pickup.

"Who's the blush for?" My mom giggled beside me and my jaw dropped and I nudged her playfully as a blush rose on my cheeks.

"No one!" I say under my breath when I noticed my dad growing curious of my mom's accusation.

"Ryder, huh?" She smirks at me, and my face gives her the answer when my cheeks light up with pink and red.

Okay, maybe it was for Ryder. Well I don't know honestly. Over these past few weeks Ryder and I have grown to be good friends and comfortable towards each other. We've hung out a couple of times, they weren't dates, no matter what anyone says about them. I don't not like him, but I'm not sure if I'm ready to have feelings for him.

My mom winked at me as she climbed into the passenger seat of my dad's pickup, and then all three of us got into the back cab and buckled up. My dad turns the radio to an AM station and then we listen to the farm reports and a couple of old time songs as we drive to church.

We park in our usual spot and then we all step out and into the parking lot. We say hi to friendly faces as we walk to the front steps of the chapel. I notice the Baker's talking to Father Brad, and I look down at my feet until we reach the top of the stairs. I look at Ryder who's dressed in a white Cinch long sleeve, gold belt buckle, and his creased wranglers. He somewhat looks at me and then does a double-take and then we meet eye contact and he smiles. He takes his hands out of his pockets and then opens the door for my family.

I'm the last one to walk through the door, "Good morning." He says to me and I give him a soft smile.

"Good morning, thank you." I say and look at the door he's holding and then I walk into the church, following my family. We sit in the third pew as always and kneel on the thing and say our prayer.

After I say my prayer, I do the sign of the cross and then sit back against the pew. My curious eyes look around the church, noticing different decorations and people coming in and out. Ending my routine of looking around, I look to my right and the opposite side of the isle and look at the second row. Every time I expect him to be there, sitting next to his brother and mother. But he's not there. He'll never be, no matter how much I wish he was. Instead a family or Desiree and Reese will replace him, setting me back into reality.

CALEB, ASHLEY, AND I stood by ourselves as we wait for my parents to finish their conversations with other families after mass. "Caleb, stop kicking at the ground." Ashley says.

"Yes mom." He rolls his eyes playfully.

"You could at least act like you wanna be here." Ashley scolds him and then Caleb scoffs and before he can say something to defend himself Ashley says, "I had to kick you to stop you from falling asleep in there."

I laughed at her because it was true. Caleb has never been one to sit for an hour and listen to someone talk, he gets too bored. I'm glad he has Ashley to put him in his place, because when I try to, he uses the "I'm older" card, and that gets old.

I look at Ashley and I see her looking at something with a smirk on her face, and then she grabs Caleb's hand. "C'mon, I wanna go ask Miss. Kale for her apple pie recipe."

"Don't leave me-!" I say as I turn on my heel in the direction they were leaving me. As I turn I see Ryder coming towards me, oh that Ashley is going to get it when we get home. "Hi Ryder." I smile at him.

"Hey DaKota," He smiles and then stands in front of me. "Did you like what Father talked about today?"

"Yeah, I thought it was a good topic to cover with all of the protesting going around the country. Did you?"

"Is that what he talked about? I wasn't paying attention." He smirks making me laugh and roll my eyes.

"Why weren't you paying attention?" I ask him as I fold my arms. Before he talks, we hold eye contact and then he looks away as he licks his lips.

"I was too busy looking at the girl in front of me." Heat rose to my cheeks instantly, and I looked at the ground to hide it as I giggled. "Yeah did Mrs. Peterson dye her hair?" He jokes with me, making me think he wasn't talking about me, but the older girl sitting next to me.

I smack his arm as I laugh at his joke, "You're lame."

"Seriously though, you look very pretty today." He gives me a sly crooked smile, making my heart skip a beat.

"Thank you," I say genuinely to him as my blush starts to come down. "Are you coming to the diner?"

"Nah, my brother and I have an arena reservation after this. Wish I could though." He shrugs his shoulder.

"That's fine."

"Wait, was that just an invitation from DaKota Jones to hangout?" He holds his hand to his chest and I roll my eyes at him.

"No, I just wanted to know so I could let the chef know who's food to spit on." I gleam my eyes at him and he laughs at me and sticks his hands in his pockets as we stand and just look at each other.

"You could start a fashion blog!" Vanessa, one of my mom's friends, says to me as I pour her a cup of coffee. I laugh and shake my head at her, "What! You seriously have the cutest clothes and a unique sense of style!"

"Well thank you, but I don't know.." I shrug my shoulders I put the coffee pot down into it's plate. Vanessa drops her head and gives me a look telling me I should reconsider, "Okay, I'll think about it."

As I scan over the diner I notice an older gentleman raise his cup at me and I nod and grab the coffee pot and head over to him. "Sorry about that, how is everything?" I ask with a sweet smile as I pour the coffee.

"Better than my friends explained."

"I'm glad." I smiled at him as I looked at him, he was a cute old man who looked to be only around 5'6, had cute square glasses and white hair. He actually reminded me of the old guy from the movie "Up".

"I heard you started this diner at the age of 16, is that true?" He leaned forward in his booth, interested in my answer.

"Yes sir." I nod proudly.

Then he leaned back in his seat and took off his glasses and pointed them at me and said, "My name is Harry Ficklelson, and I am one of the reporters for Cowgirl Magazine, how would you like to be featured?"

Is he freaking kidding me? Cowgirl Magazine is something I have been reading since I was a kid! Never would I ever thought that I would be in it! There is no way I could pass this up.

"I would love to!" I said to him and he smiled with delight.

"Take a seat Ms. Jones." He said and opened his hand in invitation.

"Um, I should probably take this back," I say and hold the pot up higher for him to see, "I'll be back!" I say and quickly turn on my heels and walk back behind the counter and put it back on the plate.

I wipe my hands on my jeans as I walk back to Mr. Fickelson's booth and try to calm myself down from my excitement. When I walk back he's already got his old school recorder out and ready for me. "Cool recorder." I compliment him.

"That's the first compliment I've ever received for it." He looks surprised by me.

"Oh I love vintage things." I shrug and then he write down on his notepad, making a note of me.

"Okay, shall we get started?" He asks me and I nod my head eagerly. "Full name, family names, date of birth, and where you were born."

"DaKota Annie Jones, mom Cheyenne Jones, dad Colby Jones, and older brother Caleb Jones. Born in Hudson, Montana on February 16th, 1997."

"YOU WILL NOT BELIEVE what just happened to me." I say as I round the corner of the counter walking towards Beau and Taylor. I stand in front of me with my hands on the counter and Taylor raises her eyebrows at me, telling me to go on. "I just got interviewed for Cowgirl Magazine!"

Taylor's jaw drops and she hits Beau's arms, "Shut the hell up!" She says excitedly and then looks apologetic at Beau for instinctively hitting him.

"I'm not kidding! He asked me about my childhood, family and friends, rodeo, the diner, my faith and the ranch! He even said that there's going to be a photo shoot!" I was being a total fan girl, but this was a big deal!

"Are you going to be on the front cover?" Taylor's eyes get wide with hope.

"I don't know, but that would be so cool!"

"What would be cool?" A voice comes from the opposite side of Beau. We all look and it's Ryder who's leaning against the counter and looking at me.

"DaKota just got interviewed for Cowgirl Magazine!" Taylor said it before I could.

"Taylor, let her speak." Beau chuckles and Taylor slouches and nods her head in realization.

"Wow, that's awesome! Do you guys mind if I steal her away for a moment?" He turns his head towards Beau and Taylor, they both shake their head to his question.

I walk with Ryder to a both just a couple steps away from Beau and Taylor. We both slide in and I ask him, "What's up? I thought you had a reservation."

"I just came from there, but I have something to ask you." My lips turn into a worried frown, what could it be? Please don't be what I think it is.. "My mom wants to know if you would like to come over for dinner tonight."

A wave of relief washes over me when he said that, "You couldn't of just texted me that?" I laugh at him, because most guys of would of just shot me a text and asked.

"Well I'd thought I'd just ask you in person, instead of some pathetic text." He shrugs nonchalantly at me, playing with the creamers.

"Well count me in, do I need to bring anything?" I ask him and he smiles with pleasure.

"Just a big appetite, diner is on the table at 5:30." He says as he pushes on the table and then slides out. "See ya then." He adds a bad boy smile, making my cheeks blush.

I slide out of the booth and look down at my feet as I walk, knowing that Taylor is staring hole in my head for answers. "What was that about?" She asks eagerly, leaning over the counter.

"He asked me to have dinner with his family tonight." I say casually, it's not really a big deal.

"So what does that mean with you guys?" She raises her eyebrows.

"What do you mean?"

"Are you guys a thing now?" She says in a 'duh' tone and halfway rolls her eyes.

"I don't know, maybe I'll know after tonight. Maybe I won't." I shrug again as I start cleaning the counter, a habit of distraction for me.

I TUCKED MY PHONE IN my back pocket as I walked up the steps of the Victorian styled home. I took a deep breath as I knocked on the Baker's door. Not long was the door opened by Ryder, who was dressed in a nice quarter zip sweater and some jeans. "Right on time." He smiled as he opened the door wider for me and I stepped in.

Ryder's mom was carrying over a pot of something to the table, where Walker and Richard were already sitting. "Hello DaKota!" She greeted me with a big smile.

"Hi, it smells great in here Mrs. Baker." I smiled brightly at her.

"Oh thank you dear, and it's Mel." She said and took off her oven mitts and wiped off her hands on her dress pants. "Please sit." She says and then I feel Ryder's hand on the small of my back. My back arcs out of instinct and I try to play it off the best I could.

"Your hands are cold." I giggle, but it turns out nervous and awkward.

Thankfully, Ryder doesn't think any of it and leads me to my seat. He sits down next to his father, and then I'm seated next to Ryder and across from Walker. "I hope you like green bean casserole and honey ham." Richard says to me.

"Love it." I give him a soft smile, as I feel Walker's eyes burning holes in my head. I turn my head and finally make eye contact on him, neither him or I say anything to each other, very awkward and I wish I hadn't done it.

"Alright, let's say grace." Mel says as she sits down in between Walker and Richard. Ryder grabs my hand and I look at Walker and he gives me a weird look and then grabs for my hand. I barely grip onto his calloused hand, trying to focus on Richard's blessing.

"Dear Lord in heaven, we thank you for another blessed day and for our special guest tonight. We are thankful for this years production and safety of our cows and their babies. We are very thankful to be able to do what we love everyday, and very thankful for your sacrifice. Amen."

We all smiled at each other and then Richard grabbed the ham and dished his plate, the rest of us following him. My plate consists of two slices of ham, two scoops of casserole, a slice of bread and some carrots. "So DaKota, how's the diner going?" Richard asks me.

"It's going good, the winter's are a little slower, but it's nothing significant." I shrug to him. Winter is a little slower because of less tourists and their desire to taste our ice cream, but like I said, it's not concerning.

"Good, my favorite is the mashed potatoes and gravy meatballs." He winks at me and I give him a polite small.

"That seems to be popular." I nod as I wipe my mouth with my napkin. "So, Mel, how's quilting going?" She is known for her warm and fabulous quilts that she sells and donates to whoever wants them. I have a couple of denim ones she made for me.

"Keeping me busy as usual, how is your mother doing? I haven't talked to her in ages!" She says happily.

"She's doing great, she doesn't know what to do to keep herself busy now that Caleb's married." Richard and Mel laugh at my joke, making me blush.

"Tell him congrats from me."

"Will do." I say and then it became an awkward silence between us. It was filled with forks scrapping the plates and the crunching of food in people's mouths, making it more awkward. I look at Ryder and he looks sorry.

"So DaKota, I just have to ask-"

"Dad." Ryder stops his father harshly like he already knows what he is going to ask me. I look at Ryder and he is giving his father the death glare.

"No, it's alright whatever it is." I say and place my hand on Ryder's arm, giving his father permission to ask away. Whatever it is, I'm sure it's not that bad.

"What did you see in that Blackwood kid?" I underestimated his question. Richard's tone was harsh and ignorant. He sounded genuinely surprised that I could have romantic feelings towards Cooper.

After Cooper went to jail, the whole town put two and two together and found out Cooper and I were dating and it spread around the town like wild fire. After that, people looked at me like I was a girl who was ready to break anytime at the mention of his name. They would come up to me and give me a hug, and say its such a shame that our high school love had to end. I knew they didn't take it seriously. The thought I was just attracted to his "bad boy" reputation. They had no idea.

"Didn't you hear about his father before?!" He was flabbergasted with my choice. My blood began to boil under my skin.

I tried to bite my tongue, but I knew what the right thing was to do. "Cooper is nothing like his father." My voice was a calm growl, with my fist clenched under the table. "Cooper is the twice the man his father pretends to be."

"Oh really?" Richard laughs, and wipes his mouth throwing his napkin on his plate. "Attempted murder is always a man's first choice to get rid of a problem."

I turn my body towards him and scowl, "You weren't there, it was nothing like that."

"Humor me." Richard leans towards me from the head of the table.

I stand up, making the chair shoot from behind me. "Bill had Cooper's mother and brother tied up and held a knife to his wife's neck! He was going to kill her in front of her sons! Cooper had to do something!" I yell at him and then the house goes silent. Everyone's face goes white as if they just saw a ghost. No one says anything, and it's painfully awkward.

As I feel a tear slide down my cheek, I return to reality and turn to Mel. "Thank you for supper, sorry I ruined it." Before I left the table, I looked at Walker and he had a strange smirk on his face while he looked at me. I decided it was best to keep my mouth shut this time. I awkwardly walked away from them and out of their house to my pickup.

"DaKota, wait!" Ryder's desperate voice says behind me. I don't turn around in response, I grab the handle of my door. As I pull it open, a bigger and stronger hand pushes it back closed. "I know, my dad's an asshole."

I turn around to face him and wipe the pathetic tear off my cheek. "No one understands." I sigh frustrated. "I loved him. I loved him so damn much." I drop my head as another cheek fell down my cheek.

I wasn't expecting Ryder to pull me into his arms and hug me tight. It took me bit to respond but I realized his good intentions and hugged him back. "I really am sorry, DaKota. I didn't know he was going to say that. I will definitely talk to him-"

"You don't have to do that, Ryder." I sniffle slightly pulling back from our hug.

"Yes I do if I plan for you to be sticking around." I perked my head up to meet his eyes. Was he serious? My jaw drops to speak but nothing comes out. "I know it's bad timing but I was planning to do it after dinner, so DaKota, will you go out with me?" I looked him deep in the eye to see if I could spot any hint of insincere. "And I promise what happened in there will never happen again."

"Promise?" I halfway smirk at him. He nods eagerly to me, awaiting my answer. "Okay." I whisper. It wasn't Ryder's fault what his father did, Ryder has been nothing but nice and kind to me these past two weeks, I have nothing against him.

"Okay?" He smiles and it makes me brake a smile out and his widens. "Okay!" He brings me closer to him and he kisses my cheek lightly. "Call me when you get home? I have some plans I would like to discuss with you." He smirks as he lets me go.

I blush at the thought of us possibly having our first date, "Plans?"

"It's all I can say for now." He shrugs and I roll my eyes at him and nod.

"Okay." I chuckle as I open my door and hop in. "Tell your mom I am sorry for dinner tonight, and that I appreciated it."

"Will do, don't forget to call." He winks as he closes the door for me.

"Of course." I smile shyly at him as I start my pickup and he backs away from me. We don't break eye contact until I turn my truck away from his house and drive away.

I groan as my alarm clock goes off, I know there is no such thing as "too much sleep". I only got a couple of hours of sleep last night because of my night terrors. It's weird, I've been getting them more lately and I have no idea why. I would of thought over time that the pain and fright would of went away but it hasn't. I don't flinch as much anymore when men touch me, so why am I having these night terrors?

If it keeps happening, I'll mention it to my mom, but for now I'll just keep it to myself. When my mom and dad found out, they didn't leave it alone for two weeks. They would come check on me during the night to see if I was okay, they've seen it twice and it really messed up my mom. She's never seen me struggle so much in my sleep, me fighting for my life when all I have to do is open my eyes and be free.

Disregarding my lack of sleep, I push the hair out of my face and turn off my alarm. It's 7:30, but I have a busy day in front of me. I have to do all my chores, pick up a shift at the diner, and then rush to the local rodeo and help out. I am being a flag girl for sponsors and the national anthem. I haven't been competing lately because I'm trying to focus on school more, because certain events in the past have been distracting me from it.

So after getting my face washed and getting me dressed in my Stetson flare jeans and a cinch cotton tee, I went downstairs for breakfast. "How'd ya sleep?" My dad asks me as I grab a plate from the cabinet.

I hesitate before I answer him, "Fine, just had a lot of things on my mind." I shrug off as I dish up a waffle and add some blackberries to it.

"Like?" My dad asks curiously, revealing his face from behind his newspaper.

"Boy stuff, dad." I make up so he'll drop the topic.

"Do I have to talk to Ryder about something?" He says with his macho tone, making me roll my eyes.

"No, it's our three month anniversary today." I mutter, because I know Ryder is up already and he hasn't texted me anything yet. I'm not that girlfriend who needs her boyfriend to text her 24/7, but it'd be nice if he would of said something already.

"Wow, three months," He breaths out and checks the date on the newspaper. "Time flies, I guess."

"For you." I whisper to myself as I cut up my sausage and eggs. Sure, I have a good time when I'm with Ryder and I really like him and all, but something deep down inside me is keeping me from having a great time with him. That something always seems to get in my way of everything I do, and I can't figure out what it is. It's like I'm trying to turn the next page in the chapter, but my fingers stop working and I am stuck on that page.

I put my hair into a pony as I walked to the pens to separate the horses. I had to seperate the horses for feeding because the older ones get fed something different, more fats and such. Our rodeo horses get more muscle building nutrients. And our ranch and trail horses get normal feed.

The horses surrounded me as I had their grain buckets in my hands, trying to get to the troughs before start to bite each other. I tossed the grain into the two troughs and let the horses settle it out by themselves. And then I went back to the barn and grabbed the other grain buckets for the other horses and repeated the same thing.

Now I had to feed the cows, which is a lot easier to do than the horses. The cows like to keep their distance when you're near, all I gotta do is put the cubes in the trough and leave. I put the empty bags in the gallon buckets on the end of the four wheeler and went back to the barn.

I parked the four wheeler and threw away the garbage. My next chore is to clean all the tack, my favorite because of the leather and horse smell.

I KNELT AGAINST THE cushion of the booth as I wiped down the table and adjusted the condiment holder. I put the wash cloth down and pulled out my phone and checked to see if I had any messages, looking for one in particular. When I saw I had none from Ryder, I sighed and looked out the window. I pulled my eyes away from outside, but a black power stroke made me do a double take. My heart started to race immediately, could it be him? I crawled closer to the window to get a better look, I couldn't see the front licence plate. He took off the back plate because he dented it with a trailer hitch.

The pickup was backing into the spot right in front of my window. My heart was going to jump out of my chest any moment now. My stomach started to twist and churn, I needed to see him. Then the door opened and I saw a booted foot step out, pause, and then jumped out. My chest fell when I realized it wasn't him. I slouched against the booth as I watched the stranger jog to the other side and open the door for a girl, who then he wrapped his arm around her.

I watched them laugh together as he said something in her ear, and then kiss her on the cheek. My heart ached to feel that again. I watched them walk in the door and then Maybell seated them in the back corner seat, exactly where we used to seat.

I finally convinced myself to look away and stop torturing myself. Through my shirt I grabbed the pendant of the necklace and took a deep breath. "You were expecting it to be him, right?" A deep and rough voice spoke behind me, making me jump.

I clutched my chest as I turned my head to look at the person, Walker Baker. "I don't know what you're talking about." I deny as I scoot my way out of the booth and grab the empty soup bowls.

"I think we both do," He said in both a serious and joking tone. "But I won't tell my brother, because I know he's really into you."

I started to smile, but then I remembered what today is. "Has a funny way of showing it." I muttered to myself.

"What do you mean?" He asked me.

I looked at him and decided whether or not to tell him. He looked at me with humorous curiosity eyes, waiting for my answer. "It's none of your business." I say as I walk behind the counter. As I ordered the cups beneath the counter, I saw him look at his phone.

"Well I would like to know to improve my skills with the ladies, especially with cute brunets." What was his deal today? Did he wake up today and say to himself, 'Today I want to bug the shit out of DaKota?'.

"Are you going to order something, or are you just going to harass me?" I snapped my head at him, giving him a dirty look.

"Sharp woman," He chuckles, " A Baker man's favorite." My dirty look increased at his comment. I hated when he made me feel like I was a competition between him and Ryder. "Ohhh now I see what you're problem is," He laughs. "It's the big three months today! And I bet he hasn't said anything to you yet! Is that it?"

My mute response gave him his answer, and he nods and then just reaches in his back pocket and pulls out his wallet. I cock my eyebrow at him and then he throws down a couple of ones. "You didn't even ha-" He cuts me off and stands up.

"Consider it a three month anniversary gift." He says with a big smile as he walks out the door and to his pickup. I resist the urge to follow him and slap him for doing this. Was he just teasing me or was he sending me some kind of message? Whatever it was, it needs to stop.

I JUST PARKED MY TRAILER into a spot next to the other cowboys and cowgirls. It was just me who drove here because my mom was going to go with Taylor's mom and my dad is judging the rough stock and cowboys. I turn off my pickup and then grab my phone and read Ryder's message, "Not sure if we'll see each other before rodeo starts :(". We've been talking for about two hours now, and he hasn't mentioned any thing about three months yet.

Maybe I'll tell him later tonight and give him a chance to figure it out. Plus I did get him a $50 gift card to Cavenders. But if he doesn't figure it out, looks like I'll be spending that $50 myself.

I go inside the trailer and untie Pharaoh's baby blue halter and lead him out of the trailer and tie him to one of the hooks. I go back and grab his brushes and treats. First I start to comb him with the curry and then brush him. Then I grab the pick and clean out each of his hooves. He's always been accepting with giving me his legs, even when I first found him.

Then I stretch his neck by grabbing a treat and getting him to follow the treat to his stomach on both sides. Then I bring the treat between his legs, both sides. I give him a nice pat and rub and reward him the two treats.

I grab his saddle pad and place it on him, lining it up accordingly. Once I released off my tip toes, two arms wrapped around me, scaring the living crap out of me. "Holy crap." I breath out and his deep laughter comes from behind me.

"Hey baby." He says happily as I turn in his arms to face him.

"Hi." I say and then he leans down to kiss me, but I turn my cheek so he catches my cheek. "I have to get ready." Then I slip out of his arms and turn my attention to my horse.

"Is something wrong?" He asks me as he hands me my saddle.

I take the saddle from him and say, "Nope." Popping the 'p' so he knows that something is obviously wrong. I begin tightening the front cinch, looping the latigo through the belt loop. Once that is comfortable for Pharaoh, I loosely do the back cinch and then grab my bridle.

I walk right past him and undo the halter and put it on his neck and then smoothly put the bit through his mouth and the bridle over his head. "C'mon DaKota, what's the matter?" He says and stops me from adjusting the throat latch.

"What day is it?" I ask him and then he smiles, and then laughs at me. I cock my eyebrows and start adjusting the straps again.

"Did you think I forgot our three months?" I turn to look at him and he has on a comical expression.

"Well you haven't said anything all day." I say quietly, looking back at Pharaoh.

Ryder grabs my hands that linger on Pharaoh's face and takes them in his own. "I just didn't want to say it on text. I got you something." He says and then I finally meet his eyes.

"Really?" I smile and then he breaks out his smile, that makes me smile even more. He drops his right hand, dropping my left, and pulls out an envelope from his pocket.

"I got you this." He smiles as I open the envelope and pull out a card and read it, 'Happy three months DaKota! Thanks for making it great by making me really happy! I'm so glad we can do things we both love to do with each other all the time! I am so blessed to call you my beautiful girlfriend! Love, Ryder. P.S. Can't wait for more!'. "You like it?" He asks me as I close the card and look at him.

"Yes, it was very sweet. Thank you." I say and kiss him on the cheek.

Who am I kidding? I can't wait to go home and rant to my mom and Ashley that he only got me a card for our three months. Don't get me wrong, I didn't expect diamonds and chocolates, but flowers would of been nice. Or something sentimental. A card is something you get a business partner or for a birthday party, not something for three months.

"I have something for you, too." I say and then walk to the drivers door of my pickup and go to the center counsel and grab the gift card, and my card that I wrote for him. I walk back to him and hand him the card with the gift card inside of it.

He pulls out the $50 gift card and drops his head down a bit, "This is too much, babe." He groans sadly.

"No it's not." I smile lightly and go over to him and hug him. He looks down at me and leans down and I lean up and our lips connect, making mine tingle with sensation.

"...HOME OF THE BRAVE." The glorious singer drags out as I kick my pony into action and he trots around the arena as the crowd goes crazy, my favorite part of any rodeo. I held a big smile on my face and lead

Pharaoh with one hand as the other was holding the greatest flag in the world.

I pull back on the reins as we came to the gate and the gentleman opened it for us, and I directed Pharaoh over towards my friends and their horses. Jessica and Reyna were the only ones competing out of them and Taylor, Molly, and me. "I wish I had your luxurious hair, Kota." Molly says as she reaches out to play with my big curls.

"What kind of conditioner do you use?" I ask her, dropping my hands over the saddle horn.

"Garner, argon oil." She replies.

"Well I use coconut oil from Renpure, if you want to try that." I suggest to and she nods her head. I don't know why she needed it, she had very pretty strawberry blonde hair that reached her waist.

"I think I might just have to." She nodded surely to herself.

"Did Ryder say it to you?" Taylor says to me and I nod my to her.

"Say what?" Jessica chimes in, I didn't mind though.

"Well today's our three months and he hadn't said anything to me all day until I got here and was tacking Pharaoh." The girls slightly gasp and I nod in agreement. "I'm not salty about it anymore, I guess it's not that big of a deal."

"Did he at least get you anything?" Reyna asks me.

"He wrote me a card." I try to say it in a happy card so they won't react to it like I did when he gave it to me.

"Like a poem in a card?" Molly asks.

"No, just a generic card." I shrug.

"Not even flowers? Most of my boyfriends have gotten me flowers on any anniversary." Taylor says to me.

"No, it's okay though because I know he's not the most romantic cowboy out there. And he probably thought I didn't like flowers."

They all start to laugh at me, "Every girl likes flowers." They say at the same time, and I know it's true. I can't but help but laugh myself because of the situation.

"Lets go get some water and food." Taylor suggests and then we turn our horses, and walk in a straight line towards the concessions, looking like a posse from the old west.

The rodeo is almost over and us girls are lounging over by the stands still with our horses, watching the bull riders. I sat back in my saddle and held myself up with my arms on Pharaoh's croup. I looked towards the crowd and looked at the people at the edge of their seats, waiting for a rider to get bucked off. But they go wild once someone gets scored over 85 points.

What caught my eye was girls lined up at the gate panels where the crowd was cut off from the arena. They all had their phones out and their fancy cameras, making sure to get the best shots of their men riding. The girl currently videoing, hooped and hollered once her man made his ride and scored 84.5. That used to be me.

God, why does everything remind me of him.

I was pulled out of my heartache when I heard, "DaKota." I turned my head and looked at the girls, with their horses turned to me. I must of not heard them say they were leaving.

"Oh yeah, coming." I say and sat up and guided Pharaoh with the horses and girls.

We went back to my trailer first, where I saw Ryder standing there with his back against my trailer and his leg kicked up. We all gave each other a look, still thinking about his card. Ryder stands in front of my horse as I get off, "Hey girls." He greeted happily as he wrapped his arm around my shoulder.

"Hi Ryder." They all greet back, we all nod our heads at each other and the girls start to turn away except for Molly, who was glaring at Ryder.

I bit my lip to stop me from laughing when she said, "Every girl likes flowers."

I get Scarlet close to the roping dummy and I give it some slack and then recoil it in my loops. I look at Ryder who is doing the same with his beautiful blue roan. "Nice throw hunny." He compliments me.

"Thanks." I smile at him when I start to head back to the header's box of my arena.

It was a great day to practice, it was really hot and there was no wind. The horses are getting a good exercise and so were we. It's 11 o'clock and we've been practicing since 9:30. I take my hat off and wipe the sweat across my forehead, while I do so I see Ryder looking at his phone. "Beau and Taylor and the others invited us to go on the lake with them today. Wanna go?"

I looked around my ranch, I had all of my chores done, but I needed to train the yearlings. I looked at them in pasture and decided they could use a break, especially in this heat. "Sounds like fun. Do we need to bring snacks?" I ask him as I walk Scarlet out of the box and towards him.

"I'll ask, let's go get untacked." He said and I nodded and followed him out of the arena.

Ryder locked his pickup behind us as we walked towards the entrance of the grocery store. Taylor put us in charge of bringing food and drinks, even if it wasn't our idea to go to the lake. But I'm happy to help. I looked down at my shorts and my flip flops, and I tugged down my shorts to hide my scar. "Your butt isn't showing." Ryder said as he cocked his head back to look.

"I know." I chuckled.

"Then why did you pull them down?" He asks me.

"It's more comfortable like this." I shrug and he does too. I haven't told him anything about my past, and I probably won't ever do it. Ryder hadn't noticed the little details about me to be suspicious of something. I was glad so then I wouldn't have to lie to him. "So what are you hungry for?" I ask him as I grab a cart when we enter the grocery store.

"Let's get some summer sausage and crackers, chips, and salsa. Little things like that." He said and it made me think of more ideas for food.

I think Ryder and I picked out every easy food combination we saw, we were definitely set for at least a couple of days. But who knows how much the boys will eat. Never can be too safe. Now we are walking towards the beverage area to finish our shopping. "I wonder if they'll let me get beer without ID'ing me." Ryder snickers and I elbow him in the side and we laugh together.

"Yeah well knowing Mrs. Watson, she'll throw a fit about be-"

"States!!" A little voice near us speaks out. I stop walking the cart and look to my left to see Reese in a wheel chair and making his way to me. Why was he in a wheelchair?

"Hey buddy." I crouched down to be face to face with him, offering him a friendly smile. Then I see two legs behind him and I look up and it's Desiree. I offer her a sorry and awkward smile. We haven't talked in a very long time, and I feel guilty standing here with Ryder.

"Who's he?" Reese says and peaks his head over my shoulder to look at Ryder.

"Reese this is Ryder, Ryder this is Reese." I say and then stand back up.

"Hi buddy." Ryder smiles at Reese, making me smile."Mrs. Blackwood, how are you?"

"It's Ms. but I am doing just fine-"

"Is he your new boyfriend?" Reese interrupts his mother with a hurt and sad question.

"Ryder, why don't you go get those drinks. I'll meet you over there." I say to him and then he gives Desiree a curt nod and leaves us. "How are you?" I ask her and she seems to relax now that Ryder isn't here.

"We're doing okay, you guys going somewhere?" She asks, looking at my outfit.

"Yeah, we're going to the lake. Can I ask?" I say and look at Reese's wheelchair.

"It's nothing serious," I take a sigh of relief. God help that little boy if the cancer came back. "He's just taking medication and makes him a little weak in the arms and legs. So the doctor recommended this."

"Look at what I can do!" He said and then spun in a tight circle in front of us.

"Wow! That's so cool buddy! You're gonna get all the girls with that move!" I wink at him and he giggles at me. I look at Desiree and my smile turns into a frown. "I'm sorry I haven't been keeping in touch."

"Oh honey, you're not obliged to. I do miss seeing your face though." She smiles and we both chuckle together. "Well, we'll let you get back to your day. See you around." She smiles as she puts her hand on Reese's shoulder.

"See ya." I smile back at them and then head back for Ryder.

RYDER AND I WAITED on the doc for the others to come get us. The lake didn't look too overcrowded with boats and jet skies, so it looked like it was going to be a lot of fun. Taylor told me that it is going to be me, Ryder, and her and Beau in one boat, and then in the other boat it's gonna be Molly and her boyfriend Jackson, Jake, and a couple of guys.

"I can't wait to jump in the water." Ryder said to me as they were pulling up the wake boarding boat.

"Hey guys!" Taylor waved as she sat on Beau's lap when he was driving. She was in a blue bikini that she looked very pretty in. Beau was sure one lucky guy.

"Hey!" Ryder and I said as we loaded the grocery bags and our towels.

"The others are in the bay, and got the grill heating up, because we are starving!" Beau said as he drove away from the doc and started driving towards the bay. The wind and water droplets felt great against my warm skin, I couldn't wait to jump in either.

Taylor, Molly and I were sitting in one boat, drinking our iced tea and having some girl talk as the boys were grilling in the other boat. The sun was beating down on me, I desperately wanted to take off my shorts, but I didn't want people to ask about my scar, it would be too overwhelming for me. "Do you guys want to jump in?" Molly asks and Taylor nods her head in agreement.

"Maybe later I will." I say as they get up from their seats.

"Really? It's hotter than hell out here." Molly says to me, I guess I can just jump in with my shorts on.

"Alright." I smile and they nod and go to the back of the boat. Molly jumps in first, gaining the attention of the boys and they start to cheer.

"DaKota, take off your shorts!" Ryder yells at me, as all his buddies laugh at him for saying something like that. The anger inside me told me just to do it and show the boys a good time, so I slowly pull down my shorts , purposely sticking out my butt, and glaring at Ryder. The boys automatically shut up and the strangers pull down their sunglasses. With a satisfactory wink, I jump in after Taylor.

The cold water felt amazing when I dove in. So amazing that I swam deeper until I couldn't hold my breath any longer. When I broke the surface, I saw them all looking at me and I smiled and then the boys jumped in with us. All except Ryder, who stood at the edge of the boat, looking directly at me.

I swam over to him and held on to the edge of the boat. "What's the matter?" I fakely ask him.

"Was that necessary?"

"Was it necessary to be a sexist jerk? If I want to keep my damn shorts on I will. So remember that the next time you want to show off to your friends." I say and his face softens, and I know he knows he shouldn't of done it, so I relax a little. "Now get in and swim with us, it feels great." I say and then splash him. He is shocked by the cold water, but then quickly reacts and dives in next to me.

I looked around me because I didn't know where he was going to pop up, and I'm sure he will do something to me to scare me. I was right when I felt my left legged being pulled downward and soon I was underneath the water. Under the water I used my right leg to kick me free, but his hands were quick and grabbed my waist and kept me there.

We surfaced in each other's arms and I began laughing, and then he surprised me when he spit the water in my face. I dropped my jaw and said, "You know people pee in here!" Trying to tease him.

"Wanna taste?" He challenged me with a smirk and a laugh and then placed his hand on the back of my head and smashed his lips against mine. We both laughed during the kiss and then we separated and swam to the others.

We all cheered when Jake face planted into the water while he was wake boarding. We all had a pretty good laugh when he resurfaced and was still holding onto his beer can. I fell back into Ryder's chest because I was laughing so hard. Ryder wrapped his arms around my chest and then I placed mine over them and enjoyed this moment right now.

I forgot everything that has happened in the past. I was living in the moment. Nothing else mattered except for me spending time with good people in good places. We were laughing and having the time of our lives. Basically we were living in a Hakuna Matata moment, and I loved it. "DaKota, wanna go?" Beau asked me and I nodded.

I floated in the water until Beau started driving. As he picked up speed, the board was on top of the water and I was easily going back and fourth. This wasn't my first time wake boarding, and I was pretty good at it. I decided to go outside the wake. When I was at the wake, I decided to jump over, so that's what I did, and I successfully landed it. Gaining some confidence, I put the handle of the rope in the middle of my arm and just held on with that. "That's my girl!" Ryder yelled and I jokingly fist pumped, laughing along with them.

"WHAT MOVIE DO YOU WANT to watch?" I ask him as I grab the remote and turn on Netflix in my bedroom.

"Lets watch White Chicks." He says and I roll my eyes because this is our third time watching it together, but he loves it so I pick it anyways. I throw the remote by the edge of the bed and then I lay my head on his shoulder and get relaxed.

In the middle of the movie, Ryder's hand slips under my baggy tee shirt and starts to run his fingers over my skin. After a bit, he hooks his arm around me and brings me up higher and turns me to face him. I look him in the eyes and I see him looking at my lips, he licks his and then he leans in on me. I hesitantly lean back but soon after his lips find mine and ours start moving together, bringing a lovely tingling throughout my body.

As things get faster, he leans his torso over me, using his left arm to support him. I put my right hand on the back of his neck, right under where his hair stops and I play with the ends. I push him closer to me and then he takes his lips off mine and trails his down my jaw and to my collarbone.

One of his hands lays on my bare skin under my shirt, and the other is still supporting him. But that changes when he again hooks my waist and he lays on his back so I'm on top. I connect my lips back with his and things move at a normal pace. His hands travel from my shoulders down my arms, my bare stomach, and down my legs and right under where my shorts ended. Then he placed them right on my tailbone, and then he slowly moved them to my butt and pressed down a little, but went back to my back.

But then he dropped them to my hips, right where my scar was. His fingers made the scar burn and I gasped and pulled away from the kiss and off him and the bed. My chest was moving rapidly as I started to think of Wade and what he did to me. "DaKota, what's wrong?" He asked very confused, and even a little scared.

"Um, I suddenly don't feel well."

"Like what? Did I take it too far?" He asks as he sits up and fixes his wild hair, created by me.

"No no- um it's girl stuff." I say to get him to think it's something he doesn't want to deal with.

"Oh." He realizes, "Is there anything I can do?" He stands up and walks closer to me, but I take a step back from him. He looks very confused, and he has a good reason to be.

"Probably just go back home, I need to do some stuff that you probably don't want to see." I lied to him, and then he nodded to me.

"Okay, just call me if you need anything." He said slowly like I was going to burst at any moment.

"I'm sorry, but I had a lot of fun today!" I say apologetically. I was truly sorry because I ruined something special and heated, especially on a really great day we had together.

"Me too, talk to you tomorrow?" He said as he turned the knob on mt bedroom door.

"Yep, lunch maybe?"

"Sounds like a date. Goodnight, DaKota." He said sincerely and I gave him 'good night' in a form of a small smile. God, that was so embarrassing. I shiver at the thought of Wade touching me and the reason why I got that scare.

Oh man here we go. I ran to my bathroom and lifted the toilet seat and let my stomach empty itself. After a couple of go rounds, I brushed my teeth and took a 20 minuet shower, that mostly consisted of me scrubbing every inch of my body three times before I felt desensitized.

Before I laid my head on my pillow, I reached below my bed and pulled out my pills. Shit. Just my luck. This is my last pill. I'll save it for another night, I'm sure there will be worse nights than this.

I tried my best not to slip on the ice as I ran to get inside my mom's vet clinic that I work in. The reason I am running is because it is the middle of January and it's cold as hell in Montana during January. I miss being able to wear a tank top and shorts, at all times of the day! But I am thankful for the snow. I love playing in the snow: ice skating, sledding, snowball fights, building snowmen, and snowmobiling!

I relaxed once I got inside the nice and warm building. I hung up my Carhartt jacket and put my gloves on the shelf. I took a sip of my hot chocolate as I walked out of the break room and into the kennel room. "Hello, pretty animals." I sweet talked all the animals in the kennels. I looked at their charts and saw their progressions and what medicine they needed to take today. I'm not sure if I have a busy day in front of me today. I hope I didn't because I wanted to work at the dinner tonight because Taylor and I need to discuss plans.

What plans? Well her wedding plans of course! That's right my best friend is getting married right around the corner. She's getting married on Valentine's day, how romantic is that!? Well anyways, I am her Maid of Honor, so we get to plan everything together! She is going to have the best wedding ever, and I am going to make sure of that.

Sometimes I wonder why I chose to become a vet. It's not that I don't like it, believe me, I love it. It's just that I wish I could take home every animal I take care of! They're all just so cute! I mostly specialize in farm animals, but from time to time, I'll see cats and dogs, and the generic house pets.

"What a good boy!" I say as I smush the face of a Bernese Mountain Dog, after I give him his yearly shots. "Alright, he's good to go. You can just go see Cindy and she'll take care of ya! Have a nice day!" I say to Mr. Wright and then leave the medical room. I sit down in my desk and start to do my favorite part of my day, paperwork. Note the sarcasm.

I notice Cindy, the secretary, come in the backroom where our desks are. "What's up?" I ask her, turning in my swivel chair.

"Desiree Blackwood just called and said her horse has a pretty bad laceration."

"Okay, I'll head out there and check it out." I say and go to the break room and grab my coat and gloves. I wonder what horse it is, and I wonder what happened. I hope it's nothing too serious, Desiree loves those horses.

I park my work pickup right next to the barn, where I assume the horse is. Desiree must of heard my pickup because she walked out of the barn and waved her arms at me. I shut off my pickup and got out and she said, "It's JW, he's cut up real bad on his hind quarter." She says in distress.

I nod to her and then open my back door and pull out my kit and then I follow her in the barn. She closes the door behind us, to try to keep in the warmth. "What happened?" I asked her as I opened the stall door and examined JW. Blood was trailing down his right back leg, she was right, it was real bad.

"Well what I think happened is that he was getting a drink next to the river, where the property line cuts off. Then I think he must of slipped on a rock next to the fence, and it tore him up pretty bad. I found a trail of blood spots next to the fence and his hair and skin on some barbed wire. Is he going to be okay? Cooper might kill me if he's not."

I stop what I'm doing when she mentions Cooper's name and then it becomes awkward, so much you could smell it in the air. "He's going to be fine, just a lot of sutures, maybe a couple of staples."

First, I handed Desiree oral antibiotics to give to him so he begins to relax. After he took it, I began to clean the wound with sterilized fluid and wipe it down the best I can without causing too much pain. As I do so, I take my stethoscope and listen to his heart beat. "His heart rate is normal, so he didn't lose too much blood."

I throw the bloody cloth on the hay underneath my feet and grab another one and dry it up. Then I grabbed my forceps and picked out any debris. Now comes the stapling. I staple the parts where I think are too big to suture together, it's usually more painful than stitching. I grabbed the staple gun and turned to Desiree, "Watch his head, he may not like it."

I wasn't scared of getting stepped on or kicked, I had pretty good reflexes and it's happened to me before. Carefully and precisely, I grabbed the two pieces of skin and lined them up and then stapled them together. JW threw his head a little bit and stepped forward, but nothing extreme. "Good boy." I said to him and Desiree scratched his ears.

I only had to give him 4 staples, and the rest was pretty easy stapling. He did really well with the rest of it. Now I just have to spray antibacterial spray on the stitches and then him and I will be done. I shook the can in my hand and then sprayed the wound, he didn't even react to it. "All right, all done." I said as I put the cap back on the can.

She examines the sutures and staples, "Wow, that is the best stitch work I've ever seen." She breaths incredulously and looks at me.

"Thank you, just make sure he don't lick at it or anything. I suggest putting a lighter blanket on , so if he rolls, he won't irritate it." I tell her as I pick up my med kit and leave JW's stable.

"Will do, I trust you." She said as she closed the door. "So who do I talk to about the billing?"

"No one, it's on me." I softly smile at her.

"Oh I can't let you do that, dear." She says dejectedly towards me.

"Consider it a compensation." I shrug to her as I walk backwards.

"A compensation for what?" She asks confused.

"Helping me get through the hard times." Me saying that seems to have struck something she didn't want to come back up. I turn my back to her and put my kit in the back with my other supplies.

"DaKota!" She calls out and I turn to look at her. She looks torn between something. Like she wants to tell me something but talks herself out of it.

There's a long pause before I answer, "Yes?"

Again, she looks like she doesn't know what to say, "Thank you." She says genuinely and I give her a polite nod and get into my pickup and drive away.

I FINALLY MAKE IT TO the diner around 8:30, I had a really busy day and I fell behind on my paperwork so I had to catch up. But it's Friday night, so that means that most of my friends will be here and so will Ryder, because he's not going to another rodeo this weekend.

As I walk in I see Taylor, Beau, and Ryder sitting next to each other and Taylor has her wedding binder out showing him things that I'm sure he had no clue about. I sneak up behind Ryder and tap his left shoulder but then I go to his right shoulder. He falls for the trick and looks behind his left. "Gotcha." I smirk and he smiles at the sight of me.

"Hey babe." He says as I go around the counter and stand in front of them.

"How's it going Tay?" I ask her as I look at the binder and she's currently looking at center pieces.

"Well I'm stuck between two, and Tweedledee and Tweedledum over here are no help at all." I laugh at her nicknames between the two friends. It's true, guys have no eye for the little and big details of stuff like this.

"Let me see." I say and grab the binder from her. The pieces are both identical to each other, but one has more of rustic pink to it than the other, and it just makes it more simple and natural. "This one. It looks more natural if you just glimpse at it."

"That's exactly what I thought!" Taylor expresses gratefully and then grabs her sharpie and circles the picture with a heart.

"You girls and your need for perfection." Beau shakes his head at us looking at his crazy fiance.

"Well somethings gotta make for it." Taylor teases him, earning an eye roll from him.

"How was your day?" I stand in front of Ryder, leaning over counter to have a more private conversation with him.

"Pretty long, seemed like every project I did something went wrong. Just glad I'm here with you now." He says and joins our hands together.

"How about after I close tonight, we can hang out for a while. I promised I'd help Maybell tonight." I offer to him.

"Sounds good, I'll just help Taylor with the wedding." We both laugh at that statement because we both know he's no good with that.

It got pretty busy after I arrived, a lot more younger people came in here after the basketball game. Even kids from the visiting team showed up here. I was all over the place. I was hosting, taking orders, bringing food out, bussing tables, and even helping make the desserts. I just told Ryder to go home because I didn't him to wait around for me in here, because it was getting somewhat louder than a typical Friday night.

I had three plates in my arms, two plates of burgers and friends, and the other a wrap of some sort. I brought the plates over to a group of teenage boys. "Here you guys go." I said and skilfully placed the correct plates in front of the correct boy. "Anything else I can get you?"

"Can I get your Snapchat?" One asked before I left.

"I'm three years older than you, kid. And I have a boyfriend." I laughed at him, not in a mean way though. I was flattered, but there was no way.

"Eh, I thought I'd try." His buddies now laughed at him, along with me.

I walk around the diner to see if anyone needs a refill of their drinks, and I see a couple of people who need their waters filled. I walk behind the counter and grab the glass pitcher and add some ice cubes to it and then fill it up with the finest mountain glacier water. My phone begins to ring so I reach in my back pocket and answer it without looking, "Hello?"

"Hey, DaKota." I recognized the voice to be Desiree.

"Oh hey, Desiree. What's up?" I say as I close off the spout for the water.

"Well earlier, when I was being hesitant I had something to tell you." She pauses and then I pick up the pitcher and start to walk.

"What is it?" I ask her with confusion. Her tone of voice starts to scare me.

My heart and glass pitcher of water drops when she says, "Cooper gets released tomorrow."

DEAR JOURNAL,

Today is the day. The day where I had no idea if it would ever come. It doesn't seem real to me. When Desiree told me Cooper was getting released, I thought I had imagined it. But no, its real. I have no idea what I am going to say to him. There are a million things I could say to him, but none seem to be the right thing to say to him. Is it a 'say what comes to mind' thing or is it a very planned out conversation? I'm just going to go with what comes to my mind when I see him.

Last night after I broke the pitcher, everyone looked at me like I was some old-crazy-loony person. And I called off my plans with Ryder because I know I would of been distracted the whole time. I couldn't do that to Ryder. Be with him, but be thinking of Cooper the whole time. I didn't tell anyone what happened, Desiree said she wasn't even suppose to tell me, so I shouldn't tell anyone else. And I won't because I know people will be all up in my grill about it. Some might tell me to go, and some would heavily disagree with it.

How will he respond when he sees me? That's what I'm most scared about. I have no idea what will happen. Something inside me begs for me to see him, talk to him, or even just to hear him. It's been a year and half since I've last seen or heard him. I just need to know.

I close my journal and throw it on my chair and then I grab my phone and open up my messages app. I created a new one and type in Cooper's name. I stare at it and start to debate with myself. What could hurt? "If you want to talk, meet me at Reza's at 10." I hold my finger over the send button, not sure if I should actually send it.

Eff it, I press send and then throw my phone on my bed, as if he'll see it right away and make his decision. But in reality, I have no idea when he gets released. I have got to find something to keep me busy throughout the day. Because if I don't, today is going to be a very long day. And I knew what to do once I looked at my sewing machine. I offered to save Taylor some money by sewing the bridesmaid dresses myself, and she happily agreed.

I haven't finished one, and there's six of us. So yeah, I'm behind. This is the perfect thing to keep me busy and keep him off my mind.

I moved my sewing machine in front of my window so I got good lighting and could see outside. Then I went to my closet and pulled out the fabric of the dresses and laid them out neatly on my floor. Next I turned on my music to a Cody Jinks music station and began sewing.

In the span of five hours, and many needle pokes on my fingers, I managed to finish two dresses. I put one dress on the manequine of the right size, and stood back and admired it. Taylor really picked out a great design and pattern. They were sexy but elegant at the same time, just like Taylor. I know each bridesmaid would look stunning in it.

I liked the shade of pink she chose, because it wasn't a light pink. I don't like light pink bridesmaid dresses because it looks to close to white and I think the bride should stand out more, because it's her day. But yet it wasn't too dark to get confused with a burgundy color.

I think I need some lunch, I haven't ate anything all day. Maybe I'll go to the diner and pick up some grub. Maybe not. I really don't want to show my face in there after last night. Maybe I'll take a picnic in the mountains, yep, definitely doing that instead.

CHAPTER 7

I watched as Gauge and Micah chased the squirrels through the trees, having the time of their lives up here. I just took a popular trail ride with Sir Lance, with my lunch in my saddle pack. I planned on finding an opening with a nice view and just stay there until I wanted to leave.

I was happy when I found a spot that overlooked snow covered trees and some of my ranch. It was a beautiful day outside, probably around 35 degrees and not a cloud in the sky. And the trail didn't have a lot of snow, so that was good.

I tied Sir Lance to a tree and untack him, and then grab bigger logs to sit on. Then in front of my log, I found some littler sticks and built a place for a fire. Adding more branches, I was ready to start my fire. I peeled off some birch bark and grabbed my lighter and started it on fire and placed it on my sticks, and the fire started.

For some reason, I loved building fires. I guess I used to do it a lot with my grandpa and he would always tell me how good I was at it. I haven't talked to him a while, maybe I'll call him tomorrow.

Speaking of that, I pulled my phone out of my pocket and checked to see if I had any service. If I do, I don't care. I just wanted to see if I got any new messages or not. I only had one from Ryder saying, "What are you up to today?" I'm not going to tell him about wanting to meet with Cooper until tomorrow, because I have no idea how he will react.

I don't even know how I will react when I see Cooper.

The smell of the pine relaxed me, it's actually a fact that smelling pine reduces stress. Maybe I should take a couple of branches home with me for future instances.

I go back to Sir Lance and give him a nice rub and then pull out my lunch, and then I pull out a treat for Lance and give it to him. I walk back to my spot on the log and open my lunch container, before I left the house I made myself a chicken Cesar wrap, and some blackberries, and grabbed a homemade chocolate chip cookie. The dogs notice my lunch and they take a brake from their adventuring and sit in front of me, waiting for me drop them a piece of food.

When I'm done eating, I like the dogs eat the ends of the tortilla and then they go back to chasing squirrels. I pull out my phone and decide to text Ryder back, "Still not feeling well, just sewing the bridesmaid dresses." I looked at the time and it was 3:30, I should be heading home so mom doesn't worry about me.

I whistled, "C'mon boys." I saw them run out of the trees and then hang around Lance and I. I saddled Lancer closer to the fire so his pad as warm and his saddle, so his temperature could rise before we leave.

After I got him warmed up a bit, I grabbed some snow and dumped it over the fire and watched it go out. I waited a couple minuets just to make sure, and it was completely out. So I stood on my log and put my foot in the stirrup and swung my leg over and carried on home.

WELL I SUCCESSFULLY made another bridesmaid dress, during my procrastination of not thinking about what can happen tonight. But as I look at the time, it's eight o'clock which means that I have to start getting ready. I looked at myself in the mirror, looking at my natural hair and my bare face. I think I'll straighten my hair because I had enough time and I wanted to look good.

My hair and make up are officially done. My makeup consisted of mascara, foundation, and even a little bit of blush. I looked at myself through my mirror, looking at my hair, it needed a braid. So I grabbed the front pieces of my hair and brought them to the back of my head and braided them together.

I had no idea on what to wear. Do I go casual or do I dress up? If I straightened my hair, I might as dress well too. What kind of shirt do I wear? Do I wear skinny jeans, boot cut, or flares? Oh my gosh there are so many options.

But every option I tried, I didn't like. My bedroom floor was flooded with different jeans, shirts, bras, tank tops, and jean jackets. I fell back onto my bed and closed my eyes and sighed frustrated. But then I started thinking of my belts, I knew which one I wanted to wear! This would make my outfit chose a lot easier!

I stood at my full mirror and added some strands of Navajo pearls, my outfit was officially made. But I looked at the time and it was 9:45! I was going to be late! I turned off my music and grabbed my phone and ran downstairs and out of the house. I got into my pickup and wasted no time backing out and speeding down my drive.

I got to Reza's at 10: 10, that is without seeing any cops on my way or I would of got pulled over for going 15 over the speed limit, and I would of been even more late than I was. I handed the security guard my fake I.D and he accepted it and let me in, and I hastily entered the bar and started looking for anything that looked remotely like him.

I stopped in a crowd of people when I saw someone sitting at the bar, wearing a denim shirt and a black felt cowboy hat. It could of been anyone but I spotted brown curly hair under the hat, and then I made my move. My heart beat rose with every step I took towards him, and I wiped my hands on my jeans, to get rid of the sweat.

"Cooper." I said courageously as I stood behind him.

My stomach dropped when he turned around, but only to find out it wasn't Cooper. This man wasn't any way near as handsome as Cooper is. "Sorry, I confused you with someone else." I say sheepishly.

"Honey, you can confuse me with anyone you want." He said as he looked me up and down. My lip discreetly curled in disgust. I didn't say anything, but walked to the opposite end of the bar.

After doing a quick sweep of looking across the bar, I settled down in a chair at the bar. I looked at my phone to look at the time, 10: 20. I sighed, maybe I was too late. "What can I get you?" The bartender asks me.

I look at him innocently and say, "Water." He looks at me like I'm weird for ordering a water at the bar, and I agree with him, "Screw it, I'll have a Coors." He smirks at me as he wipes down a glass and walks away from me.

EVERY PERSON WHO WALKED past me I thought was Cooper. And every time I was wrong. I sigh as I turn my head to look back the the bar wall and reread the old western newspapers for the fifth time. Then the clock catches my attention, 11: 15, where has the time gone. Probably when I got my fourth Coors.

I was definitely feeling the side affects of my fourth beer. I know four beers is pretty light, but for someone who barely drinks, one more and I might start dancing on the bar. I unlock my phone and look at my messages, specifically the one I sent Cooper. It said it was delivered, but that doesn't tell me anything. He could have it set to that so I won't know he read it, or he honestly could of not seen it. With that reasoning, I think I'll stay a bit longer.

Maybe I should just leave, was it even right coming here? I'm dating Ryder and to meet up with an old boyfriend? What does that say about me? Am I just doing what I did with River? Because I didn't know that I was distracting myself until Cooper realized it for me. Maybe that will happen tonight again.

Now, I was watching people dance on the dance floor, and that made me incredibly sad. Cooper used to dance with me all the time, and Ryder never does! Speaking of Ryder, I should have him come pick me up, sense I'm in no shape to drive back home. I dialed him up, and it rang about five times before he answered. "DaKota?"

"Hey honey! What are you doing?" I ask him smiling to myself as the bartender hands me my sixth beer. Yup, I was a goner in the morning.

"Considering it's 11:45 at night, nothing much. Where are you?" He asks me as I giggle in the phone.

"Reza's, you should come! I'm having a lot of fun!" It was a sad lie, a very sad, sad, lie.

"Are you drunk?"

I giggle and then answer, "You'll have to find out!"

"I'm on my way." He said groggily and then he hangs up.

Not much longer did the song, "Save a horse, ride a cowboy" by Big and Rich come on and I got really excited. I have no idea where I got the courage to climb on my seat and stand and start to sing. Before I knew it people were cheering for me. I was getting really into it. "Get on the bar!" A guy hollered out and I looked at the bartender and he shrugged. So I got onto the bar and started to sing and dance. People were lining up against the bar and singing along with me. It really reminded me of the scene in Coyote Ugly, and I loved it!

When "Friends in low places" by Garth Brooks came on, everyone whooped and hollered. This was my fifth song now, and they had even given me a mic! The bartender even thanked me because I guess I brought more people to the bar and he sold twice the beer than he usually does.

"I'll head back to the bar and you can kiss my ass!" I sang loudly in the mic and everyone cheered, "Cause I got friends in low places!" I sang more and walked across the bar. When I looked over the crowd, I saw my boyfriend standing in the back with his arms crossed and staring at me.

I waited for the song to end and then I said, "That's all from me folks! Thank you and goodnight!" Then I dropped the mic to the bartender and sloppily walked off the bar and towards Ryder. "Wasn't I amazing?!" I said as I grabbed his arms.

"You were something all right." He laughed and then brought me in his arms, "C'mon lets go home."

"Just one more dance!" I pouted to him and he shook his head, "C'mon you never dance with me!" I pouted more and stomped my foot.

"Okay, just one." I smiled triumphantly and grabbed his hand and drug him to the dance floor with the others. He wrapped his arm around my waist and I held onto his shoulder and hand as we started to do a mean two step. I think I might drink more, I am the having the time of my life!

I closed my journal and threw my head back remembering that drunken night. It was a month ago since then, and I still remember how I felt the next morning. I told myself I would never drink again. But the hangover isn't the only thing that sucked that morning. I remembered why I was drunk, he didn't show.

I didn't tell Ryder why I was there, but later the next day, people found out that Cooper was released, and then he realized it himself. I'm not sure he thinks I went there just to drink, or if I went there to meet him. Anyways, it got pretty awkward, but we're back to normal again. When the whole town knew he was out, they went back to treating me like some physco waiting to relapse.

I didn't try to ask or find Desiree the next day. I'm sure she knows where he was, he wouldn't ditch his own mother. I didn't want to know, because it would of broke my heart to know he was at home with her when he could of came to see me after a year and a half.

I still have no idea where he is. My guess is that he moved back to Arkansas and started a new life down there, he always talked about how he loved it down there. But the part that gets me is that he wouldn't just leave his mother and brother like that, but I guess it's none of my business.

I walked downstairs to a great smelling breakfast that my mother cooked up. It's weird to be having breakfast at home on a Sunday Morning, usually we go to church and then have breakfast at the diner. But there is a huge horse auction here today, so 10:00 mass has been moved to seven p.m.

My mom was making scrambled eggs, sausage, and breakfast pizza. My dad was already seated at the table and Caleb and Ashley were sitting at the kitchen counter talking to my mom. They were holding hands under the table it melted my heart. "Good morning." I say to them as my feet hit the wooden floor.

"Morning." They all greet to me.

As we sit down at the table, I catch Caleb and Ashley looking at each other constantly. Like they were communicating with their minds. I'd usually expect Caleb try to do that, but Ashley? Something was definitely going on.

I kept a close eye on them as we started to dish our plates. I took a scoop of eggs, lots of sausage, and two small pieces of breakfast pizza. I poured myself a cup of orange juice and handed it to my mother beside me. "Give me your hands." My dad says and then bow my head, ready for grace.

"Dad, wait. Do you mind if I say it today?" Caleb nervously asks my dad. My dad looks at us suspiciously before nodding his head.

"Dear the Lord in Heaven, we thank you for this plentiful meal and everything that went towards it. We thank you for another great day in the state of Montana on this great green Earth. We ask you to keep our crops and livestock healthy in order to keep doing what we love. We also ask you to keep our family safe and healthy and stronger than ever, now that you blessed us with another one. Amen." My eyes shot open to the last part of grace.

Caleb and Ashley sat there, hand in hand, smiling devilishly at us. "Are you saying that-" My mother choked on her own words.

They smiled at each other and nodded, "We're having a baby!"

I jumped out of my chair and yelled, "I'm going to be an aunt!!!!" I was so overwhelmed with joy and happiness, it was so exciting! "Congrats!!" I say to them as I engulf them in a warm bear hug.

When I pulled back, I noticed Ashley was crying happy tears and then my mother embraced her with another warm hug. "I'm going to be a grandma!" My mother cried, making me laugh.

"At least you know how to do something right," My dad actually joked and we all laughed. "Congrats son." My dad said and hugged Caleb.

Over this past year, my dad has been less harsh on Caleb and has been helping him start taking over our ranch. It's very touching to see my dad do this with Caleb, because I know it means a lot to him. And now one day, my dad will be teaching my nephew/niece!

"I'm so excited!" I clapped my hands together and they both smiled and looked at each other.

"We are too." Then they kissed quickly, making my heart melt ever more. "DaKota, we have something to as you." They said as the both looked at me. I'm pretty sure I knew what was coming, but I couldn't jump to conclusions.

Caleb broke away from Ashley and stood in front of me, "As my baby sister and my inspiration, and one of Ashley's best friends, will you be our child's Godmother?"

"Of course!" I say and hug him tighter than I ever have before.

I HAD AN IDEA TO CONGRATULATE my brother and sister in law, after church we would go to the diner and I'd have decorations up and throw a little party. I asked Caleb and he said it was a good idea, but we agreed not to tell Ashley about it. So right now, Taylor and I are just finishing shopping for decorations.

We arrived at the diner, where not to many customers where. I'm glad because then so many people wouldn't be hounding us on who the party is for. I'm sure Ashley wouldn't appreciate us telling the whole town before they did. "Hey girls." Maybell brightly smiled at us as she was cashing in the register.

"Hey May." We both smiled back.

"What are you gals up to?" She says and stands on her tip toes to peek over our boxes and bags.

"We're having a party after church." I said as we sat the boxes down on the counter.

"A party for what?" She asks, and Taylor and I look at each and smirk.

"Ashley's pregnant." I whisper to her and she gasps.

"What!" She almost screams, gaining attention to us but then she covers her mouth. "That's amazing!" She whispers, making us laugh.

Taylor, May, and I start to plan out where we would put the decorations and then the big banner. Obviously we're gonna put the banner on the wall you see when you first walk in, and then streamers on the windows and fun little party gifts around the diner.

"There's your boy DaKota." May says beside me as we put up the streamers. I smile once I see Ryder walking in the doors, looking around for me.

I scoot out of the booth and walk towards him, "What's going on in here?" He asks taking off his cowboy hat and looking around.

I don't say anything but smile and lean up and kiss him. I can tell he's shocked, but he quickly kisses back. When I pull back he cocks his eyebrows, "I'm gonna be an aunt!" I whisper to him and his eyes go wide.

"Really?" He asks me and I bit my lip and smile.

"That's great, honey! So this is for them?" He asks me as he wraps his arms around my waist.

"Yeah, I'm planning it for after church." I say to him as I play with his coat strings.

"You're the best, I'll meet you at church?" He said and ducked his head to be at my height and then kissed my cheek.

"Yep, see ya then." I smiled at him as he unwrapped his arms and then walked out the door and back to his pickup.

Ryder jogged over to me and my family was we made out way down the sidewalk to our church. "Hey Ryder." My family greeted and he greeted back and walked next to me. I nudged him in the side playfully and we smiled at each other. As we were walking I looked down at my outfit and analyzed it. I was wearing a white long sleeve shirt with criss-cross strings paired with some dark blue flares, and I wore a natural turquoise squash blossom to match my shirt. I was wearing my red Old Gringo snip toed boots and my hair was styled straight with the two front pieces braided in the back, my usual.

Maybe I should start a fashion blog or something like that. I always got complimented on my outfits ad my unique style, and people ask me for help sometimes. I could tell people how to get their clothes for cheap, and jewelry. Good jewelry is so expensive these days, it's insane! I could also teach people how to sew their own clothes, or at least how to make it their own by adding details or something like that. I'll have to get more opinions if I should or not.

I held open the church door for my whole family, even with the men's protests. I liked to walk last so I could sit at the end of the pew or near it at least. I'm sure Ryder doesn't want to sit by my protective family, even though they're pretty used to him by now. He says my whole family intimidates him, even my mother! I think it's pretty funny.

I noticed as we all walked in, the whole church went quiet. I'm talking like as soon as we entered, their whispered conversations abruptly stopped. I wonder if they were talking about Ashley and Caleb's pregnancy, but how would they know? Maybe someone heard me and Taylor talking about it.

But as I walked down the aisle, I felt eyes on me. Actually, I saw their eyes on me, almost every pew had someone staring at me. What did I do know? As I genuflected, I looked up at the front of the church and saw singers up there, so I guess it wasn't because I forgot I had to sing. So why were they staring at me?

Ryder sat at the very end of the pew, taking my spot. I stuck my tongue at him and sat beside him and my mom. After Father started the mass, I did my routine glance around the church. "Oh my God." I whispered in disbelief when my eyes landed on the the second pew on the right side.

It's him.

Now, I know why they were all staring at me when I walked in. They wanted to see how I would react when I saw him. I couldn't stop looking. It wasn't just a side eye, it was a full on head look. I mostly saw the back of his head, but some of his damned jawline. I had no idea what Father Brad was preaching about, it didn't seem to be as important than the fact Cooper was back.

I was knocked back into reality when I felt two eyes burning holes through my face. I looked to my right at Ryder who was looking at me with an unreadable expression. I couldn't tell if he was sad or mad or understanding, because I know he knows who I was looking at. I don't know what to do but look at the front of the church and pretend to be listening, when all I'm thinking about is the man who stole my heart is finally in the same room as me.

As they begin going up for the bread and wine, I keep my head down to stop myself from looking at him. It doesn't last long when I look up to where his family sits. My heart skips two beats when I find him already looking at me. I don't look away like some high school girl, I hold his gaze until he turns and walks away to receive communion. The worst part is that he doesn't look the same as a year and half ago, he's much hotter.

LEAVING THE MASS, IT was painfully awkward between my family and Ryder. No one knew what to do or say. I'm glad no one did because I wouldn't know what to say back. I'm still in shock that he's actually here, in Hudson. When we get to the sidewalk in front of the church I turn to Ryder, "Are you coming to the party?" I was nervous to what he was going to say.

"Of course." He smiled and I nodded and then jogged to catch up with my family. Once I got into the pickup, all heads were turned to look at me. They were waiting for me to say something.

"Did you not see him?" Caleb says with minor sarcasm, in disbelief that I wasn't saying anything about it. Ashley elbows him in the stomach.

"Of course she did." My mother rolls her eyes and then she looks at me to see if I'm okay.

I give her a slight nod, "I guess I'm a little shocked, but I'm with Ryder now." I saw my family look at each other and basically say, 'yeah, right' but they just turned around and kept to their own. I didn't blame them, even I didn't believe myself when I said that.

I watched for Ashley's reaction when Caleb opened the doors to my diner. She was a little confused but then she read the sign and she smiled brightly at us. "What's this?" She asked happily as we all walked in.

"Just a congratulations party." I shrugged, turning to her.

"You didn't have to do this." She said, but I could tell she was grateful.

"Just shut up and ice creams on me." I winked at her and walked behind the counter to where Taylor was already.

I went back to the ice cream machine and started to dispense the ice cream for Ashley and Caleb. "So are we not going to talk about what happened in church?" Taylor muttered to me as she leaned her back against the machine and crossed her arms.

"There's nothing to talk about." I say and cock my head, sending her a message that I didn't want to talk about it.

"Yeah, okay." She breathed out sarcastically and rolled her eyes. Usually, I would of called her out on it, but I didn't want to talk about anything at the moment.

I brought me and Ryder's food to our booth and then slide in across from him. I ordered a buffalo chicken ranch wrap, and he ordered two grilled cheeses and fries. I also got us an Oreo milkshake. "I'm sorry for what happened at the church earlier." I say to him and he looks up from his grilled cheese to me.

Again, I can't tell if he's angry or upset. He opens his mouth to say something, but then shuts it. He sighs and then says, "It's just that I've never seen you have that look on your face before." I dunked my fry in the shake and looked at him with interest.

"Like what?" I say and then pop my fry into my mouth.

"You looked like you saw a person go from lying in a casket to walking and talking the next day. You were happy and shocked at the same time." The way he explained it made me feel extremely guilty and horrible I was going to say something but he beat me to it, "I'm not mad, because I know if there was something still there, you would of told me already. You're an honest person, DaKota. I trust you." A huge weight was lifted off my shoulders when he said this, and it made me feel more secure in the current situation.

I placed my hand over his and said, "Thank you, Ryder."

"C'mere." He says and pats the spot next to him. I giggle as I slide in next to him and we face each other and then we both lean in for a kiss. It was sweet and loving. When we pulled back we smiled at each other then I leaned my head against his shoulder as he leaned against the window and we continue eating our dinner together.

I WISH I COULD SAY that when I got home, I was still in a happy mood from being with Ryder, but once I was alone in my bathroom, my real emotions came out. I was in the shower when I started to cry. I wasn't sobbing, it wasn't a heartbreak cry. It was a hurt cry.

I found it very weird that the first time I saw him would be at church. He knows that I go every Sunday, and I had to convince him to go most of the time. So did he deliberately go to church to make a statement that he's back? Did he want to see me? Or was he just trying to connect to God a little better?

But what really hurt was looking at him. When he made eye contact, I felt everything we had together. I felt everything he made me feel, the way he kissed me, him making me feel that we were the only two people in the world, and the way he would take care of me. But what I felt the most was the way I felt when I went to visit him in jail and he refused to see me. That was the cake topper of them all.

I have no idea if he's back for good, or if he's staying temporary. But if it's for good, I have to find a way to live normally when he's around me. It's a small town, there's no way we're not going to run into each other somewhere.

But if that son of a bitch would just talk to me, I feel like everything would be a hell of a lot easier. Maybe I should approach him and demand we talk about what happened. Maybe I should just leave it alone, because if he wanted to change the tension between us, he would have already. So why should I waste my time fixing something that can't be put back together?

COOPER

I GROANED ONCE MY ALARM clock went off, and I rolled over and lazily turned it off. I rolled back onto my stomach and pulled my other pillow over my head. After convincing myself to actually get up and take a shower, I toss the pillow by the foot of the bed. When I reopen my eyes, I see a frame from where my pillow use to lay over.

I picked up the frame and instantly regret it. It was the picture of me and DaKota. I remember this day like it was yesterday when we were sneaking around from her father. I smiled to myself remembering how fearless she was, God I miss her. I put the frame back where it was on the night stand and then I roll out of bed and head to my bathroom and take a shower.

Once I'm done taking a shower, I wrap a towel around my waist and then step out. I turn down my Cody Jinks station and then wipe my hand across the fogged mirror and look at myself through the mirror. My hair was starting to get shaggy but I didn't mind, as long it didn't look too shaggy. I have a reputation to uphold.

I didn't bother to put a shirt on when I went down to breakfast. My brother was at the table eating his favorite cereal, Lucky Charms.

He did the thing where you eat the other things first, and saved the marshmallows for last. "Morning buddy." I said as I messed up his hair.

"Where's your shirt?" He asks me with a funny face. I look down at my bare torso and at my jeans and my belt buckle.

"Couldn't find one that I liked." I joked with him.

"You sound like mom." He says and I laugh as my mom's jaw drops.

"Watch it pal!" My mom can't help but laugh at Reese. Man I missed him a lot when I was in jail.

Jail, not the worst place in the world, but I wouldn't recommend it. The first six months were slow as hell because of a certain someone, but after that, it wasn't too bad. My cell mate was pretty cool, he was like me, locked in for being innocent. His name is Matthew. We got pretty close in there and we talk through text daily because he's originally from Wyoming and I obviously live here. While I was in there, he let me drown him in my feelings about DaKota and he gave me good advice, some which I took other ways, but still good advice.

I flipped through the channels on TV in the living room while I ate my cereal, Captain Crunch with berries. I saw Life Below Zero and I clicked on it and starting to indulge in it, taking mental notes for future references. I always saw me and DaKota living in the mountains one day, we are both pretty handy and tough as barbed wire. We could definitely do it. I mean, we could have done it.

As I'm watching the show, I hear a pickup coming down our drive. I stand up bringing my cereal bowl with me and stand in front of the window to get a better look. I didn't recognize the pickup, but as it got closer I read, "Jones' Animal Rescue and Hospital." Then I saw her.

It brought back the feelings of when I saw her in church. I couldn't believe it when I saw her. She was more beautiful from the last time I saw her. Her white shirt made her look like an angel, an angel who could fix anyone, an angel who fixed me. When we locked eyes during communion, I felt, well I can't explain it. I felt everything: pain, anger, sadness, loneliness, I was ecstatic to finally see her. But I couldn't let her see that. I kept my face neutral, because I know she could read my facial expression better than anyone else.

I also couldn't help notice Ryder Baker scoot closer to her and see him glaring at me. I'm not sure if he was trying to look intimidating trying to get his point across, or he was trying to comfort DaKota in some way. I'll admit it, it hurt like hell to see her with him. Especially when I saw them cuddled up in a booth and kissing and laughing. It was so good to see her smile, she had the most beautiful smile I had ever seen. I couldn't ruin that for her.

"Dammit mom, you didn't tell me DaKota was coming!!" I yelled through the living room as she sat at the kitchen table. "Why is she here?"

"She's following up with JW. She's the one who stitched him up." She says as she sips her morning coffee. When did she start working on her own? Did she finally become a veterinarian?

I shake off my proud distraction and get back on track, "Well you're going to have to talk with her, I have to feed the cows." I say as I put the bowl in the sink and quickly run up the stairs.

"Why don't you just talk to her!" My mother yells at me as I'm on the stairs, and it makes me stop and look outside and look at her go into the barn.

"I can't." I say in a torn voice, because I really couldn't talk to her or else I might give in and ruin something good for her.

DAKOTA

I EXAMINE JW'S SUTURES and staples, the wound was really healing nicely, I'm proud of myself. The should be falling out in a couple weeks or less I suspect. I give JW a nice rub all around his body and give him a treat I took from my truck. I step out of his stall and the open back door of the barn was open and a movement caught my eye.

Cooper was carrying a bag of feed to the troughs for the cows. He was wearing a wool blue flannel and a black felt with a feather on it. "How's he looking?" Really good.

I snap my head towards Desiree who's bundled up in a warm winter coat and wearing some fuzzy gloves. "He's looking really good. The staples and stitches should come out by themselves in a couple weeks or less."

"That's good news, thanks for coming out." She said as she walked me out of the barn.

"No problem, always looking for a reason to work with horses." I smile as I put my kit in the back seat of the pickup. "See ya around, Desiree." I nod to her as I get in my truck.

"Bye, thanks again!" She waved as I shut my door. It was too weird being out there with Cooper there, and not even talking to him. It feels just like yesterday that I was sneaking out here to hang out with him, and Desiree being content that I was with him.

But that isn't how is anymore. Cooper is obviously avoiding me, doing anything he can to not be around me. It's so confusing! How can he go from telling me our future together to not being able to look me in the eye? As I'm driving I realize that my knuckles are turning white from gripping the stearing wheel too tight. I take a breath and loosen my grip and turn my focus on driving on the icy roads.

I park my own pickup in the parking lot of a bridal store in the town of Bowman. We don't have a bridal place in Hudson, so we had to come over here. The reason I am here today is to give the rest of the bridesmaid their dresses and make any alterations to them if needed, and Taylor still needs to pick out a dress. I might seem crazy to someone that her wedding is in three days and she still doesn't have a dress, but that's not the case. She is stuck between three dresses, and needs her friends opinions. Her first appointment was with her mom and aunt, and they couldn't make a decision, so now she calls on us.

I walked through the front door carrying the six dresses with coat hangers and covers, for protection of the harsh weather elements. The girls were waiting for me already and when they saw me they stood up and took some of the dresses from me. "I can't wait to try this on!" Molly says as she hangs the covered dress in front of her.

The bridesmaids consisted of me, Molly, Ashley, Jessica, Reyna, and her cousin Bailey. Bailey is only a couple years younger than us, so we don't have to treat her like a baby. She fits in with us because she's a cowgirl too, so she knows how wild we can get.

"Okay, ladies you can follow me." The assistant said and we all followed her to a dressing room big enough for all of us. "I've already tried it on, I'll just wait in the other room." I said as I stopped at the door and held my dress.

So I sat there on the couch with Taylor of the showing room, wearing my blue work scrubs and my hair in a high ponytail. I hear the girls laughing and I turn my head to see them walking out. My jaw drops at the sight. They looked so beautiful and the dresses looked flawless on them! I do a cat whistle and then they start to pose for me, making all of us laugh. "DaKota, you outdid yourself with these dresses." Taylor says as she gets a better look at them.

"Thank you." I shyly said. I felt uncomfortable when attention was drawn to me, I didn't like being the center of attention. Especially when it's all for Taylor.

"C'mon DaKota, put on your dress!" Reyna says and I shake my head no.

"C'mon then we get a bridesmaid picture before the wedding!" Jessica says and then I give in and stand up with my dress and go back into the changing room.

When I tried my dress on at my house, I didn't look at myself in the mirror. I just use my body sense to tell if the dress fit in the right places. But now that I'm here, I see myself in the mirror and I'm shocked. I usually never wear pink, but I'm been told I look good in it, and now I'm starting to believe them. The color of the dress made my naturally dark skin pop and it accented the color of my hair and eyes. But it wasn't about if I looked good or not, it was about the dress accenting Taylor and her dress.

I walked out with my head down, starting at my feet so I didn't trip over the dress and make a fool of myself. When I looked up they all had their mouth's open, gaping at me. "Oh my, DaKota." Taylor says as I stand with the group.

"I look okay?" I joke with them and they chuckle with me.

"A lot more than okay." They say and I then I blush.

"Group hug!" Molly yells out and then we all come together and wrap our arms around each other and embrace the love of our girl gang.

WE ALL SQUEEZED ONTO the couch that is only for four people, but we didn't mind being that close to each other. Taylor is currently changing in the room, into her third dress. The two other dresses she showed us were really pretty and really flattering, but we all agreed the 'wow' factor wasn't there. We all shut our chattering when we heard the dressing room door close and then we all cranked our heads to get the first look of her.

Holy hot hell in heaven.. She looked absolutely stunning and breath taking. Seriously, I held in my breath when I saw her. I looked at the rest of us and we all shared the same expression. "What do you guys think?" I could tell Taylor had tears in her eyes because she thought the same thing as the rest of us.

"This is the one." We said confidently and then a tear escaped her eye. I could tell we were all getting emotional, even I was starting to feel the water works coming.

"I think so too." Then she wiped her eyes to keep from ruining her mascara.

"You look so beautiful Taylor." I said as I wiped my tear away from my eye.

"Beau is going to die before you even get married." Jessica said and we all laughed, wiping our tears away.

"So this one then?" The assitant laughs and Taylor laughs and nods.

"Yes, this is my wedding dress." Then we all spill out of the couch and go over to and carefully hug her. "I love you guys."

It was about eight o'clock when we walked out of the restaurant, all laughing about something stupid Reyna said to the male host. She said some dumb pickup line like, "Are you speeding ticket? Because you have fine written all over you." Yeah, she was a little intoxicated.

I looked up across the street to see the bar Reza's, and I smiled to myself remembering making a fool out of myself. But then the smile faded when I saw the door being pulled open by the reason I was there that night. Cooper was there, opening a door for some blonde chick.

And he looked good, wearing a smile and laughing. Wearing one of his nicest pairs of Cinch jeans, wearing a red Cody James western shirt, and a gray cowboy hat. The girls must of noticed to because they all stopped behind me. "Do you want me to beat him up?" Reyna said with a drunk confidence. "Because I could and would."

There's no way she possibly take him with his rancher strength, but I appreciated it. "No, but thank you."

I helped Reyna get into the back seat of Molly's pickup, and buckled her up and cracked the window for her, in case she had to vomit. "Thanks, Kota. You're such a doll." She slurred as she closed her eyes and dropped her head and fell asleep.

"See you guys soon." I chuckled as they both looked back at her and rolled their eyes.

"See ya, thanks again for the dresses!" I gave them a polite nod and backed away from her pickup and watched them drive away.

"You okay?" Taylor asks me and I look around us to see that Bailey is in Taylor's pickup, and so I shake my head no. "Come here." She wraps her arms around me and I hug her tightly.

"I don't know what my problem is." I sigh frustratingly in her shoulder.

"You still have feelings for him," I felt horrible about it, it was so unfair to Ryder, him and even me. "And it's okay. That's normal."

"It's been a year and half, it shouldn't hurt this much."

"You know what I think you should do?" She says as she takes her arms and separates us, but still holds onto my biceps. I look at her for her advice, "I think you should write a pros and cons of each boy, and then see how you feel."

I nod to her and say, "Thank you, I had fun today." I smile through the pain and she nods and smiles.

"I did too, I'm so glad you're my best friend."

"Me too, I don't know what I would do without you."

Three of us were smooched together on Taylor's queen sized bed, and the other three were on an air mattress we managed to blow up last night. Oh boy last night.. We had Taylor's bachelorette party last night, and I can't say that we didn't have any fun, because we did. And if there were such a thing of having too much fun, we achieved it.

First we started by getting nails and toenails done, and then we went on a way too competitive scavenger hunt around the town. The scavenger hunt was based mostly about who knew Beau and Taylor the most. My team obviously won, because I am Taylor's best friend and we tell each other everything. The thing about the scavenger hunt is that when you found another clue, you had to chug a glass of champagne to find out the next one.

When we won, we got to choose what bar we wanted to go. My team obviously chose Reza's so we could dance and act as crazy as we wanted to. We walked into the bar, already buzzed from the champagne. To say the least, we were the life of the party at the bar. We were loud, carefree, and buzzed on beer and life. We ruled the dance floor, and danced with random strangers, having the time of our lives.

Then someone recognized me as the "hottie that danced on the bar" and then we had to hold up my new reputation. All six of us got up on the bar and danced for hours. It was a real life Coyote Ugly scene. We stayed there until 3:30 in the morning, it was the funnest thing I did in a while. I felt alive and I forgot about everything going on in my life. It was just me and my best friends, and I felt unstoppable.

It was fun and games, but I now have a minor hangover. I looked at Taylor's room and it was trashed with our clothes and our party slashes and party favors. I groaned as I realized that I should probably pick it up before we have to leave. I slowly rolled out of bed, careful not to wake up Taylor and Ashley. I smiled to myself as I saw that Taylor still had on her diamond encrusted crown for being the bride-to-be.

Grabbing my phone I walked out of the room to find a garbage bag to clean up the mess. I looked at the time and it was 11 o'clock, I haven't slept in that long since I was 13, it felt amazing. Excluding my headache from last night.

"Oh my God." Taylor frustratingly breathed out as she was looking down at her phone, "You have got to be shitting me." She slapped her hand on her forehead and then fell back on her freshly made bed.

"What happened?" Jessica asks, as we all gather around the bed waiting for Taylor to explain the crisis.

"Alex said he has the flu and says he can't make it." Alex is one of the groomsmen, he was suppose to walk with Bailey.

"So what does that mean?" Molly asks as she sits on the edge of the bed.

"That means that Beau has to find whoever has a tux and who is available today." She sighs and runs her hands through her hair.

"Taylor don't worry about it, he'll find someone. And if not, a lucky groomsmen gets to walk the aisle with a girl on each hand." I try to cheer her up, but I know she'll be stressing over it until she knows it is actually okay. I would ask Ryder to fill in, but I don't think him and Beau are that close to be in their wedding. Speaking of Ryder, I should see if he would be kind enough to bring us coffee, I think we could all use it considering last night.

"Yeah, everything will work out. Now don't stress, we don't your flawless skin to suddenly break out." Molly says, making us laugh.

"HERE YOU LADIES GO." He says as he hands out the cups of coffee to the correct girl. He reaches me and hands me mine, "And a venti iced caramel macchiato, with extra caramel." He said and winked at me, remembering that I liked extra caramel in my drink.

"Impressive." I smirked at him and took a sip of my drink.

"Thanks Ryder!" The girls said to him as they all savored the coffee drinks.

"No problem gals! See ya at the wedding." He said and tipped his hat to them.

"I'll walk you out." I said and stood up from my chair and walked with him to the front door. "Thanks again for the coffee, we all needed it."

"Wild party last night?" He joked.

"I think that's an understatement for what we did." I say and tip my drink to him.

"What, dancing on the bar again?" He was teasing me, but he had no idea he was actually right until I raised my eyebrows. "You guys did, didn't you?" He said astonished. I blushed and shrugged with a sheepish smile. "Wow, I just can't let you out of my sights can I?" He said and then wrapped his arms around my lower waist and pulled me into him.

"I guess you can't. It's alright because I kinda like you." I said jokingly as I leaned away from him as he leaned closer to me.

We both laughed and then he played back, "I kinda like you too." Then he placed a sweet kiss on my lips for a couple of moments and then pulled back, earning a blush from me.

I wish I could of seen what we looked like as we all piled out of one pickup. We were dressed in sweatpants, sweatshirts, messy buns, and pulling our packed suitcases and holding our coffee in our free hands. We were ready for business, and if anything got in our way, they wished they didn't.

As we entered the designated makeup and changing room, we set up our makeup stations with our mirror stands and popup tables with our makeup and hair styling tools on it. Then we all got changed into our white satin robes that Taylor ordered for us. After we took a couple of before pictures, we went back to our places. Bridesmaids were doing their own makeup, but Taylor had a professional coming to do her hair and makeup. Although I think Taylor's mom is doing our hair because she used to be a stylist back in the day.

"Alright y'all! We have three hours until Taylor walks down the aisle, so happy glamming!" Reyna says as she waves her makeup brush around and cheers happily. I walk over to the music and go to my Thumbprint and turn it up louder and then return to my makeup station.

"Has Beau filled you in on the groomsmen situation, Tay?" I ask her as I apply my mascara.

"Yeah he found someone to fill in!! But I didn't get to ask who because Molly caught me calling instead of texting him." She rolled her eyes making me laugh.

I finish doing my makeup, which was foundation, with a little contouring with the help of Reyna who was really good with makeup, mascara, a hint of eye shadow, and blush. The contouring was different from my usual makeup look, but I liked how it looked on me, and hopefully I'll look decent in all the wedding photos. "Ready for me girly?" Taylor's mom asks me as she finishes with Jessica.

"Yes ma'am." I say and sit up straighter and let her start to style my hair.

I STOOD IN THE MIRROR and examined my hair and makeup before taking before the aisle pictures. Taylor's mom did and excellent job on my hair, I loved it so much. It was half up and half down, it looked really well with the deep v-neck of the dress. She pulled the front pieces of my hair to the back and twisted it somehow and pinned it back there. I wish I could do that on my own, that would be so convenient.

I put some hair in front of my shoulders because that's what I thought looked good. Giving myself one last look, I decided that I looked good and not to fix anything else in case I ruin it. I tightened the belt of my robe and walked to wear the other girls were.

We stood in front of the changing door thingy and waited for Taylor to step out in her dress and final makeup. And when she did, she knocked me off my feet. She looked absolutely breath taking and jaw dropping. Her hair was styled in an elegant low bun with loose curled pieces of hair, framing her face gorgeous face. We were all fanning our eyes to keep our tears from ruining our makeup. "I love you guys and I'm so happy you guys could be apart of this. I can't thank you enough." I knew she was trying to keep herself from crying, and I think some girls let a couple tears escape the lines.

When we stepped back from our hug, she had her special moment between her mother and father. It was too precious for my heart, I couldn't wait to have this moment of my own one day. Could I see myself being married to Ryder one day? Could I handle his brother for the rest of my life? I guess time could only tell the end of that story.

"Alright bridesmaids, time to get lined up!" The wedding planner said, directing us with his clipboard.

Us girls grabbed the Heliotrope flower bouquets and headed out for the church entrance. As we walked, I looked at the beautiful arrangement of wild flowers. I loved the look of the white flowers with the green leaves, and some steams had blue flowers on them! It looked very elegant but also had a touch of country to them. When the wedding planner was herding us like cattle, I looked up to look at everyone in the wedding party.

You have got to be shitting me.

I was not expecting this at all. I guess the person Beau picked to fill in was no other than Cooper Blackwood himself. He wasn't looking at me, but that changed with he did the slightest head turn. He didn't seem shocked to see me, obviously I was going to be evolved in my best friend's wedding. Once again, I didn't turn away from his gaze. I was at the end of the line and he was at the beginning of his line, thank God we weren't paired with each other.

Deciding to break the awkward tension, I turn away from his eyes and look straight ahead. I didn't get him at all. Ever since he has been back, I have seen him everyday. Not intentionally. Like I predicted, he was at least at one of the places I made an appearance at. And all those places, he would look at me once and then never look at me again.

But now here is, staring me down like his head was permanently stuck in one position. Oh man, Ryder's gonna think I didn't tell him that Cooper was in the wedding party, that's gonna be a shit show. Whatever, I just needed to focus on the moment right now. I needed to put on a bright smile and help Taylor have the best day of her life.

Jake stood by my side and I loosely wrapped my hand around his bicep, "Ready wolf girl?" His nickname made me smile, no one has called me that in a very long time.

"Yes sir." I smiled and then we stepped out in the church and walked down the aisle. I smiled as I looked in the crowd, hoping my eyes wouldn't find Ryder. No doubt he's already seen Cooper walk down with Bailey.

Jake and I separated and I stood next to Molly and waited for the traditional "Here comes the bride" song to be played by the organist. Once it did, everyone rose and turned their heads towards the entrance.

Taylor looked up from the floor as she was walking with her father and she amazed everyone like she did to us back in the makeup room.

I looked over at Beau and he looked so proud and happy to see his future wife coming down the aisle. It was so romantic and heart melting, I pray my husband looks at me like that on our wedding day. As I looked at Beau, I felt a pair of eyes on me. So my gaze wandered to the last groomsmen, Cooper. Again we locked eyes until I noticed Taylor come to a stop on the aisle. I walked down to her and grabbed her much more beautiful bouquet and then went back to my spot among the bridesmaids.

Once the ceremony started, I found myself looking at Cooper again. And he was doing the exact same thing. I had no idea what the staring contest meant, but for some reason I didn't want it to end. Maybe I wanted to find out that mind reading is an actual thing, because I desperately wanted to know what he was thinking when he was looking at me. What kind of game was he playing with me?

THE CEREMONY WAS ABSOLUTELY amazing and beautiful, I was so happy for Taylor and Beau. They deserved a beautiful life together, they were a perfect couple. An even more perfect as they danced their first dance to "Deeper than the Holler" by Randy Travis, such a romantic song to dance to for your wedding song.

I sat there staring at them hopelessly, what was I doing with my life? I am satisfied where I am right now? Or am I just playing it safe by staying inside the only lines I know? I look in the crowd and find Ryder's eyes already on me. I offer him a small soft smile and then put my eyes back on Taylor and Beau.

The two love birds returned from their dance and now it was time for speeches from Jake and me. I guess I had to go first because Jake insisted 'ladies go first', but I'm pretty sure he was going to copy mine because he wasn't prepared. I stood up and smoothed out my dress and turned on the microphone, "Well first I just wanna say congratulations to one of the best couples I know, just right under Blake Lively and Ryan

Reynolds." People laughed at my joke which eased my nerves. "I guess I'll start with the ladies first, so Beau," another break with laughter, "So Beau, I want to thank you for treating my best friend with a great amount of respect and unconditional love, she truly deserves it. You and I have known each other since elementary school when you threw a football at my head and Taylor came to the rescue." I paused to keep myself from laughing, "I don't think I've ever seen a little boy be so scared of a little blonde girl with pigtails and missing teeth." The guests and myself laughed more at the true story, "Seriously I think that's the first moment he started to have a crush on her. Why wouldn't he like the girl who quote on quote threatened to 'make sure he'd never be able to throw a football again'? You carried on that crush all the way through middle school, and man aren't we all glad you decided to grow a pair and ask her out in high school." Beau and Taylor liked that joked as they laughed with the rest of the crowd. "But seriously, Beau I couldn't asked God to pick out a better man for my best friend. Thank you and I wish you luck in the future, you'll need it." I muttered the last part under my breath.

Beau gave me an appreciative smile and silent 'thank you' and I smiled back at him. "And now, my dear Taylor Ann. My best friend since the third grade. My go to person for anything. We've only been talking about this day since we were little girls, but somehow I don't think it turned out like we thought it would. For example, Beau certainly is not Brad Pitt." Everyone starts to laugh, including myself, "And we are are not retired at the ages of 19 and 20. But wouldn't that be nice? But Taylor I am so honored you chose me to be your maid of honor, that is the probably the only thing that came true from our fantasy wedding. But I do remember our eight and nine year old selves saying, 'That doesn't matter as long if we have each other.' Who knew we were such geniuses at that age? I know that if you and Beau have each other like you and I do that there is nothing that can stop you guys from living your best lives together, not even Brad Pitt." I end my speech by putting down the microphone, and I smile when I hear the laughter and applause from the guests.

Taylor mouths an 'I love you' and a 'thank you', and then I hold up a heart to her. The microphone was handed down to Jake who stood up and faced the crowd of guests. "Well I don't know if I should even attempt to top that speech or just say a congratulations and not embarrass myself." I laugh at a flustered Jake who scratches his head and looks around for help.

NOW IT WAS TIME TO dance, my favorite part of any wedding. The first couple of songs were someone couldn't really have a partner, so it was basically throw out any dance moves you have on the dance floor and dance with your favorite group of people. Of course, Ryder sat out by himself and watched us have fun without him.

But as time went on, two stepping songs came on, and none of them Ryder wanted to dance too. I decided to dance with other guys because he wouldn't and he didn't really seem to care. I was having more fun with Jake tonight than I would with Ryder. But during a dance, my eyes caught the outskirts of the dance floor and to another lonely cowboy, Cooper. He was watching me dance with Jake, again with a stupid blank expression plastered on his face. I decided not to waste my time figuring it out.

"Dixieland Delight" by Alabama came on and I jogged over to Ryder and grabbed his hand and started to pull on him. "Come one! Let's dance! I love this song!" I whined because it was too good of a song not to dance to.

Ryder just shook his head no and gently let go of my hand. I internally huffed at him and then I turned to look for Jake on the dance floor. Almost everyone who was invited was dancing, so it was quite crowded. As I walking a hand grabbed my wrist and twirled me into a hard chest.

I didn't have to open my eyes to know it was Cooper who swept me off my feet. No one had ever sent tingles down my body as much as his touch did. He held me tightly against him like we were still a couple and there was no tension between us. It felt so strange but yet so gosh damn good. I didn't know what do but go along with him. The only time he wasn't looking deeply into my eyes is when he was looking at the space behind him, widening our slow dancing steps. I opened my mouth to say something but then he furrowed his eyebrows and cut me off, "Your eyes aren't the same color anymore."

Then the song ended, and then he walked away just like that. Nothing else but leaving with wondering what he meant by that. Is that why he's always staring at me like that? To confirm that my eyes have changed in a span of a year and half? What the hell was wrong with him?

AFTER THAT DANCE, I tried to look around for Cooper because I wanted answers. But as always, he disappeared. I even ran out in the parking lot looking for him, I saw his pickup but not him. Where the hell could he have gone?

I walk back into the building and walk back into the reception room. Everyone still carried on with dancing and Ryder was still in the same spot, sipping on a bud light. I decided to go over with Ryder and sit with them. I'm sure he saw me dancing with Cooper, and I need to know he has to say about it.

So I pull out a chair and plop down beside him and look at him, he side eyes me and then looks back at the crowd of people. "That just kind of happened." I say in a sad reasoning tone.

"I saw." He said and drank another gulp of his beer.

"Are you mad at me?" I say and move my head lower, trying to get him to look at me.

"I'm mad that I don't know if I should be or not." It was an eye opener when he said that and looked at me in the eyes.

"Well I can tell you it didn't mean anything."

He stood up and put on his cowboy hat and sighed, "Maybe to you it didn't, but I saw how he looked at you. It definitely meant something to him." I didn't know what to do but see there and look bewildered. And I didn't do anything when he tipped his hat to me and left me alone.

I was awake, but I didn't want to open my eyes and ruin sleeping in with Cooper. My head was on on the soft spot of his shoulder while he was laying flat on his back, his left arm spread out for me. He was so warm I didn't want to leave him, just wanted to stay there forever.

I don't remember how we ended up in the bed, or how he ended up shirtless and me wearing his tee shirt. But I do remember us cuddling last night on the couch for hours. We didn't say much but that was okay. It was romantic enough watching the lightning in the huge sky of the mountains. It was just like the night we first got together. It was perfect to me.

Maybe I should make us some breakfast, I wonder if he had any food here. Opening my eyes, I sighed at the sight before me. The sun was shining through the blinds, making Cooper's skin glow and accenting his defined muscles. With the sun rays shining in, I could see the tiny dust particles floating in the air, making it seem like a dream. I moved my head slightly to see Cooper's head turned away from me and his eyebrows furred together, deeply asleep.

I leaned up and kissed the sharp edge of his jaw. Then I carefully rolled away from him and got out of bed and stood up on the wooden floor. I started walking the door when I heard, "Hey girly." I couldn't help but smile ear to ear at his nickname for me. I turned around and walked closer to him. "What are you doing?" His voice was so light and happy, it melted my heart. He was so cute when he looked like this, all lovey-dovey and all.

"I was gonna make us breakfast." I say softly and then he groans softly as he smiles romantically and grabs my hand lightly.

He shakes his head and pouts a little, "Come lay with me." He starts to lay back, still holding my hand in his, making me fall with him. I giggle as I fall on him, and then he wraps his arms around me and flips us around so he's on top. As we lay in the middle of the bed, he uses both of his arms to hover over me. He uses a soft finger to move a piece of hair out of my face, and then he looks at me. I wish mental pictures were a thing, because if they were I would take one right now.

Cooper's face read that he was content, proud, and in love. It was the most beautiful face I had ever seen. He was smiling like a fool, it made my heart melt into a big gushy puddle. "You are so beautiful." He whispers as he looks around my face.

I lean up and he leans down connecting our lips for another breath taking kiss. I don't care what anyone says, morning kisses are the best. Somehow you can't the notice the bad breath, how could you when the love of your life is kissing you?

The kiss was short, but I didn't care. He looked down at me and we both smirked like fools in love. Then I wrapped my arms around his shoulders and brought him down onto my body and then we rolled around in the bed. The room was full of laughter and giggles, from us wrestling and tickling each other. While I was wrestling Coop, and he was ticking me.

Somehow I got on top and straddled his waist and smirked triumphantly, "I won." His hands went to the side of my thighs and rested there.

"I'm the real winner." There he goes again making the face, the face every girl wants to see from her man.

I blush and push on his chest and then get off him and off the bed. "C'mon lets get food." I say as I leaned against the door frame.

He had his hands behind his head, looking me up and down, really making me blush. "I missed you wearing my shirts." I broke my toothless smile, to hide my blush I turned my head and left the room and headed for the kitchen.

I opened all of the cabinets to find some type of food. All I have is some eggs, cheese, and some milk. I guess I'll just make us some omelets. I go back to the cabinet where I think had the pots and pans. When I bend back up, my backside rubs against a hard body and my back his against a hard chest. I can feel his breath against my neck, and then starts to run his fingers up down my arms. "Can you ever just stop touching me?" I joke with him as I lean back into him.

"Never." Then he places a kiss right below my ear. Then another, and another, and one more at the base of my neck. I reach up and place my hand behind his neck and turn in his arms and immediately kiss him. He pushes my hips more into his and deepens the kiss. I run my fingers through his hair, slightly tugging at the long curly locks.

Then his hands run over my butt and to the the back off my thighs and lifts me up and sits me down on the counter. He slips between my legs and I wrap and locks my legs around him. He puts his hands right beside my thighs as my hands hold his scruffy face. We devour each other's lips, with every kiss, we want more than we can get.

Breaking our kiss, his lips travel down my neck, slowly sucking on some spots. He didn't forget my sweet spots. "Cooper, I really am hungry."

He moans, "Mhm, so am I." Then he hungrily kisses me again, making me laugh in our kiss.

"You're gonna suck my face off, if you don't stop." I mumble against his lips.

"Fine, but I'm just trying to make up for a year and half." He smirks as he lets me hop off the counter and start to make breakfast.

COOPER AND I SAT ON the raggedy porch in some reclinable lawn chairs. We sat them right beside each other so we could still hold hands. It was a beautiful morning here in the mountains. The sun was bright, spreading it's lights through the spaces of the branches of the spruce trees. It wasn't too frigid out, especially with the help of Cooper's sweatshirt and a blanket we shared.

Cooper was looking off in the distance, not noticing me admiring him. He had a little stubble on his face, something that will probably get shaved off later. Cooper was never one for facial hair. His hair covered the tops of his ears, still messy from his bed hair. I smiled softly when I noticed his peaceful expression while looking out on the wilderness.

I unlocked my fingers from his and reached up and ran my fingers to the top of his ear, pushing the little hair behind his ear. Then I rested my hand on the back of his neck, causing him to turn and look at me. "Where did you go?" I curiously asked him in a soft voice.

"What do you mean?" He asks me, furring his eyebrows.

"After you got out, where did you go?"

He sighs heavily and looks back at the mountains, "I went back to Arkansas for a bit, and then I went everywhere I could."

"Why?" I asked him.

"To apologize to the families my dad wronged." He said and looked back at me with sad and heartbroken eyes. I ran my fingers through his hair, trying to comfort him.

"You know that isn't your responsibility, Cooper." I know he feels bad about the damage has caused families, just like he did to his own family.

"I know, but sitting in that cell just made me realize how shitty it was to lose someone to something stupid. My dad put a lot of innocent men into jail, leaving their families behind. I just thought if I went to them and told them that he's in jail, they might feel better." He sounded like he already knew it didn't work.

But I don't think he knows how it feels to know that the person who hurt you the most can't do it again. It gives someone a sense of relief, but it still doesn't change the past. "Cooper, look at me." He sadly picks up his head and looks me in the eyes, "When they told me that they caught Wade and put him in jail, I felt so relieved and safe again. The pain I was in lessened when I heard it. That's what you did for those families. That's all you can do, and you did it." He just gave me a small appreciated nod and half smile, and then I said, "I'm so proud of you for doing that."

"Thanks DaKota." He turned that half smile into a full one.

"What made you come back?" I asked him out of curiosity. He gave me a pointed look, saying that I should know why, but I rolled my eyes. "No seriously. You could of took all the time in the world trying to fix your dad's mistakes."

"I wanted to see how you were doing." He says as he looks back at the mountains. Then he laughs to himself, confusing me. "That's a lie," he looks back at me with a goofy grin and leans towards me. "I wanted to see if you were still with Ryder."

For some reason it made me blush, I had to bite my lip to keep me from smiling. "Oh." Then I played with the blanket, distracting me from his staring.

"Which you still are," He says in a soft matter-of-fact tone. "Why do we always get together when you're with someone else?" He laughs but I decide to break the moment for him.

"Actually.." I say and look at him, raising one of my eyebrows.

He scrunches his eyebrows in confusion, "Actually what?"

"Ryder broke up with me yesterday before I came." I look back down at the blanket's frayed edges.

"Now why the hell would someone do that." He made me smile when he said that because it was quite ironic.

"He was there when I opened the gift from you. He told he basically knew I was still in love with you the whole time and that I wouldn't love him as much as I love you." I said shyly as I tucked a piece of hair behind my ear.

"Is it true?" This made me perk of my head and tilt it back against my chair.

"Of course it is." I said confidently and then moved my hand from his neck and brought it to his cheek and rubbed my thumb gently over it. "He wasn't even close."

"I know, Molly told me."

"When did you speak to Molly?" I asked him raising my eyebrow.

"At the wedding. She found me sitting alone and she said she noticed me staring at you the whole night. She told me how Ryder isn't as near as good for you as I am, and told me things about him." Typical Molly move, I love her. I'll have to thank her later.

"What things?" I ask him.

"Like he has never got you flowers and never danced with you, stuff like that." I just nodded and looked back down at the blanket. I notice him lean even closer to me, less than an arm's length. Then he put a fist on each side of my leg. "So how much more romantic am I?" He had a boyish smirk on his face, making me laugh.

"There's not even a comparison for that." I blushed as I looked into his deep brown eyes.

"Go on." He encouraged me with his eyes and amused smile. He loved making me blush and get all flustered in front of him.

"Well," I sighed, "You give me butterflies every time I see you. You do little random cute things that mean a lot more than you know. You go out of your way to make me happy. You don't feel the need to be constantly texting me. You know my dreams. You don't change when you're around your friends. You kiss me the right way-"

"He didn't pressure you into anything did he?" He says in a protective voice.

"No, no." I shook my head.

"Good, because if he did I might go back to jail for assault."

I cock my head and glare at him, "That's not funny." Then I start to pout because it made me sad to think about him being gone for that long.

"I know, I know. I'm sorry honey." He swoons and slides down his chair more to wrap his arms around my waist, looking up at me. "I couldn't go another year and half without my girl." He makes it up with his sweet talk. I look down at him and smile sheepishly, and then he pouts, "Give me some suga.'" I giggle and then lean down and lock my lips with his.

I PARKED IN MY USUAL spot in the grass of my home. I'll be honest, I was a little nervous to walk in that door. I could only imagine the assumptions they thought of while I was taking care of business. It's about two o'clock in the afternoon. It took hours for Cooper and I to convince ourselves we should go home. All we did is talk about each other, and occasionally get caught up in kissing each other. Okay, the kissing happened more then I let up.

Putting on my my big girl pants on, I walk up the steps of my porch and walk into my house. I don't see anyone in the kitchen, but as I look in the living room I see four heads peaking around the furniture to look at me. I felt like I was doing the walk of shame by the way they were looking at me. "So?" My mother was the first to ask.

I blush and stick my hands in my back pockets, "Cooper and I are back-"

"Aha! That will be twenty dollars missy!" Caleb cheers victoriously as he looks at Ashley pointedly. Ashley cusses to herself and then pulls out twenty dollars and slaps it in Caleb's hands without looking at him.

"You guys bet on me and Cooper?" I asked them.

They all looked guilty, I was waiting for someone to explain more. "We were seeing how long it would take you guys. Your dad and I thought it would be the day after the church incident. Ashley though it would be a couple of days, and Caleb predicted a week." My mom says to me as she sits back in her chair. Ashley still looks pissed she lost to my brother.

"Does Ryder know?" Caleb asks me as he tucks his prize money in his pocket.

"He was the one to walk away, last night." My dad speaks up. I furrow my eyebrows in how he would know that. "That kid looked like he made the stupidest decision of his life and he couldn't believe it himself. And your mother told me about Cooper coming in." He explained himself into figuring out Ryder and I broke up.

"Are you happy?" My mother asks as she rests her hand on her fist to look at me.

I blush even more and bite my lip, "Incredibly."

I'm currently at the clinic, doing about three hours of paperwork that I missed yesterday because it was my birthday. It was only me and a couple of other vet assistants. The VA's were checking up on all the animals we had staying over night for a day or two. Now that I am finished with my paperwork, I'm going to head over to the diner to hang out and relax. I laugh at myself, because I'll be doing more paperwork and bills.

I walk into the diner and I look around to see if I can see any eyes already looking at me. Just a few, which I was grateful for. I'm not sure if people have heard what has happened in the last 24 hours of my life, they usually know by now. Or they just didn't care. Anyways, I was glad the attention wasn't on me.

I greet May and then I go back into my office and go into my cabinet drawer and grab the most recent file. Instead of sitting in this congested office, I decide to go out in the diner and maybe order some food. Once I find a booth to sit in, I grab my headphones from my pockets and put them in my ears and start to listen to Johnny Cash radio.

From my knowledge of the paperwork, business has been keeping steady. The winter isn't our most popular time of year because of less tourists. But as the whether gets colder, families choose to eat out instead of cooking at home. Plus, we have great hot chocolate that we add marshmallows to and great coffee. As I'm reading the data on the sheet, a body slides into the booth with me, shoulder to shoulder.

Before I look up, I recognize the calming warmth and sparks. I pull out my headphones and then I look at my handsome man. "Hey." He smiles at me, and then I realize he has two bowls of sundaes in his hands. His eyes venture off mine and then to my paperwork. His smile pulls down into a grimace, making me snicker. "I was wondering what you were doing over here." He looks over them more, putting down the bowls.

"Why didn't you tell me you were here earlier?" I ask as I turn my body towards him. I look him over, he is wearing his leather rodeo jacket with a hoodie underneath it and his regular jeans and boots. His hair looked smooth and flattering on him, man I was lucky.

"I was getting ice cream." He shrugs like a little kid, making me roll my eyes. Then he takes his spoons and gets a spoonful of ice cream and a little chunk of brownie with it. "Reese is going to be so jealous." As he says this, my eyes wonder over the booth and I see almost everybody looking at us and whispering. "What's wrong?" He asks with a clear mouth.

I realize that I'm frowning and then I turn back to him and softly say, "Everybody is looking at us."

"That's because they wanna know if y'all are back together and if you dumped Ryder." Maybell's voice suddenly says as she stands on the other side of the booth with a coffee pot in hand. She must of heard them talking as she was refilling. I don't know why, but that made me feel sad. They probably just think I used Ryder to get with Cooper.

I just keep my face neutral as I look down at the table. Through my peripheral vision I see Cooper look at me with a deciding cocked jaw, and then he grabs my hand and pulls me out of the booth. "What are you doing?" I whisper to him.

He walks us to the front of the diner, where everyone can see us. We stood in front of each other and I stared at Cooper, waiting for him to do something. After he looked around the diner, making sure he had everyone's attention, he grabbed both of my cheeks and brought me in for a kiss. I was shocked, but I quickly melted into him and grabbed his wrists. I knew he was trying to prove something, but damn, this kiss was amazing.

Cooper pulled away from my lips, leaving me standing there with my eyes closed. Then he put his arms around my shoulders and pressed me into his chest. "Does that answer your questions?" He asked in a slightly frustrated tone.

When no one said anything, Cooper was satisfied and then lead me back to the booth. I was starstruck by his action, I couldn't stop thinking about his kiss. It was our first public kiss. And it felt like our very first one, a feeling I will never forget.

As I sat down, I realized how romantic that was. He just declared our love for each other in front of everyone, and he didn't even think about it twice. "What was that?" I asked him in a shocked tone.

Cooper just reached over the table and handed me my bowl of ice cream and grabbed his own. "I could tell you were upset by everyone talking about us, and I decided shut them up. Because you don't deserve to be unhappy DaKota Jones." He was so casual about it, I fell about 10 times more in love with him.

"I love you." Cooper smiled to himself knowingly.

"I love you more." He said, then I decided to eat some of my ice cream. When he was eating his brownie with his ice cream, he said, "Did the photographer take individual pictures at the wedding?" That was random.

"Yeah, I think she took a couple of each person in the wedding party." I said casually and confused at the same time.

"Good," He swallowed, "Because you looked hot." I felt my cheeks start to get warm, he swallowed again. "And I mean, really fucking hot." The color of my cheeks deepened times 100 when he added that last statement.

I smacked his shoulder for making me blush and he started to laugh. "I hate you." I laughed.

Cooper put down his ice cream bowl and then opened his arms and grabbed my body and lifted me into his lap, and I sat on him sideways as you would sit on Santa's lap. "Oh no you don't." He said confidently as

I was laughing. He wrapped his left around around my torso and placed his hand on my thigh.

"You're right." I said stopping my laugh, looking deep into his warm chocolate eyes and wrap my arms around his neck. "I really fucking hate you." I mocked him and he rolled his eyes at me and leaned up for a passionate kiss.

It was a no brainer, I really loved this man.

Cooper's point of view

I PUT MY EMPTY CEREAL bowl into the dishwasher, and as I was walking away I realize my mom forgot her cellphone here. Classic one mom. I'll remember that the next time she tells me I didn't answer my phone on the first time. I did know where she was though, DaKota's birthday party.

I spent two hours contemplating if I was going to go or not. For one, I didn't have a gift for her. Two, I would of made it awkward with all her friends and family there, not to mention Ryder. Three, I was afraid I was going to make matters worse. What that meant, I had no idea. It could of gone one way, but also a way different way.

So I decided to stay home and watch TV. But to deal with my boredom and new found sadness, I decided to look through my mom's photos on her phone. I know she only had pictures of Reese and I, so maybe it would bring back good memories.

I started maybe from three years ago, this woman needed to learn how to download her photos onto the computer. Most of them were us packing our things from our old house, and then us unpacking our things here. I smiled when I stopped on one where I was pretending to pack Reese into a box with the packing peanuts, man I loved my brother and his smile.

As I scrolling through, one picture caught my eye. As I went back to find it, my smile turned into a heartbroken frown. I had never seen this picture before. It was from when DaKota helped us deliver the calves. She was in between my legs, tired from doing all the work. Man she looked so beautiful, even with the sweat beads on her forehead, and her cow stained gloves. And my face showed it. I've never seen myself look like that, so in love.

Right there and then, that picture changed it all for me. I knew what I had to do, and I had to do it now. I stood up from the couch and marched over to where our computer was, and then I connected the phone to the computer.

I stood outside of the Jones' house and debated my whole idea as I looked down at the present I had in my hands. This was the exact feeling I had when I came here to ask Mr. Jones if I could take DaKota out on a date. That is when it all started, the greatest day of my life. This was my only chance, I had to do it.

I knocked on the door and not long after DaKota's mom opened the door, really surprised at who she saw. I didn't blame her. "Cooper." She said in a happy surprise voice, then she looked down at the gift. "Come in."

"Thank you." I said and then took off my hat as I entered her home. I automatically looked around for Colby, thank God he wasn't in here.

"DaKota isn't here, but if you want-"

"No, I know ma'am.. Uh, I was just wondering if I could put this in her bedroom." I said and motioned towards the gift.

"Yeah, go ahead." She was hiding her confusion, but I could still tell. I give her a polite nod and then make my way up to DaKota's bedroom.

I open the door and see nothing has changed, except for new photos of her and Ryder. The feelings of the old memories of me being in here flood my body, making me smile to myself. Deciding not to seem like a creep, I place the gift on the middle of her bed and then head back downstairs. "Thank ya ma'am." I said and tip my hat to her. She says nothing to me, still in shock that I even showed up.

I LEANED MY FOREARMS against the shower walls, rethinking everything. Did I make a mistake? Is this going to make her hate me even more? What did I expect will happen? Why did I come to my cabin? Now she's going to think I ran away again. I am such an idiot.

But then more confident thoughts come into mind.

I remember the way she looked at me during church. She was surprised yet happy to see me. And at the wedding, one of the reasons I fell on love with her came back to me. During the speech she made everyone fall in love with her. She is so kind, genuine, and funny. Then I remember what Molly told me at the wedding. She told me how Ryder is a shitty boyfriend, and doesn't treat her as well as she should be. How he doesn't compare to me.

I saw living proof of it. He wouldn't even dance with her! Now, that's just fucking stupid. That's why I danced with her that night. Man it felt so good to hold her again, and she looked.. So fucking beautiful it hurt myself to think that I let her go. As I looked in her eyes, I knew something was different. Her eyes were dull, but still beautiful. They were more vibrant when she was with me, but now, they were normal. And my dumb mouth told her. I really beat myself up for that one.

I knew what we had wasn't something someone was lucky enough to have. We had a real connection, and strongest bond I have ever felt in my life. She was my everything, but I couldn't have her. She was too good for me.

That's why I didn't visit her while I was in jail. I knew if I even just saw her once, I ruin her life. I would keep her waiting for me until I got out. I couldn't do that to her. She had too much potential in her future. Now look at her, she's a vet, at the age of 20. Who can say that in their life?

I pulled the tee shirt down my chest as I walked over to the burning fire and then ran my fingers through my hair. I stopped in my tracks when I thought I heard something outside, but realize it was probably the storm. I sit down in front of the fire place, and pull my kneels to my chest and then crossing my ankles and wrapping my arms around my knees.

I liked it out here, it was quiet. Quiet enough to hear yourself think, but not too quiet that you feel isolated. During my moment of peace, I jumped when I heard the front door slam open. "What the hell is this."

DaKota said in a demanding voice, holding the picture in her hand. Her body language told me she wasn't going to take any bullshit from me, it was very intimidating and sexy at the same time.

I didn't know what to do, I didn't think she was going to come up here. I didn't know what to say to her. I wanted her to explain what she thought it meant. She turned her head to the wall and bit her lip, and then looks back at me with fire in her eyes. "And what the hell is up with that whole 'mysterious' look? That's all you do, you stare at me and say nothing! You just came back from a year and half in jail and say nothing?! Not even a 'Hey DaKota, it's nice to see you' or 'how are you'? All I get is a dance with no words exchanged. Oh wait nevermind, I did get a 'your eyes aren't the same color'. So makes it a little bit better." I knew what she said was true, I was being really weird. I couldn't help it, she made me feel so nervous and scared that she wouldn't care about me anymore. But she had to know what I felt.

"They have changed color." I say in a soft confident tone.

"Yeah so what?" She restrained herself from rolling her eyes.

"When we were together they were greener, now they're more brown." I tell her gain, trying to get her pick up what I'm putting down.

"You're going to have to elaborate more for me." Man, she is a sharp woman.

I think about spilling my whole shower thoughts to her but then I realize I don't have any valid points. "It doesn't matter." I sigh and look back into the fire.

I see her walk around the couch and stand five feet away from me. "Why doesn't it matter, Cooper?" A fire lit inside me when she said my name, making me look at her.

Looking at her hurt expression made all the feelings of getting her back disappear. This is what I was afraid of, hurting her. "Because I must be wrong."

"Wrong about what?" She asks clearly frustrated.

Screw it. "I keep trying to convince myself that you aren't happier with the Baker kid, but every time I see you guys I always see you guys laughing or kissing." I knew she was going to protest so I cut her off, "I tried talking to you, but like I said, you were always with him. After church I was going to talk to you at the diner, but then I saw you kissing him in the booth. Then I realized me coming back must of not affected you." I meant it, I told myself multiple times to go up to her and talk to her, but he always got in the way.

"Not affected me?" She was really hurt now, it showed in her tone, "How can you even say that? That I didn't care?" Her tone worsened, she was crying now. Way to go Cooper. "What you can't tell that I cared when I went to visit you in jail for six months even though you never talked to me? I prayed and prayed that you would just talk to me. That I would get to see you, hear you. I cried for months over you! I put my life on hold for you! You don't get to say that I didn't care." She yelled at me, it didn't really affect me. I know I deserve it. "I should be the one saying that you didn't care. You left me wondering if I was still in a relationship. You left me questioning what I did wrong. I asked you to meet me after you got out and you didn't. I just wanted to know how you were doing. Was that so much to ask for?"

I wasn't going to meet her because I didn't want to instantly fall back in love with her after a year and a half. I knew if I saw her, it would be hard for me not to kiss her and convince her to run away with me.

But after looking at my lock screen of the picture of us, I decided to go, hoping she was still there. She was there alright, but with him instead. I was hurt to see her with another guy, especially to see her having so much fun with him. It hit me real hard to know I wasn't the only one to make her happy. "I was there!" I yelled back, she needed to know. "I was there enough to see you having fun dancing on the bar and then dancing with Ryder. Before I got there I told myself I was going to try to get you back, but then I saw that you didn't need me to be happy."

She was shocked to know the truth about that night, she even looked a little guilty, "You obviously have never seen me drunk." Drunk? There was no way she could of been drunk. She never had more than two beers.

"You were drunk? You don't even drink." I discretely scoff at her, looking back at the fire.

"That's what a massive heart break will do to you." That made me look back at her. "And guess what now? I don't care anymore." I knew she didn't mean it, if she didn't care, she wouldn't be here right now. Then the glare of the fire made her neck shine, and I remembered what I saw the other day.

I aggressively walked in front of her, close enough to make her nervous. I lightly grabbed the necklace chain and held it in front of her. "If you didn't care, then why do you still wear my necklace?"

She was completely awestruck that I even knew about it. I really got her there. "H-how did you know?"

Realizing my place, I took a couple steps back and then leaned my left forearm against the mantle of the fireplace, "I saw it fall out of your shirt when you were checking on JW." I admit.

It became silent, she was the one who didn't know what to say now. Then she sniffles, trying to clear her tears. "Did you mean it?" She suddenly asks me.

"Mean what?"

"That you're still in love with me." My heart skipped a beat at this question, it knew what it wanted.

I looked her square in the eyes, telling her I had no doubt to my answer. "Yes." She dropped her and I saw more tears fall.

"Then why are you acting like this?" She looked back at me.

I sighed as I scraped a split of wood, "My dad was right, I did and will ruin your future." I threw the little piece in the fire. "I can't be with you." I admitted to her, telling her I felt.

"Cooper, you're not thinking of the actual reason I was so depressed during those months." She says and then steps towards me. "I was so sad because I didn't have you. I didn't care you were in jail. That was the least of my problems. I knew you were innocent, I was there, with you. Cooper, in those three months, you changed my life for the better. I don't know how you did it, but I trusted you with everything. I told you things I thought I'd never tell anyone. You didn't run away, you stood there with me. I didn't even tell Ryder what happened to me, that's how scared I was that he would think of my differently." She didn't tell him? Has she told anyone? I knew she didn't feel the same way about him. "You made me feel like none of that bad stuff even happened to me. You made me feel.. alive. You gave me butterflies every time I saw you. You touched me like no one else could. You kissed me like no one else could. You loved me much more than anyone else will. I didn't think I would find anyone who could remotely make me feel the way you do. Cooper, it's you. If I had to choose from any one in this whole wide world, it would always be you." She was making this really hard for me. I felt like I had the devil on one shoulder and an angel on the other, and they were going to war with each other. Making my head go crazy inside.

I was trying to think of something to say to that. Why was this so difficult for me? I just need to rip the band aid off and tell her- "So are you gonna kiss me or not?" She made my life a lot easier when she said what she just said.

I knew what I wanted now, and I desperately wanted her. I needed her. I charged over to her and grabbed her beautiful face and hungrily smashed my lips on hers.

Fuck.

Her lips were softer and tasted better than I remembered. It's been way too long. My heart was full when she grabbed my shirt and pulled me closer to her. I tried to give her the best kiss she ever had, putting everything I had into it.

We both pulled away as we both needed air from our intense kiss. We leaned our heads together and I said softly, "God, I love you." and then I dipped my head to capture her lips again.

I put even more passion into this kiss, making it very heated and hot. My body went crazy when she tangled her fingers in my hair, I loved when she did that. I tightened my hold against her, bringing her impossibly closer. God dammit, not now. My body was getting too excited for this moment. I sadly pulled away from our kiss and breathed out frustrated. "If we don't stop now, I don't think I'll be able to later." She looked slightly down, where one part of my body was closer than other parts were.

DaKota then hugged me tightly, like this moment wasn't real, and then I heard her sniffle. "Hey why are you crying?" I ask her softly, and pull her back to see the reasoning. She looked a little embarrassed so I wiped her tears for her, I hated seeing her crying.

"I just missed you so much." Oh my lord, she is too cute for her own good. My heart was currently the happiest it has ever been.

I really tried not to smile in front of her ,"I missed you too." but a laugh did escape my mouth. She hit my shoulder, making me smile even more. "C'mon lets sit down."

Before we sat down, I moved the couch to where we could watch the storm, yet be by the fire. I realized the blinds were closed, so I opened them again. I sat down on the couch first and then she sat down on my left and buried her head into the crook of my neck, such a baby, a cute baby though. I reached behind me and grabbed my grandma's old blanket and placed it over us. "Oh and DaKota." I said remembering something.

"Hmm?" She said, snuggling closer to me.

"Happy birthday." I smirked knowing she was rolling her eyes at me.

I WOKE UP WITH THE biggest smile on my face. Why? Because I didn't have a night terror last night. I haven't had one since the night Cooper and I got back together. I know, cliche, but it's true. He makes me feel so safe and secure, that I guess stuck in my head and made my dreams go away. Now my dreams consist of Cooper and I's future, the best dreams I've ever had.

My smile faded when I realized I had to go to work. Don't get me wrong, I love my job and am very thankful for it, but I have worked everyday and been on call every night. So I've barely seen Cooper this week. But today is Friday, so I am not on call! Anyways, I get out of bed and hop in the shower.

I look at myself in the mirror and smooth out my black scrubs and move my hair to the correct place I like it to be. It was still wet, but it was going in a pony no matter what, so I didn't care what it looked like. I looked at my phone to see if I had any messages, none. Strange, Cooper usually sends me a good morning text. I shrug it off, maybe he's sleeping in.

When I get to the clinic I already see it is going to be a busy day ahead of me. I took off my light coat and put it on the coat rack and then go to my desk. I clock in and then log in on my computer to see my schedule and sigh to see I literally have no times for breaks.

It's not even noon yet, and I am already having a shitty day. My first call was to a farm to help calf and the birthing went smooth, but the mother stepped on my foot twice. If haven't been stomped on by a cow before, you have no clue about the pain if you've never felt it. So now I am walking with a limp.

Then my next appointment was a yearly check up with a cat. And what a surprise, the cat scratched my right wrist and caused me to bleed. I hated cats ever since I was a little kid. And when cats do this, it makes me dislike them even more.

Then I had to go to another farm and give a llama some arthritis shots in the joints of its knee. The injection part when smoothly, the old llama didn't really care. But when I was checking its teeth, he spit on me. I mean all over my face, it was lovely.

I should of called in sick today.

Slamming the door of my pickup, I grab a new scrub shirt from the back and walk back in the clinic to see a full waiting room. And I notice cat carriers. Just freaking great. I quickly get changed into my shirt, because now I only had a 15 minuet lunch.

Grabbing my lunch from my fridge, I sit down at my desk and try to finish reports and eat at the same time. I try not to eat that fast so my stomach will get upset and then I throw up during a surgery. "Dr. Jones, I have a concern about my baby." An unfamiliar voice says behind me.

I close my eyes, trying to be patient. Patients always think they can come back here and question the medicine we give their "babies". But as I turn in my chair to talk to the patient, I realize the patient is Cooper.

My frown turns into a smile, and it turns into a bigger one once I realize he's holding flowers. How sweet! "What are the flowers for?" I say as I limp over to him and kiss his cheek and grab the beautiful wild flowers.

"Why are you limping?" He ignores my question.

"A cow stomped on me." I said and then he makes an 'o' shape with his mouth, because he knows how much that hurts. "So?"

"We're having a date tonight." He smiles proudly as he follows me to my desk.

"We are?" I ask him as I replace my old flowers with my new ones.

"Yes ma'am, at 7 o'clock in our special spot." He winks at me, making me blush. Our "special spot" was the one in the sage grass where we went to get away from everyone, and occasionally make out. "And where something pretty." He says suspiciously.

"What's the occasion?" I eye him up and down, as he rocks back and fourth on his heels.

"No occasion, we're just having a picnic." He shrugs and then I look back the clock, crap.

I stand up and lean up and kiss his check again, and he puts his hand on my elbow as I do so. "Thanks again for the flowers, I've got to back to work."

WITH MY USUAL LUCK, my day got worse. A hamster bit me, another cat scratched me on the same exact spot, a little girl started crying when I gave her dog shots, and I had to put a dog down. That's what I hated most about this job, putting animals to rest. It was the absolute worst thing I ever have to do.

But now, I get to go on a date with my incredibly hot boyfriend who makes me forget about those bad things. But first, I gotta get ready.

So I turn on my music and turn it on shuffle. Who knows what kind of music can come on. It could literally go from Earnest Tubb to Tupac, it's not safe to say. Anyways I put my hair into a bun as I step in the shower, I just needed to was my body and shave.

I just finished my hair, and I looked at the time 7:00, I was running way late. I'm sure he'll be here any second now! But I couldn't rush doing my makeup! Well if I'm going to be late, might as well take my time.

After I'm pleased with my makeup, I look at the time only 7:15, awesome. Now I had to choose my outfit, now that might take me a while. I decide to let Cooper know I might be awhile. As I open my door

I hear him and my dad talking about something, what? I don't know. "Cooper, I still have to pickup out my outfit!" I yelled down.

"Okay, take your time!" He replies, making me smile appreciatively.

I look at myself in the mirror, pleased with my look. My hair was classically pinned back the usual way I do it. My makeup wasn't smudged and my dressed looked great with my eyes and dark hair. I decided not to wear any jewelry, so my chest was bare. I was finally ready. I looked at the time and it was only 7:15.

I grabbed my phone and headed down the steps. When I reached the bottom of the stairs, I saw my dad and Cooper shaking each other's hands. I smiled because of their new relationship. When me and Cooper got back together, my dad became more accepting of Cooper and started to treat him like family. Which I hope he will be some day.

When Cooper looked at me his jaw dropped, making me blush. The way he looked at me set my insides on fire, "You look great." The two most important men of my life said at the same time.

"Thank you." I said and kissed both of them on the cheek. Cooper also looked good. He was wearing charcoal pear snap long sleeve, creased Wranglers, a gold buckle, and a black felt hat.

"Ready?" Cooper asks me as he looks around and feels around in his pockets, and then stops when he finds what he's looking for.

"Yep, bye dad." I say as we walk away from him.

Not much was said on our drive to our special place, but I didn't mind. It was beautiful day today. Probably around 55 degrees and no wind and no cloud in the sky. It was May, so the whether was getting nicer and nicer, getting me excited for summer.

Cooper opened the door for me to get out and I thanked him and stepped out. As I took a couple of steps, I realized I shouldn't of worn hills in the country. "Cooper." I stop him and he turns to look at me and I look down at my feet.

I start to take off my heels, "Wait." He said and hurried over to me. "Get on my back." He said.

"Cooper we have to go up hill."

"Are you doubting my strength?" He jokes, "And I don't want you to stress your foot."

My foot actually wasn't too bad anymore, but I won't let him know that. So I throw my heels in the box of his pickup and then climb onto his back. He had me carry the picnic basket as he held onto my legs and then made the journey to our special place.

I laid down the blanket and Cooper laid out the food. Tonight he brought PB&J's because he said they have no food at their house, but I didn't mind. He also had some fruit and summer sausage, so it all made for a good meal.

"Should we play 20 questions?" He asked me as he finished chewing.

"Sure, I can go-"

"I'll go first." He quickly says making me raise an eyebrow. I take a bite of my sandwich and wait for him to start.

Cooper is sitting crossed legged kitty corner to me, as I use my arms to support me as I sit up with my legs stretched in front of me. He clears his throat to begin, "Do you know how beautiful you look right now?" I blush at his compliment.

"Do you know how cheesy you are?" I smile at him and he smirks back at me.

"No questions, missy." I stick my tongue out at him.

"How was the rest of your day?" He asks me and then I tell him about my problems and he tells me his idea of handling things, but I didn't consider them professional. He was mostly joking anyways.

"Do you know what today is?" I scrunch my eyebrows at him at his odd question.

"Friday." I laugh awkwardly and he rolls his eyes.

"The date, girly."

Oh duh, "Um the 19th?"

"And that is?" Well I know for a fact it isn't his birthday, nor is it an anniversary, so what could it be? I raise my eyebrows, giving up. "May 19th is the first day we met in the diner." Holy sweet baby Jesus, could my man get even more romantic? How did he even remember that?

"So is that what this date is?" I ask him and he smirks at me, making me worried.

"Sort of." Then he looks over a couple of feet in front of us, "Do you remember what I promised you over there?" He said and pointed to the spot he was looking at. I looked and remembered what happened there. It was the day we decided we were going to tell my dad that we were going out. I remember being very afraid of what the outcome would be, but Cooper assured me everything would be okay because he would be right by my side the whole time. I closed my eyes, replaying that moment in my mind, remembering how sure his voice sounded. I love him so much.

"Yeah, you promised me you would stay by my side no matter what." I say as I still look at the spot.

"So will you promise me the same thing?"

I was confused on what he meant, so I turned to look at him. My breath caught in my throat because my heart jumped into my air way when I saw him on one kneeling holding a black velvet box. My jaw literally dropped 10 feet, and I stared at the box and then looked at him. "Cooper.." I dragged on in case it was a joke.

"DaKota, you are by far the most important thing in my life. I never stop thinking about you and I always want to be with you. You are the greatest person I have ever met in my life to this day and will ever be. You are so kind, caring, loving, forgiving, genuine, empowering, inspiring, strong, smart, and perfect. You have made me into a man who I thought I would never be, and I am so thankful for that. We have been through thick and thin together and knowing that I know we can get through anything together life throws at us." I could feel the water works coming and I knew they were gonna fall if he didn't stop now. "I don't know if I told you this before, but before I met you, I didn't believe in love. But as always, you proved me wrong. I'm pretty sure I fell head first the third time I talked to you." Yep, he did it, a tear broke the barrier. "I love you so much I'm pretty sure it's a crime. So DaKota Annie Jones, will you promise to stand by me for the rest of our lives?"

I wiped the bottoms of my eyes, cleaning off my mascara. I take a deep breath and nod, "Yes." and then I laugh happily and I see his shoulders relax.

"Yes?" He confirms my choice.

"Yes!" I say and then I jump into his arms and tackle him to the ground. He tightly wraps his arms around my back, extra tight this time.

After our moment, I get off him and we sit up again. We sit knee to knee as we look at each other. I couldn't believe it, Cooper asked to marry me! Taylor, Ashley, and my mom are going to freak! I'm freaking out right now! "I love you so much!" I cry as I grab his face and smash my lips on his.

I melt into his lips as we move perfectly with each other, like we always have. He pulls away too quick for my liking, "I forgot." He laughs and then holds the box in front of me. He slowly opens it again, and I stare at the box. Holy shit.

"Do you like it?" He nervously asks me.

With my mouth open, I nod. He smiles and then takes it out of the box and puts it on my ringer finger, which is shaking. "It's perfect, did Taylor help you?" If Taylor knew about it and didn't tell me, so help me God.

"No, I stalked your Pinterest." I began to laugh because that is such a Cooper thing to do, I bet he was too shy to ask for help. "Plus I thought Taylor would of ruined the surprise, and I guess I just know my girl." He says smugly making me smile more.

"I can't wait to be your wife." I proudly say as I look at the ring that perfectly fit my finger.

"Hmm, me either." He says huskily as he pulls me closer to me and kisses just below my ear and further down. He lowers me so we hit the ground, and then he spins so I'm on top and then we start to roll around in the grass as we laugh and kiss each other.

I can't wait to spend the rest of my life with him.

Today was the day, the day I get married to the love of my life. I was already counting the hours until I get to say "I do" and become Mrs. Blackwood, it gave me chills just thinking about it. But my chills quickly faded away when I realized the amount of heat I was in from the two bodies crowding me on the bed.

It was my two best friends, Ashley and Taylor, and my two maid of honors. That's right, I couldn't choose between them. Ashley is like my sister when she married into the family, and Taylor has been my sister ever since we were kids. So to make it easier on myself, I picked both them.

Ashley is due pretty soon, she's just a couple of weeks away and she is beyond ready to get my niece and Goddaughter out of there. I knew Ash and Caleb were excited to have a baby girl, Caleb probably more than Ash because "he'll get his favorite girl in a smaller vision and then have two". I am so glad Ash came in his life because 10 years ago, I would of never saw him saying that.

The alarm clock goes off, to the sound of church bells. Classic Taylor move. All the girls groan and turn on their sides. Last night was worse than Taylor's bacherlortte party, because now Taylor was fully involved, getting really wasted. We basically did the same thing we did that night, again going to Reza's. As soon as we stepped into the place, they recognized as and they demanded we dance on the bar. We didn't disappoint them. Until I told them I was the bride this time, then they got bummed that I was officially off the market.

"Good morning girls." Molly said as she sat up in their bed. I had a similar bridal party as Taylor: Molly, Ashley, Reyna, Jessica, Taylor, and Maybell. I somehow manage to convince Maybell to be in my wedding. She said she was too old, but I told that was nonsense. I was going to include my mom too, but she wanted to enjoy the time with my friends.

"What the hell did we do last night?" Taylor awakes pushing her hair out of her face. We all just laugh at her and then I climb out of bed to stretch.

"I'm going to make breakfast." I say to them.

"No! You're the bride, we have to make it for you!" Reyna said jumping out of the bed and beating me to the door. "You just go take a bath or shower and relax. We got this." Reyna said as she directed me over to the bathroom.

We were staying at her uncle's lake cabin, it was huge and beautiful. The exterior of the cabin was made out of red wood trees, and the interior was set of beautiful western decor and antique tools. I wish I lived here.

The rest of the girls followed Reyna and I continued to go into the bathroom. I plugged my phone into the speaker and turned it on to my "Thumbprint" radio.

WE MADE IT TO THE VENUE to my wedding, which I absolutely loved with all my heart. The place was surrounded by mountains and had a huge barn, and a dance floor outside of the barn. We would be getting ready in the hay loft of the barn, it had great lighting and made it feel like home.

But being here made me nervous for some reason. I wasn't scared of getting married, nor at the thought spending the rest of my life with one man. It was because I am starting a new chapter in my book of life, it was a huge step to take. I would officially become an adult. Cooper and I would start own on family, and hopefully add onto it.

My mom handed us our turquoise robes to put over our undergarments as we started to do our makeup and hair. I couldn't wait to see the girls looking all pretty in their bridesmaid dresses. I couldn't wait to see myself in my full hair and makeup and in my dressed that I was in love with. "Alright girls let's get dolled up!" Maybell said as she clapped her hands and wiggled her body, making us laugh.

We were all ready to put on our dresses. Our glowing makeup and flawless hair was finished and ready for the wedding. The girls put on their dresses first and when they all came out together, my heart melted into a huge puddle. They all looked so gorgeous, I was so happy to call them my best friends.

I ran over to them and we all did a group hug and I said to them, "Thank you for being here. It really means a lot to me. I love you guys." I almost started crying but Taylor scolded me.

"Do not ruin your makeup!" I heard the tears in her eyes, she was restricting them.

"Now put on your dress!" Ashley said, she looked extra glowing in her dress because of her pregnancy.

I went into the changing room and slid on my dress very carefully. I took a deep breath before I turned around. I had no idea what my hair or makeup looked like, so that's what I looked at first. My jaw dropped at how radiant I looked, I blew myself away.

Then I finally looked at my dress. It went perfectly with my hair, it looked perfect. My skin seemed to glow accordingly with the pure white of the lace and my dark skin. It was July, so my skin had tanned thankfully. The front of my dress had a straight neckline, almost see through just like the back. I loved how the shoulders almost disappeared as the crossed over. It allowed to see my collar bones, which was one of my favorite characteristics about myself. Looking in the back mirror, the dress allows people to see my wolf tattoo on my shoulder, I loved it.

With a shaky hand, I turned the handle of the door and exited the changing room. I walked slowly to the group of girls and they all gasped. The moment was surreal that I was getting married, I felt the tears in my eyes. "How do I look?" I ask them with a nervous chuckle.

"Like a super model out of a catalog." Jessica said, looking me over.

"I think it's missing something.." My mother said like she already had a solution. I watched her pull out a box and then walk over to me. I grabbed the box from her and furred my eyebrows, would could it be? My jaw dropped once I opened the box and saw the beautiful piece of jewelry.

"Now you have your something blue and old." She had tears in her eyes, which made mine cloud with tears.

As I looked at the natural stones, I realized this thing must of cost a fortune. "Mom, you shouldn't ha-"

"It's my baby's wedding day, I love you so much." I engulfed her in a hug and then I felt everyone join in, making the moment even more special. My mom grabbed the necklace from me and secured it around my neck. She turned my shoulder so I looked in a mirror and a tear slipped from my eye, which I wiped right away.

"Cooper is going to have to check his pants when he sees you." Desiree says from the group of girls. I looked at her admiringly because I am so thankful for her.

"Thank you raising a great man." I said and wrapped an arm around her and she leaned into me.

"Thank you for making him better." She sighed, keeping herself from crying.

"Okay, it's time to get lined up!" My wonderful wedding planner said to the crying girls. I turned around to see my planner holding my beautiful handmade bouquet.

We all walk downstairs and outside of the barn to get lined up. Of course I have to stay behind so Cooper doesn't see me. I peek my head outside to see everyone seated in their chairs, and how nice everything looks. Cooper and I decided to have a later ceremony so the sun was so bright, and right now it was a perfect light, very romantic.

The order of the party went: Jake and Maybell, Rusty and Jessica, Johnny and Reyna, Molly and Ryan, Beau and Taylor, and Caleb and Ashley. Caleb and Cooper had became very close these past two months. I feel like when I'm not with Cooper, he's doing cowboy shit with my brother and their friends.

"Oh sorry, I thought you were my little girl." My dad's voice comes from beside me. I turn and look at my handsome father, all dressed up in a classy suit. I give my dad a sad look as he comes and wraps me in a hug, "You look absolutely breath taking." I knew he meant it because I saw the tears in his eyes. I have never seen my dad tear up before.

"Oh dad, you're going to make me cry." I hug him tighter.

"I just wanna tell you how proud I am of you, and I love you very much." He kissed the top of my forehead and pulled away from our sentimental hug.

"I love you too, thank you for everything you have given to me." I say and kiss his cheek, "And I'll always be your little girl." I smirk at him and he smiles.

He looks in front of him and then back at me, "Well, I guess it time to give you away." He says, trying to make it positive, but it turns out somewhat sad.

He offers me his arm and I loop my hand through and give him a positive nod. We started to walk at a slow and steady pace. As we were in front of the ceremony venue, I gaped at the gorgeous view in front of me. At the end were two barrels with a bouquet of unique wildflowers were on each and through out the seats, more flowers.

At the front, the rustic wooden pergola had beautiful flowers hanging from it and in the center was a huge bull skull with the most perfect horns. But what was underneath the pergola is what really took my breath away. My cowboy.

He had bought a new black felt cowboy hat to "really look sharp", his words not mine. He wore a traditional tux coat and underneath shirt. The black tie was cool because the pattern was the old west bandanna pattern, like a wild rag. And obviously he wore dark creased Wrangler Jeans, his orders. But in short, he looked smokin' hot.

He must of felt the same way because the look on his face made my stomach do flips and my heart rate increased. He looked so proud and thankful as I was walking down the aisle. We couldn't take our eyes off each other, the moment was something I hope to never forget. We finally reached the end of the aisle and I handed Taylor my bouquet. I turned to my dad and he kissed me on my cheek, "I love you." I smiled at him.

Cooped walked over to us and before my dad let me go he said, "Love you more." Then he faced Cooper and sternly said, "Take good care of her."

"Always, sir." My dad finally let go of me and then Cooper's hand instantly grabbed mine, sending tingles and sparks throughout my whole body. Cooper lead me over to stand in front of the priest and we stood in front of each other, holding each other's hands.

"Friends, we are gathered here today to witness the marriage of Cooper Blue Blackwood and DaKota Annie Jones. Let us call upon God to be with us today as we celebrate this union of two into one." The priest opened, while Cooper and I stared into each other's eyes, while the priest continued to do his thing.

"I, Cooper, take you, DaKota, to be my wife." Cooper takes a deep breath before he starts his vows. "Kods, I promise to be faithful and supportive and to always make our love and happiness my priority. And I know if I don't, you'll kick my sorry butt. I will be yours in plenty and in want, in sickness and in health, in failure and in triumph. I will dream with you, celebrate with you and walk beside you through whatever our lives may bring. I know that if I'm with you, holding your hand, that I can conquer anything. You are my everything, my love and my life and best friend, today and always. I love you, girly." So much for trying to save my mascara.

This man never fails to make me fall more in love with him, he does it every time. I take my hand away from Cooper's and wipe my eyes as I start to laugh when Father Brad hands me a handkerchief. "Thank you." I wipe my eyes and hand it back to him.

I take a steady breath and then start mine, "I, DaKota, take you, Cooper, to be my husband. I promise to be your lover, companion and best friend. Your partner in parenthood. Your ally in conflict. Your greatest fan and your toughest adversary. Your pal in adventure. Your personal chef. Your nurse during sickness. Your consolation in disappointment and grief. Your forever dance partner. Your accomplice in mischief. Your babysitter. And most importantly, yours. This is my sacred vow to you, my equal in all things. I love you, cowboy, until the mountains tumble down." Cooper squeezed my hands at the end of my vows and I smiled at him.

"You have declared your consent before the Church and this community of your family and friends. May the Lord in his goodness strengthen your consent and fill you with his blessings. What God has joined together, let no one separate." Father Brad said happily and then motioned for Reese, who was our ring bearer. He was no longer in a wheel chair, but his usual crutches. He handed Father the rings and then Cooper messed up his hair as he walked back. "Lord, bless these rings which we bless in your name. Grant that those who wear them may always do you will and live together in peace and compassion."

"DaKota, take this ring as a sign of my love and fidelity." Cooper said as he placed my ring on my finger, making my heart skip two beats.

I grab his ring and grab his hand, "Cooper, take this ring as a sign of my love and fidelity." I put his matte black ring on his finger and then connect our hands back together, missing his warmth.

Father Brad smiled lovingly at us and seemed very pleased and happy to say, "My dear friends, it is my pleasure to introduce you to Mr and Mrs. Cooper and DaKota Blackwood! Cooper, you may kiss your bride."

Cooper separated our hands and placed both hands on my face and brought me in for our very first kiss as husband and wife. I put my hands on his wrists and kissed him back, instantly melting into him. I heard

438

the crowd whistle and holler for us, and then I pulled away and we both smiled happily at each other.

Cooper again grabbed my hand and then raised our arms in the air as we started walking down the aisle. He cheered loudly making my heart extremely happy and make me laugh and join along with him. He was proud to be my husband, and I was even prouder to be his wife.

COOPER AND I'S HANDS were intertwined underneath the wedding party table in the barn. We had just finished our meals and now it was time to do our first dance together as husband and wife. We both stood up and Cooper put his hand in the small of my back and guided me to the dance floor of outside of the barn.

As soon as Cooper placed my hand in his and around my back, the song we chose together started to play, "Blue Eye's Crying in the Rain" by Willie Nelson. We both decided this was our song because it played the first time we ever danced with each other.

I laid my head on his shoulder as we closely danced with each other. I closed my eyes because of how smooth of a dancer he was. His direct contact with my skin was soothing and comforting, perfecting the sound of Willie Nelson's voice. He had his head very close to mine, I could feel his warm breath against my neck. I felt so at peace with everything, Cooper was my home.

Today was just, perfect. The ceremony was great. Our wedding pictures went great. Our diner was great. Our venue was great. Our wedding party was awesome and so supporting. The maid of honor and best man speeches were great. And now this dance, was indescribable.

The song was coming to an end, so I pulled my head off Cooper's shoulder and started to look into his dreamy brown eyes. I began to see our future together in them, I was the happiest girl in the world right now. Cooper brought our hands closer to his chest, stopping our feet. "I love you, my bride." He smiled.

"I love you, my husband." Then he surprised me when he dipped me and connected our lips in a quick passionate kiss. Everyone around us clapped for us, bringing us back into reality that we weren't the only two people in the world.

Cooper brought me back upright and wrapped an arm around my waist and brought me as close as possible to him. I laughed sheepishly and said, "Who's ready to dance their asses off?!" I knew Cooper was surprised my choice of words, but I didn't care. This is my wedding and I can say what I want to.

My guests took to it anyways, the dance floor became crowded as "Watermelon Crawl" came on and we all synced together and started to dance, making my heart as happy as it can be.

My dad had managed to get a classic '67 Chevy pickup to our wedding vehicle, so I enjoyed sitting next to Cooper while he drove. I lifted my head off of Cooper's shoulder as we reached our destination. His cabin in the mountains. Cooper turned off the engine and then opened the door and climbed out and then helped me slide across the bench seat.

Before I could firmly get two feet on the ground, Cooper swept me off my feet and carried me bridal style. "Cooper!" He laughed at me as he walked into the cabin.

He walked over to the couch and skillfully sat us down and I moved off his lap when he said, "I'll start a fire." Cooper took off his tux jacket, revealing his white shirt and black suspenders that made me giggle. "What's so funny, my wife." He said as he placed the logs in the fireplace.

I played with the ring on my finger, "You look like an old man."

He scoffs and turns to look at me, giving me his famous sexy smirk. "Old men wish they had a body like mine." I rolled my eyes at him and he continued to build the fire.

Once he placed the match under the logs, a flame started and caught onto the logs. As Cooper watched the flame get bigger, I suddenly felt the need and want do something. I walked behind him and sat down. I leaned up and wrapped my arms around his chest and laid my head in the crook of his shoulder. Cooper placed his warm hands over my arms and leaned back into me.

Then I placed a soft kiss in his favorite spot on his neck, traveling up until the bottom of his ear. He caught on so he turned his head and caught my lips with his. Cooper swiftly turned his body towards mine and then I managed to sit in his lap, without leaving his lips. I wrapped my arms around his neck, bringing him closer to me.

He licked my bottom lip and I opened my mouth more for his tongue to dominate mine. His grip tightened on me making me moan into his mouth. I started to play with the ends of his hair and then his lips left mine and traveled down my jaw to my collarbone. My chest was firmly pressed against his and then his hands traveled down to my butt, pushing me more into him as he nipped slightly against my skin, making me moan again.

Thankfully, he reconnected our lips, continuing our heated kiss. Then his fingers traveled up my sides and to my shoulders and gently pushed down the straps of my dress. I helped him out with that, and then I pushed his suspenders out of the war and began unbuttoning his shirt.

Once I removed his shirt I wrapped my arms around his broad shoulders and ran my hands down his back, making him moan slightly. Cooper propped himself against the floor with his hand as he lowered us down, leaving his another arm to support my head. What a gentleman.

Leaving my lips once again, Coopers lips kissed the right side of my jaw going to my ear. He kissed right under it and then slightly bite my ear lope, making me moan with pleasure. Then he placed slow kisses on the tender spots of my neck.

Without hesitation, my fingers grabbed Cooper's belt buckle and start to undo it. I felt his lips stop working wonders and then lift his head to meet my gaze, leaving a silence between us. I knew what he was thinking, "DaKota are you sure?"

"Yes, I want to." His soft eyes became overwhelmed with desire and excitement when he heard my confirmation. I continued to take off his belt and then he stood up and took off his jeans by himself, revealing his bright blue compression shorts.

"I thought I needed something blue too." He said once he sat in between my legs again, making me laugh in this intense moment.

Once our laughter softened, his eyes became serious and lustful. He grabbed my dressed and softly pulled it down my body, only revealing my underwear. My dress had a built in bra, so my chest was bare, but Cooper paid no attention, which sent a huge wave of relief to me.

He laid back down and whispered to me, "You are so beautiful."

That hit me on a spiritual level, making me feel truly appreciated and beautiful. I wasted no time smashing our lips together, creating another intense kiss.

Cooper's rough, but soft fingers sent chills throughout my body. He ran them over my arms, my neck, the middle of my chest, and down my legs. He created magic that isn't even imaginable unless experienced. Coming back up my legs, they found the hem of my underwear and pulled them all the way down.

I ran my fingernails across his back, feeling his muscles move with his movements. He was perfect. I used both hands to push down his compression shorts and then he helped me with the rest of it. I hummed once I felt his completely naked body against mine, it was heavenly. Cooper intertwined our fingers together, "You ready?"

"Yes, I trust you." I whispered.

He brought his lips near my neck, heavily breathing. "I'll be gentle. I love you." He said as he moved his body to bring me pleasure and pain at the same time. I let out a breath as I started to relax and Cooper started to kiss me, leaving me with no doubt that this was the best day of our lives.

EPILOGUE

My body automatically stretched as I woke up in our soft king sized bed. I looked over at my sleeping husband and smiled to myself, still loving how it amazing it felt to wake up next to him. He had just received a hair cut, but his overnight stubble showed on his perfectly structured- rugid face. I looked at the clock and it was 7:15, holy we were really sleeping in today.

I slowly got out of bed, dressed in my flannel pants and Cooper's old tee shirt. I go into our bathroom and do my daily routine, brush my teeth and wash my face and put on my wedding ring. Once I'm done, I walk out of our room and walk to Kasen's room.

Kasen Colby Blackwood was born on March 19th, coincidentally on the one year anniversary of Cooper and I's engagement. He weighed 7 pounds and 3 ounces and measured 21". My labor went perfect and I had no complications, except for the pain of course. I became pregnant on the night of our wedding, which we weren't expecting. None the less, we love our little boy and are very thankful for our little blessing. But I still get a lot of shit from Caleb about conceiving right away.

Cooper was so excited when we found out we were having a boy, he was literally dancing in the hospital and singing on the top of his lungs in the car ride home. My whole life, I had never decided on whether I wanted a boy or a girl first, but seeing Cooper this excited made me even happier.

Kasen is quite the character, definitely keeps us on our toes. He really likes to try new things and experience them on his own. I mean, what two year old doesn't? He absolutely loves riding with his dad on the tractor, and managing the ranch on horseback. He has a sorrel Shetland pony who he calls, "Girlfriend", even though he stays clear of girls. It took him a long time to get used to Addison, Caleb and Ashley's girl.

Kasen is also tougher than nails. I swear that kid is invisible. He has given me about 100 heart attacks from close calls. He has already sprained his arm and had stitches in his head. He is the king of doing michevious things, but he is also my little sweetheart. As much as he loves spending time with Cooper, he is totally a mama's boy. From the few times he actually gets scared, he runs and jumps into my arms.

I opened his door that had a huge Sheriff sticker on it and when I looked at the bed, I noticed he was gone. He never gets up by himself unless until 8 o'clock, maybe he is in the bathroom. I close the door and walk down the hallway and to the bathroom. The light is on, but no Kasen. Okay, then he's in the kitchen.

As I make my way to the kitchen, I hear nothing which makes my heart race. I finally make it and don't see my child. I run to the window and look outside to see if he is by the barn or in the arena. My stomach drops, I see nothing.

I run back to our bedroom and shake Cooper's arm under the covers. "Cooper!" I know he is awake but just doesn't open his eyes. "Wake up!"

"Only if my wife kisses me." He smugly smirks with his deep morning voice.

"Not the time Cooper! I can't find Kasen!" I throw the covers off him and throw the shirt on the floor to him as he immediately opens his eyes, looking wide eyed at me.

"What do you mean you can't find him?" He asks me as he slips his shirt on, following me out of out bedroom.

"He's not in the house!" I slip on my boots and run outside with Cooper following me. Where the hell could my child be? Lord, please let him be safe wherever he is.

Cooper is looking in the barn, where Kasen likes to hide during hide and go seek. And I'm looking in the stables and tack room. Sometimes he likes to just go talk with Girlfriend, but he wasn't there. Cooper and I walk out of the buildings at the same time, "Nothing?" He was just as concerned as I was.

Our last resort was to look in the pasture, so that's where I started running to. I climbed the gate and started to run in the sage grass. He wasn't by the horses, and Girlfriend was there, no sign of him. As I ran over one of out hills, I spotted a group of cows that were lounging around.

Over the back of a cow that was laying down, I saw a speck of red. It had to be him. I had to stop my run and start a light walk, not to scare the cows and potentially get my son trampled on. As we got closer, I couldn't see anything else.

The other cows noticed us and started to start to get up began to walk away, and the cow I kept my eye on caught on to the others, looked behind and stood up. Then I saw my child's back hit the ground. "Kasen!" I yelled as Cooper and I slid on the ground by our child.

Kasen rolled over onto his back and looked up at us, and then I picked him up and engulfed him in the tightest hug ever. "You scared me! What were you doing?" I asked him in a panic as I searched his body for any cuts or any sign of harm.

Kasen's big puppy eyes looked at Cooper who sitting behind me and softly spoke, "Well I was going to fweed the cows, but the bag was too heavy for me. So I walked out here and fwed them wike this." He said and then ripped some grass and held it out in his palm.

I let out a sigh of relief and looked at Cooper behind him who still looked scared, "Buddy you scared your mom and me have to death." Kasen sadly down at the grass, breaking my heart. "You have to wake mommy and daddy up if you want to come out here." Cooper says softly.

"We appreciate you trying to help, but these animals are a lot bigger than you and they're dangerous. You could get hurt-" Kasen interrupts me by laughing suddenly.

I look at Cooper weirdly and he returns the look, "They ain't scawy!" He continues his laugh.

"What do you mean?" I ask him.

"Elvis let me sweep on him." I started to laugh now. My kid, sleeping with cows. His grandfather is going to love this one.

"That's what you were doing?" Cooper chuckles.

"Yeah, she was waying down and told me to cuddle wit 'er." Cooper and I looked at each other and smiled.

"She did, did she?" Cooper asked amused at his story.

"Yep!" He said with a smile and then it turned into a frown, making me frown. "Are you mad at me?" He asked very softly and disappointed.

I pulled him closer to us, "Sweetie, we're not mad. Will you do something for us?" He just nods, "Will you promise to only come out here when we are with? Mommy just want you to be safe because me and daddy love you very much."

His frown turns into his father's smirk, "I pwomise!" He says proudly and then I pull him into a hug, Cooper's arms now wrapping around us. "I wove you." My heart melted in a puddle at my little cowboy hugging me.

As I was hugging him, I heard wrappers being crinkled. I opened my eyes and dug in his back pockets and pulled out two candy bars. "Kasen Colby Blackwood! Why do you have these in the morning?" I ask him in a shocked voice and then he looks like he crapped his pants, but then looks at his dad.

He rocks back and fourth on his heels and smiles and bats his eyelashes, "Mommy, you wook wery pwetty today!" He learned that one from his dad. He looks back at Cooper for approval and I see from the corner of my eye that Cooper gives him a thumbs up, and then I elbow him lightly.

"Well thank you, but I'm keeping these." I glare at him and he snickers devilishly. "Now you better hurry back home before I catch you and eat you up!" I said in a witches voice and he gets bugged eyed and takes off for home.

Cooper and I stand up and I say, "Look at what you taught him." I say as I watch our child run for his life up the hill, occasionally stopping to grab his hat that is way too big for him.

"It can't be that bad, I've found it effective." He smirks as I look at him and mock him.

"Did you teach him that smirk too?" I ask him and he laughs.

"I told him you can't resist the Blackwood men's smirk." I scoff at him and look at him, but he's giving me the smirk. I glare at him and then he wraps an arm around me teasingly.

"I'd wish you'd stop that." I say stubbornly.

"That's what you said last time, and now look at where it got you." Cooper lightly smacks my butt and I glare at him, earning a laugh from him. I looked down at my belly bump, yep we're having another on in seven months. I push him away from me and he laughs but only returns again and wraps it around me again and then brings me to his chest and squeezes me so my cheek is smushed against him.

"I'd wish you'd leave me alone." I was joking and he knew it to when he laughed and hugged me tighter.

"Oh but if I was gone, who would bug you?!" He teases me more, and stops walking allowing me to step back.

I hold his forearms and look up at him, "I guess I would miss that annoying smirk." I slightly pouted to him.

"And I would miss kissing that cute little pout of yours away." He says and then ducks down and captures my lips with his.

Out of all of our years together, none of our kisses were the exact same. I don't know how but I loved it. I pulled away from his kiss and then he grabbed my hand and tangled our fingers together and started to walk again. "I love you, my beautiful wife."

"I love you too, cowboy." I said and then used my other hand to grab onto his bicep and lean my head against his shoulder. I will never get used to this sight. Me holding hands with Cooper, while carrying his child, and watching our kid running in the hills. Even during parenthood, we haven't lost our puppy love with each other, it still feels like we just met and in the first stages of falling in love. I'm forever thankful he moved to my little small town and repaired my scarred heart.

One day I hope Kasen finds someone who he loves as much as his father loves me. I hope he showers her with the affection Cooper did with me. Shows her off to the town like Cooper did. I hope he makes her feel as alive as I do when I'm with Cooper. He protects her. Shows her what love really means. Treats her with the amount of respect his father showed me. Cherishes her. Talks to her about anything like we did, and never walks away from a fight.

I hope he learns from us.

Because if he does, he will get through anything.

Lightning Source UK Ltd.
Milton Keynes UK
UKHW010853080223
416610UK00013B/1128